Quentin S. Crisp

RULE DEMENTIA!

Quentin S. Crisp was born in 1972, in North Devon, U.K. He studied Japanese at Durham University and graduated in 2000. He has had fiction published by Tartarus Press, PS Publishing, Eibonvale Press and others. He currently resides in Bexleyheath, and is editor for Chômu Press. His novella *Blue on Blue* was previously published by Snuggly Books.

SNUGGLY BOOKS

QUENTIN S. CRISP

RULE DEMENTIA!

THIS IS A SNUGGLY BOOK

ISBN: 978-1-943813-18-6

Contents

The Second Author's Introduction to Rule Dementia!

IT'S a cold and rather dull Valentine's Day in the year 2016 and I am beginning the second introduction to my collection of short fiction, *Rule Dementia!* The previous introduction was begun in 2002 and completed in 2004, for a book published in 2005. Writing, as these dates testify, is a dilatory business. The first introduction begins with the words, "It's been a long and difficult journey," and goes on to question the validity of the journey metaphor. Now, almost twelve years since that introduction was completed, I have changed enough as a person and as a writer to think that, after all, 'journey' has something to be said for it. I am in a different place now, geographically and in other ways.

I have, at my left hand, a copy of Aldous Huxley's *Island*, which I have yet to read. As I understand it, from the synopsis and introduction, the book is about the failure of utopian ideals, but perhaps, when I come to read it, I'll discover it's not quite so straightforward. On reading the introduction, one thing in particular stuck in my mind. Apparently, not long after the novel was published, Huxley himself said of it: "[the] weakness of the book consists in a disbalance between fable and exposition. The story has too much weight, in the way of ideas and reflections, to carry."

I was struck by this because I detected behind it an attitude that now seems near extinct: that the author might be either modest or, better yet, constructively self-critical. This seemed to me to contrast with the current state of affairs in which every author is obliged to be their own publicity impresario, because of which there is no room to do anything other than blow a fanfare of hyperbole for your own work, and then step forward as if it were someone else who blew the fanfare. Okakura Tenshin observes that self-advertisement is the instinct of the slave—trying to find a master in the marketplace—and perhaps this tendency in the world of writing is a symptom of wider processes in our society that are robbing us of mental and even practical freedom.

There is something else that I glean from the contrast between Huxley's attitude and the predominant attitude of the current age, namely that we have to a great extent lost the understanding of literature as an *attempt*, an understanding that includes the perception that there is merit in making the attempt even if we never quite attain that attempt's ultimate goal.

This is, first of all, humane, since we are not forever damned if we don't produce something perfect the first time, and secondly, more conducive to producing something close to perfection in actuality, for it allows that criticism is not only necessary, but something positive that might be advantageously acted upon—if it's too late this time, then the next time.

All of this is a preamble to my saying that I have very serious doubts as to the quality of the work in this collection, not to mention doubts concerning whether the dedication of my life to writing can ever produce any results that are not painfully embarrassing. Because, however, we are living in the age of advertisement and clickbait hyperbole, I'll refrain from specific criticism of these older—which is to say, younger—stories. My life has been defined by the great attempt that is literature, and these stories, whatever their individual merit or lack of merit, are part of that attempt. If they fail, I hope they do so in a way that redounds to the greater glory of those that succeed.

I believe I will go on making the attempt of literature until I die or until the human race effectively obliterates itself from existence in its eagerness to be enslaved to its own creations, at which point I might be discouraged by the lack of readership.

When younger writers, as very occasionally happens, turn to me for advice, I like to send them the words with which Hokusai introduced his collection of prints, *One Hundred Views of Mount Fuji*. I consult these words intermittently for my own sake, too. They are both a reminder of the need for humility and a consoling encouragement to persevere in one's chosen path (or the path by which one has been chosen):

> From the age of six,[1] I developed a compulsion for sketching the forms of things, and from the time I had reached a half century or so, I produced innumerable pictures. However, until my seventieth year, nothing I produced was truly worth looking at. At the age of seventy-three, I had come to understand, a little, the morphology of birds, beasts, insects and fish and the essential life of plants and trees. And so, by the time I am eighty-six, I will have progressed still further, by ninety I will have penetrated deeper into the heart of things, by one hundred I will have attained true mastery, and by one hundred and ten, each dot, each stroke, will be as if alive.
>
> All I ask is that the gods of long life bear witness that this prediction of mine is no delirium.

At least it is not yet entirely clear (if we take him at his word) whether I am lagging behind Hokusai, and won't become clear until I am seventy-two years old, in 2044. (Forty-four, being

---

1 All the ages in this translated text are given in the traditional Japanese way, counting (roughly) from conception rather than birth, by assuming a child is one year old when born.

two hearts, or twice death, is for me a lucky number.) The sharp-witted reader will have gathered from the above that I have little confidence that I will produce anything of especial merit before that age.

If I refrain from commenting in detail on the stories in this volume, perhaps I might be forgiven for commenting on the previous introduction instead. That it was written by a lopsided child is evident. On re-reading it for the purposes of writing this, I cringed at a number of places. Still, I cannot disown the off-centre infant who, to adapt the saying, is parent to my present self. Cannot, and would choose not to. I have, from very early on, known that to amputate what embarrassed me—if I even survived so drastic an operation—would also be to remove my most vital sources of originality and insight. It has even seemed to me that this embarrassment (the capacity to be embarrassed and to embarrass others) was a golden gateway to creativity and spiritual truth, and if it appears accidental that my work is embarrassing, this is firstly because it is accidental, and secondly because if it were wholly artful it would lose the power of true embarrassment. Still, I have been conscious enough of it—conscious of?! "tortured by" is what I mean—that I have given myself over, in my braver and more honest moments, to the existential experiment of embodying embarrassment, since I know that I cannot run from it.

These days, though, I tend not to dress in the gaudy colours—the motley, you might say—that I did when I wrote these tales, and, what's more, I even think I was misguided in some things. I noticed the phrase "rational materialism" in the old introduction. It's perhaps unjust that in the very nature of things—within the stream of time, at least—one's younger self can never have the last word in a conversation with one's older self. However, I remember those days well enough to believe it would be a kindness if I could tell my younger self that he had been sadly tricked by people who belong too much to the world, and that there is little reason to believe the words 'rational' and 'materialism' belong together. I commend him on this, however: what he struck upon by furious intuition, I continue to confirm in all I study—that materialism is deadly. The outlines of the four horsemen have grown very much in definition since this collection was first published. I can almost name them now. I am close to obtaining their phone numbers and addresses.

Well, on that score, I doubt the reader will be confused if I say that I am unsure whether any of us will make it to the abovenamed year—2044—with body and soul intact. You can see those growing silhouettes yourself.

It is about a quarter past six o'clock in the evening. I have just been for a walk to Bursted Wood and back. The trees were still leafless, but the sun was setting in saffron over the railway tracks between the tree-topped banks. The bare branches looked as the cawing of crows sounded. Though the day was ending, the air had a pre-dawn quality of emptiness and sobriety, as if this were truly an interval in life when all that had been happening was a finished chapter and all that was to come was unknown; it was a meantime of quiet waiting—perhaps not even of waiting.

During my walk I noted, at the edges of the wood, a number of felled trees, the fallen trunks of which had been sawn into logs which had been left to rot where they lay. Why? Was it simply in order to thin the canopy of branches, the way that people knock through an interior wall in a house they've bought to make two rooms into one and "create an impression of space"? A horrible thought. Perhaps it was a mistaken thought, too, but that, anyway, was how it struck me.[2] Sometimes I am convinced

---

2 I am by no means an expert, but Bursted Wood might be maintained through the very ancient practice of coppicing, which would appear to fit

that humans—especially those with European roots—have an inability to let things be (combined with a capacity for waste) that amounts to a psychosis.

I came back determined to finish my introduction. I had been hoping to give some kind of bulletin regarding my personal life and 'career' by which the time between the last edition of this book and the present edition might be measured, but I have too little energy even for self-pity and so, sadly, the appetite by which I might make the most of this opportunity is missing. Perhaps that's just as well—it's so very hard to know. Anyway, in this 'meantime', what I must do is recognise my failure, that is, as usual, I must die; I must become as empty as the February sky.

When the first edition came out, I had a report back from a friend of a friend—via the friend. Her opinion, conveyed by the friend, was that I gave too much away in the introduction and that I should let the reader discover what the stories contained and what they implied and how they were meant for him- or herself. I accepted the justice of this observation.

I have been considering, lately, Poem #544 by Emily Dickinson:

> The Martyr Poets—did not tell—
> But wrought their Pang in syllable—
> That when their mortal name be numb—
> Their mortal fate—encourage some—
>
> The Martyr Painters—never spoke—
> Bequeathing—rather—to their Work—
> That when their conscious fingers cease—
> Some seek in Art—the Art of Peace—

the facts observed. As my words in this introduction suggest, I am skeptical regarding interference with nature by humans for the good of the former, but perhaps I am biased (that is, wrong). I am willing, for instance, to be persuaded that a better target for ire than coppicing is the mowing of lawns. In short, once more Confucius turns to Lao-Tzu and says, "After all, you might benefit from a little study."

Sure enough, this is a great creed. I do believe it is a great creed.

If I give away too much then, and if what I give too little resembles something worth giving, I hope I can be forgiven.

There is so little time now.

Now.

now.

now

now

now

Quentin S. Crisp
15th February, 2016.
Bexleyheath, Kent

Author's Introduction

IT'S been a long and difficult journey, typified by the fact that I first wrote this opening sentence in 2002 in Kyoto, and am rewriting it now in 2004 on an industrial estate near Reading. The original sentence went like this: "It's been a long and difficult journey, and it's by no means over yet, but at last my misshapen work is beginning to see print."

I now wonder about the journey metaphor. As I write this, the metaphor that comes to mind in its place is one that has occurred to me a number of times in my life, an absurd and miserable metaphor that goes like this: Writing is an attempt to escape from the grim prison of reality by digging a tunnel with a teaspoon. Full of dread lest the whole thing cave in on my head, or I am discovered and deprived of my teaspoon, my hands trembling, I scoop out one more speck of dirt, and one more. My heart is wracked by pain and sorrow, and I dream only of the light and the air which I may never see.

In this world, freedom is elusive, and is almost always curtailed by the need for money. However, this collection of stories is not a money-making exercise. It will not bring me material freedom, but perhaps it will afford me—and, I hope, the reader—something of the freedom of the imagination. In 2002, when I first wrote this introduction, it was for a different publisher and a somewhat different collection. That project fell through. Now I have been assured that the current publisher wishes to produce a volume as near to my own vision as possible. Seizing the chance of this brief freedom while I may, I would like to offer this re-written introduction as an explanation of that vision.

Let me start with the difficult question of genre. I sometimes have occasion to disclose to an acquaintance the fact that I squander my spare time in the scribbling of fiction, and, upon being asked what kind of fiction it is that I write, always find myself stuck for an answer. For the sake of convenience I will usually reply that I write horror, or sometimes, science fiction. However, on such occasions, I cannot help feeling that I have told something of an untruth. The fact is, I am distrustful of labels and categories. I suspect them of doing a great deal of harm in the arts and in society in general. As an example, let me ask, when was the last time that a work of horror or science fiction won the Booker Prize or any similar literary award? I would suggest, and I think there are few who would disagree, that any novel bearing the designation 'horror' on its cover would not even be considered for such a prize, irrespective of its worth as a piece of literature. Horror in particular is seen as a juvenile genre by the literary establishment, and, since I have never had any sympathy with those pompous types who consider themselves 'adult' without a trace of irony, I sometimes take a perverse pride in counting myself amongst the ranks of horror writers. I would rather be juvenile if it comes to that. But still, a part of me remains unsatisfied with the restrictions of genre.

I have nursed the dream of being a writer since early childhood, but I never thought to myself, 'I want to be a horror writer', or 'I want to be a science fiction writer.' I only ever thought, 'I want to be a writer.' It just so happens that the first stories I had published fitted well within the confines of the horror genre, and so I have been addressed as a horror writer and have come to some extent to think of myself as such. Now seems as good a time as any, however, to make the true situation clear.

Since my boyhood, when my father read me *Lord of the Rings*, if not before, I have always considered literature to be intrinsically linked with the imagination. That there are those who seem to hold a contrary opinion has come of something of a shock to me in my adult years. I dislike, I heartily disapprove of so-called realism in literature. I do not mean by that that all works of literature must be replete with elves and vampires and other such imaginary creatures. I simply mean that, for me, when literature departs from its fundamental role of celebrating the imagination in some way or another, it ceases to be literature. The realist ostensibly portrays reality in all its drabness and shabbiness in order to bear witness to 'the truth'. Yet I cannot escape the feeling that he is secretly siding with this shabbiness. I wrote a few words on this subject in my diary:

> 14/Dec/2001
> There is something smug about [the realist], and when you think about it, there's only one explanation—they actually fit in in this hideous world; they belong here. I think that is largely the dividing line between those I trust and those I don't.

This predilection for literature that conspicuously celebrates the imagination naturally led me to read much of the works usually categorised as fantasy, horror and science fiction. But my reading did not stop there. I was particularly interested in the hybrids of literature, and in my adolescence discovered one of the supreme hybrids, H. P. Lovecraft. Lovecraft has had an incalculable influence on my own work. He, too, is a writer whom it is difficult to place in any one genre. His work has been variously described as cosmic horror, science fiction, Gothic horror, weird fiction, and probably in many other terms which I have forgotten. I was particularly impressed by the strains of Gothicism and of the weird in his work. Lovecraft whet my appetite for other writers of Gothic and weird fiction, such as Mervyn Peake, Charles Maturin, Mary Shelley, William Hope Hodgson, and so on.

I'm afraid if I took time here to expand on what I mean by 'gothic' and by 'weird' that this introduction would swell to unwelcome lengths, so I shall have to refrain from definition and simply assume that because the reader holds such a volume as this in his or her hands that he or she has a working knowledge of such terms.

In my idle moments I have toyed with the idea of officially proclaiming myself—to anyone who might care—an author of Gothic or of weird fiction, such is the love I bear these genres. However, whilst I might on occasion write pieces that fall neatly into one or other of these categories, I know that they would both be inaccurate as a description of my work as a whole.

No, my reading did not stop with genre fiction or even with those authors on the fringes of genre, such as Lovecraft. I extended my reading into the realms of pure literature, though always with an eye open for the hybrid weeds that grew in the shadows of literature's great garden. Thus, in my time, I read Baudelaire's *Flowers of Evil*, Flaubert's *Salammbo*, Kahlil Gibran's *The Earth Gods*, Huysmans' *Against Nature*, Gogol's *Diary of a Madman*, Mishima Yukio's *The Sea of Fertility* and Nagai Kafu's *A Strange Tale From East of the River*. In fact, I have become something of an omnivorous reader. But the works that found a place in my heart have seldom been those imbued with the dry flavour of realism. Even a writer such as Nagai Kafu, though influenced by French naturalism and seeming to reproduce reality with photographic faithfulness, has somewhere in his works, if only in the use of language itself, an intoxicating aestheticism that sets me to dreaming. That is what I require most from literature and that is the effect I strive to produce in my own work.

Well, I have spoken a little about what my work is not, and given a brief summary of my influences, but I have yet to say exactly what my work *is*. In the course of my writing I have naturally come to form a sort of philosophy of writing, and I would like, with the reader's indulgence, to make an essay at explaining that philosophy here. The question of realism is actually quite an important one, and in that connection, I must start this explanation with something resembling a confession. The truth is, I have no sense of reality. I am quite convinced that I am congenitally lacking in such a faculty, if indeed it is a faculty. For example, I have never been able to tell good acting from bad. For me everything is as real as everything else. It's a little like being colour blind—reality blind.

I believe I can do no better in enlarging on this topic than to quote once again from my diary:

14/Dec/2001

What is realistic? Surely this is something constructed by human beings, unwritten laws such as those against public nudity (okay, so they are probably written, but let's say invisible laws). We wear clothes out of this tyrannical sense of 'realism'. Actually, it would be 'unrealistic' for everyone to walk down the street naked, just as it is 'unrealistic' for someone to go into a song and dance routine in the middle of their daily life. It is pure oppression and nothing else. At school I didn't understand the unwritten laws of 'realism' and was branded a weirdo because of it. Why only me? I still don't understand those rules. It makes me very wary. At the end of every playtime I would give out a great Tarzan-like, chest-beating ululation as if to say, 'Reality has not beaten me.'

So, anyway, my stories are not realistic either. Having no idea of the 'realism' by which other people operate, I feel a distinct lack of confidence about my characters and dialogue. I remember the comments of a certain cynical teacher—one of that dry, tedious species known as 'realists', no doubt—on the works of Katherine Mansfield. He said that no one really talks the way the characters do in 'Something Childish but Very Natural'. Well, I do! So there! Just because he's a boring conversationalist, doesn't mean everybody else is obliged to be. Still, I have no confidence on the point of realism. I'm so lacking in realism that I wouldn't even be certain of being able to recount my own life story in a realistically convincing way. I seem unable to mix with reality—like oil and water. So, I have decided to make this weakness a strength by having the whole, vague question-fraught margin between reality and unreality as the very focus of my work. And surely there is some validity in that? Although I have, as an adult, largely bowed under the tyrannical yoke of reality, in these stories at least, I try to give out again that chest-beating Tarzan-like ululation. "I am here. I will not give in to reality."

Well, perhaps there is just a touch of exaggeration here. At least, due to the insecurities mentioned in this extract, I have made a point of knowing my enemy and studying realistic techniques in literature. I have even adopted them to a certain extent, to try and make my stories convincing (not realistic). I really have no idea how far I have succeeded.

My basic approach in writing a story is to take a metaphor that interests me, to explore it and bring it to its logical—or illogical—conclusion, as if it were the literal truth. It does not matter in the least to me if I steamroller reality in the process. What is important to me is the perfection of my symbols. Stating it like that, it probably sounds a very artificial and simplistic method. Nonetheless, it is the method that suits me best.

I have come this far and I still have not arrived at any conclusion as to what genre I belong to. A part of me would like to leave that question without an answer. But, on the other hand, no matter how great may be my distaste for labels, I also recognise their usefulness and the attraction they hold for human beings. It is part of human nature to wish to name things. I believe William Blake once said something along the lines of, "I must devise my own system or be enslaved by that of another man's." Well, in the same way, I must devise my own genre or be enslaved by that of another. And so, I have decided that my work belongs to the genre of demented fiction. If you want to know what comprises demented fiction then please continue and read this collection. I'm afraid that if I frame a definition here I will be creating future limitations. However, I will stretch the reader's patience further by giving a few hints. I arrived at the term demented fiction because of my love of the flawed masterpiece and my penchant for leaving irregularities in my own tales. I also think that it describes well my tendency to start from a totally absurd premise and gleefully play the whole thing through to the end with a straight face. If I have an idea and think, "I can't possibly use that," I immediately hear an impish counter-whispering in my head telling me that I *must* use it. I shall restrict myself to these few hints for the present.

Well, I am afraid I must have bored you stiff with my nonsense, but I wanted to get one or two things off my chest.

Actually, I haven't quite finished yet. At the start of this introduction I mentioned a journey, and corrected this metaphor to that of an escape. But what is the destination I have in mind—the place I wish to escape to? I shall risk being thought a lunatic and state my aim plainly. I wish through writing to discover the whereabouts of the human soul. I believe that the soul has potential, but not necessary existence. Unfortunately, in the twentieth century and in our current century, it seems that all human endeavour has been directed towards the elimination of all routes that might access the soul. I am referring, of course, to the philosophy of rational materialism that is prevalent in our current age. When the materialists finally achieve their aim and sever all connections between this world and the world in which the soul has potential existence, I have no doubt that it will mean the extinction of the human race. Perhaps it is quixotic of me to think I can achieve anything to reverse this trend by the plying of my insignificant pen. But as far as I am concerned it is no less than a struggle for survival. As William Burroughs once observed, referring to our home, the planet Earth, "This is a penal colony which is now a death camp."

Just as I have little or no sense of reality, I really have no idea of the worth of my own stories. I can only say they have been written with the serious intent that I have confessed above. From my own point of view, there are stories in this collection that I am close to being happy with. I hope the reader will find enough of interest here to repay the time they spend with this volume, and even, perhaps, to encourage them to accompany me a little further in my efforts to pull off the great escape.

Should I leave this world soon after the publication of this collection—you never know, after all, I've been feeling a bit unwell recently—at least I can feel reassured that the bare essentials of my vision, in however embryonic a form, are contained here in these pages.

I have kept you much too long. I shall close here. Please enjoy the stories, and I hope we shall meet again.

I finish revising this introduction on the third of July 2004, in Twickenham, Middlesex, UK.

Quentin S. Crisp.

RULE DEMENTIA!

Jellyfish Joe

WELL-VERSED in the abstrusities of a thousand psi-religions was Joe, and full of moon-mystic erudition. Yet life had left him with nothing. Forlorn and empty-hearted, he threw himself away, near forgetting his name and where he came from, until, finally, fresh from a stint in a suicide sect—the only survivor—he decided to create his own scrapbook religion.

He resisted the compelling universalities of the great world religions and the compelling originality of cults and cranks alike. It was a time of recuperation, convalescence. He had a key a friend had given him long ago, to an empty, neglected house, and there he lay on the coarse grey blanket of the bed and looked out of the window into the sun-dusted, rain-miserable, overgrown garden, his eyes focusing on a leaf . . . and unfocusing.

He acquired a scrapbook, scissors, glue, and carefully cut out bits and pieces, not particularly from other religions, but from the neutral detail of life itself. He found an old, yellowing jotter and, in the manner of free association, made a list of the things he wanted his religion to include. The list is still extant. It reads:

> Vests, esp. string vests.
> Bowler hats, esp. in conj. w/ string vests.
> String.

Sieves.

Silverfish or similar primitive, lurking life form.

<u>Jellyfish</u>.

And the last word was underlined twice, as if to indicate that it was particularly inspired.

It was the obscure image of the jellyfish that Joe finally fixed upon as being as good as any to found a sect on. Feeling quite revivified by this elemental play of ideas, this arbitrary, child-like and anonymous genesis, Joe returned to what was left of the world he had half-forgotten, sold it, and bought the wreck of a hippy commune that had woken groggily from the haze of a party to find that it was in the wrong decade, and had assumed a terminal air of spaced-out anachronism ever since. He paid an absurdly low price, and rather than repair the place, made the most of its dilapidation and decorated around it. At last he had his ashram. He advertised straightforwardly for disciples, and, experienced in such things, was not too surprised to find them forthcoming.

He had taught his disciples long, diligently, and with much spiritual ingenuity, until now, the day of his last pilgrimage, when he must take leave of them forever, had come. In the morning he opened his eyes. It was yet early. Rolling from the loose turban of soiled sheets that covered his mattress he took a note of paper from the tiny chest of drawers, looked at it with satisfaction. Sleep still in his eyes, his fingers twitchy with nervousness and fastidiousness, he folded the paper precisely and inserted it carefully in an envelope. He did not seal it, but tucked the gummed tongue inside. On a couple of nails jutting dangerously from splintered beams there hung the Holy Bowler and the Holy String Vest. Joe donned them, stepped into a pair of pleated, baggy trousers, and pulled the braces over his shoulders. It was time for the Ablutions.

4

The tiny, doorless bathroom was set a couple of feet up the wall from the floorboards of the landing. Joe climbed in like an astronaut climbing into a sleeping capsule. He foamed his face and picked up a razor clogged with a mush of stubble. The razor sliced straight-edged swathes through the foam like a combine-harvester reaping a field of wheat. The closeness of the blades to his skin and the straightness of the lines gave him the tight, satisfying feeling of a ritual. He was doing all this for the last time. He glanced at the room he was standing in, the ribs of plasterboards through which he had seen the stars, the exposed pipes which had lulled him to sleep with the celestial gurgling music of the plumbing. All this had been his life. It was not exchangeable for money or goods. It was mere experience that would extinguish, that was now extinguishing. He doused his face with wide-awake splashes of cold water from the basin hanging off the wall and examined his features with buzzing detachment in the soap-blotched mirror as if finally to grasp the identity behind the name, or at the very least, to banish the efficacy of that name eternally. It was a face of indeterminate age, one might say middle-aged if it were not for the sober-pale air of youth it wore. There was a mix of quirkiness and anonymity in the features, how one might imagine a clown without his make-up, suddenly tired, serious and modest.

Joe returned to his bedroom, slid his arms into the filthy-smooth lining of the sleeves of a shabby shirt jacket. He sat cross-legged on the floor, dipped the tip of a fountain pen in a bottle of ink, took a deep breath, and penned one last poem, entitled 'Jellyfish'. Signed and dated, now he was ready. He impaled the scroll of the poem on the nail where the Holy Bowler had been.

✻

His disciples were waiting for him.

He descended the uncarpeted stairs, passed through the nook where the laundry was done and the toilets were, full of acid graffiti screaming of regressions to the bison-filled plains of America and proclaiming the obscene holiness of shit and pubic lice. Finally he emerged into the Great Hall. It had once been the dance hall of an old club, and there was even a bar at its side. Now, even in the day, it was a murky place. A little light filtered from a dormer window above. Great gauzy veils were hung about the place like giant, batik cobwebs. The patterns on them were kaleidoscopic spirals, paisley-ed micro-organisms or creatures of the deep seas such as whales, star-eaters, angler fish, lampreys. There were, of course, jellyfish, too. The walls were painted with similar designs in purples, azures and luminous greens. It was so dingy in the hall that the luminous paint glowed distinctly.

Sitting cross-legged in a row on the left side of the hall were the fifteen disciples with wooden buckets of water in front of them. As Joe entered the hall they intoned the words of the sacred mantra, "I know what I mean." Joe had adopted this as the most important mantra of the sect because he was above all disillusioned with universality. Previously, in his eagerness to communicate ideas, Joe had often irritated people with his habitual phrase, "You know what I mean?" until he realised that they didn't. Since then he had told himself over and over in his own head, "I know what I mean." It had given him great satisfaction to make it a key doctrine of his own religion.

Joe sat cross-legged at the head of the hall. "Shall we begin?" he asked, and each disciple picked up the ceremonial sieve that rested at the side of his bucket. Every morning they carried out the same ritual. They would sieve the water in their buckets and examine the mesh for flakes of gold. There never were any, of course. There was some debate among the disciples as to the meaning of this ritual. Some said that it demonstrated there was no such thing as real wisdom, since however much you might pan for it, it will slip through your mesh. Others claimed that it signified that nothingness, which by implication contains all things in their most perfect synthesis, is the most precious thing in the cosmos and the substance—or insubstance—of true fulfilment. Arguments both subtler and simpler had also been bandied about the Jellyfish Ashram.

Joe watched. It was a period of slackness in which he could relax and think of nothing. Fixed periods of waiting are always so. They are necessary in the formation of any plan of action. He gazed at the faces of his disciples leisurely. They, like him, looked anonymous and weary. It was especially tiredness that he saw in their stubble and the lines engraved on their faces, the gentle tiredness of people who thought they were nothing special, but for one reason or another had not found any place or satisfactory identity of their own in the world, and had been forced into a zone where there was only a question mark. They wanted to know who they were. Joe could only put names to faces. Lionel. Stewart. Matthew. Ralph. Lester. Barry. Mick. Gunter. Jason. Dylan. Simon. Nathan. Hugh. Vaughn. He could not tell them more than that.

The ritual was over. Lionel stood.

"Master Joe, today you are to leave us forever on your final pilgrimage. Before you go we would like to hear from your own lips the quintessence of your teachings one last time."

"Lionel, my friend, you have followed me faithfully and with a humbleness that humbles me. I will gladly teach you again, as if it were the first time."

Joe leaned sideways in an attitude of recollection, his gentle-thick, dogsbody hand poised in the air as if to pluck words from it.

"Does the world control the Jellyfish, or does the Jellyfish control the world?"

The question lit up the hall, inspiration sparking between Joe's thumb and forefinger.

"The Jellyfish has attained enlightenment. It is in a state of perpetual meditation. Think of it! You may look into the ocean and sometimes the transparent Jellyfish may be invisible, one with the water. It is utterly passive and empty. Surely, then, it is the world that rules the Jellyfish. Yet wait! Can emptiness be measured? Only things that exist can be measured. So the Jellyfish is infinity, and infinity is freedom. It must contain all things. The world projects its will and its dreams into the emptiness, but this is not control, this is what it means to be controlled. The Jellyfish is a mirror, but it doesn't reflect what is already there, it creates its own emptiness by projecting everything outwards. Then, when everything gazes in the mirror of emptiness, it is sucked back in again. Does the world control the Jellyfish, or does the Jellyfish control the world? There is no answer. One is the reflection of the other. Listen, in the beginning there was Nothingness, and Nothingness was the Jellyfish. But Nothingness is a paradox, an impossibility. No light and no dark. No substance and no absence. So Nothingness folded in on itself under the sheer weight of its own paradox and Everything was created. This did not happen a long time ago, since there is no time in Nothingness. It is happening now. Nothing and Everything exist simultaneously, are coterminous, reject each other and force each other into being or non-being."

Simon leant forward and raised a hand. He was a small man with the helpless face of a comedian, his lower eyelids dragged down and his nose turned piggishly up to expose his nostrils.

"I'd like to ask something."

"Yes?"

"Your words are inspiring, Master, but ultimately it seems like all they are telling us is that the universe is a paradox, balancing opposite forces. It reassures one to hear that there is an all-encompassing order as inevitable as mathematical truth.

But, similar to mathematics, it seems abstract. It doesn't teach us how we should live our lives."

"No one can teach you how to live your lives. I will not fall into the trap of telling you to believe in yourself. You are free to doubt yourself as well. But if you will be taught, I will do my best to teach and you must do your best to learn. In the end, whether we like it or not, we must become as a Jellyfish. We may resist, thinking that the Jellyfish opposes us, but eventually we learn that it opposes nothing. There is nothing to lose. The Jellyfish exists without heart or mind. See the Jellyfish washed up on the beach. Take up a piece of slate, I dare you, and slice the Jellyfish in half. Commit that most terrible of blasphemies! I, your Master, beseech you in the name of all that is holy, to commit that sacrilege! Do you think you can slay the Jellyfish? Look closely. Has its heart stopped beating? Has its mind ceased to function? No. Its heart never beat; its mind never functioned. Life and Death are one for the Jellyfish. Some may fear becoming the Jellyfish. That is natural. When you are still human such a thought is terrifying. Then others of you may be tired of such human terror, and you may wish more than anything to become a Jellyfish, but I tell you, only when you have ceased to fear and ceased to wish will you become a Jellyfish.

"Please, no more questions now. I should like to read to you from the Holy Jotter. My voice and your listening are more important than words. I would like us simply to be together for a few minutes before I go."

And Joe stood and walked to where the Holy Jotter hung from another bent nail on a loop of coarse, bristling string. He lifted it from its place slowly, with fond fingers, the coals of a strange, gentle emotion in his eyes. For a moment there was just his face in shadow and the dog-eared book in front of it, a moment magnified with all the respiratory closeness of solipsism. Then he turned back to his disciples.

The Holy Jotter had been written in the inchoate period before Joe had assembled his disciples. After scratching his head and stroking his nose and absent-mindedly drinking many mugs of cloudy lapsang souchong, Joe had sat down with the jotter like a draughtsman at a drawing board, licked the lead of a tiny stub of pencil, and set about the creation of his very own Bible. It had appealed to him as a stroke of genius, no, divine inspiration, to write the whole thing in pencil. Rather than being carved in stone, the Word was scribbled in graphite and liable to be erased with a rubber and revised on a whim. He had divided his gospel into chapter and verse, but the divisions and the numbers were completely arbitrary since he had been more concerned with feeling than with editorial thoroughness.

Joe sat back down at the head of the hall, opened the Jotter and read, his voice illuminating the swell of pages like a candle glow.

"Chapter 1, verse 27. It is better to play and to know nothing than to be wise and to do nothing. There are no greater fools than the teacher who believes he is understood and the disciple who believes he understands. I know what I mean."

"I know what I mean," intoned the disciples, an echo muttering low and solemn.

"Cause and effect is an illusion, a chain of the mind only. Life, consciousness, beauty, cannot arise from cause and effect, since cause and effect is ultimately sterile, incapable of creation. Long ago the dark seas waited without expectation for something that could not be named. There was a bolt of lightning and suddenly the seas were energised, full of seething, inchoate life. Why? There was no reason until the thing happened; it was a reason in itself, self-conceiving, spontaneous.

"Chapter 13, verse 2. Let us consider beauty. A jellyfish may be weighed and measured. Its beauty cannot. Yet the universe is nothing but an unending fractal pattern whose foundation is a simple equation. The pattern divides and subdivides like the reproduction of microscopic, asexual organisms. We ourselves are part of the pattern, yet we can look at it and call it beautiful. At what point did the pattern acquire the ability to see itself as beautiful? Answer: the power was already there and the pattern shaped itself to it, not according to cause and effect, but according to pregnant synchronicity.

"Chapter 3, verse 11. The Jellyfish is a living mandala. Does it know it is beautiful? In the Far East the word for 'jellyfish' is written with the characters 'sea' and 'moon'. Such perception describes the nature of the Jellyfish far more thoroughly than would the careful measuring and biological classification of the creature, since it acknowledges the existence of the jellyfish within the observer and vice versa. This is what synchronicity means. 'Synchronicity'. Sounds a bit like 'Jellyfish'. If you say it slowly. And use your imagination. Sort of.

"Chapter 7, verse 52. I know what I mean."

"I know what I mean," came the antiphonal chorus.

"Chapter 9, verse 4. 'Lightning' sounds a bit like 'synchronicity', too."

A tone of satiety had come into Joe's voice with the last few lines. He had started eagerly, as if he had a wide, tilting ocean of words to tell. But somewhere in the telling, the impossibility of the task had dawned upon him. The meaning had faded out of the words. He had reached the point of satisfaction sooner than expected because he knew he could never be satisfied.

"I've already spoken enough, I think," he said, and closed the leaves of the Jotter. "The last and most important of my teachings is not written in the Jotter and is yet to be told."

The disciples raised their faces in a fresh and wondrous expectancy. Joe looked at his watch, tapped the glass face.

"My guide will soon be here. It's time for me to go."

He stood and his disciples watched in helpless flickering amazement as a man in saffron robes entered the hall from the

11

unclosable door which opened on the stairs to the front door and the street. The man, Lobsang, was a Sherpa who had wandered far from his native land and was now inured to the cold, leaden London air. He had helped Joe through one or two difficult passes in life. Joe trusted him as a companion of few words and fewer visits. For the past few years now he had been charged by Joe with a very particular mission which involved him as confidante, advisor, scout and messenger. That mission was almost concluded and it was with an air of serene and fateful finality that he now approached Joe.

"Please come. I have what you asked for," he said.

These words meant the jettisoning of the past to Joe, and it was almost absent-mindedly that he turned to his disciples and raised a hand in farewell.

"I've got to go now. See you later."

And the two went through the unclosable door, down the steep, shadowy stairs and out into the groggy daylight.

"The train doesn't leave for a while yet. I believe we have time for a cup of tea, if you like."

"I'd love one," said Joe.

There was a greasy spoon café a few turns from the station in a street forgotten by window cleaners and exterior decorators. They sat down at a red Formica table and Lobsang put the briefcase he had been carrying on the chair beside him.

"You told me to prepare for a long journey. You're turning into a bit of a crystal-ball gazer in your old age, aren't you?"

"Not at all. You wanted me to find anything related to jellyfish that might indicate your path in life. I have done so. There is a tiny, unnamed island whose existence is a guarded secret. It is almost as if you knew of the island before you founded your sect. Call it synchronicity, but I think this place is perfectly suited to your purposes."

"Yeah. I was just joshing. An island, eh? It just goes to show that if you choose your own road, whatever it is, somewhere in the world there's a suitable destination."

Lobsang was silent.

The proprietor brought them their tea. Joe raised the cup to his lips, slurped, set it back down in its saucer and gave a gasp of satisfaction.

"Aah! Good to wet the old whistle! I'm feeling rather dry. I'm surprised something like an island can be kept secret these days, even if it is only small. One looks at maps and tends to think that everything is charted."

Lobsang paused between sips.

"The world is an ever-unfolding map. Those who are satisfied will attempt to unfold it no further. But others may find places hidden between the folds. I have all the information you need in this briefcase."

He sipped again, then set down the cup and unbuckled the case.

"Please take a look."

Joe shuffled the sheaf of papers given to him and studied them with the air of a working man applying his concentration to the form of racing horses.

"Who do I pay for the tickets?"

"The path has been cleared for you. Do not worry. Money is unimportant."

"One-way?"

"Of course."

"Of course." He thought for a moment. "You know, even when I first asked you to find out what you could, I had a feeling I was doing something irreversible—one-way. Time has been tightening and tightening till now I feel . . . rather tense."

He wiped his forehead and then wiped his palms on his trousers.

"I can almost hear the drum roll."

"You still have the choice."

"No, no, one way or another I'd only be hiding, procrastinating. Strange that fulfilment should be so . . . "

"Yes?"

"I hardly know how to describe it. So much like a double defeat, like check-mate, like admitting you were wrong all along and that you didn't really want any of the things you struggled for anyway. One imagines fulfilment as the beginning of real life, but it ends up as the final split-second in which all life is seen as a waste of time and a worthless lie. Actually, you could have had fulfilment at any time, but you preferred life. You preferred procrastination. Christ! For a guru I've become pretty long-winded. Where's my pith? I feel like I've had all the pith taken out of me."

"These are not the words of a man about to attain fulfilment. What is worrying you?"

Joe glanced about gloomily.

"I've broken butties here with my disciples, drunk a brew or two. I don't know, what have I really left them? I'm tired of religion and I'm tired of irreligion, but they both keep coming, wave after wave. It seems that every time you try to teach freedom you're just making one more chain. It's all the same in the end whether it's some smug, fat Buddha telling you that the wheel of Samsara is nothing but suffering, or some lunatic Catholic priest screaming at his boys about God striking them with lightning if they dare have a swift one of the wrist. It all ends up as a denial of life. It's bloody miserable. Sometimes I feel like saying, be vain, have a facelift, become an alcoholic, pine away for impossible love, play with money, become a sad and dirty old man, devote your life to art or to the orgasm, do anything but listen to someone who has something to tell you about life, anything but search for truth or enlightenment. Who wants to waste their life meditating in a cave when they could be going to a gig, or drinking with mates, or anything at all?"

"Then why don't you follow your own advice?"

"I can't. Not me. The waves keep coming, telling me to seek life's meaning. Those who I would teach such a message already know it anyway. Only I, the one who would teach it, am incapable of following it."

Lobsang stiffened as if he had heard a distant signal.

"It's time to go. The train leaves soon."

"How is it you're so punctual when you never wear a watch?"

"It's my body clock."

They boarded the train together and sat staring from the window in silence. It was a couple of hours till their destination and Joe was largely occupied with his own thoughts.

At one point Joe turned to Lobsang and said, "Why are you helping me?"

"Because you are my friend."

"You don't really believe in what I'm doing?"

"That is not for me to judge."

"So you don't think it's wrong, anyway?"

"You are an individual. You have an individual fate. I trust you."

"And I trust you. Isn't that frightening?"

Then Joe took the unsealed envelope from the inside pocket of his jacket.

"I want you to give this to my disciples when the thing is complete."

"May I ask what it is?"

"It's my final teaching, of course."

"Of course. I understand."

Lobsang took the envelope and put it away in his briefcase.

Gulls yelled like enthusiastic stevedores over the cargo crates in the lip-chapping air of the port where they parted. Joe was met, as Lobsang had told him he would be, by another man with a shaved pate wearing saffron robes. The two, newly met, ascended the gangway together and were soon lost to the sight of the Sherpa left upon the grey and rusty wharf. At length the ship pulled laboriously away from its moorings and churned the leaden waves under equally leaden clouds, slowly, slow-ly nosing out of the harbour into the wide embarkation of the choppy ocean. The ship gathered knots indefatigably, and moved out to where the dull, syrupy glory of a few shafts of sunlight pierced the carbon gloss of the clouds, as sonorous as a trumpet blast about the throne of God. As the ship turned into its journey Lobsang turned away and walked back to the train station unhurriedly.

The train had rattled through some minutes and some miles of countryside as dull and restful as the glass through which the Sherpa saw it all, on what was for him a return journey. He was alone with the ghost reflection in the grey of the late-day window. There was only that autumnal reflection and his own agelessness. No one knows what thoughts were passing in his corner of the universe when he absently took the enve-lope from his briefcase. It remained unsealed and he untucked the gummed tongue and took the folded notepaper out. He unfolded it and a smile pale as a watermark traced across his features. The creased creaminess of the paper was immaculate. Not a single word spoiled its symmetry.

It certainly seemed appropriate that Joe's last voyage should be made by sea instead of air, but perhaps those who had arranged it had also meant to allow him time to reflect. He gazed often from the deck at the passing waves. Their seeming endlessness and protean homogeneity lent him serenity. But beneath the sun-skipping serenity of the surface, the sea was deep and ominous. Still, he never wavered in his mind from the course that was set.

It was to a certain archipelago in the Pacific that Joe was taken first. From there his new guide was to accompany him on the final leg of his journey. This leg was made in a small fishing vessel of the kind often used to take tourists on cheap cruises around the bays of the local islands. His guide could have been taken for a mute much of the time, he was so silent. But Joe was grateful for this. He did not find it lonely. On the contrary, this silence seemed to contain some gentle reassurance in it far more profound than that of conversation.

Under a fierce sun the waters sped and shoaled like the backs of porpoises. Joe watched the way the water next to the boat's hull streaked by while the distant water of the horizon seemed a static plain. He thought of the flatness of a spread map, with its lines of latitude and longitude. He thought of that map spinning around him and wondered if it would have the same effect. As he gazed at the waves he saw something strange. It seemed that little dribbles of water were leaping from the sea and flying horizontally for some metres before rejoining the water they had come from. It was a while before Joe realised these liquid flashes in the sunlight were flying fish. For some reason this exotic discovery made him think again of maps, and particularly of old sea charts with pictures of mermaids and krakens on them, and 'Here be monsters' written in those areas as yet unexplored.

There was at last a sense of arrival in the dizzily revolving plain of the ocean, and in the waves that throbbed as hard as rock against the hull of the ship. His companion seemed to be navigating by certain signs that were utterly mysterious to Joe. The only possible reference point he could imagine was the blaze of the sun, which seemed now so low in the sky that it was as if the ocean were running into the sky and the sky back into the ocean.

Joe looked at the figure crouched in the shade of the cabin. The figure glanced back at him and by certain subtleties in his movements as he turned the wheel and scanned the field of waves ahead told Joe that their destination was indeed near. Before long Joe could see it himself, a dark dot standing on the horizon. The dot grew until it resembled something like the tower of a ruined castle overgrown with dark vines and creepers. As the island grew larger, Joe could make out that the tower wall was actually a dry, rocky cliff-face, the vegetation, sometimes massed in great hornets' nests of leaves, made up of trees and shrubs. The cliff-face was broader than it was tall, giving a strange impression of squat, concentrated power. In fact, a curious mixture of stormy darkness and glaring light made the whole island seem like a mirage crackling with inner lightning, a wonder of the ocean.

The boat slowed towards the thin shoreline which circled the island. Joe looked twice and saw a figure standing erect in front of the clear azure waves like a monolith left to measure tides, guide boats or serve some other, nautically esoteric function. The figure was wearing robes slightly different to those of his guide. They were blue, touched with white markings that could have been constellations, clouds, the tops of waves, or microscopic organisms.

The boat was lulled gently on the tiny, transparent crests of shallow, shore-seeking waves. Joe needed no instructions. There was no need to wait any longer and he climbed over the side of the boat and splashed the few remaining feet to shore.

"We have awaited your coming a long time."

Joe was surprised to hear any words issue from the lips of that iron-faced sentinel. He could imagine the living pillar standing facing out to sea for years without a moment's relenting while tides rose over his head and ebbed away from his sandaled toes.

"How long?"

"Many generations. I am pleased to have the honour of seeing the end of our long vigil."

"I'm sorry it took me so long."

"You are here now. That is everything. Please follow me."

Joe turned back to wave goodbye to his erstwhile companion, but the boat had already started away from the shore and was some distance out in the hot, dark shadow of the mid-ocean afternoon. Joe felt no regret, only a freedom as ageless and impersonal as the wide, empty sky and the air of present reality standing all around him. He turned again to follow his last guide on Earth, whose name he would never know, but whom he was trusting more absolutely than he had trusted any other being in his life. He watched the sandaled feet before him bend and twist on the rocky ground, the ankles stoically absorbing all and keeping such balance that to look at the upper body only, one might guess the man was walking on a carpeted floor.

Soon the man turned towards the parched, looming cliff-face, climbing upwards, passing a few scrubby trees, leaning forwards into the slope. Occasionally the rocks and scree slipped from beneath Joe's feet and he almost tumbled, clouds of dust drifting into the still air about him.

Joe looked up at the deep pits and lumpy crags of the rock face, shielding his eyes. Some of its formations were very curious, like the pipe-organ stalagmites and stalactites to be found in certain caves, reaching up to great, swollen masses like petrified clouds. He wondered where might be their destination amidst such seeming barrenness. It soon became clear, however, that what he at first thought a deep shadow beneath a lip of rock, was actually the entrance to a cave. They passed beneath the overhanging rock and into the cave's fossil-dry gullet. The cave continued in an irregularly circular tunnel for some distance, so that the darkness became complete and was eventually relieved at some obscure distance by the milky release of daylight at a far exit. The guide did not turn, did not light up a torch, merely trod the worthless, crumbling ore of darkness with Joe trudging clumsily behind, a temporary blind man. They emerged once more onto a sunstruck ledge of rock. Joe winced and shielded his eyes, himself crowned cruelly by the glancing, glaring, dizzy, splintered rays. Gazing thus, in the archetypal stance of the explorer, he saw a wide, flat basin below. Around the edges it was feathered with the green of sparse vegetation, but the centre was as bald as an arena. The great, frowning walls of the island enclosed the plain completely.

The guide pointed, the spray of his fingers like an eagle taking wing.

"See? In the far wall of the valley is a shadow. The shadow is the last gateway. Beyond is that which we have tended for generations, that which waits for you. Let us take breath awhile and start."

The scorching plain was behind them and the shadow of the great stone archway, shaped almost like a keyhole, sloped off their shoulders like a cloak. They had not entered another valley. Stone walls enclosed this space, too, but those walls leaned together as if in conference and allowed only a tiny fragment of sky to spill its light onto the scene below. Here the walls were damp and an ancient smell of salt lingered coolly in the air. What the slow scintillations of light illuminated was the perfect reverse of the other half of the island. Instead of land surrounded by walls surrounded by shore, here a body of water was surrounded by shore which was in turn surrounded by walls. A special breeze funnelled in reverse from above brought the waters of this long extinct volcano out in gooseflesh. The light on these quick ripples was of that perfect, silent white that seems to blur of itself into a tearful sheen. Joe gazed at the cirrus striations of white, at the pattern of their static movement.

Such a hush was upon the water as the effusion of violins at the end of an old film might melt into—the moving chill of deaf-and-dumbness. Perfect, lapping, empty silence. Then beneath the painted waters he saw it, the pattern more beautiful and alarming than any waves. It was a pattern like that kind of camouflage that is perfectly invisible until some unidentifiable switch is made in the mind and it becomes obvious, the spell of invisibility broken forever. Floating cold and sickly as a dead thing, filling the whole lake with its translucent, membranous presence, was a gigantic and almost imperceptibly pulsing jellyfish.

At first, regarding, stunned, the sober-cold rim of the god-like invertebrate as it pulsed insensately, Joe felt that this was a morbid thing, a cataract-coloured lump of pollution neither living nor dead, but constantly sluggish and twitching as a drool-mouthed dog dying of rabies. But soon the filmy, globular shape began to exert on him a kind of awe. A million years had petrified between Joe and his guide, and that guide, eyes smudged and sparking with an understanding so ancient it was reptilian, said nothing. Something in the moted cold, the inhuman realism and the slow motion of the dull, embryonic presence, made Joe's human heart withdraw as if from the slurring, warping sting of its tentacles. But that very cold, at first disgusting, became attractive, as meditation in a cool, clean cave is attractive.

Joe wanted to touch that eyeless substance, that primitive indifference, to feel the static electricity of contact with something created within an unlit sphere of events prior to and utterly unrelated to the human.

He drifted to the edge of the lake and sat cross-legged where its ripples melted into one another. The world had shrunk down to this moment. A figure sitting by a lake in a cavern, fidgeting slightly, the air around him empty and free, suggesting no action, no path, allowing anything, expecting

21

nothing. There was no waiting. Yet, in that emptiness the world had become supremely personal. Finite in space and time, Joe's memories trailed behind him in a wake, in their strict limitation tinged with the infinity of imagination. A reverse image of these memories, a mirage, opened out before him, a gateway to daydream, sentiment, fantasy. Narrowing down to this single point, life was now suggesting an eternity of all that was unlived based on what had been lived; the unfulfilment of Joe's life cast a reflection of fulfilment in his death, the vast remainder of existence. It was his own reflection he was gazing into. No waiting. He was beyond timing things, beyond making decisions, beyond waiting, when he stood, removed his clothes, and lowered himself into the cave-cool water.

His flesh was pasty beneath the refracting, shivering mystery of this transparent element. The very emptiness of the water was like death. There were no fish, only the slower-than-life pulsations of the unbreathing sea-thing before him. It was like one vast, transparent organ independent of a body, whose pulse was purely nervous, an activity more primitive than life. It was an animated mandala, a jellified lightning bolt, a self-luminous fossil, an x-ray of chaos. The filigree of the stingers swayed trance-like before his eyes. The water deafened him to all but his own respiration. One stinger floated insensibly nearer as he struggled in the surging stillness of the lake. He reached out with his hand to touch it. He caught hold of the lightning. The lacy, silvery pattern traced around the dome of the jellyfish and its chandelier of tentacles seemed to flash for an instant. Joe was momentarily as transparent as the monster that he touched—a moment of illumination and agony.

When the guide walked to the edge of the lake and peered in, he saw no trace of a body floating by the mass of unfeeling stingers. There was only the numbness of the barren water.

✳

The crabbed blue melancholy of night was on dense-bricked London, and Lobsang was following an urban trail back to the squat where he was temporarily staying with acquaintances. His hands were warm with the plain-paper grease-stained parcel he was carrying home from a takeaway. As he passed beneath a street lamp his body was visibly overcome by some silken, relaxing sensation, sinking in from the head downwards. He stopped and closed his eyes a moment. His lids flickered a little as if he were dreaming. When he opened his eyes there was an expression of glowing, elastic contentment on his face, moistly human, oilily egoless; an expression as unfashionable as his bare feet in the damp London gutter. Looking about, he mounted the pavement and backtracked a little until he came to a space between buildings where a half-torn-down wire fence girded a patch of waste ground. He raised his eyes to the sky between the dark, disconsolate eaves of the buildings. A strange constellation glittered there, brighter than all the other stars of the sky. Lobsang could clearly perceive the dot-to-dot shape of a jelly-fish, its blooming bell, its trailing stingers, clouded with its own Milky Way. And within the nebulous shape of the jellyfish, like the face on the Turin shroud, he saw a face as peculiar and anonymous as that of a clown. Despite the skeletal spareness of detail he recognised the face. Then the constellation began to wink and die like the sparkling flash of a firework after it has exploded at its zenith. A wan smile floated on Lobsang's face. He continued on his way.

Back at the squat, while the others tucked into the un-wrapped fare with grimy fingers, he retrieved an envelope from his briefcase. It was the envelope given to him by Joe on the train. He fished the notepaper from inside and unfolded it. Letters looped and crawled across the page in Joe's hand, like letters of a workman jotting measurements and estimates. It was as if the message had been written in invisible ink.

※

Lobsang was not the only one to see things that night. In a draughty passage of Joe's quondam ashram, beneath the ramshackle, carpetless stairs where the deep chest freezer and the washing machine stood, Stephen was shivering in his sack-like robes. It was his turn to do the laundry. There had been several loads and the light had faded as he stood watching the clothes tumble round and round, until he could no longer see them and had to watch the coloured lights by the control panel instead, like a solitary air traffic control officer watching the landing lights of a solitary plane while his paper cup of coffee went cold beside him.

Since Joe had gone away, Stephen, a small, dark-haired disciple, had developed first a sniffle, then a sneeze, then a heavy bout of influenza. For a while he could not leave the soiled, sweaty nest of his mattress. Finally he was up and about, but only just. When he walked his eyes fell to the ground as if he were walking in darkness, afraid he might trip. His nose was constantly running, and he had soaked several rolls of toilet paper with his transparent mucus. Even now, on top of the freezer, was a nest of shredded tissue paper such as a gerbil might make in its cage. When one length of tissue paper was hopelessly sodden and stringy, he would shuffle to the nearby toilets to retrieve some more. In short, he felt rotten. Until this miserable illness abated he did not have the energy or the will to do more than perform one or two of the humblest duties and beguile his foggy wakefulness with such things as the unending observation of a tiny green light.

As he stood, shoulders hunched, and the light before him grew fuzzy, he felt something like a rippling up his back, an airy lightness as if his flesh were responding to the gentle vibrations of the strings of an acoustic guitar. He raised his head and sighed at the light-fingered buzzing that had made his upper back into a bliss that bordered on that of non-existence. Sensing this bliss was too great and too persistent to be the mere random quiver to which his body was occasionally subject, he turned around. Behind him a strange man, a tramp perhaps, was hovering in the small passage. It must have been Stephen's cold, or some trick in the tickling grey-blue veil of fibrous darkness that had fallen, but Stephen could swear there was a faint glow to the figure. He was not afraid, not exactly, but there was a chimney-like warmth to this presence that reminded him of emotions not to be felt in diurnal life, but only with a nostalgia that visits at the time of death. For a moment, indeed, Stephen thought with stupendous relief that he was dying. This notion was brief-lived. Ripples of sudden disappointment settled into the usual disappointment and contentment of being alive.

"Who are you?" he asked, and noticing that a great string of mucus had suddenly leaked from his nose, he swabbed at it with a slimy tissue.

The figure stepped forward.

"Don't you know me?" it asked.

From something in the voice, Stephen was sure he ought to know the draggled figure, but it was as if that identity were too wide and too familiar to grasp.

"I'm sure I've never seen you before, but maybe I do know you somehow."

"Perhaps you do not know me because I am not me and never was, and perhaps you know me because you have always known me, even though we meet for the first time. Still, I told you I would see you later. It is later now. Don't you remember those words?"

Stephen couldn't remember anything for certain. His sense of chronology had become ambiguous, events spinning around him like objects around someone sick with dizziness. What he would once have deemed memories now were indistinguishable from premonitions. Another thread of mucus began to stretch itself from the tip of his nose, and amidst his confusion the glistening thread seemed full of joy, a brazen embarrassment, a helpless vulnerability. Tears fluttered behind his eyes like a bird bumping and flapping at a window, trying to get out.

"Tell the others I'm sorry not to see them in person," continued the stranger. "I've got no person to see them in anymore. They ought to understand. I'm theirs now. There's really no need to say goodbye. Stephen, it's all over."

And saying this the stranger reached forward and laid hold of Stephen's arms. The last four words reverberated inside Stephen's muffled head. He closed his eyes and burst into a lachrymose explosion of liquid from his eyes, nose and mouth. As if he had inhaled a menthol vapour, his nose, throat, brain, lungs and entire body was enveloped in a warm, crystal sensitivity. He could breathe again. His head was perfectly clear, his body light and free of weariness. The stranger, however, had gone. He had disappeared into Stephen like a ghost into a wall. And then a spell was broken and Stephen cried anew and with a quick spring of tears when he realised who the stranger had been, or, since the stranger was all that Joe had never lived, his reverse silhouette, who he had not been.

✳

He did not particularly expect the others to believe him, but he could no more hold back his news than he could have held back his tears.

The others had been gathered mainly in the meditation hall, where they sat scattered like toadstools, eyes closed, breathing bleakly under the imperceptibly flickering fluorescent lights. Along one wall, from a little above waist height, was a long line of windows. The lights being on, the outside world had been thrown into darkness, making the panes of glass appear glistening, solid-black walls. The meditation room was thus removed from all association with the outside and became an abstract, self-contained space.

Those who sat in the room were focused on a yet more abstract inner space, and there was no one to witness the room itself. Had there been such a person, and had they approached the windows, they might have noticed the glass was old and warped, that the panes shivered slightly and that there was a constant draught, like a stream of water. Standing by the black, condensation-trickling windows, such a person might have noted a sweet autumnal loneliness; the loneliness of the self, ageless, nameless, that stares forever from the cave of the eyes but never sees itself from outside, that self, grey and shadowed, whose shoulders are hunched and whose back is curled like a fallen, gale-blown leaf. The meditators, however, being essentially pragmatic in matters of the spirit, attached no value to such melancholy sweetness and preferred the crisp, moderate warmth of their bodies and their cross-legged meditation, away from the windows' cold.

The illusion of flat, solid blackness the windows created was broken when a silent eruption of light gave the damp night depth. Amongst those who meditated, some were trying to place themselves in the serene, drifting state of The Jellyfish, pulsing in the eternal nowhere of the deep sea as the self, eyes closed, pulses in the infinite nowhere of consciousness outside of space and time. Their colourful darkness was lightened and their amniotic concentration disturbed by a seeming shower of rays upon their eyelids and upper skulls. Roused from their meditation they looked about for the shining presence responsible.

When Stephen burst into the room they were crowding about the window. A silver blush was fading from the rain-streaked cheek of the night. The gaggle of masterless disciples turned to Stephen and both sides were so jubilantly keen to tell the other their news that a confused and excited babble ensued. Eventually both sides managed to tell their story. Stephen, that of his strange meeting and the instantaneous curing of his flu, the other disciples of the jellyfish constellation they had seen floating in the sky and of the dot-to-dot face that had glowed amidst its tentacles. The story of one side, with its lightning synchronicity, only served to bolster the wonder and the credibility of the other. There was no room for doubt. Joe had been true to his word. He had come back to see them again.

Two days later, Lobsang arrived at the groggy doorstep of the ashram and, finding no answer to his plying of the bell, and the door, as always, open, he climbed the shadowy stairway to the main hall. He carried with him an envelope, unsealed, in which there was a piece of paper. On the piece of paper was Joe's last and most important teaching.

The place seemed deserted, but by chance Lionel happened into the hall, recognised Lobsang and asked him what he wanted. Lobsang did not offer to embellish on his purpose or the message he carried with his own words, but simply handed over the envelope. Lionel's forehead knitted with the gravest perplexity when he read the contents. First he hesitated, but then, the burden of responsibility—of being the sole guardian of the teaching—proved too great, and he called the other disciples. The new teaching threw the disciples into a furore. There was much argument over the meaning of this puzzle and the voices raised contained variously despair, rapture, reflection, anger and awe. The handwriting was undoubtedly Joe's, so the authenticity of the teaching seemed indisputable. There was a paradox, however, in that the very authority of that authenticity refuted its own authenticity. In the midst of the uproar, Lobsang took his leave. His going was hardly noticed.

Researchers with a particular interest in obscure cults and religions unanimously attribute the split of the Sect of the Jellyfish to the contents of that envelope. Under the leadership of Lionel, half of the disciples persisted in keeping the sect alive. Indeed, to this day it survives and has started to attract serious attention amongst New Agers, occultists and other groups. The rest of the disciples dispersed and went their separate ways. Their fates are various. Gunter set up a nudist restaurant. Jason plunged into dissipation and became homeless for a time, until he managed to find a precarious niche on the lecture circuit, recounting his experiences. Ralph made a slight name for himself writing essays of a philosophical nature, though these were not taken seriously by the academic establishment. Mick disappeared and is rumoured to have been behind attacks on certain abattoirs, fast food chains and scientific research centres. And so on.

When questioned, both those who had remained loyal to the sect and those who left insisted that Joe was a great man, that he had changed their lives utterly, and that they remained loyal to his memory. Yet, despite the preservation of the Holy Jotter and the Last Teaching, written consistently in the handwriting of an unknown person, there is no historical evidence that such a person as Joe ever existed. Stories have trickled back from those who know Lobsang about an island and a vast jellyfish. But no trace of an island has ever been found where that island should be. From this circumstance many have been led to conclude that Joe and the legend surrounding him are either the product of an exceedingly lame hoax or the group hallucination of an isolated religious community and those few dubious enough to have connections with them. Others, referring to the Last Teaching, have remarked ironically, that since he was apparently not such a great man after all, his existence or non-existence is utterly, so to speak, immaterial.

These, anyway, are the words that met Lionel's eyes when he opened up the envelope given to him by the Sherpa:

The time has come for me to deliver my last words to the world. They, more than any previous words, must come from the very depths of my heart. To some, albeit a very few, I have been a teacher, even a messiah. I do not know whether other messiahs were ever tempted to make such a proclamation. But if they did make such, their disciples must have seen fit to make sure the proclamation never reached the ears of the world. However, I must not be guided by precedent. And so, my friends, I hereby declare that I am and always have been nothing but a charlatan and a fraud. In all the days of my teaching I had no inspiration but the flimsiest of whims to guide me. I just made it up as I went along,

Signed,

Joe.

The Haunted Bicycle

I MUST beg the reader's indulgence here—as I will no doubt beggar both indulgence and belief elsewhere—for a slightly unusual disclaimer. Usually in such disclaimers it is stressed that all persons, places and events within a given story are entirely fictional. Well, I don't think the events of which you are about to read need any such disclaimer. The main character, however, is based on a real person—one who sadly no longer graces the world with his presence. For this reason I have long hesitated to do anything with the scribblings under this title in my book of plots, and, if the truth be told, still feel an extraordinary apprehension here on the threshold of the story.

One might think it is difficult to invent characters *ex nihilo*, and that the lazy writer simply lifts them from his own life, but seeing the task before me, I am convinced it is actually far more difficult to draw a faithful portrait of a real person than to make things up. For this reason I must apologise in advance, both to my readers and to Les, for the dismal failure to do him justice that I anticipate. If I continue, nonetheless, with the writing of this yarn, it is only because I am absolutely convinced that if Les could read all this he would be laughing his socks off. Such conviction is a rare thing indeed for me, and in astonishment I take it as a sign and go ahead. Les, of course, is a false name. I also reserve the right to tell bare-faced lies at any point in this story, in this disclaimer and in life generally, especially to those I owe money. It's called poetic license.

Well, that's all I wanted to say. So, without further ado, may I present to you a gothic picaresque kitchen-sink novella of the Uncanny, Surreal and Absurd:

The Haunted Bicycle

Chapter I: Something the Matter

One evening, some years ago now, Les came round for a mug of tea.

I was working on a manuscript, sunk deep in thought, wrestling with designs grand and macabre, when there came the familiar sharp knock at the door. The manuscript was *The League of Hollow Twigs*, part of my ambitious and unfinished Earwig cycle. If only I could leave it to my overself to write these things instead of having to go through the painstaking process of transcribing the elusive details of a dream. How much longer will it take until the dream is captured on the page? O world, I am misunderstood! Kalpas hence this work shall be hailed a timeless classic in the whispering halls of Tau Ceti!

I let Les in and put aside the ink-stained and dog-eared manuscript with a sigh. And since dusk was falling outside and a chill of early autumn was stealing through invisible cracks in the window frame, I got up and drew the curtains.

As I rummaged about for something to serve as an ashtray, I noticed Les was unusually quiet. I never knew when Les was going to call. He just did sometimes, like a hedgehog that occasionally appears in the back garden. One thing I could usually rely on, however, was that soon after settling down and looking about the room for a while as if wondering where he was, Les would proceed to inform me that I had "missed a laugh" the other day, and go on to tell me the precise nature and circumstances of said laugh, until I quite came to regret the eternal bondage of my bookish ways. This time no such tale was forthcoming. Les was positively subdued, and I knew that something must be the matter.

At length I located what seemed to be the sole object in the house capable of being used as an ashtray, a foil dish that had once contained a tart of some description, and placed this, host-like, in front of Les. While the kettle boiled in the kitchen, he thoughtfully drew out stringy pinches of tobacco from his pouch and arranged them lumpily on a cigarette paper. His unbuttoned shirt cuff dangled from his wrist and he had to take care that it did not upset his fragile construction work. He said not a word. Being confronted with the feelings of another is like being confronted at once with the unmanageable vastness of the world and with my own contemptible inadequacy, and I therefore tend to take it as a terrible put-down, as I did on this occasion. I did nothing to relieve the silence. And why should I?

It was not until I served tea and biscuits that Les lit his rolly, looked at me with a brief, tentative smile, and broached the subject that was troubling him.

"Do you believe in ghosts?"

"Yes," I answered briefly and without hesitation.

"I thought you would. I don't know why, I just knew I could talk to you."

"What about?"

"You know that bike I got from the dump?"

"Maybe. Which one?"

Les had, in fact, procured a whole series of bicycles from the dump, giving up on each in turn when their problems were found to be beyond solution.

"The racer. The smart one."

"Oh yes."

"I think it's haunted."

His voice wavered on the last word like the breaking voice of an adolescent.

If anyone else had said it I'm sure I would have either been surprised or taken it as a joke, but for some reason, coming from Les it sounded quite natural. Yes, if anyone's going to find a haunted bicycle it's Les, I thought to myself.

"Why's that then?" I asked.

"Well, the action on it is all funny."

I only had a vague notion of what 'action' was, but it struck me as abstract enough to be the proper part of a bicycle for a ghost to inhabit.

"Could it be the ball bearings?" I asked, trying to sound as if I knew what I was talking about. Besides, ball bearings in bikes had the same kind of meaningless fascination for me as bubbles in spirit levels. I simply wanted to introduce them into conversation.

"What do you mean?"

"Well, maybe the bike's lost its bearings."

"Well, it could be that. But I don't think it is. You see, it's like the bike steers itself. It won't let me steer it. I wanted to go to the beach, but it went the other way, where the watermill is. I almost got run over. It was pretty scary, actually. Then I tried to walk it back to Beach Road, but I couldn't. And I didn't want to try and ride it again, so I had to carry it back."

"Very strange. You know what?"

"What?"

"I think it's haunted."

"Really?"

"I dunno."

"But seriously though, what d'you think? I came up here 'coz you're one of the few people I can really talk to. I'm fed up with everyone at Beach Road. What d'you reckon? You know about ghosts and things like that. Is it really haunted?"

"Do you want me to take a look at it?" I assumed my best professional manner.

"Tell you what, why don't you come round tomorrow?

Then I can show you what I mean. It's hard to explain other-wise. And I can play you my new Stryper record, too. That'll be smart!''

Chapter II: A Digression

You may be wondering how I met Les. Well, while the scenery is being changed, let me take the opportunity to fill in some background details.

After a long stint on the road, Les crashed at a certain house whose landlady took in strays of one sort or another. It was she who introduced me to Les, as I recall, on the beach. She said he needed friends and hoped I might fill that role. At the time I groaned inwardly at the thought of one more person towards whom I must feel some sense of social duty, one more compli-cation in the web of politeness and hypocrisy I wove in order to maintain a comfortable distance with the rest of the world. In the course of time, however, I came to view our meeting as of the utmost serendipity.

I am essentially a person with nothing to say. As you might imagine, this makes conversation very difficult for me. When I am lucky the other party simply thinks I am a very good lis-tener. When I am unlucky I am forced to look at myself in the harsh mirror of awkward silence. In sheer desperation I try to say something, anything, just to satisfy the other person that I am interested in them. For some reason, all the usual things that people talk about—current affairs, work and so on—seem so utterly nonsensical I find I can't even string a sentence together on them, and the only words that make it to my tongue are on subjects so impertinent, so lacking in connection to any human concern, that, if I thereby avoid all controversy, I also risk being thought an imbecile.

"Have you ever seen a sea-monkey?"

"What's your favourite deep-sea fish?"

"Do you think dead hedgehogs should have the right to adopt children?"

These and other similar questions, while hardly vexed themselves, have nonetheless vexed my listeners at one time or another.

At first I thought I had nothing in common with Les except idleness. However, I was soon to discover that our natures co-incided in another way. In Les I found someone who did not give a sea-monkey's what I said, and to whom I could happily talk drivel all day without fear of either boring or offending. The language we developed was not exactly that of in-jokes so much as spontaneous, infantile obscenity. I would make some remark so surreal and perverse I dare not repeat it here, at which he would laugh and call me weird, and then proceed generously to trump my own weirdness and obscenity with that of his own.

Well, nothing makes one's meaning clear like illustration, and all of a sudden I find myself thinking back to an earlier chapter in our shared bicycular history. Les was always urging me to accompany him on some expedition or other, and occasionally I would rouse myself from my lassitude and submit myself to the dictates of his enthusiasm. On one such occasion, Les had finally managed to extract a promise from me that we would cycle along the old disused railway line that led out of town and to the next village by a rather picturesque route. Our vehicles for this venture were two somewhat rusty pushbikes that Les had procured, as usual, from the local rubbish dump. The predecessors of the eponymous bicycle, these were not haunted by anything more sinister than a few squeaks. They were perfectly tame creatures of their kind. They were not, however, free of problems. What should have been a leisurely, even exhilarating ride, was turned into a hard slog the moment our wheels encountered even the slightest gradient. I'm not sure exactly why this was. Perhaps it was because the chains were rusty. Or perhaps the poor beasts were simply tired out, like horses ready for the knacker's yard.

The scenery on either side of the track was exceptionally beautiful, the lush trees and vegetation giving way in places to prospects of level pastureland enclosed by wooded hills. All this was rendered even more beautiful, to someone like me, by the air of disuse that hung over the place, the quiet sense of failure, of an irreversible step backwards, that seemed to cut it off from the rest of the world. There were no longer sleepers along the track, so that all that remained was the track itself, several miles of distractingly neat and hard-packed dirt, a kind of footpath as straight as a Roman road. The neatness of the dirt served now to emphasise a lack, an emptiness.

Vaguely aware that this scenery had once flashed glamorously by outside train windows, I started out enjoying its rather more sluggish passing and the pathos this suggested, from the seat of my bicycle. Before long, however, for reasons already mentioned, I found I could not enjoy anything while still on this bone-shaker. Les very magnanimously offered to swap bicycles, since his seemed to be the superior of the two, and for a while we took it in turns. But eventually I dismounted in despair saying I could not go on.

"Let's walk for a bit, shall we?" suggested Les.

This seemed like a good idea as, anyway, we had to go either back or forward. Wheeling our bicycles along in relative ease, we made fair progress and soon came to a shelter. I could not possibly pass by without taking advantage of a place to sit down, and this time it was Les' turn to yield to my enthusiasm for inertia.

"I wonder why they built a shelter here?" I mused aloud.

"Just so people can sit down, I s'pose."

Well, yes, this was the obvious answer, and perhaps it was a stupid question. It's true that shelters are not unknown in such places. But even so, I could not help marvelling that someone, designatable only as 'they', had gone to the trouble to put it there. It stood like a sentry box at a particularly straight and level stretch of the track, overlooking particularly even fields, apparently the only vertical thing, save for a few fence posts, in the vicinity.

We leaned our bikes on their stands in the middle of the track and sat on the warped, crumbling wood of the bench inside.

Being a great admirer of all things obscure and out-of-the-way—I once knew an artist who was passionate about containers, and thought this displayed a wonderful sensibility. "I collect containers," he said. "I have a great many containers. I like containers. Especially water heaters."—I immediately surveyed my new, wooden environment. Of course, my attention was soon drawn to the graffiti. No matter how dull and uninspired a single piece of graffiti itself might be, the uniqueness and obscurity that is inherent in all graffiti cannot fail to please me, and here there was the added attraction of location. What were the little vandals doing out here, and when? Something about the scratched initials and other fragments reminded me of an obituary. Among them one particular 'death' caught my interest:

Sarah Bagnall

4

Mark Bolton

Martin Pearce

James Lilley

IDST

I pointed it out to Les.

"Crikey! It's a pity it hasn't got her phone number."

"It's probably just as well," I said. "She's probably a ginner."

"A ginner? What's a ginner?"

"Don't you know?"

"No. What is it?"

"Well, if you don't know by now, you'll never know."

"Well, if you tell me I will know."

"It's someone with ginger hair."

"Oh, I see. A ginner. What's so special about a ginner?"

"Aaaaah!" I said meaningfully, which is to say, meaning-*less*ly.

"Yes?"

"Aaah! That would be telling!"

"Well, why don't you tell me, then?"

Feeling somewhat at a loss, I licked my lower lip thought-fully.

"They have ginger hair," I managed, forgetting the mysterious tone I had assumed.

"Is that all?"

"Um, and ginger pubes, I suppose."

I added this in the same matter-of-fact, reflective tone. Like having to explain a joke, it was not in the least bit funny. In fact, I felt a strange discomfort, which soon turned into an almost overpowering sense of shame. But like someone who drinks to forget his sorrows, I drew myself up, resumed my former mysterious air and launched once more into my oratory, waxing tedious.

"Have you never known the terrors and ecstasies of the ginner? Have you never felt your soul repeating on itself with a burning sensation like indigestion, the burning of madness and distraction for that endless ginger fuzz? Have you never found yourself worshipping at a copper idol, offering your finest and most sacred feelings to that which you know in your heart to be baser than a mackerel? Have you never taken delight in your own ruin, knowing that you threw yourself away for a twisted, ambiguous beauty, that which would mark you out forever as subhuman, and yet rejoiced as you fondled the very freckles that cursed you?"

Towards the end I was fairly shouting, as if relieving myself of a burden of long standing.

Les looked at me. His face frogged up with laughter.

"You're weird," he said.

And for the moment that was the end of the matter.

Just then, I spied an earwig crawling from a crack in the timbers of the shelter and a new conversation was born.

"Look! I wonder if it's male or female?" I said.

"How can you tell?"

"It's easy. Just look at the pincers. If they have little right angles, like squares, where they meet, then it's male. If they are smooth and curved then it's female."

"Is that true?"

"Yes. So now you can tell people you know how to sex an earwig. This one's female, and damned sexy, too. Just look at those curves! Almost willowy, I'd say."

"Cor, yeah! I see what you mean."

"She's coming your way. I think you're in there. You don't need Sarah Bagnall's number, after all. Look, she's juicing up at this very moment. She can't wait to wrap those pincers around you. Maybe I should give you some privacy."

My words now were deadpan, with the emphasis on 'dead', but it seemed to me all of a sudden that there flashed behind them something vicious and angry. It was not an anger directed towards Les in the slightest. What, or whom, was it directed towards, then? But any answer I can give to that question must be so general as to be inane. It is best simply to leave my words as they stand and hope my meaning is apparent. Can't you feel the anger?

Behind that hard emotion, too, as I so often find, there was also a much softer one. This was nostalgia. There is no emotion as paradoxical and enduring as the longing for that mysterious place, home. In my case, the roots I was forced to be nostalgic over were memories of rejection and humiliation, memories of living in and crawling through all the dirtiest feelings of human existence. Yes, back in the mists of time, I crawled out from under a rock called 'Weirdo'. I suppose you could say it was the romance of grime. Just as there is honour amongst thieves, so there is companionship amongst rejects.

Les was quick enough with his response.

"Nah, you can have her. She's a ginner, anyway. I wouldn't lower myself. She's probly had more pricks than a dartboard."

Somehow that little flash of obscene genius seemed to signal the end of our breather. We climbed back on our bikes and began to pedal laboriously away. After his initial unresponsiveness, Les was to take up the ginner motif with surprising inventiveness and alacrity. When, before too long, we had to start walking our bikes again, he accused mine of being a ginner and made suggestions as to the existence of a dubious relationship between the bike, myself and the earwig from which we had lately parted.

It was as we were leaving the shelter that I had, by no means for the first time, a premonitory inkling of the existence of the Listening Folk. All my life I have been haunted by the feeling that I am spied upon, but was never able to give this feeling the name of the Listening Folk until the adventure in whose telling I am now engaged.

Do you remember the kid at school, probably when you went to a new school in a new area for the first time, who provided you with your virgin experience of hate at first sight? Do you remember the horror of meeting those eyes, knowing that they saw into you, took you all in, that they *knew* you and hated you with a complete, irreversible and unreasoning hatred? You could not believe the absolute power and authority of that hatred, which turned you to jelly whenever you fell under its gaze. It seemed to you that that child, that piece of

41

walking evil, was created purely in order to hate you, and that you could never know repose of the soul while they lived and breathed. Do you remember? Well, that child was an agent of the Listening Folk. He, she or it was their avatar, sent to make you sweat and squirm.

The Listening Folk are everywhere. They exist to collect all your most shameful secrets and store them up against the day they may be used finally to destroy you. Jesus may love you; the Listening Folk hate you. It's personal.

Perhaps it was the quiet and emptiness of our surroundings, the creak of the shelter, the sunlight glinting on slight puddles, but as we got up to leave the place, and put some distance between ourselves and it, like the scene of a crime, my shame of some moments before returned with such burning intensity it seemed to bore through me in a ray of concentrated light. I could fairly hear a rustle as of invisible eavesdroppers, and I became convinced that our whole conversation had been overheard, if by nothing more than the weird emptiness.

I'm glad I took the time out for that little digression. Perhaps it was more important to my story than I first thought. It shows that just as no story ever really has an end, so no story ever really has a beginning, either. I can trace my themes back indefinitely. And what are those themes?

I think I can state without sacrificing too much in the way of subtlety, that one of them is shame.

My shame at the words I spoke to Les was manifold. I do not believe that Les had anything to be ashamed of in the least by being kind enough to respond in kind. But I, I was Artifice talking to Innocence. I should have known better. I was even ashamed to think of Les as 'Innocence', even ashamed to think that I 'should know better'.

42

But really, what had I done wrong? Nothing. In ourselves there is never anything wrong with us. Only the existence of other people makes us 'wrong'. Only the existence of other people necessitates shame.

I remember my fascination when I discovered Tourette's syndrome, and have occasionally wondered if I don't suffer from a latent form of the condition myself. The Tourette's sufferer finds him or herself afflicted with a condition that invites misunderstanding—he or she is unable to suppress the uttering of obscenities. How often, as I have sat in a lecture, or in some other public forum requiring quiet and restraint, have I felt compelled to get up and sing, to jump on tables, to shout filth and utter words I knew would be deeply hurtful to whomever was speaking? I have sat in terror, afraid I would do such things entirely against my volition, and the very terror of those things, their very taboo, was what compelled me, like the lure of a cliff edge.

I now have in my mind a picture of myself on that rusty bicycle with the shed behind me, that shelter which was a perfect trap set up by the Listening Folk, in order to ensnare me into betraying my own shamefulness. The shelter seems dark, shadowy. In front of me is Les, to whom I might say shameful things with utter impunity. He is riding into the sunshine.

Oh, how I tire of civilised company! How stifled I am by those who insist on acting their age!

Chapter III: Daytime TV

So, anyway, I went round the next day and plied the bell and knocked on the bullseye panes of the windows—the place used to be an olde tea shoppe, so the front was more window than anything else—until there was movement from the gloom within and Les opened the door.

"Yeah? What d'you want?"

For a moment I paused. Had I done something wrong, without even knowing it, between last night and today? It was quite possible.

"Nah! I'm just joking. Come in."

"You got me there."

"Have you seen my new stereo?"

"No, I don't think so."

He gestured towards a squat black stack of hi-fi equipment on the corner table. It was undoubtedly the newest thing in a room both sparse and grubby. Its very sleekness seemed incongruous in these surroundings.

"Smart, isn't it? I bought it with my sick money."

I was impressed, in the way that schoolboys are impressed by the cheekiness of their friends.

"You get that much sick money?"

"Well, I don't have much else to spend it on. And it's mine to do what I like with."

Somehow Les had managed to wangle sickness benefit for fits of anger that apparently rendered him unemployable. I'd never witnessed any of these fits myself, though I have reason to believe they were real enough. But Les himself always spoke as if he had been very clever to pull the whole thing off, and, whether his fits were real or not, I was inclined to agree.

"Do you want to hear my new Stryper record?"

Frankly, I would rather have listened to forty-five minutes of phlegm-hawking. Not that I had no curiosity. It's just that I knew Les would inevitably ask my opinion at the end and I would be forced to try and present the truth in an attractive light. After we had gone through this mercifully brief ritual, Les tiring with each track he played quite quickly, so that I never heard any all the way through, Les made tea. This was a far more welcome ritual. Les had a unique way of preparing tea. I don't know exactly what he did, but by the time it reached me, the tea was always a lukewarm beverage with too much milk and sugar and a harsh aftertaste of tannin. This was typically served in a filthy mug with a few cat hairs added for good measure. However, it was still tea, and therefore good. There is something comforting about tea. It has about it such an air of perfect normality that I sometimes wonder if anything in the world is better.

So far Les had not mentioned the business at hand, but something in the way he proffered the tea betrayed his aware-ness of the reason for my visit. All this had been a prelude, as if the bicycle was not something one could tackle casually. It required a little mental preparation.

When I had had enough of the tea, Les invited me with a slightly uncertain air—as if I might have forgotten—to take a look at the bicycle. We went through the cramped and grotty little kitchen out of the side door and into the narrow passage outside, which seemed little more than a route of access to the drains and a thoroughfare for neighbourhood cats. This was also Les' roofless garage. Here he had stored three pushbikes and one motorbike. None of them were actually roadworthy. Les' attempts to decorate them with house paint, mainly red, had failed to improve their performance, and my constant advice to apply some WD-40 had also proved fruitless. Of these four vehicles, only one even looked remotely as if it might get from A to anywhere deserving the designation B; that was the newest bike, the one which Les claimed was haunted.

Until now I had not thought very deeply about this claim. It seemed too much like an extension of our usual nonsensical banter for me to question it closely. However, I was beginning to feel a sense of vague expectation. This feeling was abetted by Les' attitude throughout. He squeezed past his other bikes, re-arranging them a little to make the passage easier for me, and stood silently before the bike in question for a while, as if making calculations. Then, seemingly accustomed to holding and moving the bike in a certain way, he picked it up in both arms and carried it carefully to the gate that sealed the passage. There he set it down again.

"I think I'll have to show you on the road out the front," he said.

The road out the front led only to the beach and was used mainly as a place for residents to park their cars, so it would not be too dangerous if anything went wrong with our little investigation. Les unlocked the gate and heaved the bike out onto the pavement beyond. I followed. He held the bike still and upright as if afraid it might escape.

"Okay, now watch this," he said.

He took his left hand from the saddle, and with both hands now on the handlebars, began to walk the bike towards the beach. The wheels had only given a few clicks when the handlebars twisted viciously to the right and Les dropped the bike quicker than a stick full of riled earwigs. From the speed of his movements it was obvious he had held the bike only gingerly and been ready to let go at any moment. The bike clanged with unsettling heaviness on the ground.

I don't consider myself particularly sceptical, but what leapt to my mind when I witnessed this performance was water diviners and their divining rods: "No, I wasn't doing a thing. The rods moved completely by themselves." "But I saw your hands move." And so it had simply looked to me as if Les had suddenly, for no reason, twisted the handlebars and flung away the bike in fright.

"Did you see that?" he said, his voice close to a whisper.

"Let's have a go," I said.

I picked up the bike. It was certainly heavy, making me think it was probably quite old. Without bracing myself, I began to wheel the bike towards the smell of the sea. I was unprepared for the violence of what happened next. Once again, after a few clicks, the handlebars twisted with nasty abruptness to the right. It did not feel exactly as if I had met some resistance within the mechanism of the bicycle. It felt more as if something outside of the bicycle was trying to control it. My reaction must have looked very similar to Les'. The difference was, I was slower to let go, and as a result almost sprained my wrist. As the bike clattered once more with nerve-jarring heaviness upon the ground, I sucked in air through my teeth and shook my hand in pain.

"Very odd," I managed finally, still nursing my hand.

"What do you think?" Les pressed me for a diagnosis.

"I think it's just a little bruised. It'll be alright in a minute."

"No, the bicycle."

Actually, just as my hand and wrist were shocked and numb, so my very thought processes were paralysed.

"Do you think it's really haunted?"

"That's hard to say."

"No it's not. Listen:'Do you think it's really haunted?'"

"Nice gag."

"Thank you."

But I couldn't leave it at that, for, from out of nowhere, a sense of intellectual pride reared its head, and I found it hard to admit my ignorance.

"What happens when you try to ride it?"

"Well, when I tried the other day it just wouldn't go where I wanted."

"But you rode it?"

"Yes. But I don't think it's a good idea . . ."

"We've got to find out what's wrong with it."

I picked the cursed and battered metal frame once more from the ground, sat astride the saddle and pushed on the pedals. The bicycle was launched into motion. For a moment there was the bliss of cool air that only riding a bicycle can give, then the handlebars were yanked to the right. Luckily, the pavement dipped here level with the road, and there was no bump as the bike was steered invisibly out between two parked cars. I continued to wrestle with the steering. I felt a strange antagonism, an anger in myself, as if directed towards *someone*. I shouted, "Stop it! You! I'll . . ." without thinking about whom it was I addressed.

The bike wobbled dangerously. I thought of the heavy frame crashing to the tarmac. I thought of the tarmac rising up jauntily to make a sharp connection with my skull. As the bike teetered so my heart fluttered, half at the thought of injury, half at the feeling that some invisible will was struggling against me, and what's more, that it was considerably stronger than me. Somewhere in the midst of this panic, as the presence of another will became an undeniable certainty, I forgot to pedal. Robbed of momentum, the bike finally toppled and I somehow managed to leap away before I was pinned beneath it.

I staggered to regain my balance, and when I had, exhaled sharply as much as to say, "That was close!"

"Are you alright?" asked Les from the pavement, as if it were the safety of shore.

I looked around. I looked up at the sky, empty but for a few wispy clouds and the wheeling gulls. I looked down again. Along the road three boys were playing with a skateboard.

"I think I'm alright," I said uncertainly. "The bike seems to be haunted, though."

Handling it as carefully as we would the remains of a mummy, we placed the bike back in the side-alley and retired once more to the comfortable gloom of the house.

The incident had left me with a disagreeable feeling. Perhaps that is understating the case, but I can't think of a more appropriate word. Disagreeable. What did it remind me of? It was a feeling such as a child has when the world violates his strict but inarticulate sense of aesthetics. I thought of the first time I had encountered a Buddhist monk, bald, soberly dressed and with an air of utterly disgusting modesty and pacifism about him. His existence was not a threat. It had nothing to do with me. And yet I found this very indifference hateful. Or other times it might have been a fat woman, desperately nervous, with quivering lips, who made me shudder. Children are not naturally liberal. It did not matter to me if she was harmless, if she had problems, if she was a decent human being. I did not want her in the same world with me. I felt as if her existence would smother me with a kind of nauseating dullness.

And so I felt about this haunted bicycle. It was ugly. Maybe it was harmless, but this ugliness made it evil to me. You might think the best thing to do would be forget about it. No one was forcing us to take an interest in it. Our lives would continue very well if we simply let it be. And yet that seemed impossible. It loomed up. It seemed inescapable, smothering. We were up against something, like an immeasurably high, invisible wall.

What are we going to do?

The question occupied us for some time, but as paranormal investigators we were hopelessly under-qualified. Our conversation was a strange cross between the whispered urgency of children when confronted with some spooky situation they can't possibly consult an adult about, and the defeated listlessness of the chronically unemployed when discussing just about anything requiring concerted action. We ended up staring at the toes of our shoes, making frustrated thinking noises.

At length I could stand it no more, and, leaping to my feet, I burst into a plaintive song, which had become something of a refrain for me of late, to the tune of 'Blowing in the Wind' (though obviously stretching the meter a little bit):

> How many earwigs does a man have to snog
> Before they will say he's not well?
> The answer, my friend, is fifteen million,
> The answer is fifteen million.

Les joined me on the next verse:

> And how many mackerel does a man have to kill
> Before they will tell him to go and have a lie down?
> The answer, my friend, is one hundred and thirty-two,
> The answer is one hundred and thirty-two.

Feeling a little better for having got that off my chest—when in doubt, surrealism—I turned to Les with new resolve.

"There's only one thing for it!"

"What's that?"

"We'll have to have a cup of tea."

And so Les went into the kitchen to prepare more of the muddy-brown panacea. I stared at the blank TV screen for a while before deciding, with sudden inspiration, to turn it on.

I have a theory about Heaven. If such a place exists it is somewhere where there is so much time—not a month, but a whole era of Sundays—that the inhabitants even have the leisure to appreciate the details and the genius of daytime TV: Such programmes as *The High Chaparral*, old matinee films, dreary quiz shows and *Lassie*. And so it is that of all people on Earth, maybe the unemployed come closest to Heaven, though perhaps they themselves don't know it.

When I flicked on the TV, *Lassie* happened to be on, and without thinking, I settled back into the armchair.

Les returned with the tea. He looked at the TV. The picture was quite bad, the colour mainly consisting of bright orange and slime-green. He twiddled with the knobs for a while, but his tweaking produced no discernible improvement, and so he gave up.

Watching *Lassie* is like going into a coma, falling under a spell of utter and perfect tedium. So we were slack-jawed, occasionally dunking our digestives, until there came the inevitable point in the water torture that passed for a script where

50

Lassie barked at a group of human co-stars and one of them said, "I think she's trying to tell us something. I think she wants us to follow her."

I stole a glance at Les. He looked at me in a curious, thoughtful fashion.

"Are you thinking what I'm thinking?" he said.

I nodded.

"I think she's trying to tell us something."

We laughed, like characters in a cartoon cracking up at some will-sappingly unfunny joke at the end of the show.

Chapter IV: Really Serious

And that is how we came to be, for a while, bona fide psychic investigators, albeit of the most amateurish and bumbling variety. (I feel like this should be the cue for music, but I'm working in the wrong medium. Never mind. Imagine something appropriately madcap for a slapstick montage.)

Enough!

I didn't feel much like going near the bike again soon, despite our canine-induced revelation, so we decided to put off further investigation till the morrow. The morrow came, unfortunately proving the old saying false, and still the same dilemma confronted us. I helped Les shift the bike's weighty frame from the side-alley to the pavement, where he set it upon its stand, and for a while it simply glinted in the mellow rays of the Indian summer. This time we had prudently faced it away from the beach. The problem was neither of us wanted to get on it and ride. Both of us had felt something ugly in the twist and jerk of the handlebars, and the very fact we could not identify that something awakened seemingly ancient instincts warning us against further contact.

"Well, it's time," I said.

"Yeah. I suppose so. No point in waiting, is there?"

"Exactly. Off you go then."

"What?"

"I'll be right here."

"But then you won't know what happens."

"Don't worry about me. You can tell me afterwards. Or I can run after you."

"What about a backy?"

"No . . . I don't think that's a good idea. To be honest, I don't think the bike likes me. I felt it yesterday. I don't want to jinx things."

"Go on! I'll ride carefully."

I don't know why it is, but I am precisely the kind of person that maniacs feel the desire to give backies to. Such is the strength of their desire that their powers of persuasion become utterly irresistible. This occasion was no exception. I found a precarious and exceptionally uncomfortable perch on the back of the bike, convinced we would keel over the moment Les took his feet off the ground. To my surprise, after a breathtakingly slow start, which seemed barely fast enough to maintain our balance, we picked up moderate speed. I could feel Les' body swing with heavy, plunging emphasis from left to right as he pedalled. The bike leaned rhythmically in the opposite direction with each plunge. In fact, this swinging and leaning was so extreme and accompanied by such wobbling that more than once I gasped as on a roller coaster, certain that something other than Les' skilful counter-balancing had saved us from torn clothes and gravelly grazes. After all, it seems unnatural to recover after leaning at an angle of forty-five degrees.

"I won't try to steer now," Les' voice came back to me.

Nonetheless, the handlebars twitched like a dousing rod in his grip and we edged, or rather veered, out into the middle of the road. Fortunately the road was quiet and empty. We already knew where the bike would take us, or anyway, in what direction. It was steering a course once more towards the Old Corn Mill, where the waterwheel was. However, we were to stop before reaching the mill.

The bike lurched over the hump at the entrance to the side road and dropped down the slope like a diving bird. There was the unmistakable sensation that Les was no longer in control of the thing. Its hurtling momentum seemed to have acquired an independent life. I held tight to Les' scrawny ribs as the bike delivered a series of one-inch punches to the bones of my backside.

We were travelling at speed alongside an old stone wall overlooking a section of the river. Where the road formed a sort of bridge we turned sharply. Suddenly the brakes were applied with great force. We were both catapulted forward. I banged my chin on Les' head and he just missed doing himself an injury on the crossbar.

We got stiffly and carefully off of the bike. Checking that everything was still in place, I was about to admonish Les for his unnecessarily abrupt halt when something happened. I suppose at first I just thought there was something a little unusual in the purling of the stream that flowed out from the fern-fringed darkness under the road. Listening to that strange purling, however, I soon forgot who I was and where. There was only a kind of chill shivering that told me to be absolutely quiet and still, and it seemed I stood outside a door in darkness hearing voices. Those voices were a loud and ugsome whispering. That is, although their tone was that of a whisper, there was something about the voices and what they said that was so monstrous I could only conceive of them as immense, or myself as miserably small. Indeed, I felt so small and lost that I would have cried if I had dared.

With the sound of these cracked, croaking whispers, I seemed to recall things, things long forgotten. I recalled primal infancy, sleepless nights of screaming and crying, voices and half-seen things that reached out from corners and were never there when my parents came, but whose language I seemed to know better than that my parents spoke. I had known that language an age ago, and knew only to associate it with fear and hatred. Those nights of living shadows, like the torturous passage of a fever.

Becoming conscious of the *faculty* of memory I lost my grip on those memories, and they shrank away like water down a plughole. At the same time I remembered my present self with a horrible shiver. I could still hear the voices, though now they seemed to be more distant and physical, an unintelligible whispering from the darkness of the underground stream. I looked at Les to see he was looking back at me with an expression of naked terror on his face.

I beckoned him and nodded with my head to indicate a retreat from the stream. Ever so lightly, we picked up the bicycle together, and, soft as thieves, crept away to what seemed a safe distance, picking up speed as we went.

Near the Old Corn Mill we dropped the bike again and stood breathing deeply.

"What was it?" I asked.

I wanted to be sure we had heard the same thing, and that this was not just some juvenile hysteria. I remember once, on the way back from a night-fishing expedition with two friends, we convinced ourselves we were being chased by a dark figure with a knife. Of course, there had been no such person—or had there?—so this time I was determined to give Les no cues.

"I heard something," he said.

"What did you hear?"

"Voices. Whispering, like."

"What did they say?"

"They said something about earwigs, and," he looked at me significantly, "and about ginners, too."

"What?" Even as I asked I felt I did not want to know the answer.

"They said they were gonna join up with the earwigs, that they know a little doorway what they can get through, and that the key is in the ginners. They said the mackerels won't help them now, but that doesn't matter anymore. There was a lot of other stuff, too, but it was all in some funny language and I don't remember it proply."

I had heard much the same things. To hear Les recount them now made them suddenly objective and real in the daylight. I was stricken by strange alarm, as if the day had become overcast with pain sudden as the crack of a whip. Interestingly, the actual words I would have used to repeat what I had heard would have differed. Where Les had said 'join up with', I would have said, 'form an alliance', where he had said 'little doorway', I would have said, 'infinitesimal portal', and so on. Somehow, even as we had heard the voices, they had been translated in our heads, as if the nature of the language were self-translating. Thus we each had our own version of the words, but the content was undoubtedly the same.

"That must be what the bicycle wanted to tell us," I said musingly, rubbing my chin.

Even in the midst of my disquiet, I somehow could not resist playing the sleuth.

"But what do we do now?"

I was quite genuinely at a loss for an answer, but seeing the Old Corn Mill gift shop and tea room nearby, I quickly came to a decision.

"How about a cup of tea? I think we need it."

We parked the bike outside and since we did not fear theft, did not bother to lock it up. Inside we chose a table in the corner. We were the only customers. I emptied my pockets of old bus tickets, tissues and so on, and, rummaging also through my threadbare Dutch tweed—picked up at an Amsterdam flea market—finally managed to assemble an adequate-looking amount of coins. When these were pooled with Les' coins we found we had enough for two small teas and a scone, which we could share.

"This really is serious," said Les, stirring his tea gravely.

I had to agree. Even as I tipped sugar into my tea, my hand was shaking. Our unspoken instinct that this was not something we could run away from seemed to have been proven true. I had the altogether nasty feeling that we were 'mixed up' in something. That there were two of us made me feel a little better, but my overall mood, and I believe that of Les, too, was one of utter helplessness and vulnerability. I was all too aware that wearing a tweed jacket and rubbing my chin in a thoughtful, enigmatic manner comprised the extent of my abilities as a paranormal investigator, and Les was possibly even less qualified. We were in a corner physically, and in a spiritual sense, too, we were cornered.

"How about if we just throw the bike in the river?" I ventured at length.

Les didn't look keen. Somehow I knew it was useless too, but I pressed the question anyway.

"I dunno. We can't do that, can we?"

He paused for a while and sipped his tea.

"If we do that," he continued, "then we'll never know what's going on, probly. But it might carry on anyway and we won't be able to do anything."

"Then we have to find out more. And the only way to do that is probably to listen to those voices again."

Les met my eyes. Clearly this was not something either of us wanted to do. There was no point hiding it from each other, and we could not have done so, anyway. We talked around the subject some more. There was a kind of nakedness to our voices, like the expression I had seen on Les' face by the stream.

"What do you think's happ'nin' then?" asked Les.

"Well, it's like you said, isn't it? The bicycle is haunted. Really haunted."

"But it's not just that, though, is it? I mean, it's everything. Like those voices and the stuff they was saying. You know what I mean?"

I did indeed know what he meant. It was interesting—terror had made many things 'interesting' in a brittle, unbearable way—that we should both feel as if everything was affected. This was not just an isolated spooky bicycle in an otherwise normal world.

"Is it just us?" This seemed a question of some significance.

"Is it just us or is it the whole world?" I finished the question for him. "To be honest, I haven't got a clue. I'm confused. Maybe this is what real hauntings are like, but you just never hear about this stuff, just because . . . I don't know, because you never really hear about how anything really is. What I mean is, we know the word 'haunted', and we've all heard lots of ghost stories, so in a way ghosts and things like that seem normal. We think we know what they are, but we don't. They could be anything. We can call them 'weird' or whatever, but even that's just a word. When we experience them we realise that 'weird' is exactly what we don't have words for. Does that make sense?"

"Sort of. I think I know what you mean."

"I'm glad someone does. Fucked if I do."

More lay-philosophising of this sort and Dutch courage in the form of tea, unfortunately only the two cupfuls, and we stole ourselves to approach the stream again, to see if we could catch more of that hideous conversation. I even had my spiral-bound notebook and biro at the ready.

Carrying the bicycle, we crept back to where that underground river emerged into daylight. As we got nearer, we hit an invisible wall of fear and for a while it seemed we could go no further. But we knew too well what we had to do. With a feeling of trembling emptiness, as if I had suddenly been drained of all content, I inched with Les to the very spot on which we had previously stood. In the process we broke through the wall that had been restraining us and, meeting no further resistance, felt unsteady and uncertain. There did not seem to be anything otherworldly about the place now, and even as we strained our ears to catch some whispering from beyond, it seemed a foregone conclusion that we would hear nothing.

My pen was poised over paper, but I could not very well transcribe the muttering of the stream.

"Did you hear that?"

"No."

"Neither did I."

After a number of exchanges of this sort we gave up.

"Perhaps we have to ride the bike first," I suggested.

This suggestion was taken up very enthusiastically by Les.

"But we can't ride here now, 'coz we're already here. We need a bit of a run up."

I concurred with this view, there being really no room for disagreement, and since our investigation was getting into full swing there was less of fearful hesitation in what we did. In fact, following through the swing of our investigation, I did not even question why I climbed on the bike with Les for a backy this time. As it turned out, it was just as well I did.

Les pushed down on the pedals with a slow plunging of his body. Then, quite unexpectedly, the bicycle turned in completely the opposite direction, for a moment resembling a dog chasing its tail, before straightening out and continuing in the direction of the Old Corn Mill, which we had just left.

Chapter V: Old Letters

Writing this account of a history I generally take satisfaction in letting lie, I find memory and curiosity stirred up in odd ways, like a snowstorm in an old paperweight. And beneath that paperweight, which has done its job admirably, I discover there are still papers. Prompted by this essay at reconstructing what can—and perhaps should—never be reconstructed, I have looked in my trusty file and found preserved there a fragment of the correspondence between myself and Les from roughly the era of which I write. I shall copy out my own letter first:

Bucks.
11.Nov.1994

Dear Les,

How goes it, my laughing coelenterate? Not much to report this end, I'm afraid. What about you? Got off with any lush invertebrates recently? I'm sorry we never got round to going out in that dinghy, like you said. Maybe sometime we will. I'll let you know when I'm down next.

Life up here is pretty boring really. I haven't made any friends. Well, I have kind of, as a volunteer. It's a thing called the befriending service. I went to this office, told them my background and they sent me round to be friends with a chap called S—J—, who happens to have been born on the same day as me and also likes Doctor Who.

Whenever I go round there we just play tennis in the garden—I'm crap at tennis—watch Dr. Who videos, listen to old Beatles records and fence with sticks and rulers in his room for ages. It's quite fun really.

Well, it's getting dark outside. The leaves are falling from the trees. Maybe it's because I grew up near the sea, but it's weird being this far inland. I feel like there's nowhere to go to. Everything is too still and solid. I can't hear the faintest murmur of waves and I can't smell the faintest breath of salt.

But obviously I haven't left it all behind. I went to sleep the other night in my hard, narrow, uncomfortable bed, hearing the traffic just outside my window, thinking how hard, narrow and uncomfortable everything was here, and how shallow . . . I suppose the tide of dreams comes even this far inland though, because just as I was dropping off I began to hear a sort of wet, dripping sound. I didn't think much about it. It just seemed very sad. Then the wet sound turned to a sort of splash, and the splash turned to voices. Of course . . . I can never escape . . . my terror, my love, my nightmare, my true home of homes . . . They had come for me. I heard them singing in a kind of benthic caterwaul. The mackerels had come! The mackerels with their lugubrious eyes and their slippery stripes!

I hardly dared move as they climbed in through the window and hoisted me on their shoulders. But that song! That song! Older than the first dynasties of China! Wilder then the music of Gypsies! I felt as stuffed and useless as a Guy Fawkes doll as they settled me onto the seat of an old bicycle. Then, so that I would not fall off, they fitted stabilisers to the bicycle's back wheels and began to pull it along the empty pavements on a piece of string.

We gathered speed and before long all the darkened towns of England, stuffed full of sleepiness, were flashing by, and yawning out of the night the empty spaces between towns, like the spaces between dreams. Even the stars in the sky were turned, every one, into shooting stars, such was our speed. Much of what passed was strange to me, but every now and then I seemed to half-recognise a place, as from some distant childhood journey. Then the sense of familiarity grew stronger and more constant, and I knew we were approaching home. My head lolled floppily on my neck. Past orange lights we sped and into the inhabited areas of whitish blue lights. Still we didn't slow.

At last I saw that we were hurtling towards Beach Road. I saw a light on at your place, but I was paralysed, as if drugged with the distilled essence of dream, and I could not even raise my voice. To the sea they were taking me! To the sea! Into the cold mystery of the nighted waves we splashed, the land shelving away beneath until no sky tilted above, and there was only the surging darkness of the ocean world where no stillness ever comes.

Still on that bicycle, they took me deep down, between the shrinking, swelling gateways of weedy rocks, through streaming, billowing veils of green tendrils, and to the grotesque splendour of their submarine palace where the emperor mackerel sat atop a throne of rusty tin cans, crowned with the living diadem of the most fantastic, luminous sea anemone—which was fed at intervals by those unfortunates who displeased His Majesty—and flanked on either side by eerily seductive dancing blennies in skirts of seaweed.

I was brought before the emperor, there to be mocked and humiliated while the entire court fell about in writhing convulsions of fishy laughter. I spent many miserable years there, imprisoned in the cage of an abandoned shopping trolley for the amusement of the emperor.

At length I managed to escape and got back here on Tuesday. I immediately collapsed, exhausted physically and spiritually from my ordeal. When I awoke I could not decide whether the whole thing had been real, but noticed the place smelt unpleasantly of fish. I just wondered if you noticed anything strange on Monday night when I passed by your place.

Apart from that nothing much has happened really. I've found a shop where they sell nice dresses, but they're all too expensive for me to own in this lifetime. Well, I'd better put the dinner on, I suppose. I don't mean I'd better adorn my body with the dinner in place of clothing, but rather that I ought to start cooking my evening meal.

Watch out for them pesky earwigs!

Q.

Now let me copy out Les' reply:

Dear Q,

thank you for your letter. I'm alright thank you very much you perverted silverfish. not much is happnin hear except that John moved out which was just as well coz hes been getting on my nerves recently it's a bit much sometimes with everyone running around making it hard to relax anyway I am O.K.

it isn't that Boring really as Ive brought Quite a few Video's Well Seven to be exact plus Ive also brought Def leopards album the Vault which is quit smart,

I think I heard those mackerels you was talking

about One of them keeps singing outside my window so I cant sleep, It was calling me the other day an it threw some stones up to my window so I told it to bugger off but it came back wiv more and they was dancing round in circles and barkin at the moon they won't get me though.

I met an earwig the other day too, he was hidin behind the dartboard so I looked at his pincers and he was a male. he said he had a message from you, but I didn't trust him I thought he mite be a ginner in disguise and I squashed him and all this milky stuff came out, but his pincers kept on movin, and he said the mackerel had takin you, so maybe he was your freid after all.

anyway, I am glad to hear you escaped from those pesky mackerels, must say Cheerio for now God bless and my best wishes for your new life up north,

Les.

I remember the time and circumstances of this correspondence well enough. I had moved 'up north'—almost anywhere in the country was north of home—in order to find some way out of the hopeless dead end of unemployment and obscurity. The move turned out to be abortive, offering me a different dead end in a colder, lonelier and altogether less friendly place. What is strange is that I find I cannot place these letters chronologically in their proper relation to the incident of the haunted bicycle. Chronology has never been my strong point, but this verges on the ridiculous. Hence the comparison I made with a snowstorm was not a gratuitous one. These memories are a blizzard in which I lose my way.

It would be particularly interesting if I could establish the proper order of things. Somehow the letters above seem written without knowledge of the whole haunted bicycle adventure, and yet, if such is the case, and these letters come first, then they are positively prescient. Then again, if they were prescient, why were they not remembered with more distinctness and surprise at the time when their prophecies were unfolding as reality? It may be easily understood why this bothers me.

The reader will perhaps observe that I have already recorded things that might be seen as prophetic. Yet, perhaps because they are still in my possession, these letters seem to encapsulate the enigma for me. They are, in a sense, out of time, like my story itself, and it is this achronology more than the possibility of any prescience that disturbs me.

Reading old letters makes me feel, in the quietest possible way, like someone is saying to me, "This is your life!" I feel the lightness and detachment of a ghost, together with a kind of sad, affectionate satisfaction that, well, it might have been a pointless failure, but anyway, it was 'me'. So I hope you don't mind if I make a few observations on this occasion. I don't intend to go into any deep psychoanalysis of the relationship between Les and I. I'll leave that to others, if, indeed, there is any interest in such an exercise. Does my paralysis in the face of the mackerel compared with Les' defiance indicate a weaker nature? Is this exchange of fantasy some form of coded seduction and rejection? In which case, who is seducing and who is rejecting? These are superficial questions whose answers cannot be found by taking the letters at face value.

I say letters, but of course, one of them, mine, is, in fact, a photocopy. It was my habit at the time to make copies of most of my personal correspondence. This habit betrays the writer's excessive concern with posterity, documentation and the storing of 'material'. The letter was written during one of the most unhappy periods of my life, and yet there is no direct mention of my unhappiness. Instead one may detect an awkwardness in the opening of the letter and the half-hearted, dutiful accounting of 'real life'. Only when I find the key to leaving behind 'real life', through mention of home and the sea, does the letter take on any fluency. Only when I abandon myself to nonsensical fantasy does it seem I have anything to say.

Les' reply is shorter, since he was never as wordy in his letters as I, but it is no less creative for that. His attention to detail is really quite touching, and that bit about the earwig's milky ichor is a marvellous piece of writerly observation, probably based on personal experience.

It occurred to me that now Les is gone, apart from a couple of poems in his hand, these are all I have left of our friendship. Looking at the letters in that light they seemed a kind of farewell. I am sure that, even if I knew I was going to die tomorrow, and I had a single day in which to say my goodbyes to everyone, I would not be able to come up with anything more profound or adequate to the occasion than the desperate drivel scribbled in that letter. That's the kind of guy I am.

Chapter VI: Under English Skies

We sped past the Old Corn Mill and onto the narrow, overgrown footpath that ran alongside the river downstream from where we had heard those voices. Every loose pebble seemed to jolt the bicycle into the air. We were whipped by brambles and low branches until we forgot to keep our balance, and more than once seemed in danger of toppling through a breach in the wooden fence and the matted river weeds beyond to the muddy water six or seven feet below. However, for all the roughness of the ride, the bike seemed as if running on a fixed track, and we arrived at our destination with only a few weals and scratches. Of course, we did not know it was our destination until we actually arrived. Just as before, the brakes were applied with neck-breaking suddenness. My jaw hit the back of Les' head and he just saved himself from an injury on the crossbar. We were next to the local electricity transformer, opposite a sign saying, "Danger, No Cycling", with an arrow pointing the way we had come. This was where the footpath met the main road, and from here we could see Les' house.

The bike would not budge an inch, the brakes biting the wheels as if with lockjaw. Strangely, the bike's stand had also become locked, so that we were unable to let the bike stand free as usual. Instead we leant it against the wire fence, some four or five feet high, surrounding the transformer, and waited. There was nothing unusual in our surroundings, but something as abstract and trifling as the stubbornness of a bicycle had lent them an air of mysterious expectancy. The day was overcast now, with that special greyness I'm sure is peculiar to England, as if there are no actual clouds, but the sky itself has changed colour. Some day I must write an essay on that grey sky, as it is nothing less than the most lucid mirror held up to England's soul.

The mirror held in an atmosphere close and oppressive. And yet, nothing happened. We stood listening, watching, hands half-raised as if to hush the world the better to hear what we were listening for. I suppose we thought that voices would come once more from the stream now half-hidden by the rank and utterly unchecked rampage of convolvulus, nettles, hogweed, buddleia and other vegetation. However, although the very purling of water had come to seem eerie to me, neither of us heard anything more definite than this.

There were sounds in the silence, as if the day itself were a creaky old house, but these were merely the sounds of our waiting. At length they seemed to convey a kind of uncomfortable boredom. I looked at Les. He made an ambiguous face, half-acknowledgement, half-question. I suppose I must have had a similar expression. We held this attitude for a while then shook our heads.

"Nothing," I said.

"I wonder why the bike stopped here, then."

"Maybe it's not voices this time. Maybe there's something else. We should have a look around for clues."

And I took out my notebook and biro once more. As if the bike's stubborn brakes had been applied to our own hearts, we could not shake off a certain tension, and our voices were subdued. Perhaps because it was nearest at hand, we turned to the transformer first. I'm not an expert on these things, but I presume the job of the transformer is to collect electricity from some more central source and relay it to the houses and businesses within a small, given area. They are not an uncommon sight, but then again, given the amount of houses and businesses in the country, I'm surprised they're not more common.

There seemed to be nothing remarkable about this one. Small concrete posts supported the wire mesh erected to keep people away. The wire was rusty in places, and dead, withered bindweed was tangled here and there in the interstices. On the side facing away from the footpath there was a gate secured with a padlocked bolt. There was a sign on the gate. I had seen this kind of sign before. In a triangle was a stylised silhouette of a man in a kind of sinister swoon. A black zig-zag tipped with an arrow was striking, or piercing, his chest. The legend below the triangle read, "Danger of death. Keep out." The whole thing was executed in those poisonous, wasp-like colours of warning borrowed from nature, black and yellow. It seemed hard to believe that Death itself was kept in by this flimsy wire fence. If I climbed over this, now, in broad daylight, and approached that cluster of grey, metal boxes, would I really be inviting the terrible and final nothingness that makes of our lives an absurd and despicable lie? Is death so mundane?

I have always been attracted by those things left unnoticed in the corners of our lives, and there is no doubt that this transformer was among such things. I cannot even think of the proper names for those grey boxes, such is their obscurity. Are they modules? Terminals? Surely it is something like that. A number of curved bars, like pipes, protrude from the sides of one of the boxes. What are *they* for, then? I've no idea. This, and the dullness and opacity of the boxes, makes them mysterious to me. That they should contain death seems of great significance. Yes, the whole mystery of our life and death is here, like this—a nameless, grey box I don't understand, stands like some particularly dreary sphinx under grey English skies. If I were to touch it in the wrong place, no matter how casually, that would be the end of me.

While I had been sunk in such reflections, Les had started to poke about the weeds around the transformer. He picked something up from the midst of the litter and held it up for my inspection. It was a polythene bag.

"Is this a clue?" he asked.

"Er, no," I decided, in what was, I realise, quite an arbitrary manner. What do clues look like, anyway?

Les' industry reminded me of the job at hand, that it was not enough to stare enigmatically at transformers, and I too began to poke about in earnest. While Les searched the area around the transformer, I returned to the footpath and looked there. The encroaching foliage did not so much suggest luxuriance as utter dishevelment, like a bushy, uncombed beard. Much of the path was in the shadows of a tunnel formed of this green fuzziness. I noticed where the arch of an ivied bough curved over the path, seeming to hook onto the leaning, half-obscured fence. Where there was no tunnel there reared up beside the path a vista, a veritable tidal wave of convolvulus. For some reason this vista fascinated me quite as much, if not more than, the local transformer. If I looked long enough I was overcome by the uneasy sensation that this tangle of stringy weeds went on forever. It was not simply that I wondered if there was anything behind the convolvulus, succumbing momentarily to the illusion that the entire hill, in whose shadow we stood, was nothing more than weed, as the planet Jupiter, I believe, is nothing more than gases. I also wondered if this might actually be a single convolvulus plant grown into mystical profusion, a perfect moebius tangle without beginning or end. As I looked upon the dark galaxy of heart-shaped leaves constellated here and there with white, trumpet-shaped flowers, this thought became maddening.

At last, in something like disgust, I turned away, deciding to take a closer look at the riverbank instead.

I don't know why it was, but both Les and I became thoroughly engrossed in our mission. In childhood I had often lost track of time foraging in rock pools or digging up ants' nests, but in adult life to lose track of time doing anything at all was a rare occurrence. It was not as if either of us found anything to encourage our search. Occasionally Les would come over to the fence and I would climb back up to it to inspect a broken bottle or an ice-lolly stick with a silly riddle on it. I had decided to give up the least pretence to authority, and when he asked me if such objects were clues, I simply replied:

"I don't know. What d'you reckon?"

To which he would shrug, eventually concluding they weren't clues after all.

Despite all this, we did seem to lose track of time, the juicy, grub-ridden earth yielding up to us the wondrous secrets that usually only children have eyes for, even if they have no words for them, as indeed, I had no words then and have none now.

One discovery, however, did elicit words from me and awaken us from our pre-verbal trance of rooting. I kicked something solid in the leaf litter.

"Aha, I have struck gold!"

Les rushed to see what I had found. It was a one pound coin.

"What a stroke of luck! With our newfound funds we may purchase viands to stave off our hunger and weariness."

"What?"

"I thought maybe we could get some grub from the garage."

I was so impressed with the brilliance of Les' response to this that I shall write it down verbatim:

"Why don't we get some biscuits?"

I nodded my head slowly as the genius of this suggestion sank in.

"Okay. But in that case we'll need something to drink, too. Any preferences?"

"Nah. It's up to you."

There was no one behind the counter when I entered the shop. I went straight to the shelves where the biscuits were stacked. However, I had an unexpectedly hard time choosing. The biscuits were either prohibitively expensive or decidedly unattractive. It looked like I would be unable to buy decent biscuits *and* drinks for both of us, and I suppose my tuts and sighs of frustration and disappointment must have been fairly audible. At length I settled on a small packet of digestives and two cans of ginger beer. Even these modest provisions could only be purchased with the addition of some very small change left over from the tea and scone. As I walked to the counter I noticed some of the prices in the dairy section. A pint of milk, 36p. Two pints of milk, 75p.

The shop assistant was now at the counter. He was a beefy young man with one of those heads that somehow seems wider at the bottom than the top. I had seen him here before, and felt vaguely that I knew him from somewhere else. Was it just because we had grown up in the same area? I set my goods on the counter. The man reached for a bag.

"I'm sorry the manager's such a nazi rip-off bastard," he said.

"Pardon?"

He repeated himself.

"It's okay," I said. This seemed a bit lame under the circumstances. Would it be friendlier to complain, I wondered, to show my sympathy?

I paid and took the bag from the counter. I made to leave, but as I did so the man's expression changed—sorry, I cannot go on calling him a man; that's far too neutral. He was a bloke, if ever there was one. The bloke's expression changed and he obviously made some decision on the spur of the moment.

"Do you know who that bike belongs to out the back?"

"The one by the transformer?"

"Pardon?"

"The electricity doodah."

"Yeah, that's the one."

"Yeah, that's mine."

"Really?"

Why was he so surprised? Surely he had asked in the expectation that it was mine? He must have seen the bike from the back room, and probably saw myself and Les, too, and wondered what in God's name we were up to.

"Well, when I say it's mine, I mean it's my friend's."

"Where did he get it from d'you know?"

"The dump."

"I knew it! It's weird, but somehow I knew it was that bike. Are you in a hurry?"

The bloke began to talk, hesitantly at first, then with a kind of excited ease, like someone lately released from a vow of silence to whom language is a freedom and luxury still strange, wrapped up in shyness. Even though Les was waiting, I had to listen to the end. In our digging around outside I had thought we were getting lost in the normality of the day. Seeming to drift further away from mystery, we were drifting further into it. Thinking we had found nothing, we had dug so far we could not see we had found everything. This is what I felt as I listened to the bloke's narrative.

A couple of times customers came into the shop and he would stop talking, resuming his tale after they had gone. When he finished and told me to be careful, I thanked him and left the shop. Les asked what had taken me, but without answering I told him to try riding the bike. The brakes had been released. In fact, even the steering seemed free of anomalies. Since I did not want to hang around in that place any longer than necessary, I suggested we eat our feast elsewhere. We took the bike home and strolled down to the beach. There I told Les all that I had just heard.

Chapter VII: The Testimony of the Bloke in the Garage

Are you in a hurry? It might take a while to tell the whole story. No, it's okay. You're not bothering me. It's a pretty boring job, anyway. No, not boring. That's not the right word. I feel isolated, you know? That's what it is. You might not think it, but when you've actually got to work here, sitting in the backroom all day, it's real isolation. Things are completely different this side of the counter. You wouldn't believe half of what goes on here. Most of the time people come in and go out and I just have to pretend everything's normal, say "thank you" and "come again" and stuff. There's not much you can say to customers without them thinking it's weird.

Anyway, that bike's a good example of what I'm talking about. Do you know Stuart? I don't know his second name. Everyone just used to call him the Lone Ginger, or Mad Stuart. You've probably seen him about. He is, or was, a local character, if you know what I mean. He always used to wear the same clothes, a plastic cagoule, like a one-man tent, you know, and bicycle shorts. Well, you only knew he was wearing shorts 'cause you could see his legs. They were pretty hairy. Lots of ginger hair. Yeah, that's the one. Glasses. Dead white. Always riding his bicycle and stopping for no reason at random places, like, I don't know, next to the stile by the horse-riding track, for instance, and writing stuff down like he's taking notes. Yeah, Mad Stuart, they called him. He was meant to be a bit funny in the head. Well, he did wear bicycle shorts *and* bicycle clips. That was a bit funny. But I don't know if he was mad exactly. I think some people just have a different way of looking at things, do you know what I mean? Anyway, everything's mad really, isn't it? I don't see why we should just point our fingers at one or two people and laugh and call them mad and stuff. See, I'm open-minded, you can tell me anything, and at least I'll listen. At least I'll think about it.

I spoke to Stuart once, actually. I was taking the short cut home along the footpath round the back, and he was stood there with his bike between his legs, like he was listening to something in the hedge. Then he'd write really quickly in his notebook. Then he'd stop and listen again for a while. It looked like he was taking dictation or something. Well, he was blocking the way, 'cause it's quite narrow. I said "hello", just so he'd know I was there, but he just nodded and kept on writing. I didn't want to get annoyed or anything, and I wasn't in a hurry, so I said, "What are you writing?" He didn't answer straight away, though. He kept writing, almost frantic, but also sort of neat and precise. Then, when he'd finished he said, "My work is very important, but I can't possibly explain." He said it just like that—what you'd call a cut-glass accent, I suppose. Somehow, the way he said it impressed me, so I can remember it pretty much word for word. So then he said, "This may sound strange, but what I'm doing may save the entire human race from its natural and rightful doom."

You know, sometimes when you talk to mad people, people who talk to themselves in shopping centres and stuff, you can look at them and see something's not right. I don't know, maybe they're dirty or something 'cause they don't look after themselves, or maybe they've got a weird look in their eyes, but anyway, sometimes you feel repulsed, like you just want to get away from them. Well, Stuart wasn't like that at all. He sounded polite and civilised, like a vicar out of one of those old Ealing films or something. You know, he just didn't sound mad. So anyway, I was quite interested and asked him some questions. He didn't really want to talk about it, you could tell, but in the end I got him to explain a bit more. He said that he was the only person in the world, as far as he knew, that was aware of the problem and working on it, and that he didn't have time to care about appearances. See, what it was, right, was that for some reason he had developed the ability to see and hear secret things in the world around, and, he said, a lot of what he saw and heard did not "bode well" for the human race. So what he was doing was going around and collecting and collating as much data as he could. You know, I wish I could say all this the way he said it. I know it sounds kind of stupid the way I've said it, but somehow there was something to what he was saying, like, behind the words, that really made me think. I can't explain. It kind of made me see things around me a little bit differently. By the end of his explanation he seemed to be getting nervous, and I can tell you, I felt pretty nervous listening to it. So the conversation just ended in awkward silence. I said something like, "Excuse me, must be going," and that was it.

Anyway, what I'm leading up to is, that bike used to be Stuart's. About a year ago the manager saw it from the backroom window, leaning up against the fence around the electricity doodah, almost exactly like it is now. When I saw it like that today I couldn't help thinking about Stuart and what happened to him. It made me feel weird seeing it like that. I thought, that can't be co-incidence! So, as I was saying, the manager saw the bike out there, and he's a right nosy bastard. You know, he's into binoculars and telescopes and things. He always wants to know what's going on everywhere and goes on about "Knowledge is power, my son," and stuff like that. Naturally, this bike drives him mad. He has to find out what's behind it. Somehow he can tell there's something a little bit odd going on, see, but he can't go out there and look 'cause he has to mind the shop and he's too fucking stingy to close up for two minutes. So what he does, he phones me up and asks if I can do an extra shift. I say okay, as I'm not doing anything else, and the moment I get here he goes round the back to take a look at the bike. I didn't know what was going on, so when he came back in I asked. He said there'd been an accident or something and we'd better phone the police. I kind of shrugged and started to dial 999. But then he said, "Wait a minute!" and he took out some rubber gloves from the backroom and went out again. After a while he came back and said, "Okay, you can phone them now."

So I dialled and passed the phone to him to do the explaining. It turns out that Stuart has parked his bike there, climbed over the fence somehow and has fiddled about with some of the equipment inside. By the time the police got here, with an ambulance, it was too late. The medics said it looked like he had died of a massive electric shock. No one saw him climb in there, though. No one really knew what happened. The coppers asked the manager some questions, and I heard them discussing stuff while they were waiting for the doctor to come and declare Stuart dead, and apparently, all the units in the electricity doodah were intact. There was no sign that they had been tampered with at all.

The police knew a bit about Stuart already, and there was no next of kin, so it was really just a case of the body being disposed of at the state's expense. Stuart had a reputation for snooping around in odd places, so they just thought he'd gone in there 'cause he was away with the fairies. They didn't really need a motive, and though it was all a bit strange, it was all put down to Stuart being strange himself, and somehow everything else got swept under the carpet, too. One of the constables, though, said, "'Ere, what do we do with the bike?" Since they already had the whole thing pegged as death by misadventure, and there was no next of kin, there wasn't really a lot they could do with it. It wasn't lost property exactly, so no one would come to claim it. They thought they might possibly need it in the unlikely event that the coroner's report turned up something odd and they found out this was not a straight-forward case, but then again, it seemed a lot of bother. Then the manager piped up and said he'd look after it. He kept it in the back room for months. He never actually did anything with it, though, and the police never came back for it, so he ended up selling it off to the dump.

Now, my manager really is mental. I wouldn't be staying here, but him and my old man are old friends and it's all a bit complicated. Anyway, I'm not going to be here forever. No way. Not with that mentalist. You'd have to spend a day with him to know what he's like. For instance, he came in here one time when his ladyfriend chucked him. Well, I don't know if they were ever going out properly, but anyway, something must have happened, 'cause he came in red as a beetroot, eff-ing and blinding, "That slag Maureen, how dare she say that to me!" I've never seen anything like it. He went into the back-room and started banging about in there. After a while I went in and he was having a Scotch. He started lecturing me in this really weird tone of voice, like, suddenly really cold. He started off not making sense, like he's totally lost it. Kind of like, "Insects, eh? Insects? The trouble with most people is they don't know what they're talking about. They think as long as they know how to be popular that they're clever. What's wrong with insects, anyway? Women are strange creatures, you know. Whose side are they on, d'you think, then, kid? Think about it, eh! Everyone's working for someone, whether they know it or not. Everyone's somebody's agent. Now, the way they act, you've got to wonder who's orders they're following. See, they think they're better than us. Oh dear, oh dear! It's worrying, is that. If a woman says you're an insect, that's because she is fundamentally—fundamentally, mark you—convinced of her own superiority. What she is in effect saying is, I am a member of the human race, and you are not, therefore you are inferior and not fit to wipe my arse. But think about it. Just 'cause you're the member of another race doesn't mean you're inferior, does it? See, they're perfidious, that's what they are, kid. But I ask you, what's so good about the human race, anyway? Full of tarts who can only speak in lines from soap operas. We'll see who has the last laugh, eh, insects or humans."

And he kept going on about how much better insects are than humans. I thought that was pretty random, but it's like, there's method in his madness, or something, or a pattern, anyway. The back room is infested with earwigs, right, horrible little things, they make me kind of itch when I see them. I suppose there must be a whole nest of them or something, under the garage, where the riverbank is. I happened to swat one of the little bastards one time when the manager was there and he went ballistic—"What do you think you're doing? Whose side are you on, you murderer?" It's like he really identifies with these earwigs now. But it's not just that, either. After that there seemed to be even more earwigs using the backroom as a shortcut. There was one crawling across the table one time. I thought to myself, the bastard's not here now, I can do what I want, and pretty much just to spite him, I took off my shoe and pulverised the little fucker. Then I kind of got cold feet, I must admit, and I cleaned it up so there wasn't a trace left. And then I forgot about it.

The next time the manager came to the shop his face was dead white. I could tell something was wrong, but I didn't want to know, so I just looked away. Then I realised it was me he was angry with. I couldn't think what was wrong. He just started laying into me—verbally, like, but it was a close thing. I thought it was going to come to blows—about what a snot-nosed, backstabbing, ungrateful hooligan I was. It turns out that somehow he knew about the earwig. Well, that's when I left the first time, but the manager had a word with my dad, and anyway, I ended up coming back. I'm not going to be here forever, mind you.

Well, as if this wasn't weird enough, other things kept happening so that it just got weirder and weirder. But, you know, when you spend most of your time in the backroom of the shop, thinking to yourself, and the only company you have is from your headcase of a manager or the few customers that come and go, after a while it's hard to tell what's weird and what isn't. I kept thinking maybe I'm making a lot of this up, or making connections between things when there is no connection. You know how they say that no two witnesses ever give exactly the same account of the same incident? Well, I keep on wondering how my version of things might differ from other people's. But there's one thing that I can't work out, and it's to do with the whole bicycle incident. You remember the manager went out with the rubber gloves? After the police left he took me into the backroom, laughing like he's really pleased with himself. "I've got something to show you. Look what I've got!" And he took out a notebook from the desk drawer. I had a look at it, and it just seemed to be full of bollocks, like someone had written stuff down when they were off their head. So I said, "Yeah, what is it?" He'd only gone and stolen Stuart's notebook off his body. So I had another look at the book, and then I got this weird creeping feeling, like everything was fitting into place, but maybe into all the wrong places, because I realised that all this stuff was, I don't know, let's just say it fitted in with the manager's interests. As a matter of fact, I can show you. He keeps the book locked up in one of the drawers, but I know where the key is.

The bloke disappeared into the backroom and returned with a small, spiral-bound jotter. He handed it to me as much as to say, "Take a look at this and you'll see what I mean!"

I opened it at random and read the following:

11/02/'93   near the old coal bunker

> There is absolutely no room for an affinity to develop between Mackerel Nioux and the Earth Inner Circle. I have said for many times. Strictly speaking Nioux never knows them. Nioux is confused about the robbery and aggressive behaviours all the time. They do not behave themselves. They are usually infringing upon their own human rights. They are eternally located far away from zero point in the negative direction on the digit line. They are seriously illusive for Nioux's real estate on Earth. They are paranoiacs to a man. Nioux has never told these invaders about the personal property. You must pay more careful attention to the earwigs.

There was more, much more, but even if I could remember it all, I'm not sure there would be any point in reproducing it. The bloke had described these jottings as the kind of thing a person might produce at the height of a drug-induced reverie. I found this a peculiarly apt comparison. Without wanting to go into too much detail, I am familiar with such writings, both as a reader and an author. Many times the key to the whole universe has seemed within my grasp, and I have thought how perfect it would be to write it all down, so that I don't forget. But it is as if everything written in such a state is written in a very special kind of vanishing ink. With this kind of ink the physical tracings of the words themselves remain; it is the significance of those words that vanishes. When the drugs wear off and you return with the special weariness of come-down to a daylight world like cold dregs in the bottom of a teacup, the key to the universe you so cunningly recorded at the moment of perfect understanding makes no sense whatsoever.

I had a similar reaction to the words in that notebook, like waking up in sober daylight to the ashen taste of nonsense. Clearly you would have had to 'be there' at the time to have felt the true potency of these words. This, I supposed, was what happened when Stuart tried to take down in English things properly belonging to some language entirely other.

However, even in this ashen nonsense there were elements that stirred me. The mere mention of certain words in this cold, alien context gave rise to what might be called a spine-tingling sense of mystery. There was the impression of the overlapping of realities that really ought to have nothing to do with each other. This was an impression also given to me by the bloke's whole story. At certain points in his narrative I could not help looking at him to try and gauge whether this were not some kind of elaborate joke. But how could he have known those things that would spark my paranoia without some form of spying or surveillance being involved that was itself redolent of paranoid fantasy?

80

Finally, I was overcome by such a feeling of 'things clos-ing in' that I found it hard to pay attention to anything else the bloke said. I remember he told me to be careful, and that I had wondered exactly what he meant by that, and that I had also used this as a cue for immediate escape. As I left the shop, hearing the shop bell ring behind me, I felt somewhere inside a kind of dismay at abandoning the bloke so abruptly to the isolation of which he had spoken. More than this, though, I felt a contradictory relief at having fled a presence that had become claustrophobic.

Chapter VIII: Personal

The bloke's mad little yarn gave Les and I a lot to talk about. The air became a little chill, and we retired to Beach Road. It seemed too late to do anything else that day, but anyway, we needed to talk, and we needed the comfort talk brings. We didn't want to *stop* talking. When Les' landlady and some of the other tenants returned, we withdrew to Les' room up-stairs. Thinking about it now, the conversation was almost in-distinguishable from our usual nonsense, but it was perhaps the most profound, intimate conversation I have had. Our talk was wide-ranging, full of much fear, much wondering and much laughter. We just couldn't seem to reach the end of it. And yet, I had to go sometime. So, reluctantly, I stood up to leave and we made arrangements to resume our talk and our investi-gation as soon as possible. In the meantime we would both rack our brains as to what we should do next.

Outside, a pale darkness had descended and there was a va-porous mizzle in the air, making the night strangely close and intimate, almost . . . personal. The dampness and the early glow of the streetlamps rendered my surroundings vivid, as if freshly turned, with a special vividness at once redolent of fertility and decay. It occurred to me that the world was naked, quite obscenely so, and this inspired a corresponding sense of nakedness in myself. I felt quite unbearably nervous just to be alone in the world. I trembled and looked about me as I walked. Still, I made it to the top of the road where I lived without mishap. By that time I was sunk in thoughts I don't rightly recall. It was then, as I crested the hump at the mouth of the road, that it happened.

"Oi! Twat!"

My heartbeat suddenly doubled. Two syllables had been enough to startle my fight-or-flight instincts into sickened wakefulness. But it was more than that, even. After all, I was suddenly robbed of the power of either fight or flight. It was as if someone had called me by my secret name, not the one I was given at birth, but the one I had before, the one that *was* me. No one can resist when called by their secret name. I spun round, my cheeks already stinging with shame. There was no one in sight, but the voice came again, echoing the thoughts playing on my mind, and thus sardonically re-confirming its own authority.

"Know yer name, dontcher?"

"What do you want?"

I felt pathetic. I was already preparing to humiliate myself in order to worm out of whatever unpleasantness threatened. I felt extremely uncomfortable at the fact that this was happening so close to home. If I escaped, I calculated, I should change my direction immediately, so that my enemy would not find out where I lived. All the while I looked around slowly, trying to locate the source of the voice.

"Nothing you've got, tosspot," sneered the voice.

Now I became certain that the voice was coming from the old cement mixer at the edge of the track. There were houses on only one side of the track. On the other side was an extensive slope, largely unused and unusable, half-covered in Japanese knotweed. I don't know who the cement mixer belonged to. I suppose it was left over from some building that had taken place here. But it had not been used for quite some time, as evidenced by the bindweed creeping up its legs and over its back.

"Don't think you've got away with it," the voice continued.

"What have I done?" I asked.

"'What have I done wrong? What have I done wrong?' Right little Mummy's boy, aren't we? It's not what you've done. It's what you *are*. We're gonna tell everyone all about you."

"No, please don't."

"D'you think they won't find out, anyway? It's all going to come out. We're only doing what we have to do, like seashells."

"Seashells?"

I found this last remark a little obscure.

"That's right. They spend so long in the sea that its echoes are trapped inside them forever. Listen to this."

I listened. At first all was silent. Then, from the darkness inside the cement mixer, came the distant sound of waves, a muffled, underwater restlessness, like the hiss of a blank recording. Slowly, as if rising to the surface of this endless watery static, there came a percolation of voices. They were familiar, yet it took me a while to place them. As if echoing close and dank at the bottom of that vast well, the ocean, they were the voices of myself and Les. It was the conversation we had had in that shelter at the side of the disused railway line. Obviously these moments were all recorded somewhere to be reproduced perfectly, as if they were still happening, at any given time. But now I was eavesdropping on them from the outside they sounded strange. I felt a sense of dislocation. What was it I had been thinking earlier about nonsense in the cold light of day? How uncomfortable it was to hear my own voice in this way! How it set my teeth on edge! Your voice does not sound the same from inside your head as it does when it comes from outside. Why should this be? I know I am not the only person who cringes to hear their own voice recorded, but perhaps the feeling is extreme in my case. Now, listening to my voice in this way, I could do nothing but plead guilty to my crime. And what was that crime? But it had no name. It was as unique and obvious as my personality itself. It was in the words I spoke and the very tone of my voice. For some reason the particular scene that was being replayed expressed my crime with painful clarity. I hung my head. I could not defend myself. My own voice was the charge, the evidence, the trial, the sentence and the punishment. And it was the omen of worse to come.

Then the wash of ocean drowned the conversation between myself and Les once more, and the other voice returned.

"We've got plenty more where that came from. You shouldn't talk about things you don't know about. In your case that means you shouldn't open your mouth at all. It could get you into trouble. Ginger pubes? We'll give you ginger pubes."

"What, literally?"

Strange the way our personality, no, our many personalities, often do things that surprise us. Here was one I had not seen for a while, putting in an appearance quite out of the blue just to deliver that ridiculous line. I was to regret that random appearance bitterly.

"Listen, clever dick, we know where you live."

I thought the voice was going to say more; instead there came another sound. It was quiet at first, like the faintest of whispers. Then it grew louder, a rustling, scratching sound, as of the rapid movement of uncountable legs. Then, from the shadow-clogged mouth of the cement mixer, came the very tips of two thin appendages. Exactly what they were I will never know, but they seemed to feel around the rim of the metal mouth in a blind, sensitive way. Others joined them.

I ran.

Despite what the voice had said, I did not run directly home. I pegged it back to the top of the road, then up the dark, narrow, hedge-crowded lane that ran behind the backs of the houses. It could be that the owner of the voice and the vague 'we' it had mentioned really did know where I lived. In fact, considering they seemed to already know so much about me, it stood to reason they probably knew my address, too. Nonetheless, and even in my state of panic—a state of panic, I might add, that was a black mixture of hatred and disgust so powerful it was outright fear—I could not run straight back home. My very instincts told me to take this shadowy, indirect route, as if there might have been some protection in so doing.

I reached the warped and peeling door that led to the back garden. It leant, half off its hinges, the unkept garden beyond bursting through the gaps in wild, green profusion. I looked around to make sure no one was watching, then scraped through. When I got into the house at last, I immediately locked the doors, shut the windows and drew all the curtains.

My house could not even keep out a draught. Anyone or anything that could break through the mental barrier of trespassing in a stranger's house would have no trouble with the physical barriers. I was all too aware of this fact and felt on edge all that evening. The sensation of nakedness I had experienced earlier had penetrated to my very home. Where else could I go? Nothing could distract me from this feeling. At last, thoroughly miserable with fear, I went to bed.

I didn't like leaving the ground floor empty below, but there was no helping it. It was my habit to sleep with the window open, so that I could breathe the night air, but tonight I could not bear anything of the sort. My bedroom window was at a level where anyone up in the garden might be able to peer in at me. Suddenly this thought and the vast darkness of night outside made me extremely uncomfortable. I kept the window shut and the curtains drawn, but what I could not see also made me uneasy. I wished there were no window there at all.

It seems strange when I think about it, but I soon fell asleep. Perhaps fear itself can be exhausting. Perhaps there are others reasons. Could it be that there is a very determined kind of dream that creeps into the waking world in order to drag you back down with it into the dark depths of sleep? For whatever reason, sleep took hold of me and did not let me out of its grip for some time. Even when I heard a tapping, scratching on the window and struggled to regain consciousness, sleep kept me in its paralysing bonds, so that I floundered and sank again. Just for a moment I had drawn close to the surface and wondered with sleep-slurred thoughts whether that tapping, scratching came from a bramble that needed cutting back, or whether . . . but the slurred thoughts became wordless stirrings of apprehension . . . the vast night, air on my face, my unprotected face . . . but I must breathe . . . helpless . . . sleep, sleep . . .

At the time, knowing how quickly beached dreams die in the light of day, I kept a dream diary next to my bed. When I finally awoke, after I had managed to collect myself to some degree, I snatched up that diary and wrote down all I could remember, fragmentary as it was. I am not sure how appropriate it was to write these things in the dream diary. It is true that I seemed to have experienced them during sleep, but I can't help thinking they were something other than ordinary dreams. For a long time afterwards, whenever I leafed through the diary and saw these notes, the handwriting suddenly large and frantic, the contents matching, I had a nasty feeling, as if someone had invaded my bedroom and written the notes themselves, just to spite me. Even now, looking at them again to reproduce them here, I am afflicted with the same dark feeling of violation. Perhaps after I have done what is necessary for this story I will dispose of that notebook.

I have my doubts as to whether linear time exists in the realm from which the notes are taken. And so, although I have attempted to arrange them in chronological order, I cannot vouch for the accuracy of this. Anyway, here, in slightly expanded form so as to render it comprehensible, is the burden of those notes:

I was being carried. My head lolled on my neck. Being carried makes me think of childhood, but despite my drowsiness I felt no comfort, no warmth. I began to wonder exactly how I was being carried. I realised I was gripped at a number of places on my body, including ankles and wrists, but not by human hands. Whoever or whatever held me, I knew they did not care for me at all, but handled me like an object. I have never felt such a sense of spiritual cold.

Gradually, I felt myself attain to a level of consciousness at which I could open my eyes. I believe there was a moment of hesitation before I did so. Then, for an instant, I exposed myself to my visual surroundings. It was a mistake. I shut my eyes as quickly as I had opened them. My surroundings had been nothing like I had expected. Indeed, there was no way I could have expected them. My glimpse had been too brief for me to understand much, but I knew we were in a kind of corridor. I use the word 'corridor' as I might use the word 'window' to describe a black hole. About us, enclosing us, were eerie-coloured patterns like the gases of a nebula. But the patterns were not fixed. They stirred, and as they did so they began to turn into something else, like camouflage revealed by movement. I was aware of intelligence there, but of a kind that only made me feel lonelier—horribly lonely. That's when I closed my eyes again. Of course, the 'us' I mentioned was something else that troubled me. As a strange drowsiness vexed my brain I heard the voices of those who carried me. They were the same whispering voices I had heard with Les, coming from the underground stream. Or they were the same kind of voices. Even of the fragments I remember there is little I can reproduce in English, and even what I can reproduce seems inaccurate, somehow slightly off-beam. What I heard was something like this:

"...too long touching this poison. How far..."

"...this one. The one we've been working on. It is even weaker than the others ... full of the madness of I ..."

"...How did you bring it here? I've never seen one like this ... unbelievable ... too soon ..."

" ... while we are waiting for the Mandate we may still prepare our pawns ... strange to see one of these clothes-wearers in Tau Ceti ... shocking ... it doesn't even know it is evil ..."

"... the clothes-wearing dichotomy of the excreting beast ... even now, unconscious, it would try to suck off us ... love-me evil of the mouth, the voice, behind it all the sucking-me ..."

"... Operation Gay ... this is the one ... this golden, fringe-flicking abomination is what we must ... a baby, sucking, love-me, cannot possibly be wrong, grows from the sick roots ... blind ... cannot leave anything alone till it is loved, the milk-puking ..."

"... why we must go back further, before the roots, the dichotomy, the blindness ... back to the single evil ..."

Then blackness. Something was being prepared in the blackness. The lights came on simultaneously with my awareness, stark, sudden. I was awake, and once again, somewhere totally unexpected, somewhere that seemed by definition unexpected. Dark screens made up the facets of an irregular polyhedron. The angles did not seem quite to meet each other, so that wherever I looked, even though I felt quite sober, my vision had to sway drunkenly to accommodate the shapes around me. The light seemed to emanate from the very blackness of these surfaces, at once invisible and glaring, so that it made me wince.

A figure moved from one facet to another, seemingly inspecting them and making adjustments of some kind. It worked in silence, its back turned. I remember I felt imprisoned by that silence. I was sure I was awake, in a state of absolute sobriety. Yet I was paralysed. The harshness of the light, the lucidity of my own faculties, insisted upon the mere reality of my surroundings. And yet I was blank, ignorant of what those surroundings were. This blankness was my paralysis, and at the back of it, some dark knowledge of my situation, too, seemed to bind me tighter. And that figure, surely that should not have been real?

It dawned on me slowly that even if I had not been paralysed mentally, something was holding me in place physically. Then, its work complete, the figure turned round to face me. I knew even as it started to turn that I was in the presence of evil. I almost heard it, a single rising note of evil that transfixed me poignantly. And then the being was facing me full on, and the half-articulate hostility I had sensed in the reality around me became suddenly explicit and inescapable. One should not stare at the sun for fear of losing one's sight, and one should not dwell on the nature and appearance of the Whispering Folk for fear of losing one's mind. Knowing this, I suppose, my memory drew a curtain across what I saw. And yet there remains a glimpse, as if, however fast that curtain was drawn, it could not be fast enough.

It was a twisted thing, and spiky, like a thorn bush, with somewhere about it a horrible air of death, as if a crocodile, worshipped as a god, had been expertly mummified and was now exhumed after thousands of years. Perhaps that was the key to its noisomeness. It was something at once dead and yet living. Imagine a chair, or a table, or a chest-of-drawers come to life. It is not a happy thought. For some reason it is immediately sinister to think of life in that which should not be alive. If a wardrobe comes to life it can only be for evil purposes; it can only be part of some plot, some great nightmare revolt in which all the crimes you thought would go unnoticed for eternity return to bury you, avenged by slaves once so low they were inanimate, mere furniture.

There may be no such thing as a guardian angel, but I now know that there exists something entirely opposite—a bullying demon, or a persecuting devil, perhaps. I knew it as soon as I recognised mine. We were irreconcilable. Quite simply, we were made so that the existence of one must be anathema to the other. To place us side by side was the genesis of primal hate in all its darkness. But it was I that seemed the weaker for this encounter.

At length it spoke. Once again, I remember only fragments:

"... have our own way yet ... winning side is patient ... truth is important, is it not? ... your undoing, quite literally ... surgery ... that you call home, the lies ... start to get behind them ... your own insidiousness against you ..."

The separate facets or panels began to collect images, as a plastic sheet collects dew. They were images I knew well, a butterfly's eye view of a past so distant it was half legend to me. I was drowning in images scalpel sharp.

Now, wherever they came chronologically, the fragments that were at the very core of this ordeal ... In the summer meadow, in the classroom, in the room of the one who was meant to be looking after me ... the cousin who was not a cousin, the spiteful girl who tormented me, the nice lady who gave evening classes ... it didn't really happen, it didn't really happen ... just a wrong turning, the world taking a left into a child's speechless wet dream ... wet nightmare ... I wanted this, but somehow, now it's come to get me, I'm not sure ... the hand on my leg and I'm paralysed in terror ... I hate myself ... it's happening ... and now, and now ... the lies ... I can see where I've been all along ... it was creeping up on me ... that whispering voice—"And here's something just for you ... whatever comes out of your mouth, we hear it all, just like your fairy godmothers ... you asked for it ..." ... creeping up ... it's on me, like a bad joke ... the insect ... even my violation is so sickly ridiculous I am afraid it will only meet with laughter when confessed ... it slithers away and now the facets are all mirrors, I see myself, ten thousand shattered, shivering reflections, and I scream.

Chapter IX: The Taste of Ashes

With a tongueless cry I jerked myself awake. I cannot be sure exactly where my dream ended, because I had a more immediate concern—a sharp pain in my right ear. This pain was acute enough to make me cry out again. Just as all experience centred around our heads seems magnified, the pain in my ear seemed to occupy a space bigger than my head itself. Terrified, I clutched my ear and shook my head. Something was muffling my hearing in that ear, and I feared the onset of deafness. However, the pain became a definite movement, a kind of furious wriggling. Then the muffled sensation was gone, as if a cork had been removed. I could hear again. What I heard was a scratching, scrabbling, like that from the cement mixer the previous night, and something dropped from my ear to the pillow. It stood for a moment as if stunned, its pincers raised aggressively, a rusty-brown, onion-skinned earwig! I couldn't believe it. I clutched my ear again as if to reassure myself it was still intact. I felt fragile and I wanted to vomit. Somehow I did not dare squash that earwig, and in a moment it had regained its equilibrium and scuttled off. Why is it that something falling from my ear made me feel like I myself might fall apart at any moment? A vandal had gained access to the private space of my head and I was left in a state of shock.

Apart from the physical shock there was something else that disturbed me. Of course, I had heard when very young that earwigs do crawl into people's ears, to feed upon eardrums and possibly even grey matter. However, I had long since been apprehended of the truth, that this was an old wives' tale. For an earwig, an insect, to be acting in accordance with some sinister old wives' tale suggested a kind of deliberation that was not natural. And then I remembered what I had been dreaming, and the significance of the thing that had crawled from my pillow was magnified again. I was frantic, dumbfounded.

That was when I saw the dream diary on the floor.

After I had scrawled down as much as I could, in no particular order and barely coherent, I laid the book to one side again. I could not possibly go back to sleep. I sat on my bed, hugging my legs, shivering, till dawn. Dawn, in fact, was not far off, and with its coming I descended to the ground floor to go through the morning rituals that would help me meet the day. When I first looked into the mirror over the basin I felt a powerful relief that, after all, I was free of hair, or anyway, of unnatural hair. My face, thankfully, was the one I knew from before I went to sleep. Nonetheless, this relief was mixed with a new fragility, as if I'd had a close escape that I could not bear to think about. More than that, there lingered a feeling of gluey disgust and dirtiness even in the absence of what I had seen in those dream mirrors.

I continued to shiver as I washed, dressed and breakfasted. These rituals may sound casual, but at the time I struggled through them as if they were ordeals that would decide the fate of my soul. How can I explain? There is no beginning and there is no end. That shivering was the rising to the surface of a struggle that I had known for as long as I could remember, and doubtless longer. That night, with its dream, seemed like the beginning of the struggle, but perhaps it was more like the centre, its ripples spreading backwards and forwards. Certainly, since that night I have become more conscious of the struggle. It has become my life. Sometimes, in the stillness of an empty room, perhaps, or at any given moment, for no reason at all, I am visited by that same shivering—a trembling so violent I cannot bear it—and I do not know how to make it stop. I must simply wait and hope it will pass, though I know it will always come again and again until its promise is fulfilled.

And what is the nature of this trembling? What does it feel like? What is its essence? I'm afraid that my answer must sound very eccentric. Nonetheless, for some reason it is important for me to set down on paper, in some little corner of this universe, that secret snowflake of words that is my very soul.

The power of words is paradoxical. A single word might capture perfectly a certain meaning that it is impossible to explain precisely using many other words. It is perhaps appropriate that my soul had been nailed by a word that, to my knowledge, does not appear in any dictionary, and probably never will, a word that has currency only in the obscure little nook of space and time that is England of the late twentieth, early twenty-first century, and that only amongst a certain section of a certain generation. That word is 'gay'. The particular nuance I have in mind has nothing to do with homosexuality, but is closer to a painful naïvety, which in me has become a painful self-consciousness. There is no more embarrassing, shameful thing to be, but why should I confess, "Yes, I am gay", when anyone can see it's so at a single glance? I close my eyes and I see a trail of golden stars glittering across space, twinkling, then I am wrung inside at the twisted horror of it. I do not belong in this world. I should not exist.

Let me be more personal, but hopefully less obscure. I am ugly. Once again I use the word to express something other than the dictionary meaning. This time the circulation of the word is even more limited. It is my own idiolect—the dialect of an idiot, perhaps?—and it has nothing to do with physical looks, nor anything to do with any moral sense of evil or sin. Even if the twisted creature that thrashes inside me in a straightjacket of its own flesh is spotlessly innocent, it is so utterly naked and vulnerable—let us say 'pink and raw'—that it is too hideous to look upon.

I remember . . .

Yes, even before that night there were times, visiting a friend perhaps, when I would look down at myself and be struck with such horror I felt I had turned to stone. I bowed my head. I kept my mouth shut and waited for a chance to leave. Then, walking home, my head still bowed, I suffered the agonies of a million needles piercing my flesh, aware that my ugliness was on view for the whole world to see.

Ashes.

That is what I saw, tasted and felt as I put on my jacket, locked the door behind me, and walked slowly up the road, hoping someone at Les' would be awake to let me in.

Ashes.

Chapter X: Jeepers, Creepers, Ouija Get Those Peepers?

"Sorry to get you out of bed so early."

Sorry.

I would get down on my knees and say it a thousand times. Sorry for everything I've ever said and done. Sorry for everything that's yet to come. Sorry that my very presence is taking and not giving. Sorry that I've never spoken a word of truth in my life. I would say all this but I do not even have the right to say sorry, since I can never be forgiven. Much better to say little and know my debt can never be paid. Much better to say little and not burden you with my voice, only leave myself to your mercy.

"That's alright. Sit down. How are you, my friend?"

"Fine, thanks."

Is that voice solid and dead as a lump of stone? Listen more carefully. What seems to be solid is made up of a thousand thousand trembling cracks, so close together you can hardly hear them.

95

"Shall I make a cup of tea?"

"Yes. That would be great. Thank you."

How can I accept your kindness, a worthless parasite like myself? Yet, I cannot refuse. To bear my guilt in silence must be my punishment.

"Here you are. I hope it's not too strong."

"No. I like it strong, I think."

There is a kind of plant that lives in the desert. I believe it is called the Jerusalem plant. Years may pass without rain. Its leaves fold in on themselves. It withers. It looks like a scrap of tumbleweed that will crumble in your hand. But once it feels the touch of water again, its colour changes. It begins to unfurl.

"I had a dream last night," I said.

Apparently I was not the only one who had dreamt. Les, too, had had a nocturnal experience that had shaken him to the core. He too had felt he had no other choice than to wear a brave face when morning came. Let me draw a veil over the conversation that ensued after I mentioned my 'dream'. All that need be said is that it cemented the feeling that we were 'in this together'.

With this feeling, and with our renewed desperation, there came a sudden, increased creativity of ideas. Perhaps because we no longer had any choice but to believe in our plight, we were reacting to it with greater spontaneity. The idea we finally settled on, however, as the most prudent plan A, was to hold a two-man séance.

It just so happened that I had a virtually brand spanking new ouija board, a trophy of my trip to the United States of America. When I was living on about £32 a week—fortnightly payments—I saved up. You think it's impossible? Well, I did it! Think spuds! Think supermarket own brands! Oh yes, I did supplement my diet with the spoils of shop-lifting, I suppose, so I'm not quite sure what the moral of this story is. Those bastards at the DSS wouldn't have liked me going on holiday, so I had to sign off for two weeks and pretend I was going up north looking for work. As far as they're concerned you shouldn't set foot outside the door if it's not to look for work. I could give a hardy lecture on the way a gentleman of leisure, such as I was, is treated by a ruffianly society of illiterate clerks and bureaucrats. But I won't. After all, no one would take me seriously. It's not as if I occupy any sort of moral high ground.

Anyway, in America, in the same shop in which I discovered that sea monkeys really do exist, a toy shop, as a matter of fact, I found a ouija board and couldn't resist making a purchase.

Ouija boards are fascinating items. I have known people who are perfect materialists claim bad experiences with the ouija board, talking about those experiences in a tone that communicated the seriousness of their fear. The wrong voice answered to their knocking. Such things are not to be meddled with, they seem to imply.

No, this is not a toy.

So much the better, because now I wanted it for anything but playing games.

Sometimes I think there is nothing in the world better than the company of a single friend. That is how it started—an evening with a friend. Since we did not want to be interrupted, we decided to hold the séance at my place. I drew the curtains and locked the door. The ouija board had never been used. Les reclined on the carpet, leaning on his palm and smoking while I read the instructions and sipped at my tea. There might have been no world beyond that room.

The instructions were written in a slightly campy way to match the kitsch of the pamphlet they were printed on—black ink on red paper, with little silhouette illustrations vaguely reminiscent of Aubrey Beardsley. I found the mock-serious tone irritating, as it made me feel less than confident of the authority of the method described. Nonetheless, I read the instructions thoroughly, as if we were about to play our very first game of Monopoly, because I was sure any sense of sanctioned ritual, of doing things right, that we could achieve, was important. According to the pamphlet, the optimum number of people for a séance was three, but we would have to make do. No one else was going to be in on this.

No, this is not a toy.

At last I felt I had gained all I could from the instruction pamphlet. I still felt more than a little uncertain, but there was no point in delaying further.

"Are you ready?"

"Ready."

We moved the table into the centre of the room and placed the board on top of it. I lit some candles and incense because I felt anything I could do to create a mood would help.

The board itself was smart and shiny, what you might call 'posh'. The letters of the alphabet were arranged on it in a semi-circle, printed in a deliberately antique typeface. The other half of the circle was made up of numbers, punctuation and useful, time-saving words such as 'and' and 'the'. Instead of a glass tumbler there was a vaguely theloditic implement which the instruction pamphlet termed 'the planchette'. I didn't know much about ouija boards, but somehow 'the planchette' didn't seem to fit in with my image of them. I didn't like it. I thought of a certain poem by Sylvia Plath in which spirits rose to the surface of the ouija glass like moths to a flame. We decided to swap 'the planchette' for a glass.

I turned out the lights and we sat facing each other across the ouija board. We joined hands, left over right. I almost said 'held hands' but realised that is the wrong terminology. Yet, emotionally, perhaps, the latter phrase is more accurate. It was not at all self-conscious. We had a task to perform that absolutely demanded we should hold hands. Perhaps for that reason it felt very comfortable. If you are a naturally tactile person, perhaps you will not understand how very rare it is for me simply to feel comfortable touching or being touched by another.

Despite this comfort I also felt extremely nervous. It was a feeling akin to stage fright. I had to hear my own naked voice speaking some very unnatural and embarrassing lines before our work would be done.

So, with two hands joined on the glass and two joined at the side of the board, so as not to 'break the circle', we began.

"O, spirits of the aether, hear my voice. We are here to beg your assistance in seeking Stuart, the Lone Ginger . . ."

I did not use his nickname gratuitously. I simply did not know what his surname was and felt the need to be specific.

Les began to speak. I saw he had closed his eyes, and he spoke as if in prayer.

"Stuart, my friend, we want to help you. Please Stuart, if you can hear us, tell us what you want. We are your friends. We want to help you. We're waiting for you here. Let your spirit come into this glass and tell us what you need."

He carried on in this way, half in a chant, repeating himself now and then just to keep up the flow of words. I closed my eyes, too, and listened. With nothing in the world but darkness and that prayerful voice, the hair began to prickle on the nape of my neck.

Then the glass moved. It moved an inch, jerked, entirely of its own accord, and we both opened our eyes. Once again it began to slide. It was a curious sensation. Although both our hands were on top of the glass, it felt to me as if I were not touching it at all, merely watching. Then the rim of the glass bumped against a letter—it was 'f'. I don't remember the letters that came after that, because they were gobbledegook, a bad Scrabble hand, but the feeling of will that they conveyed, of something trying to communicate, had the prickling spreading from my neck to the rest of my body. The glass came to a halt, as if dying. Something had come and gone. Les began his chant again, but was soon interrupted by the glass being galvanised into movement once more. This time it was spelling actual words. Next to the board we gripped each other's hands more tightly.

For the first quarter of an hour or so—I really cannot be sure of the duration—the spirits came in dribs and drabs. Each new voice came and departed like a wave of shivering. I use the word 'voice'—although they were silent, somehow the atmosphere of each was so distinct that it was like hearing voices. Those first minutes were a revelation. I never knew until then the extent of the noise, the ghostly traffic that passes around us at all times. Don't ask me the exact nature of the thoroughfares they travelled. I cannot even be sure of the nature of the travellers themselves. I only knew they were out there, that they are always out there, beyond the range of our everyday senses. Myself and Les were like blind men at an intersection. We seemed to be catching mere snatches of a world in which we were utterly lost.

"... there's a place in the pampas grass. The cats know. Behind the old woman's blind eye. The feral gate. Why don't you slip away with us? Such games there ..."

"...June, June ... always here, like this, in the summertime ..."

"...I finger. What you want? You call finger want him touch you good? Finger touch you good ..."

"... inside you are time of us ..."

" ...Remember me! The world has torn us apart. Remember me, or we're lost ..."

"...where did they get to? Sorry, do I know you? I thought this was Sarah's party ..."

These were a few of the voices, the moths that were visible momentarily in our candlelight.

Then these voices were scattered. Their signals were over-ridden completely by one much more powerful. I am positive that the same strong current pulsed through both myself and Les. The glass was filled with the disembodied will of a single, energising voice. Stuart had arrived. Our hands gripped each other even tighter, as if we were on a fairground ride. As the glass slipped across the board we lurched with its movement. The world itself was tilting to make the glass move. It was a peculiar, queasy sensation, not at all pleasant—a delicate, riveting fascination like watching your innards being taken out before your eyes. We had no choice but to hold on tightly to the end.

"It's me—Stuart! They weren't watching and I got away. Must be quick. Not much time."

The most unnerving thing about Stuart's arrival was the very simple, familiar sense of another person being there, even though all we had was a moving glass and letters in order. The very normality of the conversation, despite the content and the circumstances, was eerie.

"Where are you? Who are 'they'?" I asked.

As the conversation slowly, painstakingly unravelled, this sense of normality gave way to something infinitely heroic, or else infinitely desperate. Something without arms, without legs, without substance of any kind, some incorporeal imperative, kept itself focused in a single, sustained effort on such a mammoth scale it was as if someone single-handedly dragged blocks from far-flung quarries to erect a monolithic SOS before us. It plunged itself into this labour to such an extent that it soon abandoned even the shorthand it started with and martyred itself to sentences monumentally complete.

"Can't explain where. No time. They are the Whispering Folk and their cousins, the Listening Folk. How much do you know? My death?"

"We know you died by the local transformer."

"The what?"

"The electricity doodah."

It was hard to believe that something 'out there' could hear our naked voices.

"Didn't die. Tried to die, but they got me. Where to start? Okay, listen. I'll explain.

"The world is full of secret languages. The rocks conspire with the clouds, weeds with windows, paper with drawers, clothes with blood. All is conspiracy. The great weakness of man comes from his unbending sense of what is absurd and what is realistic. The world is divided by a veil. Beyond the veil mackerel and earwigs are mobilising, pebbles are holding orgies, we are a laughing stock. On this side of the veil animals are mute, rocks on pavements are silent and still."

"But that's absurd," I put in.

"That's just exactly what gets on my tits!" the glass continued its spectral telegraph: "Why is it absurd? It's so arbitrary. You're just believing the whole sham of the world. Anyway, the veil deceives and protects us at the same time, but the Whispering Folk want to tear down the veil."

"Why?"

"They are vindictive. It's not just that. It's some vendetta. The rest of creation doesn't care. It needs a stock for its laughter and man, in his ignorance, happens to be it. But there's something I don't understand here. I see the mackerel creased up in laughter as if they know what is to come. I do not like it. I think mankind snubbed or double-crossed the Whispering Folk long ago, so now they want to mobilise all of creation to humiliate us. They resent us because we do not even remember them. They've been taking it out on me . . . but I must get to the point.

"They plan to use me. Through me they will find a way to the human race. That's why I tried to kill myself. They were coming for me. I was too late. Only my body was left behind. But I've been clever. I know a way to escape. Do you know the old railway track? There is a shelter there. Tomorrow at three twenty-seven, for seven minutes, the door will be open a crack. Wait for me there on the bicycle. This time we will be quicker than them. You must take me to the electricity thing. I must not talk too long in case they overhear. It's been a long time already. They will miss me."

"What will happen if we fail?" I asked.

"I cannot tell you—the torture, the madness . . . on this side of the veil things are different. If the veil comes down it is the end. No, worse, it is the beginning. I cannot say more. I must go. I think they are . . .'"

But the last sentence was never finished. The glass moved away from the row of letters and towards the word 'goodbye'. It stopped halfway, suddenly lifeless, nothing more than an empty vessel again.

Chapter XI: While the Tide Comes In

The sound of waves is sleep without tiredness. More than that, it is going back to a time before you were you. There is no sound on Earth like it for making you forget the world. This is especially true at night.

This night, however, I could not help remembering a certain conversation that had seemed to have the sea for background, and I was uncomfortable. I felt that 'overlapping' I have mentioned before.

We sat in the sand by a rock and talked. At first we talked about the morrow and the uncertain mission with which we had been charged. There was surprisingly little to say. Of course, the whole affair was riddled with questions and doubts. Our most obvious concern was with what had happened to Stuart. There was also the great, over-arching doom of what *would* happen if anything went wrong. I also had certain suspicions that I saw no need to voice. I could not help wondering how Stuart had been able to stay so long from the clutches of his captors. However, since it was clear that we had absolutely no choice but to do as Stuart had asked, I kept these tormenting suspicions to myself.

The subject came to its natural end and we were washed up once more on the shore of silence by the sound of waves. Perhaps it was because the subject was so vast, so imminent, like the cloud-laden sky above us, that we felt no more need to talk about it. Now all we could do was wait. The waiting and uncertainty had brought us to an island of something indistinguishable from peace. A thousand eavesdropping realities may have been overlapping, threatening me once more with that incurable trembling, but now the pricking of invisible ears was the same as the prickly silence of intimacy. Not despite the fact I felt so exposed, but because of it, there seemed no point in hiding anything. Our murmuring voices in the darkness were like the last flames of a dying fire that kept the wild of endless night at bay.

Les had some straight cigarettes—'straights' we called them, as opposed to the cheaper 'rollies' that were our usual diet—and he gave me one. The flame of his lighter leapt from nothingness and passed between us, leaving two glowing circles hovering in the darkness where it had been. Maybe it was these—all we had by way of real fire—or maybe it was the events of the past few days, but something seemed to remind Les of one of those mysterious memories of his, and he pointed to part of the headland enclosing the beach.

"See that rock over there?"

"Yeah?"

"I was down here one time at night and I saw lights moving in the sky above it. I couldn't really tell how high up they was, but they were green and they looked quite big. I don't think they was an aeroplane, 'cause of the way they moved. They went round in circles, kind of slow at the top, and quick at the bottom. Do you think they were UFOs? I don't know. Maybe they was just an aeroplane."

"Well, they *were* UFOs, because UFOs are Unidentified Flying Objects. You don't know what they were, therefore they were UFOs."

"Yeah, but were they aliens, d'you think?"

"I really don't know. Maybe. After all, it wouldn't be strange, would it? I think that's what Stuart was saying earlier: nothing is strange."

"Yeah, that's true. And this area is weird. Loads of people have seen things round here.

"You can climb up that rock, you know. Up over the grassy bit. There's lots of birds' nests round there. Then at the top there's a kind of maze with a path that leads to that little car park opposite the golf course. D'you know it? We should climb up there together some day. Maybe that's where the UFO lands, up there."

"Yes, we'll definitely have to climb up there sometime."

My eyes still lingered on the blue-black void that Les' finger had indicated. The stars glittered, cold and ancient. Now my gaze moved across to the sky above the sea, and the star-bedizened clouds that had before seemed the symbol of all our troubles. They were the intricate face and wings of a gargoyle made of smoke. Hovering as they did between Earth and space, they made me see there was really no separation between the two. We were *in* space. The alien lapped at our very feet in the glistening waves. Such wonder! Ah, nothing matters, after all. I may be doomed to madness, tears and obscurity, but anyway, I have looked upon the sighing mystery and alien beauty of the night sky. I am smaller than the last dying twinkle in that sky. I have felt my loneliness swallowed up in it, like white breath disappearing into darkness. Surely this is a sweetness greater than love or lust. Take me, cold sky! Do what you will with me!

When I was a child how often would I amuse myself—but perhaps 'amuse' is not the right word—how often, then, would I make myself sigh and shiver by turning the beam of my pocket torch out into space, imagining it travelling at the speed of light, mostly obliterated by dust and particles in the atmosphere, but maybe, just maybe, one day, millions of years hence, in an almost invisible pinprick of light, crossing the interstellar void and arriving at another world—a message from my long-vanished childhood.

As I sat on the beach with Les I thought of the reverse of this—of the light from aeon-dead sources that was now reaching us. What obscure and sad light is this, from what single star of what far quarter of creation, that now falls sighing upon the silver crucifix around Les' neck?

I suppose he must have noticed me looking at it.

"Thanks for the cross. I wear it all the time. I take good care of it, don't worry."

"I'm not worried. It's yours now. You can do what you like with it."

"Why did you give it to me, though? I mean, I am grateful and everything. I was looking for one like this. It's just that it's a really smart one. I thought you might want to keep it for yourself."

"No. I think it's better if you have it. I don't need it."

Les paused thoughtfully before speaking again.

"What do you believe in?"

"What do you mean?"

"Well, all the stuff that's happened in the last few days—it makes you think, dunnit?"

"Yes, it makes you think."

"But you never talk about what you believe in."

It was true. No matter how intimately I might have talked with a person, I never mentioned those philosophical areas usually called 'belief'.

"Ah! There's a good reason for that," I said.

"What's that?"

"I don't believe in anything."

"Really?"

"No. Not really."

"What do you believe in, then?"

"I don't know."

"You don't know?"

"Well, no, perhaps I do. That's just it, you see. I just can't talk about what I believe in. This is what happens when I try to. Actually, I believe in everything."

"What do you mean?"

"I believe everything that I'm told. For instance, when I'm talking to a Christian I believe in Christianity, even if I might argue with them, and when I'm with an atheist I believe in atheism, even though I might argue with them. I have no intrinsic convictions of my own. I'm like a chameleon. It can be very confusing and disturbing. You end up hating people, wishing they'd just keep their mouths shut. Five billion people, all believing different things and thinking they are right and everyone else is wrong—I have never, never understood where anyone gets that sense of certainty and authority from, to believe that they are right. I just feel like I'm torn in five billion different directions. That's why I really don't like to talk about my beliefs."

"Nah, I don't really like to talk about mine, either. Well, you know I'm a Christian."

"Yes, I know."

"Well, my landlady is too, and you know she always goes on at people that they should be Christians, but I don't agree with that. She just nags. That puts people off. I just think that Jesus changed my life. Before I used to hate everybody. But now I don't. Now I love everybody."

"Really?"

"Yeah. Well, I try to. So being a Christian is good for me."

"I'm sure you're right."

"Isn't is lonely not believing in anything?"

"I suppose so."

I let the sand trickle through my fingers. The silence seemed to beg a question.

"Well, we're here, now. That's what matters," I continued, "Everyone else is asleep and we're here awake, talking."

I said that, but looking at the glowing tip of Les' cigarette I became suddenly desolately lonely. I felt like crying. I felt as if I were shrinking, turning cold. I did not want that tiny point of light to go out, but I knew that it would, soon, and there would be nothing left but ashes.

Ashes.

Les drew on the cigarette. It glowed brighter. I could almost hear it burn. Something drew the tiny furnace backwards—an in-breath of combustion—and closer to its extinction. Something drew on the waters, and the tide was dragged back over pebbles and sand. Something drew on me. I was alone.

There is something that I must say. There is something that I must do.

Sometimes I find everything comes down to this. It is the most urgent thing in the world. I must find some way to give myself to another. No, I must find a way to give another human being to themselves—the gift of 'you through my eyes', 'you though my heart'.

I am alone.

I began to sing in a quiet, unsteady voice.

"How many earwigs does a man have to snog
Before they will say he's not well?
The answer, my friend, is fifteen billion,
The answer is fifteen billion . . ."

Les joined me when I got to 'the answer', but before I could complete the verse I had dissolved into tears. If only they had been quiet tears I might have preserved my dignity—such as it was—but they were not quiet. I choked, gagged and hiccupped on my tears. I knew if I tried to talk I would not be able to, that my voice would come out in that strange, childish, tearful stutter which is the sound of all our pretensions in pieces. Yes, I am gay. But why confess the obvious? I had ambushed myself with that song. It had touched that sick, secret snowflake at my heart.

I felt a hand on my wrist. I was paralysed. At that touch the tears gushed with renewed strength. I was an ugly, helpless, snivelling thing.

At last they seemed to subside.

"Are you alright, mate?"

"Yes, I'm alright."

I was glad to get through the three words without my voice leaping unexpectedly, as if tugged on a fish-hook.

Determined, I started the song once more.

"And how many mackerel does a man have to kill,
Before they will tell him to go and have a lie down?
The answer, my friend, is one hundred and thirty-three,
The answer is one hundred and thirty-three."

The tide was coming in. Our little island of time had shrunk down to almost nothing.

Chapter XII: Orgasmic Climax

The next day was cold and wincingly bright. I donned my fingerless gloves against the nip in the air.

Perhaps that nip was not due entirely to the weather. After leaving Les I had not passed a peaceful night. In fact, I had barely slept at all. It would be redundant to repeat in detail all the abuse that the world had stored up for me since the evening when the voice had addressed me from the cement mixer. But perhaps I should mention that things were waiting for me, like bullies waylaying a schoolboy on the way home from school. There were whispers, many of them quite poisonously distinct, and there were snares of waking dream. Many of these made reference to what had recently passed between myself and Les. Strangely, though, they did not mention our mission.

I arrived home feeling pinched and bruised, and it did not stop there. But enough. There is no need for me to write everything, after all. Only, the next day there was still a doughty nip in the air.

With the coming of morning, I found it impossible to stay in the house on my own, and went round to Les' earlier than I had intended. If I am waiting for something I find it impossible to concentrate on anything else. Waiting with someone else was slightly less torturous. We still had more time on our hands than we knew what to do with. We kicked about Les' house in a mood of strange tension, like schoolboys playing truant, until finally we could stand it no more, and we went out into the bracing air to release the bicycle from its dormancy in the side passage.

Most of our debate the previous evening had centred around how many bikes we should take. Presumably speed was of the essence. If we only took the one bike our speed might be reduced enormously. But then again, we were in this together. It hardly seemed tolerable to be riding separate bikes at this stage of events. Besides, none of Les' other bikes were really built for speed. Or if they were originally, you'd never guess it to ride them now. So we might as well just ride together on the haunted bicycle again. There was a good chance, anyway, judging on past experience, that Stuart would supply any speed we lacked. And so there was nothing to do now but make sure we were at the appointed place at the appointed time and hope for the best.

I do not believe I have ever been more sober in my life than I was on that day. The day's sobriety and mine were one. Despite the hour, the general mood and the crispness of the air made me feel as if we had risen especially early to prepare for a long journey. In a way, we really were going on a long journey, into the utter unknown. Everything reflected the completeness of this uncertainty.

As we checked the bike's tyres, the sunlight gleamed weakly on the saddle. Les rode the bike up and down the pavement a few times experimentally. It seemed to be completely normal. There was not so much as a wobble in the steering. I had never seen Les ride such a normal bike. I was reminded of the glass we had used on the ouija board and how it had suddenly stopped, empty. We were alone.

Les squirted WD-40 here and there for good measure, and, though we would probably arrive so early that we would have to wait at the other end, we no longer had the patience to wait at this end. Les gathered together some biscuits, a lump of cheese, some ginger beer and a penknife, put them in a scraggy plastic bag and gave them to me to look after. Then we set out.

Since we had plenty of time and wanted to conserve our energy for later exertions, we started off walking the bike up the hill. Once we got to the top we stopped. Les mounted the bicycle and I climbed up behind him. With a downward plunge of the pedal we were well and truly launched on our mission, the streaming wind a reminder that from here on our balance would be tested in ways other than just the physical.

The way through the town to the disused railway line was long and involved, and then we still had to cycle some distance to the shelter in question. We stopped while the shelter was still some distance off. The time by Les' digital watch was two fifty-eight. We did not want to approach too near before the time Stuart had given, in case our premature arrival somehow jinxed things. Instead we sat down at the side of the empty track and ate the goodies I had held onto. We hoped this rest and light repast would boost our strength for the task now imminent. We spoke little.

Finally, we had eaten all we could. Actually, it seemed neither of us had much appetite. Rather than carry something that might get in the way, I hung the remainder of our food from a barb on the barbed-wire fence. I wiped my mouth with the back of my hand. A few minutes and a few dozen yards—that was all that was left.

We waited in silence until three twenty-six. Then we got on the bike once more and Les pedalled us to a point in front of the shelter. We did not dismount. Our backs diagonal to the little wooden hut, we rested with our left feet upon the ground. We waited, not knowing quite what we waited for. Surely we would know it when it came?

It was three twenty-seven by Les' digital watch. We looked over our shoulders at the shelter. There was no discernible change in its appearance. In my imagination, however, this empty and ramshackle wooden structure had become an open gateway. I almost thought I could feel a draught. For some reason I kept expecting some thumping impact on my back, like something leaping on me. I saw nothing. Looking intently back over my shoulder, I did not notice that Les had turned to face the front. His voice surprised me.

"Quickly! There's no time to lose! Hold on tight!"

It was his voice, but certainly not his intonation, and not his choice of words. With a stabbing feeling of confusion become fear, I gripped Les' sides. His foot thrust down on the pedal and the bike was launched on its final, imperative race. When I touched Les' ribs through his shirt I almost drew back. It did not even feel like Les. A shiver ran through me like static electricity. Les faced forward. I only saw the back of his head with its rat tails of hair. The feeling in my hands seemed to contradict this visual information. All I could do, though, was to hold tightly, as the voice commanded.

Les pedalled like a demon, and after we had got up a bit of speed I dared to ask what had happened.

"It's okay," came the voice. "It's all going to plan. Sorry about this. A good head start is essential."

It was such a bizarre sensation to hear Les' voice used in that way that I did not dare ask anything else. I kept a frightened silence, as if only clinging to this alien thing could save me from plunging into a bottomless chasm.

We did not seem to be pursued, but who knew how long we had before pursuit began? Or perhaps we were pursued already, invisibly. Or perhaps some trap lay ahead. There was no telling. Speed. Distance. Faster. Further. It never seemed fast or far enough.

We had a long way to go. Les continued to pedal furiously in determined silence. There was no room for slacking. This unrelenting effort to keep nosing at the highest possible speed coupled with the very emptiness behind us made me extremely uneasy. And where was Les—the real Les? What a weird and utterly lonely position I was in on the back of that bicycle!

Eventually we came off the railway track and onto a narrow country road. We were making good time and as yet there was no sign of pursuit. We still had to negotiate these twisting country roads for a while before hitting the main road back into town. And then, of course, we had to cross right to the other side of town, and whichever route we took, some of it would be uphill. Suddenly the madness of the whole venture struck me afresh with a despair that was actually dizzying. If we were pursued at all, surely everything was lost. Everything! I watched the tarmac flash by beneath the spoked wheels as I contemplated just what this meant.

We turned one high-hedged bend after another. As we cycled swiftly by a primrose-dotted hedge the bike gave a wobble. For a moment we lurched out into the middle of the road and I thought we were going to end up in a tangled heap. However, the bicycle was swiftly brought under control again. I had more than a slight impression that this was achieved *despite* Les' suddenly confused movements. By rights we should have gone head over heels. I heard Les' voice again.

"Crikey! I wasn't expecting that."

It was his normal intonation. I realised that his body, too, felt normal again.

"What was it?" I asked.

"Stuart was talking to me. He told me to let him steer and pedal. Then he said he had to hide."

"Where is he now?"

"He's still here."

"Really?"

"Yeah. Can't you tell?"

I thought about the quickly curbed wobble and it did seem to me there was still something of that presence with us, though it was hard to say why I thought so. Then I wondered why he might have felt the need to hide. It did not seem a good omen. And if both myself and Les could detect his presence with our feeble human senses, then what about entities with senses different and possibly more acute?

Perhaps because of Stuart's withdrawal, or perhaps because I had distracted him with questions, Les' pedalling had become a little more moderate.

"I think we should go faster," I said. "Can we go faster?"

"Yep! Watch this!"

And Les raised himself off the saddle like a jockey, pedalling furiously in a half-standing position. We came to a roundabout that I recognised, covered with a bright mosaic of flowers. Slowing a little, we took the first turning. At last we were on the road back to town. For the first time since we had started this race against doom I felt a slight sense of relief, a slackening of tension. The road now was all downhill, the gradient fairly steep, until it hit the first traffic lights. Les dropped back into the saddle, still pedalling hard. Traffic began to pass.

Perhaps it was the momentary slackening of tension, with its reckless suggestion of hope, that brought on a backlash of intensified panic. Cars whizzed past, hard and deadly. Hope and despair seemed buffeted about in the dull, whirling sky above. In the fields to each side, horses munched indifferently on grass. The veins in my head were throbbing. I could even see transparent veins pulsating before my eyes. As if a heavy cloud had suddenly smothered the feeble sun, a dark anxiety closed in upon me. I seemed to hear a whispering in my ears. I looked behind.

Even as I turned my head I knew I should not look.

There it was, actually visible on the air, as if the juggernaut further behind had thrown up black veins of fumey smoke before it—the whispering. The whispering—all twitching feelers at first, like those that had obscenely caressed the rim of the cement mixer's mouth, then taking forms of things I had seen before, between sleeping and waking, and things I had never seen.

We were hurtling towards some terrible collision, I was certain. Everything froze in a pulsing hush, and the whispering took over.

I suppose in that moment I knew a great many things that I have forgotten. I still remember much. This was the torture and madness from which Stuart was trying to escape, this the unbearable absurdity. If I attempt to describe that moment now, in retrospect, the first thing that springs to my mind is a certain children's book called *Struwwelpeter*. Perhaps you know it. On the cover is a picture of the 'Shock-Headed Peter' of the title. This naughty boy has refused to have his hair and nails cut, and now his hair is a tangled mane and his fingernails are long and twisted. He weeps at the state he has brought himself to in a kind of self-crucifixion of shame. Inside are a number of gruesome instructive rhymes with nightmarish illustrations to match. A boy sucks his thumbs and as punishment the Scissor Man snips them off. A girl plays with matches and ends up a pile of ash. Another boy refuses to eat his soup, and starves to death. But these are not the rhymes I am thinking of. In amongst them is another rhyme a little more enigmatic, and what instruction it is meant to give is obscure. It features a hunter who sallies forth one day with his hunting gun in search of hares. The foolish hunter takes a nap, and while he does so, his quarry, the hare, steals his clothes and his gun and waits for him to wake. As a child I found the inky little sketches that accompanied this rhyme peculiarly dark and disturbing. What was it about the hare in hunting cap and glasses that made me thrill as to the presence of evil? The very lines of concentration above the hare's nose, as it fired at the fleeing hunter, seemed wicked. But that hunter is the whole human race. We sleep. We dream. Secure in our belief that we are the hunter whose reason holds dominion over all nature, our sleep is deep and undisturbed. But dread the moment when we wake and see the reversal that faces us!

That is what I saw looming above us, behind the bicycle—a rent in the veil of our slumber, and beyond, vista upon vista of sadistic, inhuman laughter. There were the Whispering Folk and the Listening Folk, there the earwigs, the mackerel, there the hideous intelligence of rocks and crabs, there things of which I had not heard or dreamed, a jeering Bosch-like crowd to Tau Ceti and further. Further still. Sad-eyed and naked, men, women and children were ridden like mules by giggling fish. Humans wept in cages and zoos. They were goaded on to war, unknowing, like dogs in pits, or bred to weird, topiary shapes, like pigeons or poodles. But all this is only the melancholy allegory for what I saw, since, I am afraid, I can do no better than to express it by such means. I felt all the cold sickness of a beast in an arena.

Ah, what sickness! When animals wear clothes we find them comical, ridiculous. How much more so does the universe find we who clothe ourselves, straight-faced! It is man's sense of the absurd that makes him absurd. It is because he takes himself seriously that he is a laughing stock. It is man's aloneness, his snobbiness in the face of all creation, that makes him risible. Surely we deserve what is coming. We strut around on our two legs, po-faced, saying 'poppycock' and 'nonsense' to all we do not understand. We do not deserve to be saved. And yet it's understandable that we should wish to ward off the nightmare of our own absurdity with such words. This is our only defence. And, after all, I am human, too, to some degree, and I can't help being on the side of humans in this and thinking of those who would tear down the veil to spite us as evil.

The moment that had frozen unfroze. The rent in the veil now reached up to the sky and the sky was about to crash down upon our heads. Before I knew what was happening we were enveloped in a quaking darkness of choking fumes. The massive lorry thundered past us, and, pummelled by the wind of its violent wake, we were almost thrown into a mangled heap at the side of the road. Fumes swirled around the back of the lorry, sucked in after it. The world reeled. I gave a whoop of terror that turned into hysterical laughter. The rent had disappeared.

We were going at such a speed that it seemed the slightest wobble, the slightest jolt, would send us into a deadly spin. I thought of the hard tarmac and my own unprotected head. I thought of the violent contact of the two, the fizzle of pain, knowing something was wrong, some unidentifiable damage, the damage itself being part of the reason it could not be identified, like a kind of numbness, an amnesia; I thought of the feeling of blood, slick to my touch, flowing, matting my hair in a kind of trickling itch. I thought of all these things, and they seemed to embrace me, so gently it made me cringe and shiver. The promise of impact, damage, blood, embraced and caressed me as we careened tightly around the bends in the road. My laughter was unstoppable, jagged. Tears crept from the corners of my eyes. The wind pushed them towards my ears. Les whooped too, as he pedalled. I felt reassured. I held tight and thought of nothing.

We passed the first houses of town and soon we hit the traffic lights. As if waking up I said, "The seafront! Go by the seafront!" I was about to explain why, anxious Les might not listen, but, freewheeling through amber, he steered without argument to the seaside turning. That route usually had less traffic and was generally flatter.

Sunk in a daze, I clung. We traversed the town. Downhill again, we were almost there. Les steered us onto the track that ran from the water mill to the local transformer. The bicycle bumped on stones. Almost there.

With just a few yards left, Les' voice came again, half-strangled. Something told me that it was not Les at all.

"Jump!"

Les jumped from the bicycle and I jumped after him, into the undergrowth at the edge of the river. I looked up to see a curious sight. The bike was continuing of its own accord. A strange, nauseous convulsion travelled from my stomach to my head in a wave. The air darkened. The bicycle parked itself against the wire fence of the local transformer. I could see shapes moving on the air, like shadows of smoke. Stuart, or something that had once been Stuart, was climbing from the bicycle and over the fence, pursued closely by a slinking, homogenous pandemonium of visible whispers.

These phantom shapes danced before my eyes for a matter of seconds, or split-seconds. Shadows lengthen and distort the shape of that which casts them, but there was something wrong with the distortion of these shadows. Stuart was not as I had remembered him from life. In fact, he could not have been described as human at all. His arms flailed, seeming to lengthen and broaden into paddles, or claws. His head swelled bulbously. There was something of the insect about him, and yet he also seemed to be covered with a repellent mass of curly hair. I thought back to the feeling of depression I had experienced after my first attempt to ride the haunted bicycle.

It was hard to tell whether Stuart was hunted or whether he dragged the other shapes after him by some form of magnetism, for there seemed to be an affinity between them. But whereas Stuart, lone and separate, seemed to express fear and desperation in all his parts, the agglutination of shadows behind him expressed mockery. Here again was the rent in the veil, the rampaging of secrets that should be hidden. Demons of humiliation were joined grotesquely like a thousand Siamese siblings. But now I saw them as something else, a kind of fleshy snowflake shot through with twitches and spasms of a twisted ecstasy indistinguishable from ultimate disgust. Each twitch and spasm was an orgasm of nausea and sickness. They seemed to be building towards a peak, some meta-orgasm. As I thrilled to each orgasm in weird sympathy, I was overcome by images that filled me with reeling horror.

I saw a foetus in the womb, a mixture of tears and semen and other bodily fluids, its umbilical cord seeming to turn it inside out. I saw a baby suckling at a breast like some hideous, incestuous parasite. I saw clothes conspiring against their wearers, whispering in their thoughts like manipulating devils, cultivating madness. I saw bodies contorting together fearfully when that madness was stripped naked again. I saw all things partake of this alternate concealing and revealing—doors taunting with their leading somewhere, air with its transparency, ground with its gravity, animals with their whatisit biology, pens with their waiting to write only what they're made to, bits of cardboard with a sense of nameless dread like a child's nightmare wolf, food with its necessity, forcing us to consume it, excrement with its why-ness, eyes with their seeing-ness, paper clips with their unassuming silence, like camouflage, flowers with their deliberate prettiness, and so on to infinity. The orgasms quivered and rose, kept rising.

And in the seconds that I saw all this, Stuart had reached one of the boxes inside the fence. For a moment he was obscured by the other shapes. Then I felt, rather than heard, a scream, and I closed my eyes. When I opened them, some time later, the shadows had gone.

Chapter XIII: A Funny Thing Happened on the Way to the Doss House

I paused outside the door of the house on Beach Road and looked it up and down, wondering if I should knock. It is not unusual for me to pause in such a way. All too often the company of other people is an ache reminding me of responsibilities and past sins that I would rather forget.

It was dark and my breath showed on the air. Now it is well and truly autumn, I thought.

A narrative ran in my head.

"And the man who had so lately saved the world from the madness it deserved watched his breath evaporate and plied the doorbell . . ."

Man? Somehow that wasn't quite right. Boy? Closer, maybe. Fop? Gaylord? Subhuman? Lump of sticky repulsiveness?

Well, I knew which one was most accurate, but sometimes we must choose the word that sounds best.

"And the fop who had so lately saved the world . . ."

Saved the world? Ridiculous! Absurd!

" . . . looked around nervously at the utter quiet and aloneness of the night in which he stood unknown . . ."

I plied the doorbell, and knocked, in case the former did not work. I knew that very likely my aloneness would come to an end in a matter of seconds. I savoured what was left of it.

The narrative still ran in my head, but now the nervousness with which I regarded the empty road had become pronounced, and, almost afraid that my thoughts were audible, I wished that narrative would stop.

At last the curtain that hung behind the door was drawn back a little. Les' face appeared with an expression of happy recognition on it. He unlocked the door and told me to come in.

"Sit down. I haven't seen you for a while. Where have you been?"

"I've been a bit busy," I answered non-committally.

Actually, it hadn't been so very long since I had called last. It was not unusual for me to go a few weeks without visiting, despite our proximity. I suppose that, after the whole bicycle incident, during which we had met every day, and which had been, shall we say, quite intense, a sudden absence of a week or two seemed strange.

Our last conversation had centred around the scene at the local transformer. Apparently we had both witnessed the same thing. We discussed at some length the meaning of that final scream. Was it Stuart's death cry? Or was it something worse—a sign that he had been captured again? The bicycle no longer seemed to be haunted at all. Perhaps we had succeeded. But an element of doubt, comprised partly of certain words read or heard during the ordeal that stuck in my head, and partly of a number of incidents that had taken place in the intervening time, led me to conjecture about our failure, or—something more disturbing still—the possibility that we had not failed, but that our success had been planned by our enemies. For two weeks I had been lost in the gloomiest introspection.

"D'you want some tea?"

"Yes, please."

Les made the tea and brought it through from the kitchen.

I sipped at it, but could not think of anything to say. A couple of times I was on the verge of saying something, and even opened my mouth. But since all I could think of were ridiculous, made-up anecdotes about wasps and dolphins, I thought better of it.

Les started rolling a cigarette and I watched him intently, all the while thinking of other things. At last I came back to the present, and, licking my lip thoughtfully, I asked, "Do you mind if I scrounge a fag?"

"No, that's alright," he said, licking the rizla. "Do you want me to roll it for you?"

"No, thanks. I should practice, really."

The roll-up gave me some respite, gave me something to do. The silence would not feel so awkward to me if my hands were occupied with something. And when I had finished rolling, I would have a prop with which to diffuse my awkwardness, and that prop would give me a slight nicotine rush, to boot.

"So what have you been up to?" I asked once I had managed to roll something, if not aesthetically pleasing, then at least smokeable.

"Nothing, really."

But he didn't look at me as he spoke. His eyes were cast downwards. He flicked his cigarette. I thought momentarily of those fits of temper I had never actually seen. Something was troubling him. Then he looked up at me.

"Has anything weird happened to you since the bicycle stopped being haunted?"

"What sort of thing?"

"Well, you know, weird things, whispering and things?"

I nodded. I blew smoke.

"Me too," he said. "So all that stuff that happened could happen again at any time and there's nothing we can do about it."

"It didn't actually happen."

"Yes it did."

I hesitated, inhaled smoke deeply and exhaled again before continuing.

"No, I've been thinking about this." My voice became strangely assertive, "Listen to me. I'm chronically unemployed and you're on the sick and our stories about mackerels and earwigs and ginger pubes just got a little bit out of hand. We just made the whole thing up! And if you ever hear whispering from a patch of bindweed, I suggest that's what you tell yourself. Don't stop! Don't listen! Just remember, we made it up! That is what I intend to do."

He sighed. He was not satisfied with my conclusion, though, perhaps understanding that what I said made sense, he had no answer to it.

There followed a long silence. Smoke expanded and swirled on the air.

"We got a new cat recently," Les began, breaking the silence. "The vicar's cat had a litter and he wanted to get rid of them, like, but the person who had this one decided they couldn't look after it, 'cause it was too naughty, so we took it instead. So it hasn't been properly housetrained yet, even though it's not really a kitten anymore. It keeps pissing everywhere and stuff. It's called Jason. It's a stupid cat, really, a fuckin' idiot, like . . ."

Les continued his rambling account of their new cat. I nodded and gazed at the dirty, threadbare arm of the chair in which he sat. Why did this spiel about the delinquent feline, which seemed to back up on itself repeatedly as if trying to find its way to some conclusion, make me feel so utterly miserable?

We could not go on like this. There was something very urgent I had to say. I felt poised.

"Yes, that's interesting," I said, still nodding, as Les finally found the conclusion he had been in search of, to do with the complete unsoundness of the cat's mind.

"It reminds me of something that happened to me the other day."

"What's that then?"

"Well, I was walking down the road, looking for snails' eggs, you know, thinking it's about the right time of year and anticipating the wondrous sight of a hatching, the little snaillings born with ready-made shells as translucent as runny jism, when, all of a sudden, I was approached by a strange, segmented figure in a shawl. At first I thought it was trying to overtake me, then I realised it was keeping pace. I was a little disturbed by this, especially when I saw, protruding from the folds of clothing where the feet should have been, a pair of pincers big enough to pierce a man's head and meet in the centre.

"Aha! An earwig! I told myself, and examining the pincers more closely I saw that they were female, and curved in a gentle, elegant way that reminded me of that time, long ago, when I first saw the exposed bones of the skeleton and lay dreaming in the field while my cousin, Arabella, pissed by my head. Well, naturally this turn of events sparked my interest. I greeted the earwig courteously and there came a rustle of antennae from beneath her shawl that fairly set my heart a-flutter. Perhaps it was the shawl, or the faint black gleam of bulbous eyes that came from within, like the lustre of grinning death in the eyes of a fresh corpse, but it seemed to me as if there were something serene, perhaps even holy, about this being. What was it she reminded me of? The Virgin Mary? The Mona Lisa?

I could not be sure. And then, softly, in her sibilant insect voice, she hissed my name and told me that she was with child, or, more accurately, with spawn, and that I was the father.

"Strangely shocked by this news, I grimaced. It would not be the first time I had been harassed by the female earwig community. Looking fixedly at the ground I said under my breath, 'They're not mine. You can't prove anything. I don't even remember you. Try some other sucker.' 'You do remember me,' she said, and raising two of her hooked legs, she drew back her shawl to reveal all the curvilinear mystery of the female earwig visage. I was dumbstruck. I felt like melting. From a long way off something seemed to be coming back to me. 'Sylvia?!' I said suddenly. 'Yes! Yes, my darling only one,' she said. 'Fuck them!' I said. 'Pardon me, my most delicious one,' she said, 'but what do you mean?' 'Fuck them!' I said. 'I don't want the fucking brats, my God, writhing about in your insect womb like maggots in a corpse. They're not mine! I don't want the disgusting sound of their legs and wings in my head all day. Fuck them! Fuck them! Horrible insect bastards! Get rid of them! Abort the segmented, exoskeletal shits! Abort the fuckers!' And then her hooked legs rose to my cheeks and she bent her face to mine. 'How can you say that?' she asked. 'We are bound by eternal vows.' 'No,' I said. 'Fuck off!'"

I was actually shouting this now as I related the incident to Les.

"'Fuck off! If you don't abort the little, mulchy, semi-translucent parcels of pus, then I fucking will! Fuck off! Get that mandible shit out of my face! I haven't done anything, you fucking earwig bitch! I haven't done anything! Just leave me a-fucking-lone!' 'It's too late,' she said, caressing my face with her hooks and ripping my cheeks open. At that moment there was a squelching sound that turned my stomach and a stink worse than a thousand putrefying cats. Suddenly the whole road was full of the slimy litter she had dropped, all hissing and slick, half of them born dead, devoured by their brothers and sisters. Then the little earwigs began to slither up my legs towards my face. In a terrible, blind panic I tried to brush them off, stamping on those that had fallen, screaming, 'Die you little shits!' But soon I was covered in them and fell beneath their weight, seeing in their faces a terrible likeness and hearing their tiny, hissing, squeaking voices saying, 'Dad-dyyyyyyyyyyyyyyyyyyyyyyyyyyy!!'"

I finished on a scream.

For a moment there was silence, then, "Really?" asked Les.

"No, not really. I just made it up," I said.

Les laughed, his face frogged up.

"You're weird!" he said. "Actually, though, something a bit like that happened to me the other day. There was this wasp, see, and you know that wasps have pricks they can sting with more than once . . ."

Les continued, and I felt an enormous relief, so that I hardly even listened to the content of his narrative.

In a life haunted by voices it sometimes seems there are only two difficult things—being with other people and being alone. Les had that silver crucifix to protect him, but what did I have? If I needed a charm, something homely to ward off the whispering demons of paranoia, then I could think of none better than the tepid, milky, sugary mug of tea in front of me, served by the welcoming hand of a friend.

The dim yellow light indoors made the night outside, glimpsed through a crack in the curtains, seem solid blackness. Speak on! Yes, keep talking. Let's have another cup of tea, another cigarette. I'm not ready for the walk home. Just another five minutes. And another. I don't want to be alone anymore. I wish we could just stay like this forever.

You probably think this is the end, but it's not. There is no end. There's no beginning, either.

Zugzwang

(Dedicated to Liz)

Who is this for?

Am I writing this because the page is the last place in the world I can be alone and free? No, even here I am neither alone nor free. Or am I writing this as a proclamation to the world? But what is the use of that? Why write to a hostile world? I cannot expect it to indulge either my pleas or my wishes for revenge.

I'm sure this paper and this pen have been waiting for me. Perhaps they know better than I do what I shall write next. Can I possibly do anything unexpected? Can I possibly catch you out? Oh, I'm bad at this. All right. All right. I'll make my move.

It's like this. I have no way of knowing what goes on out of my sight. Maybe that's what has always caused that creeping feeling at the corner of my eye, as if I'd just missed catching sight of something strange and sinister. But now the creeping feeling has spread to infect everything. It's everywhere I look. How can I describe it? My senses are a windowless cell made up of distorting mirrors. My vision is ingrowing. It is furred and hooked. Everything I lay eyes on seems to curl and melt and twist. To think, to move an inch, is to struggle against a tide of mockery. The very words upon which I try to stake my sanity are a series of grimaces on the paper. They are my enemies. And all this is a delirium.

Of course, I don't *know*—do I? That's what all this is about—isn't it?—not knowing. That and the fear that I will be a fool if I make a certain assumption, or that I will be a bigger fool if I don't. Well, this is the turning point.

I suppose I should start with the germ of the fever that brought this delirium on. Perhaps it's appropriate that the details are unfocused. There is a certain old pub in London which seems to exist more as a rumour than a concrete reality. Once in a while, according to the rhythms of some unknown calendar, the existence of the public house seems to coincide with the existence of whoever is seeking it, and ways that previously seemed to conceal themselves now lead plainly there. And it was there, at a gathering of friends, that I first met her.

We were already drunk before we set out for the place. In fact, it was an idea born of drunkenness. Tommy joined us later. She had had nothing but a phone call to go on, but she seemed to find the place without any trouble. I remember distinctly the moment she stepped through the door. It was as if I had been expecting her, and yet, at the same time, was surprised. I seemed to think to myself, "Ah, she's arrived, then," but I didn't know who 'she' was. Perhaps this is an exaggeration, but I am unsure how else to put the feeling into words. At any rate, I felt suddenly that the evening had become more interesting.

Lorraine made room for her with the result that she sat down next to me. I was actually a little put out by this, as well as pleased. She was clearly far too good for me and her proximity made me feel self-conscious and downright self-loathing.

She was what you might call a honey blonde. Her hair was tied back, but wisps of it escaped from the rest, drawing my eyes with a kind of abstract fascination. She wore a broad-brimmed hat, which actually suited her admirably, and she drew one of her legs up to her chest as she sat on the chair. She radiated generosity and confidence, and I began to feel I was being positively perverse in not talking to her.

With some diffidence I asked her name.

"Tommy," she said, as if that one word were a winning line. Indeed, it was.

"Isn't that a boy's name?" I half-slurred the obvious—too obvious—question. I was unsure whether I had suddenly become considerably more drunk, or whether I was exaggerating my drunkenness as a sort of defence mechanism.

"Well, usually it's a boy's name, but not in this case. I'm not a boy, you see."

"Yes, I can see that. It's unusual, though, isn't it? I mean, I've heard of Charlie, and even Terri, for girls, but I've never heard Tommy . . . "

"Yes . . . They used to call me Tom-boy at school, you know."

"I'm sorry to hear that."

Somehow I could not believe that she was actually talking to me, that my existence had a place in her awareness. That awareness seemed to take a far stronger hold on me than that of other people. It was as if I had suddenly ceased to be invisible. I felt stammeringly uncomfortable. In the drunken haze of that evening everything I said to her was like some reckless confession. Later I looked back on the first meeting and tried to work out exactly how it had all happened. I developed a theory that appealed to my own self-image. Somewhere in my mix of desperation and resignation, somewhere from the bottom of the deep hole that I dug myself into with every word I uttered, something must have shone out with an alcoholic glow and attracted her to me.

The conversation even reached such depths that I remember slurring such pitiful words as these:

"Okay, so I'm a bit drunk, it's true. I'm sorry 'bout that. But that doesn't mean I'm stupid, y'know. I'm not stupid, and . . . I know what I'm saying, and, what I mean to say is, I'm sorry . . . but it's all true. I really mean it. I'm not stupid, you know."

Even at the time I thought, if it's come to this I've blown it all again—she must think I'm an idiot. I remember a silence in which I stared for some time at her mouth, and particularly the curve of her laugh line at the side of that ellipsis. Her face, turned towards me, was in shadow. I threw myself utterly on the mercy of that silence, trying all the time to fathom the meaning of that smile.

We exchanged phone numbers. A friend of a friend of a friend—after that she became first and foremost *my* 'friend'. I did not bother to enquire too closely into the bloodless lineage she had eclipsed.

At the age of eight I fell in love with the cello. I think to fall in love is to find something or someone that cannot be reduced to any more fundamental symbol, so to try and describe one's love with words is probably useless. Now it is not only useless, but must be a kind of torture to me. Nonetheless, I feel the need to explain a little. The cello seemed to me to embody, in both shape and sound, and even in colour, all that was most beautiful in life. The glib and all too common association of sadness and poignancy with the violin was, I believed, a mistake. It was the cello, an instrument of much greater depth and resonance, to which such an association properly belonged. It seemed to me that if I could take a bow to those strings and control the deep, welling, elegant sadness that came out, I would be the master of life itself. I suppose that, in recognising the genius of the cello, I recognised the unformed genius in myself, and awoke the will to shape that genius. I wished for nothing other than to play the cello, to immerse myself in the fountainhead of all possibility.

Of course, in the end, the genius of life I had thought to play through the cello, proved beyond my control. For some reason, it is hard to pinpoint the exact cause of my downfall. Something in its very vagueness haunts me. I suppose, for one thing, I was foolish to have such individual ideas about the instrument; they tended to isolate me from those who might have helped my career. I had what I believed was a unique vision of the cello's potential, and even wrote copious notes on it. To think that those notes still exist makes me sick at heart.

I was very much influenced by such composers as Messiaen and Urbanner, and of the latter's work, particularly his *String Quartet No.3*, which happened to have been composed in the year of my birth. I felt that Urbanner was doing with music something very similar to what Braque and the other Cubists did with painting. With his creaks and corkscrews of sound, it was as if he were taking linear melody and refracting it through some bizarre and sombre crystal. What was different about my theory was that I felt Urbanner had placed method first in producing such effects. I was aware of some ultimately abstract world, somewhere 'out there' with its own settled reality, that was waiting to be expressed, and for which I had to find the method of expression. This world was very much a 'corner of the eye' world, a sinister and melancholy Cubism that crept away the moment one tried to look at it directly. But if I could look at it directly, and capture it in sound, even in its Cubist fragmentation, it would have a more compelling unity to it than Urbanner's work . . . That was what I strove for.

But, as I got older, I became less and less sure of the soundness of the musical philosophy I had developed, until it seemed there was no logic to it at all and I could not even explain it to myself. It had been merely a child's vision, after all. I was classically trained, and tried to find my way within the musical establishment for some years. But this did not suit me, and I wonder if, in a way, when I found the world was not as I had wanted it to be, I didn't simply give up on my dreams of my own accord.

I wandered through the world in obscurity, occasionally lashing myself with the scourge of ambition to try and rouse myself from my torpor. My efforts always foundered. I remember having heard somewhere that 'when one is tired of London, one is tired of life.' Perhaps because I associated London simply with 'life', and made the resolution finally to meet life, I came here. My situation changed little. After all, that *is* life, I thought. Here in London I worked at any job I could find—so many jobs that in the end I did not know who or what I was any more. Maybe that is what I wanted. In that way I could pay the rent for my shabby flat, fill up my time and wear myself out so that there was never really any need to think. Life was just a matter of washing the dishes when there were no clean ones left, killing the fag-end of a groggy evening with booze, trying, but not caring too much, to make it on time to work—in short, a series of helpless, stumbling confrontations with the next moment, all deadened by hopelessness.

Occasionally I would get work as a musician, paid or otherwise, but seldom as a cellist. The cello is a specialised instrument, and in the meantime I had learnt to play more popular instruments, such as the guitar and even the mandolin. After a while, I ceased to play the cello in any company but my own.

When the world outside had turned to blackness I would sit beneath a naked light bulb and stare stupidly about my rented room. As if deliberately, the glare showed up the stains on the mostly bare walls, making the place seedier still for its lack of softening shadow. Discarded clothes and leaves of sheet music littered the floor. I would look to the window—whose curtains had never closed properly since I tugged one of them too hard and tore it half off the rail—seeming to discard the world with this action. Outside, two roofs met in a kind of lead-bottomed gutter. Here puddles glistened and cats led their rough, secret lives. Above, if rain clouds did not obscure them, were the stars and moon, glinting like shards of broken glass.

Wearily I would take the cello out of its black sarcophagus and sit with the bow hanging before the strings, waiting for the will to play. Then the bow would touch the strings and that deep, welling lament would begin, vibrating through my body and nagging in my chest, a sonorous, dirge-like serenade proper to the distant, sterile moon which was my audience.

I remember the last time I played in this way. I took up my bow as usual and put it to the strings, and the dirge began. I must have played the same loop for so long that I was hypnotised by the notes rising up into the unpeopled night. At last I seemed to become conscious of them again, as if waking up in the midst of a dream. At some point I had slipped the loop, straying into variations and strange, plangent improvisation. These notes were my voice, speaking from my heart once and forever. That was it—everything that I wanted to express, and there was no one to hear it except for the moonlight on the tiles, except for the stars that even now could be extinct in the sky. It was the sound of worlds dying, the voice of absolute loneliness and defeat. I was playing the end of my music. How could there be any audience for this? If I had any genius, then it was the genius of failure. I lay down my bow and I knew I could never put it to the strings again.

At first I avoided inviting Tommy back to my flat. Away from my flat, with someone new, I could be anybody. I could have only just arrived in the world. If she came back to my flat I would necessarily become someone in particular—the wrong person.

I maintained this floating, in-between situation for as long as I could. All this time I felt I might be on the edge of something great and wonderful, something I had never imagined. It frightened me. As the currents of life had sucked me mercilessly into despair, so now they seemed to be sucking me just as helplessly into the fulfilment of a dream that had never been mine. This dream was quite as incredible as the dreams of success that now lay wrecked at the bottom of a cold, dark ocean. But it was entirely different. I was utterly lost.

I woke up in warm, crumpled blankets, like an animal's burrow, a quilted, furry heap. Some living, breathing thing was curled up beside me. Daylight fell on the carpet and the bedclothes, as blissfully peaceful as light reflected from the surface of a slow river, marbled with the shadows of invisible eddies. I felt as empty as the light.

Where was I?

Who was I?

When Tommy woke up, the warmth pooled in the palms of her hands seemed to have the same gentle intensity as the light. It was good to be no one, nowhere.

Tommy seemed to think I was being deliberately mysterious. I suppose, in a way, she was right. In the beginning she laughed at my evasive nature, but soon enough it became the cause of our first argument.

We were sitting at the corner table of a certain café. I watched strangers passing by on the street outside. When, occasionally, I turned back to Tommy, I felt a little uncomfortable. I was impressed, as by a brilliant piano solo, but I was not particularly happy. I wondered exactly what *she* had to do with *me*. She broke the silence.

"We're quite near your place here, aren't we?"

"Not far."

"Why don't we stay the night at yours for once? I'd really like to see it."

"Hmmmm."

I hoped she might forget the idea if I didn't say anything.

"Is that 'hmm-yes' or 'hmm-no'?"

"Well, I'd rather not. I mean, I'd rather stay at your place, if that's okay."

"Don't you want me to come to your place?"

"No. I don't want anyone to come to my place."

"So, you never have guests?"

"No. Well, a few friends, maybe."

"I see. And I'm not your friend, is that it?"

Just in that last sentence the tension that had been lurking in the conversation came sharply to the surface. I knew she was no longer in a joking mood. My own temper flared up in turn.

"To be quite honest, no. I only invite people back to my room who can accept me for what I am, not people who emotionally blackmail me."

I said it probably more to spite myself than to spite her. Somehow she appeared to me so wonderful, so perfect, that it simply was not fair for her to get angry with anyone, ever. How could they—meaning me—ever be in the right against her? How could they—meaning me—do anything but hate themselves? And so I hated myself and played a hateful role.

For a while it looked like being an early end to our relationship. Tommy called me the most selfish person she had ever known and accused me of having no idea of the effect I had on other people. I hung my head sheepishly and mumbled half-hearted yet stubborn words of defence. Just as it looked like she was about to leave, I found I could not bear it any longer.

"I'm sorry. Please stay at my place tonight. I'm really sorry."

I supposed it was my tone of voice more than the words themselves that saved the situation.

As we walked up the creaking, uncarpeted stairs to my flat, I felt wretched. I hardly spoke, but walked ahead of her, suddenly shy again, like a mere acquaintance. Once again in my life I was back on the wrong side, that is to say, my own side. Tommy, of course, was the right side. Well, I had tried to stop her from seeing the truth, but it was inevitable that it should come to this. I felt resentful, but overlaying this feeling was a consoling, fatalistic sadness.

We reached the landing. I put my key in the lock. She smiled at me. I did not smile back.

"Well, here it is," I said, opening the door and raising my hand limply in a pathetic parody of display.

As soon as we got in I slumped down on the paint-spattered wooden chair and lit up a cigarette, as if exhausted. As far as I was concerned the deed was done. I had no energy for the aftermath. As I blew out smoke and Tommy looked around in childlike curiosity, I surveyed the scene. It seemed to me I had never known a stilllife more eloquent of neglect and despair. The dust, the empty bottles, the unwashed plates and mugs that had become ashtrays, the holes in the plasterboard from some drunken rage, the very position of a dog-eared paperback—*The Last Man*, by Mary Shelley—on an otherwise vacant shelf—all this was as faithful an expression of melancholia as desert sands are an expression of the wind. All this had a history behind it, a history which was symbolised by the battered collection of sarcophagi enshrined against one wall as the centre and focus of this inner sanctum of hopelessness and shame.

Tommy seemed quite unaffected by this.

"What's so bad about it?" she said at last.

I shrugged slightly. I gestured feebly to the window.

"Look. The curtain's coming off the rail."

"Oh, so *what!*" she said. "Is that all?"

"Well, no. I don't know. It's not a very nice place, is it? You know, I don't have much money, and that, and it's kind of dirty."

She made me feel positively self-indulgent for being so ashamed.

"I don't care about that. Is that really what you think of me? Do I seem that shallow?"

"I suppose not."

"Actually, I quite like it here. It makes me feel relaxed."

I couldn't detect any trace of a false note in her voice.

She launched herself backwards onto the bed, bouncing on the mattress. Drawing her feet in she sat cross-legged, her whole body as supple as her smile. Yes, she was on my home ground now, so to speak. I think it was only at that moment, as I looked at her beaming face in these familiar, squalid surroundings, that the truth of her impossible presence in my life sank in. Even the light that fell on Tommy's hair seemed somehow seedy. The light on her hair—surely that, more than anything else, signified the merging of these two worlds. Tommy herself, though strange, in this light became familiar, in a way that thrilled me to my heart. Failure makes you utterly alone. Now this girl had entered the solitude of my failure it created a mysterious intimacy, as if we two were the whole doomed human race. The cloudy-paned window, the endless extinction of the night, and a few empty cobwebs stirring in the draught, framed her as I moved closer. Now those lips and the whispers that came from them were a ghostly holocaust, quiet as dust.

It seems I have no choice but to turn over memories of happiness that now can only bring me infinite pain. Even in quality this pain is not ordinary. The more I turn these memories over, the more twisted they become. Now I'm drawn back again, with unquenchable remorse, to the bleak landscape of my room and to the glaringly beautiful shape that became its foreground.

I had no idea why someone so positive, who clearly had so much choice, should chose me. But then again, even though I couldn't understand it when she said all that nice stuff about liking me—in connection with Tommy, silly words such as 'nice stuff' and 'liking me' came to take on the thunderous profundity of the Bible—wasn't there a part of me that said, 'of course!'? Wasn't there a feeling of, 'Well, that's because it's *me*—

me, the centre of all things—and no one else!'? Don't I deserve this? What have I done wrong? Better things happen to worse people, don't they?

My memories twist and twist again. Here's another one.

I wrote before about the last time I played the cello. Actually, it wasn't quite the last. Eager to draw me out, I suppose, Tommy often asked me to play something for her. Most of the time I would play something simple on the guitar. In the process of drawing me out, however, she learnt that the cello was my first instrument. After that she was constantly trying to cajole me into demonstrating to her the fruits of my first love. I protested—by which I mean, I lied—that the cello is best played in combination with other instruments, but she began to sense my old evasiveness, and, fearing a repeat of the scene in the café, I finally gave in.

I had no idea what I was going to play, but when I put the bow to strings I thought I had laid to rest for good, I found myself, quite naturally, playing an eerie, mournful theme in the same vein as the last piece I had played. The thought I had had before, that this music was not meant to be played in company, came to mind again, and I felt uncomfortable. In fact, I felt as if I were unwinding my own intestines with that bow and twisting them up in knots again before Tommy's eyes. When I looked at her face she was watching with a faraway, unreadable expression, a faint smile playing at the corners of her mouth. Somehow I could not stop until I had brought the piece to some sort of satisfactory resolution, but finding that resolution under that gaze proved to be torturous. At last I drew the final, dying note and laid down my bow. I was right. The previous time should have been the last.

"Please don't ask me to play the cello again," I said.

She must have sensed my seriousness. She never did ask after that.

The next time I went back home, she came with me.

It was summer again and from the ancient, clacking train rabbits could be seen frolicking in the fields of the Norfolk countryside. The amber sunlight on the serried ears of wheat seemed to give the crops a patina of age, as if they were of polished wood, the creaking furniture of an old house. We chugged in and out of the many familiar, unmanned stations, at which I had never once alighted. Time seemed to extend infinitely before us. All this had to me, perhaps because of deep childhood associations, an element of inexpressible pathos. And perhaps because she was beside me, there was also a strange freshness to it all.

It seemed to be a lifetime since I had last been home.

The house was large and detached, of a kind that it once seemed everyone should have the right to, set in its own grounds and back from a leafy road connecting two tiny hamlets.

What was that feeling when, with Tommy beside me, I stepped through the door of the home I had known since birth? It was something between sadness and relief.

As we took our luggage into the kitchen and sat down at the wooden table and Mother fussed around Tommy and I drank a glass of water, I can remember thinking, "This is what love is. This is what life is." For perhaps the first time in my life I felt embraced by the wondrous glamour of normality.

Strange how easily glamour turns into sadness again.

Now I saw Mother and myself half through another's eyes. Mother took on the charm of an actress as she fingered her pearls, and the family history that she related to Tommy became intensely fascinating, like the lights of a town seen from a distance.

When I climbed the stairs with Tommy to our room, tired as if drunk, Tommy said, "Your mother is lovely, and your house is lovely."

"I'm afraid she'll have to sell the house soon. Since Father left she can't afford to live here on her own."

'Our room' was in fact my old room. Nothing had changed since I had lived there. It was not the first time I had been back since then, but stepping under the lintel I was struck again by the same feeling as before. The past is still here, but I myself have moved on. I can never return. I have entered the stream of time and now there is no such thing to me as home. This room belongs to someone now dead.

I smiled sadly at Tommy and sat down on the bed. The person now gone, to whom this room belonged, had always slept alone. For the first time tonight there would be two people in this narrow bed. How strange it all was. Saying nothing Tommy drew closer and put her hands on my head. I pressed my cheek against her belly.

We went for a last walk in the surrounding country and then retired.

In my old bed, with the heart of another body beside me in the darkness, I sank into a sad confusion of feelings that became sleep and dream.

I don't know exactly when it was that I woke up. I only know it was pitch dark. Such darkness seems to exist outside of time. I was alarmed. Not for the first time, I forgot quite where I was and I cringed at heart as if the darkness might strike me. Then I heard the voice, and froze. It must have been the voice that had woken me. It was a sort of hissing, whispering. There were no words, but there was a kind of modulation and articulation, as *if* there were words. For a moment I thought this voice was addressing me, and a thrill of terror seemed to grab me with greedy claws. Then I realised that the voice belonged to Tommy, and my confusion reached a kind of paralysing ecstasy. Of course, my rational mind soon kicked in and I knew that she was talking in her sleep. I had heard sleep talk before and been surprised at the weird things people said, and in a tone of voice that suggested consciousness. I had even had bizarre exchanges with sleeping people. But I had never heard anything like this. It was like an alien language.

The voice continued for a while, but even after I realised what it was, I found it eerie and unnatural. I was relieved when at last it stopped and was replaced with silence. As I thought to myself before sleep finally overtook me again, I realised that I *had* heard something like it before, once.

It was when I was living in Paris. I had rented a tiny flat at the top of a tall and rickety old building. The stairwell was narrow and winding, the wood of the treads and the banisters dark, worn and warped. In fact, the whole building seemed to be warped. One night, returning home drunk and melancholy, I heard a voice from one of the rooms about halfway to the top. In that instant my blood froze. What was it? It sounded something like a rat having its throat slit, but there was an intelligence to the sound which made me think it must be human. I could not decide whether it was a scream or laughter; I only knew that it made me pause for a while and shudder before hurrying on up the stairs. For some reason Tommy's sleep talk reminded me of this.

The next day, with the house to ourselves, while we were having a lazy late breakfast, I brought the subject up as something I had suddenly remembered. Tommy, of course, said she had no memory of talking in her sleep at all.

"I'm not sure you could call it talking," I said. Then, in my most impressive, sinister voice, "At least, it wasn't any *human* language."

I even found myself shivering as I said it.

"Stop it. That's horrible!"

It was true. It did seem somehow an unlucky thing to say.

Anyway, that is when the conversation began.

"You know," I said, "when I was younger I'd often walk down the streets, looking at all the houses, and wonder if they were real, if people could actually be bothered to carry on the ridiculous masquerade known as life behind the scenes—that is, when I wasn't there. What if I burst in on this house, where I have absolutely no right and no reason to go, and catch them unawares? What will I find? But then, I knew somehow that even if my suspicions were true, I would never find anything. They are too clever. They know my moves before I do. The whole of existence serves for their eyes and ears, keeping me under surveillance."

"Why would 'they' want to do that?"

Tommy smiled in a bewitchingly teasing manner as she said this.

"Of course I can't be sure. Their reasons are mysterious, but I think it goes something like this: The universe is a practical joke. That joke has to be on someone, and that someone happens to be me. In fact, it was inevitable that it should be me, because I am *me*, and no one else is. It's like, life must have a meaning, but if you twist it into some joke, then it's just a matter of having a punchline. I think that punchline might destroy me."

"And everyone is in on this joke except for you?"

"Yes."

"Including me?"

I hesitated before answering, but I knew there was only one possible answer.

"Yes."

Then I felt the sudden urge to pursue my theme.

"You see, I've caught you out. I heard you sleep-talking in your true language. I know what you're up to."

"But you haven't caught me out, have you? If you really

believed what you said, you wouldn't be so naïve and trustful as to tell me about it like that."

I thought about this and nodded.

"But what if I did catch you out in some way, if you let your mask slip and I saw behind it?"

"But according to you we've got it all so perfectly sewn up that that could only happen if we wanted it to."

"That's right. In fact, that would be the worst thing that could happen. It would mean that I was going to find out what the masquerade was all about, or anyway, you were about to make your next move in the whole cat-and-mouse game, letting me know as much of the truth as was necessary for your purposes."

During this conversation I became strangely animated, and even aroused.

The time we spent together there was a kind of limbo. It was time such as I have experienced it when convalescing or playing truant. Such an atmosphere, when I have suddenly been free of the endless distraction of what I 'should be' doing, is really the first intimation of the static-filled blank that is reality.

There in time's no-man's-land we took plenty of country walks, and I showed her the spots where the pale ghosts of my childhood still lingered, now sad, washed-out afterimages. On these walks we met not another soul. Occasionally we would stop to rest. Sitting down on the dusty path at the edge of a field, we carried on a conversation that seemed to have no beginning or end, but was all middle. I gave out my autobiography in disparate fragments. I gazed off into the midst of the wheat as I spoke, saw the sun gleaming on hard, shiny ears. Somehow this put me in a cold sweat. I felt as if I were drowning in shadow. I wiped my brow. The days were so dry and silent.

Sometimes Mother came back from shopping or in from the garden and simply took over, as if this were part of a prearranged programme of entertainment. She took down old photograph albums from shelves, made tea and sandwiches and generally transported us back in time to some ideal England that had never existed. Tommy and Mother had become 'close' without me even seeing how it had happened.

We were due to make the journey back to London on the Monday, so it was decided that we would have a special dinner together on Sunday evening. Tommy volunteered to help Mother prepare it, and would not be dissuaded.

Sunday came soon enough and, in the afternoon, I took the opportunity afforded by Tommy and Mother's being occupied with cooking, to sort through my personal effects. In my bedroom I had left behind books, tapes, clothes, all manner of things, and now I was thinking of taking a few bits and pieces back to London. In the end I found it was not a chore I could get over with quickly. Many of the relics I sorted through brought back memories and set me to daydreaming.

Finally I settled on a number of items to which I felt the strongest attachment and lay them on one side. Then, sighing at the completion of a strangely dreary task, I descended the stairs again and moved towards the kitchen.

The kitchen door was open, but, even some distance away along the central passage of the ground floor, I was struck by the silence. That made me curious and I, in turn, approached silently. Just as I was about two feet from the edge of the doorway, I heard a voice from within. It came as if it were the natural continuation of a quiet, pause-laden conversation. The effect it had on me, however, was violent and extreme. It was a voice I had heard a few days before—when Tommy had been talking in her sleep.

I stood stunned, listening to the weird hissing whispering. Then came a moment of terrible silence, then the voice was answered by another of the same kind, yet different—a voice at once utterly alien and sickeningly familiar.

Suddenly I was standing in an Arctic waste, burning all over with the icy cold. I could not run away. There was not a single safe corner in the world for me to crawl into. Even my own heart was no hiding place. Everywhere the same horrible whispering seemed to wait for me, like the distilled presence of evil. Around me was the air, light falling on the floor. These things were hostile and scouring. I was alone.

Can't move forward. Can't move back.

I stood helpless. As if to save me by drowning me, memory took me in its tide. Something I had forgotten came back, as real as the present, for, in a way, it was the present.

I must have been very young—maybe three or four. Anyway, it was an age at which the world is nothing but a vague conglomeration of wonderings and misconceptions that adults must answer and put right until everything finally becomes concrete and one becomes an adult oneself.

I was in an open-air swimming pool, and standing a few feet away, in a bathing costume, was that unique and mysterious figure, my mother, her identity obscured forever by her relation to me. There were a number of other people in the pool with us, too, but I have no idea who they were. My mother was young then, though I didn't think in such terms at the time. Even the water itself was strange to me, an alien substance, and I felt at a loss as to what I should be doing in it. Then my mother looked at me and smiled. She moved into a graceful crouch and backed away, gradually slipping deeper into the water. Still smiling, she spoke.

"Bye bye," she said, and she waved her hand. "Bye bye."

I was struck cold. I could hardly speak. Where was she going? What did it mean?

"No . . . Mummy . . . Come back!"

The people looked on complacently, and my mother continued to laugh and wave and back away.

"Mummy!"

It was no good. Her goodbye seemed like a command to me to stay. I could not defy it. A huge gulf seemed to open up between us. I could not move in the horrid water. I was half-naked and my feeble voice was completely naked—the voice of absolute distress. Then, even this failed me.

One of the other adults spoke.

"Such a serious face," he said, and they all laughed.

I wanted to cry. I felt tears come like a bubble expanding inside. But the bubble burst and no tears came. Two leaves, brown and yellow, were floating on the slopping water, half glossed over by the dull, slack reflection of the daylight. I looked at them and was overcome by a strange desolation.

That desolation brought me back to the true present.

Until that day, standing paralysed outside the kitchen, some nameless trust so deep I had never questioned it had formed an imaginary umbilical cord attaching me to the world. Now the trust was broken, the cord was severed. I cried as if newborn, tottering, the world appearing pinched through my stinging eyes. My tears were horrible to me, since I now understood there was no such thing as sympathy in the world. The very inanimate matter of the world at once proclaimed my utter, chilling isolation and simultaneously invaded that isolation with its cruel mockery.

The voices in the kitchen continued with their conversation. What were they talking about? I could almost tell just by the sound. Surely they were talking about me. They must have known I was there. I tried to imagine what kind of monsters could have voices like those.

I made some attempt to dry my eyes and quiet my snivelling. There was nowhere else for me to go. With the heart of a tiny child about to face the most terrible punishment of his life, stiff with awe, I moved forward and stepped through the door.

There was a moment of shock. Mother and Tommy were standing there by the stove, preparing the meal. For an instant this perfectly normal scene was unspeakably sinister. They were talking, mid-flow in some trivial conversation in English. They looked my way casually as I entered the room. Something seemed to take hold in their expressions.

"What's wrong?"

There was such spontaneous concern in their voices that I could not stand it. I ran from the room and fled to my bedroom.

Tommy followed soon after. She found me on the bed with my face hidden in my arms, as if the world might not see me if I could not see it.

"What's wrong?"

She repeated the question.

I could not fault her performance. There was not a hint of irony or knowledge withheld. Unfortunately, I could not believe in it either. It was not simply the fact that I had heard those voices—it was the voices themselves. I could never have imagined anything so horrible. She *knew* that I knew.

Taking a deep breath I sat up.

There is no sympathy in the world.

"Everything is fine," I said. "I just get like this sometimes. I'll be alright in a minute."

My voice was too empty. I could hear the evil pretence of the whole situation in it. I had to put on a better act, a perfect act, like Tommy's.

I closed my eyes. I opened them again.

"It's okay," I said, my voice suddenly natural,. "Really. I'll explain later. There's really nothing to it. I just need to be alone for a moment."

A perfect act. It was the only way to keep control.

She knew that I knew. She came closer. I braced myself. Then I let myself go limp. Her hand stroked my head and face like a loathsome flame. I did not resist.

"Okay," she said in tender doubtfulness. Then she left the room.

Silence.

I had finally woken up to a nightmare from which I could never wake again. For the rest of the day, and beyond, I was tortured, as if red-hot needles were being inserted expertly into the most intimate parts of my brain. I lay on my bed while the wildest thoughts rampaged through my mind, first making, then abandoning, any number of insane plans and conjectures.

In the end I came to the resolution on which my sanity depended. Just carry on acting as if nothing has happened, and in the meantime, examine your surroundings in the light of your new knowledge. It was as tenuous as that.

At length I stood up. I looked out of my bedroom window. The first traces of dusk were touching the landscape of fields and trees. It seemed the loneliest and most frightening thing I had ever seen. I knew I had to face my fate. I opened the door and walked downstairs.

We had a candle-lit dinner, the spread glittering in the light of the wavering flames. I had never exerted such a force of will as I did then simply in order to appear natural. I was astounded anew by the consummate skill of Mother's and Tommy's performances. There was not a hint of overstatement, nor indeed, of understatement, in any of their words or actions. The completeness, the perfection of this charade, recreating before me the flawless illusion of the Mother and Tommy I wished they were, held an aftertaste of pure terror. Conversation went on at intervals between the clacking of cutlery and crockery, and I strove to meet their faultless acts with that of my own. In my attempts to appear cheerful, however, my tone sometimes came dangerously close to falsetto.

"Tommy tells me that you've given up the cello, dear."

"No, I haven't given it up. I've mastered it, so there's no point in playing it any more."

"I think it's such a shame. You used to love playing the cello. You had a gift for it. You know what they say, 'Use it or lose it!'"

"I've heard him play it. I thought it was amazing. It's like seeing inside someone's heart when they have a gift like that. I wish I could express myself in music or art or something. You mustn't give it up! Tell him!"

Tommy's voice was indescribably sweet. I struggled to keep back tears.

"No, dear, you mustn't! How's the artichoke, Tommy?" Mother glanced sidelong at Tommy as if she might particularly understand this question, and I repeated the words of the sentence in my head, weighing them for hidden meanings.

So the torture went on and on.

After dinner, out in the passageway, came what I had dreaded most—the return of that intimacy with Tommy which once would have been a thrill of excitement. She held my hands. She had noticed that I was 'not myself' this evening. Would I please tell her what was wrong? She was worried. In my turn, I found myself falling into a strange sincerity. I pleaded with her to let things be. Sometimes the sadness of the world overwhelmed me. When it passed I would be able to explain much better.

And then we climbed the stairs together. All the time I was thinking, 'Can't move forward, can't move back. Can't move forward, can't move back.' If only I had been able to believe that I was fooling her with my pretended trust, then there might have been some kind of grim satisfaction in thus rejecting and shutting her out. But I knew she was not taken in for a moment. In fact, I was only doing what she wanted. There was nothing else I could do. This was not resistance any more than the movements of a puppet crucified upon its strings.

In the bedroom she closed the door behind us. She turned the other way as she undressed and I allowed myself a grimace. I would have to get into bed with that monster! How could I?

Numbly, I too undressed. Allowing myself no hesitation, I slipped under the covers after her as if leaping into a furnace.

Then came darkness. When I felt lips on mine, and the tongue in my mouth, it was as if the darkness itself was pinning me down, the darkness itself was exploring my nakedness, turning me inside out. I surrendered to everything. More than that, I threw myself now into my own debasement, pretending this was what I wanted, while inside I was choking on tears of misery. As if this scene were lit by the flames of hell, I seemed to catch glimpses of us from above, or from the side, glimpses of something utterly grotesque, and was sickened with horror. Enslaved, all I could think was, 'She knows I know. She is making me do this.'

The bullying and the torture, all achieved with the simple, I might almost say 'elegant', nonchalance of carrying on as normal, continued from that day.

When left alone I planned suicide. But the thought came back to me always, 'There is no sympathy in the world.' It was like a wretched core of darkness kicking in my gut, kicking back any hope of deliverance through death. So I drank. In company, too—and now, of course, all company was odious to me—a little drink helped make me a better actor, and I remembered it was not so out of character for me to be gloomy, either.

As the weeks passed and Tommy continued her horrible intimacy with me, unable, perhaps, to bear the psychological punishment I was taking, I felt myself growing far away. The reality I had once known, of basic trust in some unknown something, and this new reality, of trust in nothing, became both equally dream-like. I lived in a state of thin unreality like someone who had grown so used to the drug they are addicted to they no longer know if it has an effect or not. It was not a pleasant state by any means. Is this the kind of grogginess the victim of a vampire feels? I wondered now and then. I neither trusted nor distrusted the vampire with whom I shared a bed. I was simply distant, watching her and the victim in her thrall who existed where I once was.

Perhaps it was this distance that allowed me to wonder if I hadn't imagined those voices, after all. Everything since then had been perfectly normal, except in my own head. Clearly something extraordinary had happened in my emotional life, something the like of which I had never heard before, but perhaps the event had never had any reality beyond that. Perhaps it was a kind of insanity. I had lived through it with enormous self-control, half due to the nature of the madness itself, and now, perhaps, I could come out the other side. Perhaps, someday, I could even tell people about this incredible chapter of my life with confidence.

These tepid thoughts came to me one evening as the sun was sinking. I turned them over like someone reading the same passage again and again, unable to take in the words.

Not long afterwards, Tommy turned up unannounced. This was not an unusual occurrence and I was not surprised. I let her kiss me and watched her blankly for a while as she sat down on the bed.

"I'll get some wine," I said at last.

"Fine," she said. "I'll be here."

I was glad she didn't offer to come with me. I needed time to think. Or, no, I needed to be able to put off thought, to let my unconscious work things out for a while, to see if I couldn't shake free of this without thinking.

I walked alone to the corner shop and selected a cheap red wine without too much consideration. I couldn't rid myself of the feeling that the flinty-faced man behind the counter was watching me strangely. To say my mind had been prone to such suspicions of late would be an absurd understatement. Once I have known such bottomless distrust, can the world ever be free of its shadow again? That I could ask such a question illustrates well the twilight I was inhabiting. Perhaps it was the crepuscular hour, not before nightfall, but before dawn.

I entered the shabby hallway of the tenement building and started up the stairs. As I climbed I caught the sound of deep, discordant notes from above. Tommy must have been attempting to play my cello. I was irritated at the thought she would open that case and tamper with the instrument that I had wished to rest in peace. Something in the sounds themselves irritated me, too. It was not just that she couldn't play. The notes filled me with a sense of smouldering gloom. What was it? Anger? Fear? Sadness? It sounded as if someone were pulling nails out of floorboards or taking an axe to the door. Violence muffled by time until it becomes a ghostly melancholy ... unspeakable deeds whose mad, deformed offspring are locked away in attics to starve to death ... Such were the notes I heard.

As I climbed higher, the music became louder and clearer. Then something odd happened. The discord began to take shape; from the chaos the notes began to flow into a theme of some kind. Music is a language without words. You can hear the intelligence in it, the intent. Something was speaking. And then I recognised what it was saying. It was note for note the improvised piece that I had played for Tommy. There could be no mistake. I slowed my pace, unsure now how I could ascend into the sly challenge of that dirge. The music did not merely express intelligence, it was positively sentient of itself. Pretending to be lost in the maze of its own unravelling up above behind the door, in fact it was with me on the stairs. It was the very sound of my tread, the very feelings with which I moved forward to meet it, and at the same time, it was the dire mockery of those feelings. It measured my every hesitation, my every shudder. It was a mirror of sound. But though my every movement was pantomimed in that mirror, the eyes that looked out of it, back at me, were not mine.

The theme shifted seamlessly. It took on a tone of sepulchral triumph as if to march my soul slowly to the dark and ultimate place where it would be buried alive. Yes, this theme, too, was known to me. It was the theme that should have been my last, which I had played alone to the night one evening before I ever met Tommy!

I stopped still, my hand on the banister, my head bowed. Now the notes coiled round me in dark serpentine loops, constricting tighter and tighter in a twisted, knotted bitterness, tighter and tighter, twisting and twisting, until it seemed that all I could do to end the misery was to throw myself over the edge of the stairs, trailing the sneering notes behind me and letting them heap themselves at last on my crumpled corpse below.

That kicking in my gut, telling me that no one and nothing cared, stopped me. There was a force field of evil between me and my death. When I did break free of the coils that held me, it was instead to dash on up the stairs. With only the door between myself and the player of the cello, I hesitated again. Then I threw the door open. Tommy was sitting on the chair, holding the cello and bow inexpertly, playing random, childish notes. The flow of the dirge had ceased. I stood there in the doorway, and after a couple more halting notes she looked up at me. As usual her performance was flawless. She looked a little bewildered at my obvious anger.

"Put it away," I said. "I don't ever want you to touch my things without asking again."

She looked wounded, but, saying nothing, carried the cello back to its case.

If only she had been angry in turn or given herself away, my own anger might have been fuelled. This act of delicate sheepishness only created in me a backlash of fear.

She closed the lid of the case. For a moment, when her back was turned, I looked at the rounded back of her honey-blonde head. I had a sudden impulse to take the weight of the bottle now in my left hand, lift it high, and bring it down hard on that head. She paused. I felt a rush of horror. Then she turned around.

"I'm sorry. Maybe I should go," she said in a quiet voice.

153

I could no longer control my trembling.

"No. Don't go. It's my fault. Please stay here. Have some wine."

The thought that she might leave me alone cut me deeper than if she really had been the girl I loved.

I sat down on the now empty chair and poured the wine with shaking hands. There could be no doubt of what I had just heard. Only a single door had stood between myself and her as she had deliberately taken the thumbscrews to my soul. No matter how good her act was, I knew it was an act. She had made sure of that. And yet she carried on with it now. I was sure that she even knew of my urge to brain her with the bottle from which I now poured. I was a mess, a quivering jelly. I was her helpless prey. That night was worse than any before. That night the darkness devoured me utterly.

That was two days ago.

Tommy left early the next morning. I too got up early as if to go to work, left the house, then doubled back. I did not want to see or be seen by another human being. I did not want to move. Later I phoned her, was relieved to find she was out, and left a message that I would be staying with a friend that evening. Of course, she would know I was lying, but she would have to act as if she didn't.

The night came on and still I didn't move. I just stared at the landscape of my room. I doubt I can ever express all that went through my mind. As darkness was a paralysing fear when I was very young, so was the whole world now, in darkness or in daylight. I clutched at the thin blanket I crouched under, but even the blanket was somehow sinister. I tried to make no sound, instead terrified of every sound I heard. I thought, perhaps, I would stay like that forever. I waited, long and sleeplessly. I waited, bullied by *this* shadow, threatened by *that* crack in the wall. Most menacing of all was the black sarcophagus in which there rested the instrument of my downfall. It seemed a woeful symbol of bad luck. Once I had thought it was elegant. What sad perversity had led me to take up that hideous instrument? What sardonic fate had guided me towards it, watching over me all the while like a black-hearted tutor? Now it was only grotesque.

In my head, while other lunatic thoughts ranged near and far, there repeated, like a mantra, the words, 'Can't move forwards, can't move back.' With these words for a cane, I beat myself. Maybe some answer would come from this impossible riddle. Maybe I could disappear into the space between forward and back.

Then, towards dawn, it came to me. I took up this pen and paper and began to write. This is my move!

I know you can hear me! I know you are listening to my silent words even now. Well, I have a message for ALL OF YOU! Take off your masks! Let's stop playing this game! Perhaps there really is no sympathy in the world, and yet such an idea, such a feeling, exists somewhere deep in my heart, and in the name of that feeling I beg you all, please, stop the masquerade! Don't you have the freedom to decide this matter for yourselves? Can't the plan be changed? Am I really so beneath you that you could never dream of letting me into your circle? Can't we communicate simply, showing each other what is in our hearts? Would that be so bad? Is this some joke? Well, then, okay—let's get the stupid joke over with and then get on with life together! Please! Speak to me! Talk to me! Show yourselves!

I know you can hear this, and . . . Suddenly a chill has run through me. I feel like I've raised my voice and been met with hideous silence. That sympathy in my heart had led me to misjudge the situation. I shan't address Them any more. But still They can hear me. They know all that is in my heart. If only I could have secrets, too.

Who am I writing this for? Even the pen and paper I write with are traitors to me, leading me on to some terrible conclusion I could never imagine. Perhaps I should stop now. Perhaps I should burn this and carry on with the masquerade. What is the truth I am so eager to avoid?

She will come soon. I can almost hear the laughter. Up the stairs comes hungry laughter, buffoon's laughter, gut laughter, lunatic laughter, the laughter of something whose mouth is too big and whose arms are too long, something that lopes and bounces naked as a child, something that melts as it moves, like a plastic doll, something back to front with a hairless vulva for a stomach and buttocks where its groin should be, a living Picasso, a living Dali. Here it comes, laughter like a little girl's but deeper, pink laughter, hairy laughter, not-by-the-hair-of-my-chinny-chin-chin laughter, laughter that makes me sick because I once knew the creature that it now comes from.

If I make this move, what move will They make in Their turn?

I can't even imagine.

Should I stop now before it's too late, or . . .

It moved! I swear it moved—the sarcophagus! The notes are starting up again. Like an alien language. Building a staircase. Mad. Twisting.

One arm is as thin as a stick and slides back and forth over tangled tendons of belly, playing her laughter, an alien language, twisting, building a staircase, mad, to the door, the door of the sarcophagus.

I must destroy the cello! I must destroy her! But I do not dare open that door.

Who am I writing this for?

I can see myself now from behind the page, everything curling round, looking back at me like a living mirror, and my past trailing away like a staircase of laughter.

Who . . .

The Tao of Petite Beige

(Dedicated to Mr Aaron Nobes)

AT last the two of them crested the hill, emerging from the shady footpath onto an area of flat concrete next to The Temple of the Phoenix. Sun-filtering trees framed a view of Keelung harbour and beyond it the dizzy, concave horizon, like the rim of a golden discus in flight. They paused, relieved after their long exertion, breathing heavily in the sticky heat.

Paul cast his eyes over the temple while Arthur looked out to sea. The temple was a skeletal structure with no innards. It made up for this lack by the brilliancy of its colours, like a peacock's tail. There was also something of the totem pole in the designs that decorated these architectural bones. Paul wondered if they had always been this way, and what purpose they had been erected to serve. At last he left off looking at the temple and joined Arthur in directing his gaze to the cityscape below.

From here the water of the port was a shimmering incandescence with no hint of the litter, dead rats and foul scum they had seen at the water's edge. As Paul drank in the panorama it seemed to him that he was looking down on his own life from some lofty vantage point. Distance made the scenery bracing. A ship was now in the offing, leaving a white wake that looked stiff, static. There was a sense of infinite potential in the view. And between Paul and it, a boundless space full of intoxicating

157

breezes. But despite this potential, and despite this intoxication, the view was empty. It would never actually become anything. The battered gold of the waves was somehow sad.

Paul drew his gaze closer in, to the office blocks and apartment buildings of the city, shockingly white in the sun. Closer at hand, on the flank of the hill, protruding from the lush canopy of trees, were the curved eaves of another temple. The elegant curves contrasted strikingly with the box-like angles beyond, and Paul found himself reaching into his bag for his camera in order to capture the contrast forever on film. Perhaps it was the name of the temple beside them that put the idea in his head, but those curves seemed like the very tip of a phoenix's wing.

Paul had come to Taiwan because he had heard it was the 'real China', traditions surviving here that had been swept away on the mainland. But since his arrival he had found precious little that corresponded with the China of his imagination. If ever such a country had existed, it was no more. There was nothing left but the ashes of industrialisation and, here and there, a few glowing embers such as this temple. What would rise from these ashes now?

Paul put his camera back in his bag and the two of them continued on their way. The path led them eventually to what they had come to see—the statue of Guan Yin, the goddess of mercy. It stood some seventy feet or more tall, looking out forever to the ocean. In the fierce heat the statue appeared pale and cool as the moon. Her face was round and her body and hands plump. She wore an inscrutable expression that could indeed have been mercy, but could just as easily have been any number of other things.

In the base of the statue, at the back, was a doorway. The two of them passed through this and were confronted by steps leading upward. The statue was divided into a number of floors. The heat inside was intense, and as they climbed, sweat dripped off them.

"I've never been inside a goddess before," said Arthur. "Or not for a while, anyway."

"I wish some goddess would have mercy on me," said Paul.

At length they arrived at the top, where they found an altar covered with coins left there by previous pilgrims. A window in the goddess' throat gave another view of Keelung.

They both placed money on the altar. Paul thought of his words of a few moments before.

After descending the statue again they retired to a nearby teahouse, found a table and took the weight off their feet. A young girl with olive skin so smooth it looked waxed, came out from behind the shop counter and took their order. They asked for tea and some peanuts to nibble on. The girl set a glass container full of water over the flame of a paraffin heater on their table and brought them a bag of tea leaves and the tea utensils. As the girl returned to the counter, both pairs of eyes followed her perfect, pear-shaped behind, outlined neatly by her parti-coloured cotton trousers.

"It's enough to distract me from my training," remarked Arthur.

"Your training?"

"Yeah. You know I'm taking kung fu lessons, well, it's not just about learning how to fight. Well, it is, I suppose, but part of it is about building up *qi* energy. If I want to get into this properly, I've got to learn how to store and direct my *qi*. That can make all the difference, you see. If I just hit you normally, it will probably just hurt you and make you angry. But if I use my *qi* it will knock you down so you can't get up again. That's how the great kung fu masters could kill people with one finger, 'cause they knew how to direct their *qi*. So . . . I've forgotten what my point was. Oh yeah! So, going with women is bad for your training. Women steal your energy. The female nature is draining. They feed off your essence."

"I don't know. I mean, it's natural to have relationships with

159

women, isn't it? In fact, I think it's more unhealthy not to. No one can be one hundred percent celibate."

"No, it's true. You think about it. After you have sex you're tired, aren't you? And if you have too much sex it shortens your life. It's like drinking. It affects your health and your overall condition. If you drink too much it does your liver in, or whatever. But not just that, it destroys your brain cells and gives you the shakes. It's like, if you get caught up in any of these things, sex, drink or whatever, it destroys your reason. It's important to keep your reason intact and not give in to the passions. That's why when people go mad they spend all their time masturbating. They've lost their reason. It's all connected, see."

"I'm not convinced. I don't think there's anything wrong with masturbation. I mean, that's like the old 'you'll go blind' or 'you'll get hairs on the palms of your hands.'"

"No, I'm not saying there's anything wrong with it morally. But for the sake of your health it's best not to do it. You lose your essence when you do."

"You mean your sperm?"

"That's right. Your sperm is your essence. The Taoists used to withhold their essence in order to achieve longevity. But if you train you can learn how to withhold your essence while having sex. That's what the Taoist masters used to do. They'd spend years in some cave somewhere, then for one day they'd come down to the town and sleep with all the prostitutes in all the brothels without losing any of their essence."

Paul looked out of the open window by which they were seated and down to the small courtyard below. The arches that surrounded the courtyard, the windows above these, and still higher, the curved tiles of the enclosing rooftops, suggested to Paul some ineffable mystery that he would never grasp. What was the use of this view? It seemed to call to him, but what would it ever give to his life? He felt irritated without knowing exactly why. He turned back to Arthur.

"I don't know. That's all very well if you're into that kind of thing. I just think there are too many people in the world already telling us how to live our lives. 'Do this. Don't do that.' We don't need yet another philosophy telling us we've got it all wrong. Why can't we just be what we are and forget about trying to be something else? What's wrong with just follow-ing your natural inclinations? All this stuff about training, it seems kind of artificial to me. It's reaching for something that's impossible. It's bad enough having to endure celibacy through sheer bad luck, I don't really see the appeal of bending over backwards to be celibate."

The water had boiled and Arthur had set to with the tea utensils like a conjurer setting up his props. Now he poured a little of the green liquid into the egg cup-sized vessels they had been given.

"Oh, you just carry on with your wicked habits," he said as he finished pouring.

"It's not so much my wicked habits, it's more the wicked things I'd like to do given half a chance."

Arthur chuckled.

"Ah, this is jolly nice. More tea, Vicar?"

"Don't mind if I do."

Paul was an onanist of the first water, a confirmed physical fantasist, an erotic trainspotter, a devout believer in self-consolation. He had long ago calculated that even if he became a Don Juan overnight and slept with women at the rate of one a day, in his entire lifetime, the amount of times he had resorted to self-abuse would still outnumber the amount of times he had had accompanied sex by more than five to one. In the much more likely circumstance that things continued as they were, or grew worse, the figures were even more depressing. Faced with such crushing statistics, Paul had first despaired, then resigned himself, then, by slow degrees, had come to awaken to and explore the squalid little cell that was to be his for life.

During his exploration he had developed a rudimentary philosophy to help him cope with his solitary confinement. Sex was the meaning of life—that was as obvious as a dirty joke. But in the absence of sex what was left was masturbation. This was a somewhat ironic pleasure. There were two contradictory sides to it. On the one hand, so to speak, it was total abandon, total freedom to indulge in fantasies that, in their unspeakableness, isolated one absolutely from the rest of existence. On the other hand, these fantasies were just that. They were insubstantial. They were not real, and they left behind a maddening aftertaste of tantalisation. But during the fantasy, if he could only forget the real world, if he could focus on his isolation, that total freedom, even if it were an illusion, might be enough to keep him living day after day. He had to give himself up to it so that it grew and blocked out everything else. It was a question of how you looked at things. After all, the solipsistic 'I' always comes first. The real world is nothing.

When Paul got back to his small, top-floor flat after his day-trip with Arthur, he locked the door, lifted up the hood of his laptop computer, and logged on. There were the usual reassuring whirs and hums as the computer stirred into life. The logos flashed by and an electronic flourish of sound, like the parting of great, feathery fans, ushered him into the perfectly ordered, unreally glowing world of his virtual office, his bedroom within a bedroom. And there to greet him, the very wallpaper of this pixelated grotto, was the goddess of all his seedy fantasies, Petite Beige. The wallpaper was a black and white photograph in which Petite was dressed as a slave for auction at some imaginary Oriental bazaar. Actually, it was hard to tell whether she were meant to be a slave or some kind of princess. Although she was scantily clad in golden breastplates—these like a bikini-top forged by melting down a golden calf with some heat the like of that produced by the test explosions at the atoll from which the bikini acquired its name, thus creating an object even more idolatrous than the bovine blasphemy that formed its material—and a seraglio loincloth, there was something majestic about her. It wasn't just the gold encrusted on her bosom and glittering in her ornamental headgear. It was her very figure that was regal. In the background of the photograph had been drawn cartoon minarets and turbaned characters with piggy eyes wide in astonishment at the wares on sale. The background figures were tiny and ridiculous in comparison with Petite in the foreground. And should one of these sweaty little caricatures purchase her, it seemed a foregone conclusion that he would soon find himself not master, but slave, with Petite as his feared and beloved mistress.

Paul looked more closely at the breastplates. They seemed to be made up of interlinked scales, like armour. But the scales were feathers in the outspread wings of a fierce-looking bird, almost a dragon, which seemed to be composed of leaping flames. He remembered his thoughts of that afternoon. Of course! This fiery bird, with its head nestled below this vintage cleavage, must be a phoenix. Why had he never noticed this before? His eyes ran over the rest of Petite's timeless figure. She held her arms up in a curious manner, almost as if they too were wings, and seemed to be pointing at her breasts as if indicating some secret of cosmic significance. He followed the sloping lines of her flesh from beneath her armpits, into her hourglass waist, and from her waist out again to her tightly brimming hips. He traced her ribs and the shapely shadows of her stomach. He lingered where the dividing of the ribcage formed an estuary of shadow that dipped eventually to the elliptical pit of her navel. The difference between her waist and her hips seemed fantastic, unbelievable, and the loincloth was stretched taut around these full curves as if about to snap.

The legs inclined inward towards the knees. Paul noticed with admiration the shine on the thighs, as if they had been oiled.

These lines and curves corresponded precisely with some immemorial code written in Paul's being. Mighty inner portals swung open, accessing the treacherous realm of lust. A hot, scorching wind howled from the portal and twisted into the figure before him, taking hold as a glow in that figure's outline.

Whenever Paul was confronted with an avatar of sex in this way, and the portal opened to the void of ecstasy, the first emotion he felt was a kind of dirty fear. It was like standing helplessly by watching a dear friend being beaten up by thugs. (He well understood why sex and violence were associated with each other.) If he reduced that fear to a philosophy, it seemed to be something like the revelation that pornography was the true face of life, and, moreover, that this was a life from which he was eternally barred by some mocking violence. The reason that those who were in on the great conspiracy of sex enjoyed it so much was that they knew in the process they were trampling on the likes of Paul.

Paul let the thorny wind howl around him. He was exposed. He was alone. The demons that scavenged in the realm beyond the portal could pick him off on a whim. He trembled. He was rigid with terror. This was freedom. In the midst of it all he focused on the sacred, the blasphemous outlines that crowed over him in triumph. He wanted to possess them. He fixed them in his mind as if to absorb them utterly. He reached into his trousers and took hold of his throbbing terror.

His hand began to move in an unseemly, dog-like rhythm, demolishing the poise he usually maintained as a human being amongst human beings. It seemed incongruous that he was still wearing clothes. He had shifted gear to some nameless mode of life that had existed long before there were any such things as clothes. Something in the hunched repetition of his movements had the look of self-mortification, or some other diseased religious habit. He did not resort to imaginary scenarios in which he was an actor. He did not think of the crude act of sex at all. All his efforts were bent on identification with the icon before him, that he might attain to the mystical experience that was direct knowledge of the curves and lines. These curves and lines passed through him like a procession of ghosts, so that he could almost taste them. But still, like ghosts, they slipped through his grasp. They haunted him and lashed him with phantom whips that were at once ecstasy and denial.

He made intimate, animal noises. Inflamed, he felt something in him rising higher and higher. The ecstasy and the denial both became so great that they could no longer tolerate each other. The cries came like a cloudburst. A lacerating thunderbolt shot through his scrotum. Warm jism looped into his hand. He gasped and cried out like a child caught in a nightmare. Then came a feeling like falling rain. He sagged suddenly, exhausted. He felt naked and ashamed.

In adult years Paul had become sexually jaded. He virtually never had a spontaneous erection. He attributed this to the fact that real sex had come to seem such an impossibility to him that he could hardly even imagine it. In order to revive his libido he had devised various tactics whereby he could trace his way back to the sexual excitement of adolescence and before. One of these tactics was to abandon the more explicit pornography he had come to rely on, and instead to use material that left more to the imagination.

It was whilst trawling the annals of erotica for such material that Paul had come across Petite Beige. Petite was a pin-up idol of the 1950s and favourite of the American girlie magazines of that era. She was like some 'good-time girl' creation of Elvgren or Varga—or else some fetishist creation of John Willie or Eric Stanton—come to life. Her work with photographer and ex-model Honey Baker brought her a certain kind of fame. With her raven locks, her defiant eyes, her wicked, pointed mouth, and a figure that seemed full to bursting with untamed sex, she was a living archetype. She didn't dance, she didn't act, she didn't sing, but the presence she projected on film, in still photographs, was surely enough to earn her the title of genius. At least, Paul thought so. He had never seen sex personified so consummately as it was by this tigress in the many thousands of photographs she had bequeathed the world. In fact, that Paul and many others like him had come to worship Petite on the strength of these two-dimensional images alone was testament to the strength of the personality with which they were imbued. In determining what kind of person Petite was, there was little else to go on. She had disappeared mysteriously at the height of her fame and no one knew her current whereabouts, or even if she were still alive. It was as if her photographs had taken her place, freezing her in the era of her greatest beauty, guaranteeing her eternal youth. Paul had often thought that she had quite literally become her photographs. That was why they seemed so alive.

Another of Paul's tactics for rejuvenating his libido was to write down his fleeting thoughts on sex in a jotter in the hope that this would re-sensitise him to the sexual messages with which the world bombarded him every day.

After masturbating to the image of Petite as slave girl, along with his exhaustion, Paul felt a kind of disquiet, as if he could not possibly get away with this sort of thing and would have to face terrible consequences at some point in the future. But what those consequences might be he had no idea. He thought of Arthur's words of that afternoon. It was no good. He was what he was. There was no point even considering reform. He pushed his anxieties to one side. Perhaps there was something

166

in what Arthur had said, though. What if he continued to masturbate, but simply 'withheld his essence'—a kind of tantric masturbation? It might even go some way to revitalising his sexuality. He liked the idea. He decided to start his tantric masturbation by writing a little more in his jotter. He took the jotter out of the desk drawer, and, after pausing a moment for thought, put pen to paper:

> What is the essence of the female? In many ways we're very similar. We have two arms, two legs, a head on our shoulders, and so on. Yet a woman's face can, in most cases, be distinguished instantly from a man's. Somehow 'female' had been stamped on every inch of her. How often, when I masturbate, I mistakenly separate the obvious sexual attributes—breasts, bum, vagina—from the rest of the body, and they lose their potency, become mere objects. I have to let the female essence circulate through these parts from the rest of the female being. I have to see it as a whole.
>
> Boys are instinctively aware of the difference in the sexes without knowing the details. At that age we associate girls with flowers and butterflies and ribbons. They are far too sweet for our taste. They make us feel sick. But as we grow older, almost against our will, we feel drawn towards this ultimate sweetness. We cannot help ourselves. We need to have it. When we get a taste of the pink, gooey thing that is the female, we can't believe our luck. Does such a thing really exist? But somewhere there remains more than just a trace of the disgust that we knew when we were boys. In such pink nakedness disgust and ecstasy are one and the same.

Now that I've written all that, I can't shake off the feeling that this 'female essence' is half illusion. After all, there are occasions when I might see a pair of legs and find them alluring for an instant, until I suddenly realise that they belong to a man. Yes, half of the attraction is projected by an indeterminate something in my own head. It's a question of associations. That must be why a half-naked woman is more attractive to me than a naked one. What is covered up gives that indeterminate something in my head room to play. Women's underwear is often decorated with the flowers that we have come to associate with the female. Sex is an invention of civilisation, created by the act of covering and disguising nature. The underwear that covers this nature and makes of it a mystery becomes sex itself. The association of concealing underwear with sex has become so indelibly printed on my brain that underwear itself, quite separate from womankind, provokes a deep and aimless feeling of lust in me. My attraction to women themselves may be no more than this kind of mechanical association.

At this point, Paul felt he was dealing with a chicken-and-egg conundrum beyond solution. He laid down his pen and returned the jotter to its drawer, perplexed.

The next day, when evening came on, Paul quit his flat and wandered the dirty chaos of the Taipei streets in search of a meal. As he emerged onto the main thoroughfare the confusion of neon and Chinese characters assaulted his senses. An aeroplane roared low overhead, shaking the buildings and adding to the churning din of the lawless traffic. He hesitated as if overwhelmed by all this.

He was tired of eating a greasy chow mien at the cockroach-infested noodle joint on the main street and decided to find somewhere new tonight. He turned right where the corrugated iron hemmed in a tiny patch of waste ground, and strolled out across the little park where drunks lazed in the gazebo and mangy dogs fought and roamed. He passed through an intersection where seafood glistened on crushed ice in a shop-front display, and night stalls sold chicken feet and other lurid delicacies. Weaving in between the constant rush of taxis and motor scooters, some of them supporting entire families and their dogs, he came to an area he had not yet explored.

On the awnings of some of the shops here were tangles of stringy, creeper-like weeds, as if the original verdure of this island could not be entirely suppressed by the steel and concrete. Paul remembered that the Tropic of Cancer ran through the island. The chaos of these streets made him think that this was a concrete jungle in the most literal sense, the abundant foliage that must once have existed turning, as if at the wave of a wand, into the steamy, squalid hotch-potch of shops, tenements and high-risers.

He passed a temple whose eaves were hung with yellow paper lanterns, and stopped at a corner where guava were piled outside a fruit shop. To the left the street became narrower and dingier. Feeble yellow lights shone in tiny windows half-obscured by grime. Pot plants crowded untidily in narrow balconies. The alleys leading off from the main street suggested a secretive life lived among shadows. Paul was naturally drawn in this direction. Here there was something of the sleazy colour he had expected to find in this scion of antique China, a colour like that of a faded and threadbare tapestry abandoned on a rubbish heap. From the dilapidated buildings there seemed to issue a thin, plaintive music, as of some half-forgotten song played on a broken instrument.

He turned right at the next corner and saw, just a few yards ahead, a narrow little shop opening onto the road. A small group of people sat at a rickety table, eating and talking. He approached uncertainly, not wanting to get drawn into the shop if he did not like the wares, but not knowing how to appraise those wares without going closer. He stood before the bleary glass counter, inside which were displayed a variety of dishes, none of which looked particularly appetising. A woman stood behind the counter in an apron. She addressed him in Mandarin, and, flustered, he ordered the single dish on the menu that he knew how to pronounce—*danhuatang*, or egg-flower soup. The woman motioned for him to sit down at a table against the wall inside the shop, and he did so.

The shop seemed to merge with the living room of the family who ran the place. Inside were a number of empty tables, children's toys scattered on the floor and piles of newspapers and magazines. An electric fan in the corner swung its head slowly back and forth. There were newspapers on Paul's table, too. His current reading matter, *Orientalism* by Edward Said, was giving him a major intellectual and ethical headache of late, and he had left it behind. Instead, he picked up one of these newspapers and studied it in a desultory manner, unable to read more than a few of the characters. Before long a young girl, slender as a sapling, obviously the daughter of the family, came to the table with his soup. She smiled at him nervously, and he had the impression that the fact he was a foreigner conferred on him a sort of celebrity. He had just begun to eat his soup when this impression was apparently confirmed by a man greeting him from a nearby table. He returned the greeting with a nod, and the man got up from his seat and came over. He sat down in the empty seat next to Paul's. The man looked to be in his forties or fifties. His hair was still thick and black, but his wide face was seamed and had about it an air of tiredness.

"Hello. How do you do?"

"How do you do?" Paul returned the formal greeting.

"Are you American?"

"No."

"No. What is your country?"

"I'm from England."

"England? Ah, that is better."

Paul smiled. He was not sure how to respond to this.

"American English is broken English. Just slang. England is gentleman's English."

It was hard to tell if this were a statement or a question, so Paul remained silent and smiled again.

"You come here on holiday?"

"No, I'm working here."

Paul told the man the name of the English school where he worked as a teacher and the man nodded in recognition.

"I work in Chinese puppet theatre. You know?"

"Yes, I've seen it on television. The puppets jump about and fight and stuff."

Paul imitated the stylised gesticulations of the puppets.

"Yes. There is special skills we must learn to make them jump and move in certain way."

The man pointed to a poster on the wall showing puppet characters from some Chinese romance.

"This is me. We tour with puppet theatre. It is very interesting Chinese culture. Are you interested Chinese culture?"

"Yes. I don't know much about it, but I'd like to know more. Actually, since coming here I've seen little temples everywhere, on the corners of streets and in alleys, and I'd like to find out more about them. They're not Buddhist temples, are they?"

"Yes, Buddhist."

Paul had been told that he might get this response.

"If you like, I will show you. There is a temple near. I take you, okay?"

The temple in question was almost directly opposite the one with the yellow lanterns which he had passed earlier. It was flanked by two stone lions—the one on the left with its paw upon a sphere and the one on the right with its paw upon a cub—between which stood what he believed was called a '*ting*', one of the three-legged incense braziers with the cauldron-like bellies that had become such a familiar sight to him. The temple itself was no larger than a shed. There was no door, the front being open to the street. Paul and his guide waited for a worshipper to finish his business before stepping inside. To the left and right the walls were lined with what looked like tiny glass drawers, each containing a single light. At first these lights appeared to be candles or 'tea lights', but on closer inspection it became clear they were electric. The back wall was decorated with shelves full of dusty effigies in ornate robes, their faces painted with striking patterns. Most of them were about the size of a child's doll. The old puppet master pointed to one of the larger effigies.

"Guan Yin," he said, and Paul recognised the serene features of the goddess of mercy.

In front of the effigy burnt a candle and some incense.

The puppeteer began to expound on the various deities represented in the temple, but Paul's attention wandered and he caught only half of it. He wished that he could grasp something of substance behind the mystical display of the temple and the tattered tradition that hung about it. He wanted very much for this to be the ornate gateway to a world where all things partook of the same odour of incense, where all was a magnificent brocade woven of the same rich and mysterious colours. But it seemed to him the mystery began and ended with the physical structure of the temple itself. It was nothing but an attractive, empty shell.

172

"Her name means she hears everything in the world," the puppeteer went on. "That is why many people come to the temple, come *baibai*." He put his hands together in a mime of worship to indicate the meaning of his last word.

Something caught Paul's eye. On a low table near the front of the temple were stacked a great many sheaves of square paper. The paper was edged with gold and carried designs in red and yellow that Paul could not quite make out.

The puppeteer picked up one of the bundles.

"This we call 'god money' or 'ghost money'. We burn it so that our ancestors can have things they need in heaven. That is ghost money. Or if we have problem, maybe, we ask the god to help us, and we burn god money."

Paul looked at the ghost money in the puppeteer's hand. He saw that some of the designs were of articles of clothing, furniture, small personal items such as combs, and so on, like cut-out accessories for paper dolls.

"What do these pictures mean?" he asked.

"These are offerings for the ghosts. Sometimes they are for the ancestors. But the temple is also—how do you say?—sanctuary. There are homeless spirits who come to the temple for sanctuary. Sometimes we burn ghost money for the homeless spirits and give them clothes and things they need."

On hearing this queer explanation, Paul regarded the ghost money with even greater curiosity. For some reason he could not define, he had become strangely covetous of these gilt-framed and otherworldly bills.

The puppeteer returned the wad of ghost money to the pile on the table.

"Excuse me. I must go," he said, and bowed slightly in a nervous fashion.

"Yes. Thank you."

Paul thought it strange that the puppeteer, who had seemed so keen to hold forth of the intricacies of Chinese culture, should suddenly depart in so sheepish a fashion. Still, in truth he was grateful for this withdrawal. He watched the man shuffle off back the way they had come and, looking around to make sure he was not observed, took one of the sheaves of ghost money from the pile and slipped it into his jacket pocket.

✳

Apart from spilling his seed in vain, Paul had one other salient pastime, and that was nothing more than the exercise of his legs in the simple act of walking and the simultaneous exercise of his eyes in taking in the details of the passing world. In the same way that he kept notes on his erotic inner life, he also kept notes on observations made on such walks. He had dubbed this second notebook 'The Noctambulist's Jotter', 'noctambulist' being a word he believed he had coined himself. The notes were deliberately written in a somewhat high-flown style in order that Paul might persuade himself that there was something romantic in his evening excursions.

The day after purloining the ghost money from the temple, Paul took the evening air again on another of his excursions, and, upon returning, eagerly took up his pen to record his latest observations:

17.Apr.2001

Sometimes it pays to forget about timetables and duties. Sometimes it pays to forget about tomorrow and just get lost.

I don't know why it has taken me this long to abandon the little nest of streets I know and stroll further afield. I've been pre-occupied, I suppose, and very inward-looking. But I must not waste my chances. I must try to look outwards, and notice things.

174

Well, that is what happened this evening. Now I am back in my top-floor flat and sweating. The night is rather hot. A sign of things to come, no doubt.

I say that is what *happened*, but perhaps 'happened' is too definite a word. I know how changeable my moods are and I don't want to be too hopeful about turning points that turn out to be nothing of the sort. Only, for a while it seemed that merely walking abroad in the world, and especially at night, was an adventure. And since it has inspired me, I should act on that inspiration.

Quite simply, I was restless. I took unknown roads, and this was a virtual revelation. I saw a number of things which would have been reason enough to go back in the day with my camera. Unfortunately, such is my ignorance I lack the language to properly describe them. I suppose, basically, they were shrines set in back streets. The first that caught my attention was three or four storeys—I wish I had counted now—of idols and lanterns. Of course, it must have been a shrine, but to someone like me who knows so little about these things, there was a strange ambiguity about it. Do people inhabit the higher floors? Can you gain access to the balcony-alcoves? Of course, you must be able to, but, well, what happens here, exactly?

I think I'll be able to find my way back. But that was only the start. I saw a family at a table outside another shrine, and at the back of the decorated altar there was a black idol with red eyes that I swear were glowing. Of course, there's nothing impossible about that, but it certainly caught my attention. Further and I saw another shrine in which there played a mother and child. A crowd of red paper lanterns hung from the long peak of the eaves. The two guardian lions were particularly fascinating, and I had to have a closer look.

It was as I was moving back towards familiar streets that I saw the final thing. I could easily have missed it except that I was newly awakened to my environment and looked down each unknown way. Down a narrow, gloomy alley that almost appeared to be a dead end, I caught a glimpse of unwonted colour amidst the grimy grey. I looked closer. It appeared as if two costumed figures were frolicking or tussling at some curtained entrance. I might have passed on, but I decided to try and get a closer look. The two figures looked like characters from Chinese opera. Was this a religious ceremony, or was it a performance of some kind? As I got closer I saw a number of people sitting around watching the two figures. They looked like old people for the most part, sitting in a kind of slummy courtyard amongst converging alleyways. This courtyard extended out of my sight to the right in an area like the parking space of a hotel. Was this the back entrance of a shop? Was this a public or a private event?

I watched the figures, unwilling to approach any closer. One was taller than the other, dressed in turquoise robes. I believe the shorter one was in red. Already memory fails me. The turquoise figure was quite regal, and I immediately thought it must be a king. It swung its arms from side to side and appeared to be walking, and yet it did not get any closer. The illusion was rather eerie. I guessed that this was one of those puppets worked from inside by one or two people.

Some of the spectators looked in my direction and I grew uncomfortable. After a while I left. But I thought I might be able to get closer from another direction. I circled round the block of buildings and found another alley. At an intersection was a cornershop. On the yellow lantern outside was the name 'Li'. I made a mental note of it, in case I should wish to find the place again. I went further, turned left, and sure enough, a little distance away from me was the swaying turquoise king. He was taller than I had thought. Perhaps twelve feet tall. I stayed there only a second. I was too close and afraid my behaviour was intrusive or suspicious. I departed swiftly.

Probably, if I had dared approach anyone in the group of people, and if I had asked and been able to understand the answer, I would have found a very prosaic explanation for the whole thing.

I wonder if half the reason I left with only glimpses, apart from the simple fear of intrusion, was a fear that I might destroy the mystery I had discovered, or perhaps, created.

Anyway, I had never suspected that such things were happening so close to me. I walked back along the streets I knew, surprised at how seamlessly they joined with the mystery I had just quit.

I must find out more about the life around me, the shrines and the ceremonies and the customs. There must be some true mystery lurking in these streets somewhere.

In the following days, this suspicion of some indefinable mystery in the streets about him, by turns beckoning to and hiding from him, strengthened its hold on Paul. He was aware of its subtle presence even during the daylight hours.

Finally, this sense of obscure mystery seemed to call to him at every waking moment. In answer to its nebulous summons, he would quit his flat and wander the alleys aimlessly, even during the mornings and afternoons when he should have been preparing lessons. Certainly the alleys had a peculiar charm, squalid though they often were, not to be found on the main streets. Especially when it rained and there was a mist of moisture in the air, but also when the sun was shining, to walk in these narrow, decrepit crannies, looking up at the merest sliver of sky to be seen between cage-like balconies crowded with potted plants and washing, almost made Paul's coming here to Taiwan worthwhile on its own.

On the ground floors of many of these buildings were tiny shops, hardly distinguishable from private homes. Paul also noticed a phenomenon that quite intrigued him. There seemed to be amongst these alleys a great many metal doors—shiny metal doors—their surfaces lightly inlaid with various exotic designs. Most common was the landscape design of beetling misty mountains. There were also designs featuring dragons and so on, and once Paul had paused for a long while outside a door whose design was that of a teratogenic bird rising from wild flames as if in triumph.

One day Paul took his camera and captured a number of these doors on film. Each time he took a photograph of one of these doors, he glanced up and down the alley nervously, and when his work was accomplished, walked quickly on.

While engaged in this activity, Paul fell to reflecting on his fascination with these doors. There was no doubt it was another facet of the sense of mystery that had come to haunt him of late. Seeing a door chased with the design of twin dragons, splendid as a clash of cymbals, he could not help wondering what might lie behind it. No doubt it was just an ordinary family sitting around a television set in a grubby front room. But as long as the door remained closed and he had only glimpses, there remained a certain dream and an undying, unquenchable allure.

Thinking about it this way, Paul's disgust and disappointment with Westernisation in the Orient was perhaps nothing more than his craving of Orientals that they should somehow be the slaves of his imagination and turn his daydreams into reality. He required that they should conform with his image of a mystical East. And following close upon this thought came the rather disturbing conclusion that he was essentially evil. His attitude was no different than that of refusing to take any interest in a woman unless she aroused his carnal desires. But it could not be helped. He had been born white and male. He was bound to have certain dreams about a sleepy-eyed beauty on a silken couch that he called the Orient, and the Orient was in turn bound to disappoint him. He just had to give up and accept his own evil.

Back in his flat, in his idle moments, Paul brooded over the ghost money that now sat upon his desk. He had felt compelled to pilfer this glittering treasure, but now that he had it, he did not know what to do with it. Only, as he turned it over and over in his hands, he felt certain of some potential contained within this otherworldly currency, like the potential of a key to unlock a door, if only one knew the whereabouts of that door.

It was while Paul was out on another of his walks that the idea occurred to him, and he wondered why he had not thought of it before.

That occasion in the temple with the old puppeteer as his guide had not been the first time that Paul's eyes had met with the sight of ghost money. The folk religion of this island, hiding behind its flimsy mask of Buddhism, called for observances and festivals to be carried out on the myriad dates determined by the archaic lunar calendar. Paul had often noticed, without paying too much attention, the tables set out on the pavements in front of shops and businesses on seemingly irregular dates, and had occasionally cast his eyes over the offerings heaped on those tables. In the main, those offerings consisted of burning incense, a cornucopia of fruit, and, to the side, a neat stack of ghost money. Until the puppeteer had explained to him, Paul had not known what these sheaves of curiously decorated paper were. Now he paid closer attention and observed in a number of places that a shop keeper or business employee took the ghost money from the table and burnt it in the kind of metal bin often used for the incineration of rubbish. This burnt offering was no doubt intended to buy the favour of unseen gods that the business in question might prosper.

Was there no god whose favour Paul wished to buy? In fact, there was. Not a god, but a goddess. And rather than seeking her divine patronage in securing the success of some business, he wished her to stoke the flames of his concupiscence with her own, exalted and lubricious hands.

Today was clearly one of those days marked on the lunar calendar for sacrificial offerings. He did not want to let this chance slip by. He returned to the flat and stuffed the ghost money in his inside jacket pocket. Then he looked through his stash of Petite Beige postcards and pictures for something appropriate. The image he finally settled on was a peculiar one. It featured Petite in a beret and leopard-skin bikini roller-skating down what appeared to be the streets of New York closely pursued by a gorilla—very obviously a man in a furry suit—on a child's scooter. Below the picture was the caption, "Petite goes ga-ga over outré apeman!"

Paul did not know why he had chosen this postcard in particular. Simply, when he came to this one it seemed that none of the others would do. A vague suspicion that the decision had somehow been made for him caused an uneasy squirming in his stomach. For a moment he thought of exchanging the image for one in which Petite radiated her usual unbridled sex, like some ravishing beacon for all priapic sailors lost upon the seas of eternal tossing. But somehow he could not bring himself to do it. Usually Petite's body, her shoulders, breasts, belly, hips, her soft-svelte legs, seemed to be one sultry pout. In this picture her body was a smile, sweet as vanilla. And yet something in the relationship between her and this pantomime gorilla lent the picture an obscure frisson.

Armed with this material, Paul took to the streets once more in search of flames in which to burn his offering.

At first he thought of making his offering in one of the metal bins he had seen, but since these all seemed to belong to a shop or other business, and to be placed directly outside the premises in question, he felt awkward about making use of them. He was all too aware of eyes upon him and was afraid his offering might constitute some sort of trespass. He wandered the streets for some time in the hope of finding a bin in a place where his actions might not be observed. Eventually he came to the temple from which he had originally taken the ghost money, and against the wall of a building in the street leading away from the temple, discovered a kind of furnace with a tiled exterior. Obviously this was where temple-goers made their offerings. As luck would have it there were still some flames amongst the ashes inside. He glanced about nervously. No one seemed to be paying him any attention. So as not to smother the flames inside, he took the postcard of Petite Beige and laid it carefully in the heart of the furnace, watching as it curled and blackened at the edges. This little ritual, he hoped, would stimulate his erotic imagination and contribute greatly to the effectiveness of his tantric masturbation. With the addition of this new fuel, the flames quickened into life. To these flames Paul added one sheet of ghost money, then two and three. His lingering sense of indecision over the choice of the exact postcard to be used had given Paul an idea. He had cut out the costumes and accessories from certain of Petite Beige's pictures and attached them to the ghost money in imitation of the designs that were already printed there. When the flames looked strong enough he relinquished the entire wad into their consuming heart. He had simply burnt a quantity of paper, and yet, because he was borrowing from forms of ritual and superstition that had come down through centuries, surviving in their own shadowy way quite without the sponsorship of governments and officials, he felt as if he had committed some act whose significance dwarfed him.

He stared at the flames, half in a daze, and watched his little sacrifice blacken and burn with the colours of leopard-skin. The ashes that leapt up and danced about on the currents of heat looked to him strangely like the wings of some fabulous bird.

That night, voluminous and rococo curtains rose for Paul upon the most outrageous and phantasmagorical of dreams. When he awoke, he remembered it all in such glittering detail that he wondered exactly how he had been transported from the world of his dream back to the infinitely removed and far less vivid world of his familiar flat. He attributed this unprecedentedly sumptuous nocturnal vision, this rising of some oneiric Atlantis, to the obscure kindling of his imagination by his pyrolatrous act of that afternoon.

In the dream, Paul first found himself in some unknown area of fusty darkness. He was somehow aware of being in an enclosed space, like the backstage of a theatre, cluttered with unseen objects. He groped about uncertainly, afraid of stumbling on something. Eventually, flailing in this void of ultimate unknowing, his hands brushed up against something. He felt a tingling shock, as if he had been discovered by that something rather than the other way around, but soon he decided that the thing was inanimate. Exploring further with his fingers, he found the item to be cold and silky, making him shiver wonderfully in his belly. There were other items, too, of fur or gauze or velvet, all of them strangely seductive to the touch and to the smell—the perfumes they gave off as various and suggestive as their textures. This must be some sort of costume rack, he concluded, only half-consciously, and as he did so, he knelt and buried his face in the fabrics hanging there, so that the smells and the textures would be more closely and more deliciously combined.

Then he ceased his movements and held his breath, for he had become certain that he was not alone. Somewhere in the tenebrousness, and close at hand, was another presence, shapeless and awful. In the midst of his breathless suspense, Paul must have forgotten himself, since the next thing he remembered was stumbling along a gloomy passage, lit uncertainly by some glimmering ahead.

A number of times he felt himself in danger of losing his balance and falling, but something seemed to be supporting him, jerking his arms and legs to move him forward against his volition.

Eventually he seemed to have come to a point where the glimmering surrounded him, but he was perhaps even less sure of his surroundings than before. If this were a corridor then it did not seem to be made of wood or stone or any other material that he knew. Instead the glimmering wove a web of gloopy phosphorescence in festoons of marbling that even seemed to twitch and stir. Sometimes, when he reached out his hand, or rather, when something extended his hand for him, he felt that it must brush against this web, but it didn't. The web was obviously further away than it appeared. In its light he noticed what seemed to be thin sticks coming from the downward-facing palms of his hands. These must be what were moving him along. But who was moving them?

Paul continued in this way, helpless and bewildered, while striations of weird light moved across his face. Without warning he bumped into something. Ripples spread from where his body had struck and radiated shimmeringly throughout the whole web. Paul did not stop. He walked through the rippling web, which now washed over him like waves and closed behind him.

There was a magical sound as of the glissando of harp strings and Paul opened his eyes to find himself in another world. At first what he saw was too rich and strange for his eyes to take in and he was blind through lack of comprehension. Then, slowly, he began to assign meanings to things and to build up some idea of where he was. It appeared to be a palace of some kind, but everything here was made of materials he had never seen before, materials that were purer and somehow more real than any materials to be found on Earth, so that merely to stand here and drink everything in with his eyes was to be transported to another plane of consciousness. There were gauzy curtains here, and incense braziers. The smoke from the incense rose up in myriad unearthly colours to create misty mountain landscapes above, and the curtains cascaded down from these landscapes like sparkling waterfalls. Far, far above the landscapes of smoke there seemed to be the dome of a ceiling, shining a beautiful nacreous colour. But it was hard to tell whether this were really the ceiling or some marvellous alien sky. Beneath Paul's feet the floor appeared to be a kind of marble made up of delicately shifting colours. But there was a strange depth to the floor. It was as if the floor were actually a sheet of polished glass fitted in place above some weird coral reef and the reef itself were moving as smoke does, its colours so ancient and rich he could smell them.

Paul was so absorbed in his dazzling surroundings that for some time he did not notice another presence in his vicinity. The figure was standing by one of the incense braziers, seemingly waiting for something. When Paul's eyes finally rested on this figure and took it in, he was stunned. It was the character he had dubbed 'The Turquoise King' in his jotter. It stood some twelve feet tall, swaying slightly, like someone on stilts. Wearing a mask of striking black and white markings and swathed from head to foot in turquoise robes, not an inch of its flesh was on display.

The figure bowed slightly and indicated that Paul was to follow it. Then it turned and swept away between curtains. Paul trailed in its wake.

Paul was escorted through a veritable maze of these pastel-shaded curtains—a maze of cloisters and courtyards that swallowed each other in shifting perspectives. Every step he took brought him fresh astonishment. The place was alive with the paradisiacal song of birds and the gentle murmur of streams from the smoky landscapes above their heads. Paul saw great tumescent fish splashing in those streams. One of them seemed to roll its grotesque eyes at him in mid leap. He was aware of whispers in these landscapes too, as of a wind full of voices, though he was unable to place the source of the whispering. It seemed to come at once from the birds, the beasts, the leaves, the streams, the mist, the very rocks themselves, and he had a very uncomfortable feeling that whatever they were whispering about, it concerned him.

When Paul looked carefully to see if he could determine exactly what was holding up these curtains and the acanthus-like landscapes above, he noticed what appeared to be a network of beams, intricately carved and brilliantly coloured, with something of the totem pole about them.

At last Paul's escort paused momentously before the opening in another pair of curtains, as if to announce that they had arrived. He took the edge of each curtain in his hands and flung them wide. When what lay beyond was revealed to his eyes, Paul felt himself in the presence of wonder too thick, heavy and honey-sweet for tongue to tell, like the impossible backwards flight of the humming-bird. This was the jewel in the foil of all the more-than-earthly wonder through which he had wandered to get here, and he blinked, as if at the threshold of a throne room at the heart of the sun.

At the centre of the magnificent chamber now visible between the curtains, was a great divan with a jewel-bedizened canopy on which reclined the celestial form of Petite Beige herself. She wore the golden headdress and breastplates and the loincloth—tight on the hips, diaphanous between the legs—with which Paul was familiar from the slave-auction picture. Paul was reminded instantly of Boticelli's Venus. The divan was the gigantic clam-shell, and Petite was the pearl of divine beauty within. And as if the whole chamber had only lately risen from beneath the billows, everything seemed to drip with golden light.

Circular steps led down from the divan, and on the level floor at their foot were a myriad flaming braziers and incense burners. Between these, servants moved sedately to and fro pursuing unknown errands. The servants seemed to be black and white in equal numbers, but all were over six foot tall, naked but for gold-lamé codpieces, and possessed of such fine muscular physiques as to make one gasp.

From the far ceiling hung candelabrum and censers, and also a number of ornate, shiny cages, which seemed to contain some species of monkey. In fact, more of these cages crowded away into the shadows at the edges of the chamber, most of them resting atop great poles.

But it seemed to Paul that it was the queenly figure of Petite that lent all this a splendour that it would not otherwise have possessed. Even at this distance he could feel her presence, sensual and divine, like the heat from some primal flame. Her worshipful flesh was before him, living and real, animated by some proud and untamed soul. Some instinct he had never known existed told him to fling himself to the floor in veneration. But he was not in control of his own movement. The sticks kept him upright.

His escort advanced into the cavernous boudoir and he followed involuntarily. The sinister sticks attached to his hands, and, he now noticed, his feet, were beginning to bother him greatly. He felt a kind of antagonism in the way they yanked him and he was mistrustful of whatever unknown power manipulated them. But there was much to occupy his attention apart from these bullying wands. As they passed in the midst of the servants, Paul's eyes were drawn ineluctably to their codpieces, which seemed to him unnecessarily large. For some reason he could not help taking the size of the servants' genitalia as a personal affront. Then there was the cool composure with which these servants glided by. Paul was convinced that this composure was a mark of contempt for him. He decided to ignore them in return, and focused his gaze upon the majestic embodiment of desire ahead. As he watched, two black servants fanned her with large, feathery punkahs on poles, and one well-oiled white servant, sporting a pony tail, brought her a chalice of wine and some fruit on a platter. Her movements as she took the chalice were like the wild, graceful movements of a leopard. In Paul's eyes there seemed to be a bright outline of unreality around her, as if she were superimposed onto this scene.

As they neared the divan on which flesh had assumed the shape of its greatest possible glamour, Paul became increasingly aware of something that disturbed him even more than the sticks and the servants. He felt naked. It was not right that he should stand in the presence of the exalted queen of cheese-cake with no barrier between them, both as a mark of respect to her and as protection for him. What he felt towards her was as obvious as it was shameful. He was *a priori* bound to feel as he did, because she was who she was. And because she was who she was, and because he was, too, he also had no earthly right to feel this way. His presence before her was by definition an offence. And he feared what his punishment might be.

His escort began to ascend the steps, and, having no choice in the matter, he followed, feeling himself drawing closer and closer to the symbol of his ultimate delight and his ultimate fear. At last they gained the head of the stairway. His escort bowed deeply and spoke in a hollow voice.

"He has come, Your Majesty."

"So I see."

She delivered her line in a manner at once smart and corny. Although there was nothing clever in the content of her words, somehow the tone made it clear that there was no one more chic or sophisticated within a ten-thousand mile radius, and maybe even in the whole fiery-orbed cosmos. It was impos-sible not to be impressed. This was star quality.

She turned her gaze to Paul and he was instantly overcome by a curious sensation. Until now his relationship with Petite had been entirely one-way. She had been a part of his visual world, of his awareness, but he had been no part of her world. Now the image was seeing him, too. He felt as if he had come into existence for the first time ever—and that existence was immersed in the awareness of a sex goddess.

"So, my chamberlain has brought you here safe and sound. Why don't you take the weight off your tootsies?"

She patted the divan beside her, making the silk sheets ripple.

In some confusion, Paul did as she bade him. He was embarrassed to find himself floundering clumsily in the sinking luxury of the divan. It was at this point that he realised the sticks had disappeared. He had climbed onto the divan entirely of his own volition. While they were there the sticks had been a source of irritation and disquiet, but now they were gone Paul found himself doubly embarrassed to realise that he was in charge of his own actions.

He sat awkwardly on the divan with legs sprawled, his back against a heap of cushions so soft they seemed to be lulling him into sleep. There was a gap of one or two feet between himself and Petite. Her proximity seemed supernatural. The voluptuousness of her body was on an entirely different scale to that of any woman he had seen; it was a body that in its perfection truly belonged to legend. It was as if a force field of sensuality surrounded her; this impression was heightened by her perfume, a spicy potion that seemed concocted to bring the senses under its sway. Coming into contact with this force field, Paul felt himself smart all over with sexual excitement the like of which he had never known and had only imagined dimly at the dirtiest peaks of his adolescent sexual awakening. After his first glance at Petite reclining next to him, he trembled and did not know where to look. He found himself gazing around idiotically as if surveying his surroundings with great interest.

As his gaze swept the chamber, he caught glimpses of the creatures in the cages. They appeared to be a type of hairless ape, though it was hard to tell whether they all belonged to the same species or not. On the one hand their grotesque features displayed a variety that would seem to argue for a number of different species. But, on the other hand, they all seemed to possess certain features in common. They were all as skinny as spider monkeys—skinny to the point of emaciation. Disproportionately large heads with wide, thin-lipped mouths and deranged, bulging eyes lolled on necks like knotted ropes.

Their long and creeper-thin limbs were tangled in the confines of their cages. Their faces bore expressions that were extremely unpleasant, making Paul wonder if they had been bred that way artificially, because he had certainly never seen such expressions occurring in nature. Many of these scraggy simians were actually drooling, and Paul noticed more than one playing with itself, letting its rancid jism splatter onto the floor below. Finally he found these ape-creatures too revolting to contemplate further and he transferred his gaze glumly to the tightly-muscled and gleaming buttocks of a black servant closer at hand.

"Hey, Buster! Am I so hard to look at?"

It was Petite Beige. She was clearly becoming impatient with Paul's coyness. Since it now seemed it was rude to do otherwise, Paul turned his eyes in her direction. He was afraid of how squirmingly naked he would feel when he looked upon her beauty again, but it could not be helped. There she was, her hands now hooked playfully around one of her dainty knees, giving a smile that all but twinkled, and bathed in a light of ambrosial eroticism. Now it seemed that she had taken on the pastel hues of nostalgia, like the fading colours of an old film. A spray of soap bubbles blew up behind her as if from nowhere. In that instant Paul became dizzy. The image before him blurred. He saw something white and gooey, like a bee larva wriggling in its cell of wax. Then the dizziness passed and Petite came back into focus again, this time even more vivid than before.

Paul was struck by the paradox of the sex symbol. It was as if she were clothed and naked at the same time. Or to put it another way, it was as if she were holding a conversation upon something completely unrelated, such as gardening, whilst vigorously bringing him to climax. Now, whilst going along with the pretence that sprang from clothes and words, Paul let himself soak freely in the unspoken sex behind the pretence, as in a deep bubble bath.

"Don't you remember me, Homunculus? You seem a little stiff."

Paul could not tell whether she were mocking him. In the dream, the word 'homunculus' was a simple term of endearment, like 'honey-pie', and Paul did not think it at all strange. At Petite's urging to remember, though, vague recollections of some other, infinitely remote life, were stirred up that were completely lost upon waking.

Disorientated by strange memories that threatened to drag him down like an undertow, Paul found himself unable to answer. His lips moved, but no words issued forth. He simply gazed at the collection of living curves that were Petite and felt himself disappearing from the toes up, until only his eyes were left, these existing only because they were witnessing Petite Beige.

"Relax, Kiddo, the vaudeville's about to begin. Don't you want to watch the show?"

A limelight cut across the chamber and threw its circle into an area of darkness opposite the divan in the general direction from which Paul had come. In the centre of the circle was a speck. Burlesque music struck up and a jazzy pattern, like a species of Paisley, began wriggling from the outside of the circle towards the centre. Paul was reminded of the web of phosphorescence through which he had passed earlier. The pattern grew more distinct, as if being magnified by a microscopic lens, until a number of long-tailed things could be seen struggling towards a large nucleus that now occupied the centre where the speck had been. Some of these tadpole-snake things were white and some were black. At the same instant a white one and a black one penetrated the nucleus with their noses and an explosion filled the circle, shooting up in a column and creating a cloud like a great toadstool, before finally clearing away to show the two tadpole-snakes flattened into a strange pattern taking up the entire area of the circle. One of these flat Paisley tadpoles was black with a white eye, and one was white with a black eye. Together they formed a pattern like a '69'.

Now it seemed the 6 and 9 were doors. Through the black 6 there stepped an imposing Petite Beige in black leather and suspenders, cracking a whip; through the white 9 there stepped a winsome Petite Beige in a nightie. The music slowed. Paul found it familiar, but was unable to place it. The two Petites began a duet, dancing in a strange, writhing fashion, half burlesque and half allegorical mime.

"I'm closer to the Golden Dawn ... " purred the first.

"Immersed in Crowley's uniform," trilled the second.

They continued the song in this manner, eventually joining their voices in the lyric, "I'm torn between the light and dark, where others see their target—divine symmetry. Should I kiss the viper's fang, or herald loud the death of man?"

The limbs of the two Petites became entangled as they continued their interpretive dance in accompaniment to their song. Soon, like contortionists, they formed a 69 themselves on the floor of the stage.

"If I don't explain what you want to know," sang black Petite, from below, before the two rolled over.

"You can tell me all about it on the next Bardo," sang white Petite, having usurped her partner's position.

The two of them then proceeded to roll over and over in their 69 position until it was hard to distinguish one from the other. From somewhere within this Catherine wheel there came the wail, "I'm sinking in the quicksand of my thought," and with the word 'quicksand' a reverse-swastika flashed out from the spinning wheel in a black and white strobe-light effect.

Finally, the 69 wheel ceased to spin and a single Petite, who had been curled chin to ankles, got to her feet, dressed in a leopard-skin bikini. Still singing, she walked over to an open-topped sports car that in the dream Paul somehow knew to be a Porsche Spyder 550. She sat behind the wheel and panto-mimed driving until the very climax of the number, when the limelight was filled once more with the flash of an explosion and a mushroom-cloud, and bikini-clad Petite and car both vanished.

Beside Paul, on the couch, Petite was clapping delightedly.

She spoke again. As Paul looked into her pellucid green eyes and heard those first words he was gripped by a weird panic and sense of helplessness. The reality of his situation closed in on him, and there was nothing he could do but sit paralysed as words continued to flow from those tantalising lips, the words themselves gradually echoing out of time with the lip-movements.

"You are sleeping now. You are sleeping, and when you awake we must part again. But there is a way that you can come back and be with me forever. Remember me! I am your eter-nity. All you ever wanted. We shall be together for ten thousand years and more. We shall command the oceans and the fire shall burn forever in our palace. My chamberlain will show you the way . . . Through the corridor and the dark serpentines . . . You will give me every last drop of your love and I shall be queen again. Come . . . closer! Before the time is up . . ."

She made a motion with her hand, and a servant brought forth a platter, on which there rested six small glasses.

"Ten thousand years!" said Petite, raising a glass and look-ing into Paul's eyes. Shaking, he took a glass and held it up. Then Petite moved her arm forward in a hooking gesture, and Paul, thinking she was indicating something behind him, looked round. He saw nothing of interest and looked back in-quiringly. She made the same gesture and he understood. He tried to make that gesture in return, but mistimed it and almost knocked Petite's glass from her hand in a collision.

"No, no," she said with a sigh. "Look!" And she held his arm still while she hooked hers around it so that their arms were now intertwined for the toast. They drained their glasses and repeated the procedure with the remaining four. The liquor they contained almost made him choke, but in the midst of all this confusion his excitement grew like a furnace.

The servant took the platter away. Shadows had begun to close around Petite, but out of those shadows her lips glistened a deep, dark red. Her limbs were like flames. Some part of him warned that what he was about to do could only lead to catastrophe, but he no longer cared. Just one kiss of those red lips! Just to be enfolded in those arms! Just to let his hand roam across her stomach, and down! Something warm and fragrant engulfed him. In the shadows he saw the phoenix on Petite's breastplate spread its wings. A strange urgency took him. He felt around in quest of the flesh for one taste of which he would lay down his life. His hand closed on something soft and round. He was about to melt into ecstasy. Then his fingers seemed to go through something, as if he had clutched a soggy tissue. He drew back and raised his hand to his face. He caught a whiff of something unpleasant. It was semen.

Paul awoke to discover he had had a wet dream. For an instant, when he opened his eyes, it seemed the whole room was bathed in a ghastly red light. Then darkness rushed in and he was trembling violently. In this trembling it was impossible to distinguish lust from terror. He leapt out of bed and flicked on the light. His whole body was shaking and he felt a kind of hot, sick pain in his lower abdomen, as of diarrhoea. For a while he was completely at a loss as to what to do. Because he had to do something, anything, to diffuse his panic, and because it was, after all, the obvious thing to do, he decided to have a shower and clean himself up. During this procedure his thought processes became a little more ordered, but his fear did not abate in the slightest. As he washed himself he naturally became turgid again, and then rigid, and before he knew what he was doing, he was wanking furiously. He came with a cry, as if something had been torn out of him. Then he slumped against the mildewed tiles. At last the fear began to fade.

Excerpt from Paul's erotic notes:

It is no co-incidence that Petite Beige wears leopard-skin bikinis and bodices in so many of her photographs. It is an image that harks back to the stone fetishes of the 'thunder-thighs' Earth goddess of the Palaeolithic era. But even if we go back that far, it doesn't mean we are any the wiser.

I wondered before whether sex is an intruder from without, or whether it is projected from within. But the sexual meaning with which, for instance, the looming buttocks of a bending female figure are imbued, goes beyond all considerations of first cause. There is no without. There is no within. It is simply overpowering. It is the lightning of synchronicity. The same goes for seemingly artificial sexual signals. Consider the timeless wonder and excitement generated by the simple juxtaposition of the lines of a pair of knickers with the lines of the gluteal folds. How can such sensations be traced to a first cause? Even a relatively obscure phrase such as 'gluteal fold' contains enough association to pique my sexual appetite. Before the mind boggles trying to trace the erotic potency of this phrase, it is best simply to utter the shibboleth, 'synchronicity!' and stop the boggling where it starts.

And if there is so much power in an obscure phrase such as that, what about a common and time-honoured word like 'girl'? The hard 'g' dangles its legs out of the skirts of the word. The 'ir' in the middle is full of fuzz and bubbles. Then comes the clean, virginal 'l' at the end.

Paul arranged to meet Arthur outside the sky-scraping department store opposite the main station. The rattling bus was packed, as usual, and Paul had to stand all the way. By the time he alighted, darkness had fallen. The neon of the monolithic buildings all around flashed and rippled, seeming to Paul to proclaim the stupefying numbers that inhabited the city. "Millions! Millions!" screamed the lights. They were monument to a multitude of strangers whose existence was too much for any single brain to comprehend. The seething population whose Gestalt they were, in its vastness at once engendered the impenetrable, disorientating strangeness of modern life and recalled the ancient mystery of the origin of race.

A great coagulation of human shadows swarmed across the bridge from the station, on which beggars dressed in rags writhed for alms, losing themselves in a public display of agony. The shadows spilled from the steps and crowded the wide pavement outside the tallest buildings. Paul had become rather nervous of late, his senses too susceptible to stimulation, and for a while after he stepped down onto the pavement he felt the whirling panic of a child lost in a strange town. He waited on the steps of the department store building, making a conscious effort to calm himself.

By the time Arthur arrived, a few minutes late, Paul was somewhat more collected. However, he suggested they stop somewhere for coffee before heading on to Snake Alley, their destination. He feared the crowds there, and the garishness of the marketplace, would trigger a relapse into panic if he did not first compose himself properly. There were a number of cafés nearby, and as the two ex-pats headed in their direction they passed a man in a faded T-shirt and a broad-brimmed hat giving out flyers of some description. Without thinking, Paul took one, folded it and stuffed it into his trouser pocket. He did not notice at first, but for some reason, the man with the flyers was following them.

"Hey, wait! Hey! You speak English?"

Paul turned his head briefly to see the man half a step behind him. He did not know what the man wanted, but in the split second that he turned his attention on him, something like the whiff of desperation in the man's manner told Paul that here was trouble. He turned his head to the front and pressed forward, anxious to lose the man in the crowd. Arthur seemed to be abetting him in this escape by quickening his pace.

They crossed the road and slipped through the glass door of one of the cafés. With the danger apparently over, they took a table near the entrance and ordered their coffees. Just as they were settling down, the door opened and the man in the hat leaned in.

"Hey, Mister! You read the message? It very important. You read it?"

Paul opened his mouth to answer, but the man continued his babble. Suddenly Paul's anger flared up.

"I'm not interested!"

There was silence. The man looked at him for a moment with a hurt expression, and Paul regretted his lapse in courtesy. Then the man disappeared back into the human fog from which he had come.

"I think he has some kind of mental problem," said Arthur. "Anyway, what's the message?"

Paul took the flyer from his pocket, unfolded it and flattened it out on the table top. Silently he followed the lines of print with his eyes as if sidling down the zig-zagging corridors of some crazy labyrinth.

Do You Know The Way?

For those who are intelligence.

Gentlemen,

You have waited for a many long times. As you will know the candidate was arranged the mystical behind-the-scenes car crash in 1957. If you are intelligence you will know the inside-out of this message. The Beloved approved this body with the perspiration of fire. In the inside city, behind the buildings, the pigmies congratulated with the cabals. They are not ashamed of their deviations as well as abnormalities. Nobody realises the gist of the fire bird. Nobody exceeds She forever. She knew about the bloody revolution packaged with "white robe". She was not afraid of the political quacks nor of the exaggerated gangsters who repeat their schemes for her property on Earth. Those who are intelligence gave worship and fabricated the beautiful software for the access to the black spaces of the inside city behind the buildings where the fire bird incubates her every time. She is actually identical and homogenous to the shadows of the civilised societies on Earth. Do not be misled and agitated by those rumours and vilifications of the demons and bandits. Only

The Beloved knows the way to up-side-down the dimension of super logical reality. Only the kidnapped and innocent victim, lost in the dark serpentines, can know the frequency. To them are the tangible directions to the earliest fire. In essence, The Beloved infects the political plagues. She mazes the interceptors and the paranoiacs. She milks the insidious. Who was detained for more than one month in the private psychosis clinic.

Paul read this far before being overcome by a strange, mental exhaustion. He had the feeling that the labyrinth of words had somehow led him to a dead end. He tried to start again from the beginning, but it was no good. At the heart of Paul's exhaustion there seemed to lurk the disturbing impression that the contents of the message were addressed to him personally. Then there was the phrase 'dark serpentines'. Probably, he told himself, his memory was playing tricks on him and inserting that phrase in his dream retrospectively now. Or perhaps dreams exist somehow outside of time. His thoughts grew blunter the more he tried to cut an explanation out with their edges. The words of the flyer seemed in danger of opening out like umbrellas or mushroom clouds inside his mind to reveal some uncontainable truth. He withdrew from them instinctively.

"Well?" prompted Arthur.

"It seems to be some sort of political tract," muttered Paul.

He handed the flyer to Arthur and studied his face for reaction as Arthur read it. He was anxious to discover in Arthur something of his own surprise at the flyer's contents. From what he had read himself, he was a little unsure whether its strangeness was not the result of bad translation, although, as far as he could judge, it seemed this was not the case. He hoped that Arthur might dispel this disquieting strangeness by confirming it. At the same time he was afraid he had made a mistake in letting Arthur see it at all, as if what was written thereon somehow reflected on himself.

Arthur's expression did not change and he only gave an indifferent 'hmmm' before returning the flyer to Paul. An inexplicable dread descended upon Paul as he took it. For a while he simply held the flyer in his hand, his mouth open. The shadows on the paper were as if made of lead, and the words were a blur, ominous in their uncertainty. At last Paul managed to speak, stammering at first, his voice unexpectedly low.

"What . . . What did you make of it?"

Arthur gave him a sidelong glance.

"Have you been indulging in your hobby again? You seem a tad nervous today."

Paul drew back a little. Where did these words come from? They seemed to swell with some ambiguous intent. Were they a warning? An insinuation? A deliberate mystification? A subtle probe? He felt the unease of a chess-player whose opponent has made a bold, sacrificial move for which there is no apparent explanation. Before he had even thought about it he replied in kind with words unwontedly provocative.

"Actually, I tried withholding my essence for a while, as per your suggestion, but then something came up unexpectedly."

The silence that followed these words was indescribable, full of the moist ambiguity that had seemed to permeate Arthur's words a moment before. Then Arthur slurped at his coffee and gave an appreciative gasp and the ambiguity vanished as if it had never been. The two ex-pats finished up their coffees and went on to Snake Alley as planned.

※

The trailbacks from the figure on the screen gave the impression of some many-limbed Indian goddess. Or perhaps this was some fleshy tunnel, a human-shaped continuum with the figure at its centre, the final destination. Behind and between the trailbacks were glimpses of a profound darkness that sucked in the eyes, and across that darkness the trailbacks seemed to weave a kind of phosphorescent web. The figure was Petite Beige, of course. At the moment she was attired in the gauzy sleeves and pantaloons of a concubine in some fantasy harem. Gold shimmered—or shimmied, perhaps—on her breasts. Gold ran precious into the V-shaped canal where her legs joined her body. A ruby shone darkly in the firmness of her belly.

Paul had expected something like this. That his expectations had proven true only magnified his excitement a hundred-fold, just as these trailbacks multiplied Petite's body. Somehow, somewhere, without his noticing exactly when it had happened, Paul's life had been diverted onto a track where it was hard to distinguish between imagination and real life. The track was circular and it seemed there was no getting off it again. Paul remembered his notes on the impossibility of finding a first cause for certain associations, and this set him to wondering about his present situation. But the more he wondered, the further he seemed to stray from anything resembling a conclusion. He was inside the circle now, and it was too large and too dizzying for him to analyse it.

As he gazed in fascination at the figure on the screen, he tried once again to retrace the course of his current confusion. After he and Arthur had finished their coffees, he had folded up the flyer and put it back in his pocket. Then they had gone on to Snake Alley. He did not know if what took place there had any bearing on the matter in hand. They had wandered awhile through the market. He remembered the medicine stalls selling dried insects and reptiles. Then they had entered the arcade of Snake Alley itself. They had watched the snakes being slaughtered and perused the various shops selling sex aids and aphrodisiacs. Once there had been brothels along here. The snake cuisine was supposed to increase one's virility. They had stopped in one little shop and ordered snake soup, which they chased down with shots of snake blood and snake bile and some whitish liquor, in six small glasses on a tray. Perhaps, after all, this had no connection with his current condition, but he could not help turning these details over in his head.

When he had got back to his flat he had remembered the flyer and extracted it from his pocket with a strange feeling of apprehension. He was alone now. This fact was a source of both relief and unease. He read over the contents of the flyer again, his agitation even greater and his understanding even dimmer than before. At the foot of the text was the following caption, followed by a URL:

> Why is the super logical brain software defined
> as a psychotic by those sticky and corrupt people
> in Taiwan????? Beautiful software richly bless you.
> Last exit zone for those who are intelligence:

When he typed in the URL, he had hesitated before punching 'enter'. As yet the computer was innocent of the information it displayed in the little navigation window. Such a delicate, such a fatal difference between displaying that information and absorbing it! The cursor flashed at the end of the URL like a guillotine waiting to fall. Then down came the suspended blade, dyeing the URL blue as it inputted the information and activated the dormant elements therein. The screen pulsed darkly. The navigation window disappeared. First came the unfathomable night of inner space, and then the enticing super nova of lust that was Petite Beige, weaving a tunnel out of the trailbacks of her lubricious limbs. This was an ultramundane, cursorless zone that seemed to have nothing to do with the usual functions of the computer. Such functions had been entirely over-ridden, so that the computer was now nothing more than a window onto a realm otherwise utterly removed and inaccessible.

Paul continued to stare at the screen. Everything had changed because of this image. It was no good, after all, to try and trace that change, since it exerted its influence back as well as forward in time. Even the seemingly unrelated past now flashed with different colours that were a reflection of this image.

A new question occupied Paul's mind. Was this figure moving? Of course, it must be moving. How else could there be trailbacks? And yet, the harder he stared, the more difficult it was to detect that movement. It was as if he were so hypnotised by this opiate dance that each position the body assumed was eternal. No, she was moving! Surely! Slowly—slow as the movement of distant galaxies. Then, suddenly, hectic and wild, bucking and writhing like a disciple of Dionysus, working up to the frenzy of ecstatic trance. Then the speed was so great that it seemed static, merging back into awesome slowness.

Something like the tingle before a shiver, some piquant nervousness of the flesh, mounted in Paul's chest as he watched. What was this feeling? Was this not the burning and slippery essence of the female, turning him inside out with his own shame and self-disgust to reveal all the stickiness of fluids and guts that were his inner workings? The words of a certain poem sprang to his mind—"a *hortus siccus* of tits and knickers." He was a thief and these images were the spoils of his burglary, a guilty treasure trove he could not bear to leave. There was danger in his leaving it unguarded. There was danger in his walking the streets where other human beings were. They would surely know on sight that he was guilty of burglary. It was as obvious as if he were a wet-dreamer wandering in a reality where everyone else was awake. And then, he *wanted* to stay. He wanted to gloat. He wanted to abandon himself to his shame.

He locked the door of his flat. For the moment just to watch the screen was thrill and fulfilment enough. He could not believe he had got away with this crime. Ah yes, he had really pulled it off this time! That night he slept little. Even after he turned the light off, the screen shone in the dark, bathing the whole room in its sensuous rays. Whenever he awoke, Paul would sit up in bed for a while and wallow in that radiance.

When morning came he gnawed on a loaf of bread and took some swigs from a water bottle. He sat vacantly for a while and then phoned the school where he worked. He said he was sick. Well, it was true enough, wasn't it? He felt as if he had cut all links with the world. Now there was only him and the sweaty-palmed secret of the wish-come-true on the screen.

The image itself changed from time to time, transforming seamlessly from within to reveal a different Petite in a different costume and a different attitude. None of these images belonged to the photos that Paul had already seen. They were instead something like the ideal that his imagination had hungered for after seeing those photos, which it was itself unable to supply.

On the screen now, Petite was crouched on all fours with her bum in the air, like a rabbit. Her knickers seemed so smooth and tight that they were actually smaller than the abundance they contained. Their lines curved like the shore of a lake over the halcyon hills of the buttocks. The shoreline narrowed as it poured into the white vale that led eventually to the exquisite infolding of the entire landscape in the sweetly shadowed gorge of the perineum, where flesh rubbed against flesh in all directions. Of course, it was impossible to have a lake flowing over hills in such a way, but this was a moebius landscape of blushing flesh in which such anomalies seemed utterly natural. More than natural, it was perfect. These curves, these shadows, this complexion, this smoothness, this fullness—all of it said, "perfection". For some reason, as he contemplated this landscape, Paul was reminded of Easter—the sweetness of the decorated eggs, spring with all its freshness of new and frisky life, and somewhere in the background the sense of a greater resurrection.

Paul had the impression that this image was more than two-dimensional, that there was actually no screen here at all. But when he reached out to touch it, his hand encountered a barrier and the soft, shadowy indentations at his fingertips showed that a screen still stood between him and this bursting ecstasy, after all.

Still, touch seemed to be the only sense that was denied the juicy knowledge of this fruit. His vision was enraptured. He seemed to hear music, like a drum, and smell a fragrance, sweet on top with a musky tint beneath, as of deep places. He could even taste those curves in his mouth.

At last this knowledge was too much for him. All alone, he expressed this solitary knowledge and the excess of sensation it brought in the only way he could. Not once, but again and again, urgently or lingeringly. As the day drew on, the room was dotted with scrunched tissues whose odour was an incense offering to the sugary pink idol before him, and which kindled a mood fitting for his further self-abasement.

A day passed. At least, when Paul thought about it carefully, it must have been a day. As far as his feelings were concerned, however, there had been darkness outside and there had been light, there had been fierce heat and muggy clouds, and rain, and he seemed unable to put all these phenomena in any sort of order. Many days might have passed, or the whole cycle of day and night might have broken down, leaving in place of time and weather only rootless, drifting changes of mood.

At some point there had been a sunset. Paul did not remember taking time to observe it in a conscious fashion, yet there remained in his memory the impression of mellow liquid gold spilling across the buildings outside. There was a peaceful wincing sheen of light, like perfect silence. It seemed to blind without hurting. It left incandescent blushes of purple, green, red and orange behind the eyes. The sunset seemed to be saying, "This is the time when nothing matters and everyone can be alone at last." This sunset had sunk down deep inside him. Its liquid gold seemed to spill across everything still. It made the world remote and inconsequential.

It must have been early afternoon. Paul had slept very little, something in the stimulation of the screen freeing him of tiredness. Yet now it was as if he were just waking up, hovering somewhere between dream and reality. All the bread and water was gone. He was aware vaguely that he was hungry and thirsty, yet these sensations lacked all urgency, as if they were nothing to do with him. He was thinking that he should probably go out and have a meal somewhere. But he was unable to form clearly any idea as to why he should do so. As if it were a rumour he had heard long ago, he told himself, without conviction, that food and water were vital to his existence. It seemed an absurd idea. If eating and drinking were so much a part of survival, surely they would happen unconsciously, like breathing. The very fact that he was thinking about sustenance seemed to rob him of any motivation actually to seek it. The threat of extinction remained a dull and muffled nagging in his head, but he was not getting any closer to doing anything about it.

It was then that he heard the deep, rhythmical throb of drums passing by outside, like the tense, primitive pulse of the city itself. Then came the noise of firecrackers, so sharp that it hurt his ears. There must be some kind of festival taking place, he thought.

At last he came fully to his senses. He crawled across the bed and slid open the window, then the mosquito screen. The window was framed by aluminium bars, so that he could not stick his neck out far. But between buildings he just caught sight of some sort of procession. It lingered for a moment where it was, then, as at some given signal, moved on.

The sight of this procession, as well as the sound of drums and firecrackers, somehow gave Paul the urgency he lacked. He swung his legs onto the floor, stood in the centre of the room and surveyed his apartment. The tissues scattered everywhere depressed him. They seemed to signify something terrible, like the aftermath of a war, or incarceration in prison. The screen glowing on the desk attracted him, but this very attraction disturbed him. He had to get out, clear his head!

Because he did not want to feel empty-handed he took his umbrella from where it leaned in the corner. He checked his pockets and stepped through the door, locking it behind him. By the time Paul reached the streets, strolling like an archetypal ex-pat, with his umbrella for a cane, there was no sign of the procession. However, the drums still beat somewhere in the distance, and occasionally there came the aural whiplash of the firecrackers. Paul listened, ascertaining what he thought was the general direction of the vanished procession, and decided to cut through the alleys where he usually took his walks in the hope that they would take him closer.

He felt strange walking out boldly in the daylight like this—somehow dislocated. This, he thought, was the slightly sad, somewhat empty feeling that you have when visiting the school of your youth, recognising none of the faces, knowing you no longer belong. Only now, it was the whole world to which Paul no longer belonged. He had severed connections with it somehow. And yet, he was still here. He was ready to drift away. Surely he could not remain? But where on Earth could he drift to?

He walked through the same alleys, past the same dingy little shops, the same clutter of mopeds, the same children gathered outside the temple on the corner, but all of this he observed as through the remote, mellow light of the sunset he still carried with him, so that the brightness of the afternoon seemed faded and dim.

He came to the intersection where stalls and shops formed a little carnival of colours and smells with the various foods they displayed—fruit, fish, vegetables and meat—in amongst them a shop selling incense in neat red boxes. He lingered awhile outside an eaterie whose front was that of a fishmonger's—fish, crabs, shellfish, even toads, all wet and vivid on crushed ice. It seemed to Paul that all the bounty of the Earth was laid out before him, the dripping treasure of the ocean deeps. He became quite dizzy as he took it all in. He considered, for a moment, stepping inside the shop and partaking of this bounty. He was still hungry. In fact, his hunger had become fierce. He leant on his umbrella and tried to bring himself to the resolution to eat, to consume life as life itself consumed. However, the whole idea seemed ridiculous, impossible. All life had to offer him now were these rich, glistening colours, these mysterious patterns as shatteringly fresh and abstract as an empty blue sky. This display seemed to have nothing to do with eating, a peculiar enough habit in itself. It was set there merely to dazzle the eyes, a puzzle or an illusion.

Paul wiped his mouth in perplexity and regret. He raised his head, listening. Only the drums—only they could mean anything to him now. So thinking, he hurried away from the shop outside which he had hesitated, and weaved recklessly through the fume-belching, crazy traffic of the main thoroughfare, the world tilting as he did so, a taxi driver honking as he narrowly missed Paul's retreating form.

This was the area in which there stood the temple from which Paul had purloined the ghost money. He looked about, getting his bearings. The sound of drums seemed to be coming from some area vaguely ahead and to his left. He pressed on in that direction. He passed the temple and noticed the shells of firecrackers in the road. He turned left at the fruit shop on the corner. He was approaching the place where he had met the puppeteer. He came to another turning and looked to the right. Somehow he felt this road would only take him further away from his quarry. He stood blankly for a moment. Then his attention was caught by a dank little alley he had not noticed before. It was so narrow and dingy he wondered if it could lead anywhere at all. However, without further thought he slipped into the alley and followed its seedy twists and turns towards the unknown. Before he knew it, the alley brought him to sunlight again, to a place he recognised, and—to his great surprise—to the present location of the procession.

For a moment he was simply bewildered, as if the alley had taken him to some unexpected and unfamiliar place halfway across the world. Little by little, however, he pieced together what was happening. A crowd had gathered and were throwing some sort of paper, like confetti or ticker tape. Firecrackers were being let off with a deafening report. In the midst of all this, a number of celebrants in ornate costume were carrying what looked like a kind of palanquin, but which Paul judged to be some species of portable shrine.

The portable shrine was decorated with tiny, doll-like effigies of the kind that Paul had seen adorning the altars of many of the local temples. They were the lifeless passengers of this palanquin. The shrine-bearers jigged from side to side with a deliberate, aggravating drunkenness like that of traditional fools and tricksters the world over. It seemed to Paul's eyes that this clowning disguised a darker insolence and aggression. These pagan clowns at intervals made lunges towards a tiny temple in front of them, as if the shrine were a battering ram and they were using it to lay siege to the temple.

But these figures did not hold Paul's attention very long, for behind them stood two figures of much greater interest to him. One of them was the character that Paul had dubbed the Turquoise King at his first sighting, and who had later been introduced by Petite Beige as her chamberlain in a dream. This figure towered, swaying, above the crowd, its long, embroidered sleeves flapping darkly in the sunlight. Paul had the impression that inside this colossal puppet there must be a puppeteer on stilts. The second figure was the shorter character that had accompanied the Turquoise King in whatever ceremony had been taking place in those back alleys. Paul remembered this shorter figure as wearing red robes, but now it was all in black with a smooth black and white mask covering its face. It stood about five feet tall and was immensely fat. These two characters watched the spectacle before them and waved their arms about as if all this were in their honour, or as if declaiming grandly to the crowd.

Paul's first sensation on seeing the two outlandish figures again, at such close quarters, in broad daylight and while the crowd looked on, was plain astonishment. Somehow he had associated the characters with a kind of secrecy properly belonging to the realm of solitary experience; he had almost believed they were figments of his own imagination. Now it occurred to him that what he had witnessed in those back alleys had merely been a rehearsal for this festival. Still his sense of wonder remained undiminished. This wonder was an ominous thing. In the sunlight itself there was darkness. In the cacophony of the crowd and the firecrackers there was silence.

Paul attempted to get closer to the two figures the better to inspect them. During this walk he had felt remote from all that he witnessed, and even the idea of eating had seemed meaningless to him. Only in the presence of these two figures and the procession that accompanied them did that sense of remoteness disappear. He had found the only thing remaining on this Earth that held any significance for him. Exactly what that significance was he could not say, only he had been drawn here as if by the pull of gravity when all other centres of gravity had vanished. Still he was drawn on.

As he emerged from the shadows at the mouth of the alleyway, he sensed some reaction in the crowd, as if he were somehow part of the festivities. A number of spectators smiled at him, quite as if they knew him. He felt uneasy about acknowledging them, and instead pretended he had not noticed. He walked on until he was only a few feet from the giant and the dwarf. From this position he examined the costumes of the two minutely. With his eyes he followed the golden threads of the Oriental arabesques that laced their robes. Within the loops and waves of the arabesques were woven certain mythological figures—dragons, deities and so on. When finally his eyes arrived at the pill-box-like headgear that crowned each, he felt a terrible vindication of his fears. There, rising from the tangled flames of the arabesques, were the unmistakable figures of two phoenix. When he saw these, Paul felt his blood drain from his head down to his feet and away into the Earth, leaving only a cold emptiness inside him.

Meanwhile, the shrine-bearers had laid down their burden in front of the temple and were now standing back. From amongst them one came forward with a taper and set it to the fuse of a bunch of red firecrackers on the ground. Once again there came the deafening reports of the firecrackers, some of which exploded directly beneath the portable shrine so that it jumped and looked as if it might fall apart. There were cheers from the crowd and the shrine-bearers moved in again to resume their burden. It seemed the procession was about to move on, perhaps to repeat this strange ritual at another temple.

As Paul turned his head to observe this, he caught sight of a shaven pate in the crowd on the other side of the shrine-bearers. He knew that pate. Surely it was Arthur! An acute, almost tearful desire to speak to Arthur welled up within him. Paul made an unsteady lunge in that direction, against the movement of the celebrants and the crowd, who were now starting to flow the other way. For a moment he lost sight of Arthur. Then he reappeared, visible through a gap in the crowd. He seemed to be talking to someone. The person he addressed was tall and thin and wore a broad-brimmed hat. Paul realised that this person too was familiar, but suddenly it seemed to him that he could not bear to have his suspicions on this point confirmed, and he was gripped by an equally sudden fear of *Arthur* seeing *him*. He turned abruptly around and followed the direction of the crowd.

For some reason, as Paul foundered amid confusion and fear, only the giant and the dwarf, themselves not precisely auspicious presences, provided any sense of a stable reference point, and it was they that Paul fixed on as the stars by which to navigate this sea of bottomless doubt. He tried to keep them within his vision, craning his neck like someone struggling for breath amidst jostling waves. As he cast his eyes about in this panicky, floundering manner, he saw ahead of him the sad, philosophical face of the old puppeteer. Had everyone known about this festival but he?

The crowd continued to surge forwards. A hand took hold of his left arm, then his right. Two robed celebrants were smiling at him from either side. Perhaps, pleased at the novelty of a foreigner among them, they had decided to adopt him as a kind of mascot. Paul felt a curious relief, as if their support had saved him from drowning. But mixed with this relief was a new, indefinable dread. He was now bound to the authority of their guidance, wherever they might lead him. His presence in the festival had been officially recognised. Something irrevocable had been decided. The course was set.

The procession came to a confluence of roads, and seemingly without discussion turned into a scurvy little alley similar to the one that Paul had slunk down a while ago. The procession had to narrow considerably in order to squeeze into the confined space. Paul could see the swaying head and shoulders of the chamberlain rising above the mass of human beings, now entering the mouth of the alley, like the swaying mast of a ship steering into a narrow estuary.

Now that the festival was moving, the drums had started up again, low and heavy, on either side. The previous urgency was gone. In its place was a slow, solemn rhythm lending the shuffling march of the celebrants and the crowd a dignity almost regal. So much did the drums seem a part of the mood which now stole over the procession that they were almost subliminal, their rhythm no rhythm at all, but a thickening of the air into a congeries of bottomlessly resonant beats. Paul felt that resonance in his chest like a summons or a memory. These bass vibrations seemed to deepen the sunset he had been carrying with him to evening, with all its nervous sense of half-pleasant expectation, and then to night. This was *his* night, the night of his lifetime.

He could not keep from seeing the parade as a fleet of boats jostling together on the waves of some coastal sea where it became a great river, penetrating to the heart of some famous and immortal port. And now, superimposed over the view of the daylit streets, he saw waters black with night, fires burning on the decks of the boats casting long, broken reflections on the waves, columns of light that moved without moving, that were shattered and remained intact, that writhed like snakes over the sands of a desert. And the sound of the drums was perhaps nothing other than the solemn beating of the water against the hulls of the boats.

Paul was on the deck of one of these boats watching their slow, stately arrival at this destination of destinations without impatience, but only with the deep satisfaction of one who stands awake in the night of fate.

213

He remembered words he had heard in a dream. Surely they had brought him the gift of himself. His real self had been long forgotten. It had no place in the world. It would have starved here in the midst of the stark loneliness and terror, the wasteland of mere matter. It had been banished to the nethermost corners of his consciousness, from where it did nothing but look on helplessly in mute and sighing sadness. Most of his life it had been that way. Now that real self was emerging from its obscure and lofty corner, it was settling back where it belonged—in Paul's heart. And, after all, hadn't this long quest for mystery, for adventure, for romance and glory, however vague and confused it might have been, hadn't it all been for the sake of his real self?

Paul floated, seemingly without volition, closer to the mouth of the alley, the two celebrants still holding his arms. The crowd slowed in its approach, like backed-up water, the trickle that passed through picking up speed again. As Paul observed the movement of bodies at this bottleneck, a word rose inexplicably to the surface of his mind to describe it—'fulfilment'. His life was narrowing down to this single channel. Soon he would be sucked in. All the wide, glittering detail he had come to think of as his very life would be jettisoned as redundant. When he thought about 'life' becoming 'fulfilment', about an aimless ocean becoming a stream, he could not suppress a sharp sense of loss, something like the dizzying panic he had been feeling of late just walking the streets of the wide world. Here in the eddying before the final entrance to that fulfilment, the sad waters of the ocean he was to leave forever seemed to toss and pitch, like water about to run away through a crack in the Earth's surface. In those waters he saw so much, he never realised his life had contained such heartbreaking detail—his long years of failure, Mother, drunken conversations with friends that had to end somewhere and yet still seemed to be going on, relationships that never started, loves and lusts never told (just count them), studies that were never made use of, clothes worn and thrown away, music listened to and tired of, places seen from the window of a moving train and never visited, letters lost or gathering dust, days wasted—all this was running away down a crack in the ocean floor. And though there was panic and sadness attached to this wide world, that too was running away. Paul was feeling more and more detached. Fulfilment!

At last he came to the entrance of the alleyway and his two guides urged him into the gap open before him, which, in his dazed condition, he might have let others fill. He was strangely passive now, allowing himself to be tugged and jerked just as his nameless escorts saw fit. All but a slim shard of sky had disappeared. The buildings on either side seemed to emanate a grey darkness. As he was being impelled along in the current of the crowd, he noticed his escorts exchanging words with other celebrants. Objects of some sort changed hands. Before he understood the significance of what was taking place, something was being dragged over his head, as if by sleight of hand. It was a robe, as worn by some of the other celebrants, he realised. Then a mask was being fitted over his face. His vision was suddenly reduced to a keyhole view of a confusion of limbs and faces. Just as falcons are said to become perfectly docile when hooded, so, wrapped up like a puppet in these robes and mask, Paul felt no urge to struggle.

He was led on again, this time more forcefully than before. The alley seemed to be growing narrower still. There were some turnings, and Paul had the impression that the sky had disappeared altogether. Now there was only a murky darkness across which vague, robed shapes flitted like bats. A silence had descended. There were no more drums, only the sounds of scuffling and breathing, and Paul wondered if they had separated from the main procession. After a while it seemed to Paul that they were no longer in an alley at all. He was being led along a corridor of some kind. The walls of the corridor were not straight. They formed a tunnel, an oval web of dust and murkiness clinging to a goo of eerie phosphorescence. Paul watched the glowing patterns swirl. Was he still being guid-ed? There was the slightest suggestion of movement and noise around him. Then, in an instant of panic, he felt sure that he was utterly alone.

✳

When Paul came to, he was in his flat again, standing upright, blinking. He looked about, nonplussed.

Silence.

There was no sign of the mask or robes with which he had been adorned. He was wearing his usual T-shirt and chinos. Crumpled tissues were still scattered about the floor like votive candles. He turned his head, slowly, warily, as if he might catch out someone or something that was hiding and as if he were half-afraid to do so. There was nothing. And yet his feeling of suspicion did not subside. The procession, the drums, the faces in the crowd, the alley—had all of this been real? And if so, how had he been transported from the alley back to the flat without the journey leaving any trace in his memory? Or perhaps these events were not consecutive. Perhaps it was futile to try and order them in terms of linear events, cause and effect.

The flat looked, well, flat, like an envelope. It was hard to imagine that there was any such thing as outside. As Paul sur-veyed the room he was overcome by a feeling of nostalgia that was almost chilling. This flat no longer belonged to the world, it seemed, and he no longer belonged to the flat. Yet it re-mained vivid in his vision, somehow artificial, as if it were no more than an extension of the firework sheen of the image on the computer screen, which still silently displayed its mandala of erotic trailbacks atop the desk. Philosophers have speculat-ed that nothing exists without an observer. At this moment it seemed to Paul that the room would not exist without that image. Now that his gaze had rested on the screen, he could not tear his eyes away. The trailbacks were a tunnel, yes, but more than that, they were an implosion, sucking him in.

He moved, or rather, waded unsteadily, towards the screen. As he did so, he noticed the flickering pulse of trailbacks from his own limbs, like dust from the wings of a moth, as if he were leaving layers of himself behind on the air, as if he were dissolving with the effervescence of self-combusting energy. He kneeled before the desk and fixed his eyes on the image of Petite Beige on the screen. They were dissolving together, continually breaking through the upper atmosphere of here and now, arriving deeper and deeper in the moment. The chilling nostalgia that Paul had felt when surveying the room was now concentrated in the slow-dancing, quicker-then-the-eye dancing body of Petite. She was the intoxicating source of all nostalgia, all passion. The twist of gauze between her legs—surely this was nostalgia itself, insupportably, inexpressibly, nauseatingly sweet. This time, at last, he would rend himself asunder, he would explode his disgust, and his desire would be consummated. His hand involuntarily began a familiar motion and he felt a power greater than himself mount behind him at his stoking, and immense, banked-up energy such as that which sends a rocket into space.

A complete identification with this soft, delicious idol sank deep inside him, spreading a gamy taste. He continued to whip at the wet head of his dog-like joy with a rhythm borrowed from some invisible, primal dimension that calls all life to leap and surge upstream to sex and to death. The rhythm escalated in ever-tightening spirals, the power behind it spreading, building, gargantuan and dumb. Then the voiceless moment before the squirming, ungraspable instant of the peak. The energy could no longer be contained. The spiral went wild. The vast silence and breathlessness became a whimpering in Paul's throat. The energy whooshed through him, like a take-off. In a second of weak and queasy ecstasy he was wrenched inside out and emptied.

For some moments he was stunned by his wild, hurting joy. He felt some part of him was missing. It had whizzed away like a violent wind. But where and what was it? As he looked about, an injured animal, he saw that the walls of the flat, that the very air around him, was dripping away. It was disappearing swiftly in sticky dribbles of absence. And as the flat was eaten away in gooey festoons, something else was revealed. There was a vast darkness irradiated by the spicy scintillations of gold. Flaming braziers and incense burners stretched across a marble floor. Steps led up to a great divan. Through the soggy, collapsing image of Paul's former flat, like a fireman crashing through a burning door, there stepped a majestic and sultry figure. It was Petite, looking every inch the haughty queen that she was. She stood before Paul, legs astride like some horny colossus, and looked down at him, scornful and triumphant. He tried to move towards her, but he was weak, so very, very weak. Her body now appeared to be brimful of, to be made of, the shivering ecstasy that had lately ripped through him. Here was all his squirming inside-outness, his dribbly, drooling transport, his unbearable, ticklish vulnerability, his sticky self-disgust, towering above him on two mouth-watering legs. He put his hand out to try and crawl closer to her feet. As he did so he noticed his hand was now nothing more than a withered paw, the veins and bones protruding grotesquely. He felt like one of the squidgy, crumpledup tissues that he had scattered across the floor of the flat. With a great effort he raised his head. There, beyond the wicked, heartbreaking smile on Petite's face, suspended from the darkness of the far ceiling, was a shiny new cage. It was empty and the door was open.

The Waiting

there are only two hours in this long and tedious life
dying   and then being forgotten
                                        —Yang Lian

Something to do with violence
A long way back, and wrong rewards, and arrogant eternity.
                                        —Philip Larkin

NOTES *addressed to whomever finds them. Phones that ring in empty phone boxes. Strangers who introduce themselves on the urgings of an uncommon impulse. These things have been a fascination lurking at the periphery of my vision for some time—these things that until now have belonged largely to my imagination.*

In fact, I have picked up phones in empty phone boxes, and strangers have entrusted me with weird confidences. For some reason I now remember with especial vividness a sheet of paper I once picked up from the edge of a road. On it were scrawled the most whimsical of questions and exclamations. I could not help thinking it must have been written by a very young person. They themselves did not know what they wanted to say. But they had a desire greater than all the world to say something to someone out there. At the time the note seemed as bright as the sun and as fresh as the breezes of that day, albeit touched with a wistful longing. I even looked around as if the author might be watching. Now the brightness and freshness appear to me eerie and lonely and I wonder what has happened to that unknown person who tried to reach out to me.

The periphery has become the centre. A few days ago I found not just a note, but a whole manuscript. It was stuffed into a milk bottle and half-buried in the earth and dead leaves of the wood that separates this town from the next. I had been walking away from the footpaths, as is my habit, enjoying the luxury of solitude, when my toe struck an unseen object close to the roots of a tree. With something of the excitement of a child discovering a treasure worthless in the adult world, I brushed away the leaf litter. Usually such excitement ends in disappointment. However, when I saw the bottle I was not disappointed. The excitement increased, and something else flared up inside me, a fleeting sensation of dark certainty, though when it passed I could not say what it had meant. Perhaps it had been inspired by the damp darkness of the earth clinging to the glass.

The bottle had been bunged with shreds of polythene bag, but the crudely folded wads of paper inside were damp and soiled. I fished them out carefully and saw that they were covered with writing in a hand that suggested tension and racing haste. I began to read, first standing, then sitting. I read the whole manuscript before I left the wood. Even in my excitement I had never really anticipated or imagined anything like this. Not only did my excitement continue to grow, but that dark sensation of 'certainty' returned and spread until it was one with my excitement. What did my discovery mean? What had motivated someone to go to such lengths, expend such efforts, on a manuscript that no one might read? Words such as 'joke' or 'hoax', which might have explained the manuscript, just did not seem appropriate. Though I had to consider it something of the kind, and occasionally even chuckled as I read, there was also an unquestionable seriousness and consistency to it that made me uneasy. Here are the words that all too easily met my eyes, words that should never have seen the light of consciousness:

We think—no, already I am employing my habitual confusions, there is no 'we'—*I* thought that who we are is settled in the first few years of our life, if not before. But I have changed suddenly, and utterly, in my adult years. All that remains of the 'I' once held so dear are this body and, perhaps, memory. This change was simultaneous with knowledge of the truth. The lie that I was could not hold out against it. I disappeared. I reverted to the foundation upon which I was unknowingly built. Where I once was there is now an empty and fragile illusion, waiting to burst, to crumble, to disperse. Waiting.

Yxthahl—the Waiting. Stephen translated it for me. Literally, 'the Black Flame'. He told me it was a word resonant with many meanings. Now when I think of that word I see the Black Flame, and the image splits up as if seen through compound eyes, becomes many images, ever-circling. The Waiting is a corpse that will not rot. It is a darkness of a thousand eyes. It is the beating of an inhuman heart. It is the many set upon the one, brutal and bloodthirsty, in a dirty alley. It is the cold pornography of cash, lust like a boot in the stomach. It is an alarm clock that must be obeyed, an idol demanding sacrifice. It is dreamless sleep. It is drudgery and it is violence. And its eternal triumph burns in the Black Flame like a beacon of darkness.

Yxthahl. The word is a curse. To know it is to be damned. I can speak the word only with hatred, as if spitting. The Waiting. This is the nasty cold feeling in the pit of my stomach. This is what I have reverted to. The Waiting has already won. In the meantime I write.

I was never anything special. If anything distinguished me from others perhaps it was even a complete lack of any sense of destiny. (Now, in a strange, reverse disillusionment, I find I may have been mistaken.) Instead of riding out to meet my destiny, for some reason, my greatest instinct in life has always been to keep my head down and myself to myself. My parents were taken from the world and from me in one sudden, arbitrary stroke when I was only fourteen. They died in the flames of a wrecked car on the motorway on their return from holiday. I never saw their bodies. I never even saw the car. I had been staying with an uncle, and suddenly I was living with him. The world seemed very precarious and empty.

I was never really close to my uncle, and after going to university and finding a place of my own I did not keep in touch. Then, two years ago, he died of cancer. I have been very self-reliant and have had virtually no one to talk to in my life.

I say that I never had a sense of destiny, but even I must have had some expectations of that highly charged word 'life'. However, I passed through university without making any lasting friends or having any romantic interludes. Because of a certain natural advantage I graduated with an excellent degree, but before I knew it I had landed a job at a bank, and that was it. I had arrived at my life, only to find there was nothing waiting for me. It was a shock that left me bewildered and tongue-tied in the way that only nothingness can.

There was something unreal about my new life. I would be jerked out of soon-forgotten dreams at six a.m. by the grating alarm, my eyes sore and almost weeping with tiredness. I would force myself to shower, eat and dress in haste, all the time uncomfortably aware of the constricting tightness and neatness of my suit. And then the daily purgatory of commuting. Then the bank itself. I was just a junior administrative clerk, so I felt all along I was working in an institution that I did not understand. Perhaps because of this I developed the sense that there was something odd about the bank, my imagination playing strange tricks with the unknown workings hidden from me. Yes, I had been instructed on my most basic duties, but everything else I had to pick up as I went along, always with the feeling I was lagging behind everyone else. Those duties did not bring me into direct contact with the public. Instead I spent every day under the same strip lights as strangers oddly intent on their various tasks. Was I the only one who looked around with a question on my face? There were no answers, only a kind of surreal discomfort as I continued stupidly, strangled by my tie, scratched by my starchy clothes, and straightened out by caffeine. The hands of the clock would creep tortuously round the clock face, seeming to tighten the basic tense silence behind all that took place in the building.

In the evening I returned to this satellite town and to the silence and emptiness of my flat. Somehow I could never relax, as if even these hours at home were just another part of my work timetable. I felt restless and uneasy, but strangely enervated, so that it was the best I could do to fling off my jacket, loosen my tie and sit in front of a flickering screen for a while. Nothing held my interest. When I switched off the television the inrush of silence would strike me afresh. Sounds from outside made me nervous: the scraping of heels on the pavement, snatches of conversation that passed into the distance, the growl of cars. They were all, without exception, lonely sounds, suggesting a half-life of strangers ticking over all around me.

Feeling vulnerable in my own home I would sometimes cautiously open the curtains an inch or two. A chill came from the window. Outside was a streetlamp, and further, the blackness of night, a few stars here and there, glinting like cracks. I would shiver. It seemed impossible to get to know anyone in this town. Even if I went for a walk, there was nowhere to go.

So this was life, this empty waiting for some nameless thing that might never come. And then sleep—another blackness. Sometimes it came dreamless and exhausting, as if I had ceased to exist. But sometimes I would run abruptly into a great reef of dreams, looming up in terrifying, glittering complexity, dwarfing my waking life as I myself was dwarfed by the skyscrapers of the city where I worked. And suddenly the morning alarm again and the hellish confusion of half-consciousness in which reality mixes with dream, and both are paralysed. That I should forget my dreams so easily, though a certain aftertaste of awe remained, was to me a great and significant puzzle.

I suppose almost three years passed in this way. Although it was so dreary as to be unbearable, there was something so stupefying in the life I led that somehow I was unable to come up with any plan to combat it other than to wait. Towards the end of my third year at the bank, where every day I was as bewildered as if it were my first, something happened at the periphery of my awareness that was to be the catalyst for real change. The branch manager had a stroke and had to quit his office suddenly. It was uncertain whether he would return, but in the meantime we had a new manager, a very young-looking man called Stephen Colby. I saw him often in the office. He was tall and thin, immaculately groomed, and crowned with rather striking auburn hair. Although I did not give his appearance much thought, I had the vague impression of him as the son of a wealthy family, someone who had probably known since childhood that he was an heir, and had grown up in the expectation of taking the reins of business. I never did learn if this was factually accurate, but certainly I smelt power on him, and connection.

It was after his arrival that I began to have the conscious feeling that something was awry. I couldn't quite say what it was. Perhaps part of it was that I remembered some fragments of my dreams, images of flames and twisted metal that I felt sure had something to do with my parents. The dream-sense that clung to these images I struggled to articulate to myself. It was the sense of things not adding up, of something missing. And this, when I thought about it, was also the feeling that continued to irritate me in my waking hours.

In fact, there is little that could disturb me more than things 'not adding up'. I have always thought of myself as a supremely ordinary person. In fact I have one ability that many would consider almost supernatural, though to me it is the apex of normality. I have what is sometimes called a photographic memory. Those people whose memories do not keep such precise accounts of their experience perhaps do not even notice when the books are not balanced. They might think something odd; they had the feeling there was more of that or less of this, but they haven't been keeping track, so who is to say? The thought of living with such vagueness and uncertainty, to consider it natural to have all your life a nebulous cloud of heterogeneous memories, to be ultimately uncertain even of what happened yesterday, or a minute ago, I can only conceive of with the deepest horror.

This is why a very little thing came to bother me greatly. Not exactly next to where I sat, but at what might be called a knight's move away, I noticed an empty desk. Nothing very unusual in that. What troubled me was that I realised I could not remember how long it had been empty. If there had been a person there once, I should have been able to recall them, and if not, I should have been sure it had always been empty. Instead there was this glitch, this hair in the gate of my memory.

The empty desk began to preoccupy me so much that I even made sure to pass it whenever I had to go anywhere, though I was a little self-conscious that someone might notice my odd behaviour and wonder what I was up to. The chair was always pushed in tightly, neatly. When I saw the back of the chair and the general bareness of the whole desk I was assailed by a sensation resembling nostalgia, which made the hairs prickle on the nape of my neck. This sensation was like that of a familiar perfume smelt after an interval of years. But in its wake there came no images, no memories at all.

This was the most definite focus to my sense of the world being askew. Perhaps the mystery could have been easily solved if I had only asked who had last occupied the desk. Perhaps. However, it did not even occur to me to ask. Since I first discovered that not everyone possesses a photographic memory, I have kept a perfect silence about my own, as if it were a weapon I did not want confiscated. In a similar way, a sense of guilty secrecy hung about the empty desk, and it seemed better not to mention it to anyone.

My life really was so barren that my infatuation with the back of a chair was something like an event. Humanity, as it bustled around me, was strangely subdued and hazy, like the distant sound of waves. Then I was surprised to find another presence on the shore of my existence. Stacy, who worked at the desk behind me, was now leaning over my desk, trying to coax me into taking some tedious load of work off her hands. I knew very well there was nothing in it for me. At school the only time a girl would ever talk to me was when she wanted help with her homework. The 'rewards' always went elsewhere. Just as I was reflecting that nothing much had really changed, someone else appeared behind her. It was Stephen.

"It's no use trying your feminine wiles on Brendan," he said. "He's pining."

These words had a very peculiar effect on me. From the hazy sea of humanity, Stephen suddenly stood out with an almost feverish lucidity and closeness. First of all, I had never expected him even to have noticed me, let alone know my name. Also, there was his tone of voice. On the surface it was nothing more than the pseudo-cynical banter of any office. I have always been annoyed by the lack of respect apparent in such banter. But usually it is quite meaningless—repartee designed to allow the speaker to appear charming or witty without disclosing the least part of their true self. The ring of humour here, however, had an altogether different hollowness to it. I felt as if the words he had uttered were the vilest, most hateful obscenities, oozing a deadly contempt for both Stacy and myself. Those last two words, in particular, had something enigmatic about them. They echoed and re-echoed in my head as the two of them stood there. Just as a child, told they look like they are about to cry, will find it hard to hold back tears, so those two words convinced me, I was indeed pining. At that moment I loathed Stephen with an utter fury of the heart. And at the same time I admired him and might have flung myself at his feet.

"I wasn't trying anything," said Stacy feebly. "We were just talking, weren't we?"

I didn't answer.

"Forget it, Stacy, you're not even his type."

"Oh yeah? What would you know about it?"

"More than you think. In fact, I think I know his type very well. And it's not you. Well, am I right?" He looked at me.

I was so stunned I simply nodded, even with Stacy standing watching.

Everybody likes to have someone to dominate. But amongst human beings the chain must end somewhere. In the office, for some reason I could not fathom—though, thinking about it now it must have been my lack of aggression—I was the last link in that chain. As well as having to perform my own duties, I was somehow unable to refuse a number of people who thought they could use me to eliminate whatever menial tasks they did not care for. I really didn't notice any exceptions to this rule of dominance. Anyone who could take advantage of it did, unquestioningly.

After the day he had appeared at my desk, Stephen too began to assign chores and errands to me. I did not mind this so much. An errand for Stephen had priority over all other errands and was often a convenient escape. Both the loathing and the admiration I had felt for Stephen on that first occasion cooled as I had more to do with him, though neither disappeared.

One day he called me to his office. As I arrived he was just getting up and putting on his jacket. I thought that we were about to leave, but Stephen made no move towards the door. He looked at me as he shrugged the jacket onto his shoulders, and then smiled strangely, pausing in his movements. I could not help feeling as if this meeting were the continuation of an exchange that I had forgotten, or, since I could not forget, an exchange of which I was somehow ignorant.

"I want to show you something," he said.

What was it? Was it something in his movements? Whatever it was, that sense of the world being awry came back at that moment, like ripples visible from Stephen's figure. Something had winked in and out of existence. A fish's tail. An optical illusion.

"What do you think that is?" He pointed to the corner of the office.

I saw only the wall, but thinking quickly, I said, "A safe."

"Almost right."

He walked over to the wall, raised his hands and then, speaking in some ugly, sibilant tongue, he made a series of complex genuflexions in the air. At once a section of the wall sprang open and stood slightly ajar. The hairline that must have framed this door had been entirely invisible, and so sharp were its edges now that it looked more as if the matter of the wall had been refracted than as if a door had appeared. When I saw it I realised that's what I had felt at Stephen's first words when I entered the room—something like a door opening.

"This way."

A strange foreboding came over me at that moment at the sight of the portal to which Stephen ushered me. But somehow that foreboding seemed to push my reluctant body from behind. I really could not back out.

The section of wall closed behind us, leaving not the least indication there had once been an opening. We stood in a tiny, metallic cubicle, facing the doors of a lift.

"Do you know much about the history of this bank?" Stephen asked as he punched in a code number with the speed of habit. I watched his fingers intently.

"No."

"Not many people do. Actually, this is a very old bank, and a little bit unusual. Not just the institution in the abstract, but this building in particular."

The lift doors slid open and we stepped inside. We started to descend.

"Your workmates are . . . really of little interest. Mere background." He was beginning to mumble, as if he did not expect me to understand, but simply felt like letting his words wander, "but you, Brendan, you have a tiny little clue, don't you? What a strange thing it is—a tiny little clue. I thought, anyway, it would be amusing to dispense with all the tedious conventions of detective work that lay before you and give you a denouement so huge you forget what the clue was in the first place. Far more interesting to sabotage the story, don't you think?"

The attention Stephen was paying me had an unfathomable quality to it that was paralysing. Neither did I know what to make of the outlandish sequence of events that had led here— the strange language he had spoken in the office and the hidden door. As if trying to follow a stronger swimmer out to sea, I found that the further he led me from shore, the less able I felt to turn back, though I did not know where he was going and only managed to clutch the bubbles and swirls that formed his wake.

The lift stopped and the doors swished open. We stepped into a brightly lit, windowless chamber at whose centre there stood what looked like a coffin draped with a black cloth atop a funeral bier. The air was chill, and I guessed we were deep underground. Actually, we could have been anywhere, such was the isolation of the room. We could have been floating in outer space. Stephen glanced about sharply. He had taken on a briskness of manner that made me nervous. Then, without further ado, he whisked away the black cloth like a Matador's cape and threw it to the floor.

What was revealed astonished me more than any coffin would have. Standing before me, like one of the wonders of the world, the perfectly preserved monument of an ancient civilisation, was a ziggurat of bullion. I had quite simply never seen so much gold in one place before. I was struck by conflicting impressions. First of all there was the cold, prosaic fact of the metal ingots in front of me, not especially attractive, indeed, rather ugly. But the knowledge of their economic and political value shrunk down so compactly to fit in this space, like a neutron star, had about it the nasty impact of a jackboot. Then, when I stared for too long, the metallic ugliness began to take on a glorious lustre, and I could see the ingots even as the steps of some pagan temple down which ran the blood of ten thousand human sacrifices.

Stephen had been watching my face and clearly was able to measure much of my reaction.

"Interesting, isn't it?" He observed. "It makes a difference seeing it. This is what makes the world go round, here, a hard, tangible fact. Touch it. Go on."

I did as he said.

"There. You see. Anything is possible. Now, why do you suppose gold has been considered so precious all over the world since antiquity? After all, it's only a metal, with very limited practical use."

He didn't wait for me to answer.

"It does not tarnish. It does not rust or decay. Permanence! Gold represents permanence, and permanence is the foundation of true power. The money that we deal with is nothing without this. Money is only tokens and promissory notes. Its value fluctuates. With time one currency supplants another and the old becomes worthless. Gold outlasts the rise and fall of nations and economies. You may well have thought about this before, but I am telling you now because it may help you understand what I show you next.

"This, by the way, does not yet officially exist. It has been vouchsafed us for services rendered. I don't think I have to tell you to keep it to yourself."

As he spoke Stephen set about covering the gold with the cloth once more. I looked around the chamber. The artificial light glared on white tiles. One wall was lined with square, metal doors, like safety deposit boxes. Apart from that the place was bare. Perhaps it was the lack of visible exits, but the room seemed strangely divorced from all context, and I was soon in the grip of an airless, suffocating feeling.

I grew restless. I wondered what Stephen was going to show me.

Once the cloth was settled on the bullion, Stephen glanced at me again, approached a featureless section of wall and proceeded to go through the same gestures and evil-sounding incantations as he had in his office. Exactly as on that previous occasion, a section of wall 'refracted' to reveal a coarse, raw darkness. It was not a distilled, empty darkness, somehow, but a sort of ore in which were mixed all manner of amorphous impurities. The chill in the room increased. I shivered, and not only with the cold, but also because that chill had laid upon me like the heavy hand of death, that could crush me on a whim. There was also an odour wafting from the opening, a pungent odour—some sort of incense. But somehow, perhaps because of the black shape in the middle of the room, it only made me think of funerals, and I did not like it.

At that moment, as if to try and puncture my involuntary awe, the only remark I could utter was a stupid one that sounded hollow on the air.

"Is this something to do with the Masons?"

"The only reason you've heard of the Masons is because they have relatively little power," said Stephen coldly, and stepped into the darkness. After looking about me again, I followed.

I found myself in a passage of considerable size, its walls and ceiling obscured by darkness. I faintly saw something ahead that I knew must be Stephen, and I ran to catch up. The ground beneath my feet felt gritty. I gained Stephen's side and slowed down, a little relieved.

"This passage seems to be carved out of rock. How far down are we?"

"We are not underground. We are Outside."

"I don't understand."

"You will."

Something in Stephen's phrase, 'Outside', awakened in me a sense of indefinite wonder, and I searched the chaos of shadows about us all the more, to fathom his meaning. As I did so I noticed for the first time where the faint light was coming from. There were wall brackets, and in these burned torches. But their flames were not natural, yellow flames, else I would have seen them before. They looked as flames might look in the negative of a photograph, flickering with a black and greasy light.

I had become very aware of my own heartbeat, and of the vulnerability of the life it sustained. And now something fell upon me, heavier than the most terrible darkness of depression I had known after the death of my parents—a kind of desolation. I thought of the word again, 'Outside'. Yes, it seemed to me the passage was lonelier than the most far-flung of uninhabited isles, and the stirring of air here was more eerie, closer to the quick, than the waves and wind around such an island would be.

The passage turned to the right. Soon we came to a descending stairway. At its bottom was an arch lit by more of the black-flamed torches. Beneath the arch was the immense slab of a door. Carved in its surface, with an ancient dolour that belied its simplicity, was what I soon saw to be an open hand with an eye staring from its palm. In the background to this representational design were more abstract figures that I took to be some kind of mandala or map of the heavens. When I looked closer, these designs took on a curious resemblance to the cogs, wheels, springs and so forth of some clockwork mechanism. For an instant I thought of how my ignorance of the bank's hidden, inner workings had played on my mind and related that vague uneasiness to these images.

On either side of the door were small alcoves in which burned incense. This must have been what I had smelt before. I had no idea how long torches burnt for, but I knew incense burns fairly quickly. These sticks could not have been lit long ago. I stared, fascinated, at the door, until it seemed to me that I could hear my own heart booming from the other side and see the stone bellying with each beat.

"What is it?" I asked finally.

"*Qioxtl*, the Seeing Hand."

With these words Stephen dropped to his knees.

"Kneel!" he hissed at me.

I obeyed, as if forcibly thrust to the ground.

Stephen uttered more sounds, this time different, in the now familiar tongue, whose words were as spiky and poisonous as a scorpion's sting. (I had even started to think of it as the Scorpion Tongue.)

There was a rumbling and the slab opened before us.

I followed Stephen again through another passage, this time quite narrow, and then, suddenly, we emerged into a spacious chamber, lit gruesomely by more of the torches, yet still retaining a swarthy darkness, like smoke, upon the air. Also heavy upon the air was a long-entombed, gangrenous odour, somehow offensive to the moral sense as much as the olfactory. This stench seemed to emanate from the pit or pool that took up most of the floor space. In this pit something black stirred vaguely, like a pitch bog. On the far side of this pool of blackness there appeared to be the shadow-choked openings of other passages.

Before I could ask any of the questions that rose ominously within me, as if my gorge were rising, Stephen had dashed around the walkway surrounding the pool and was grovelling at the foot of an idol placed at the room's mid-point. Unsure what to do, I followed tentatively. There seemed to be nothing of ritual or show in Stephen's performance. This was genuine obeisance, such as ritual is later based upon. I had not suspected Stephen was capable of such a thing. My disgust at this spectacle increased the loneliness of our surroundings. However, I did not like to stray far from Stephen's side. Soon I was quite close and could see the nature of the idol clearly. Like so much else in this strange realm it was composed utterly of darkness, so that it was almost a concavity, an absence, rather than a presence. My heart sickened when I saw the features of this sculpted darkness at whose foot Stephen still abased himself like a dog slobbering at a bone. It could not have been called anything other than a demon. The body that crouched atop the plinth was anthropoid in as much as it had arms and legs attached to a torso. But its sinuousness made me shudder, and its limbs ended in webbed talons. Its head was that of a beast, though not any I could name. Something between a bull and a hound, with small horns and ears that hung down, goat-like. I was reminded, more than anything else, of the pantheon of Egyptian mythology, of beast-headed gods such as Bast and Set.

At last, completely unselfconsciously, Stephen got to his feet and looked at me craftily. For the moment I ignored him. This was not mere awkwardness on my part. I was still too fascinated by the statue to tear my eyes away. There was something horrible about it, though I could not work out how a mere inanimate object, in three measurable dimensions, could be so horrible. An absolute aura of the forbidden emanated from the thing, so that I did not dare approach too near. Was it the posture, perhaps? Or the fact that such a sinister object had been expressly created for some sort of worship? The closest I could come to what I thought was the truth was that this aura was something to do with the material of which it was made. But what was the material? Surely it couldn't be onyx?

Finally I turned away, unnerved. Since my surroundings put me on my guard, my eyes crawled over everything in searching and urgent fascination, and my attention moved naturally to the pool of darkness not so far from my feet. I drew back from it instinctively as I might the edge of a cliff. And just as one feels giddy, liable to be sucked over the edge by some perverse accident, when standing on a cliff top, so I felt in danger just standing in that room. This was the source of the evil stench, and the sight of it was just as morally offensive. I could not decide whether it were a single object or a body of liquid, whether it were alive or 'inanimate'. Certainly it moved. It bubbled and rippled and occasionally sent out tendrils like the horns of a slug.

Stephen took advantage of my dumb fascination to recommence his stony oration.

"We have passed through a mirror. On this side, the Outside, things are on a larger scale. And of course they have greater substance than the tiny surface world of reflection we are used to. On that side you saw bullion, on this side you see 'black gold'. Not oil, of course, though, come to think of it, not dissimilar. This is the physical, three-dimensional manifestation of the eternal stuff of the universe. This is the permanence that is the foundation of all true power. *Yxthahl!*"

I heard those cursed syllables for the first time and Stephen began his slowly unwinding explanation of them. His words seemed to ascend, at once bleak and grandiose, like a stairway from whose top the whole universe might be viewed. What was before my eyes gave those words a dizzying reality, and each turn of the stairway held some silent shock for me, a forgotten exhibit in a ruined museum of horrors.

"The Waiting . . . The Black Flame . . . What you see here is a scale model of Eternity. Of course, it all exists simultaneously. Everything is already over. Once you actually see it like this you know that our human notions of progress, of travelling towards a light, are nonsense. Look at it! It is stagnation itself! It is a blackened morass. It is a corpse that will not rot. Waiting for Eternity. Waiting. Craving. Hungering. You understand? There is nowhere to go, and so the Waiting turns inward. All those things that the human race think evil or unnatural, gratuitous destruction, joy in the infliction of pain, the brutal wasting of life, disorder and despair, these are the very things the Waiting feeds upon. They are its only means of fulfilment."

As Stephen spoke and I gazed at the inscrutably stirring darkness, I began to see, fleetingly, the images he conjured up. No, indeed, they were not images; they were realities. The things I glimpsed, the work of human beings, I do not wish to describe, even in order to execrate them. Of course, history has left to us reports of atrocity, but they are vague, or where they are explicit, our imagination is vague. To know that such things can happen even once would have made me despair for the human race. As yet, however, I did not 'know' anything. The enormity of what I saw was belied by its flickering nature, so that the impressions I received were only a little above subliminal. At length Stephen's hypnotic monologue came to a halt, and I seemed to wake up. But when the parade of sneering evil had passed, such was its insidious stealth that it left me feeling confused and violated.

"But this is really just the entrance hall here," Stephen said. "There is much more to see. So much more."

After his voice and that tarry pool had made for me a magic lantern of nightmares, I should have had enough. Why did I continue to follow him? Was it because, now that I knew a lit-tle, my ignorance was beginning to terrify me? It's true I felt the need to know more. But that was not it.

"Wait here," said Stephen. "Don't worry. You'll be safe for the moment. I'll be back very quickly."

He walked briskly, yet cautiously, to the openings at the far end of the chamber and disappeared into one of them. I waited. It occurred to me to escape the way we had come, but apart from my strange desperation to learn what I did not want to know, I felt Stephen's confidence was something I had to han-dle very carefully, like blackmail. And above all else, yes, I was simply paralysed. There was no choice. I watched myself as if trapped in a body I was unable to control.

I suppose that Stephen was only absent for a few minutes, at most. When I heard footsteps from the further darkness, how-ever, I felt a virtual paroxysm of fear. I had almost forgotten that he would return. He walked halfway back towards me, then hissed, "Come on. All clear!" and turned around again. As we wandered between ominous walls, my scattered wits began to gather themselves and I wondered afresh, with a new sobriety, about our surroundings.

"Where are we?"

It was as if I had only just managed to frame the question.

"I told you, we're Outside. There's not much more I can say than that. Outside all you ever knew. Outside the world. Outside space. Outside. More than that you learn by looking. These passages go on forever, but it's dangerous to go too far without knowledge of the right shibboleths and so on. The more you learn, the more power you have, the deeper you can go. Some, who attain great power, go in deep and never return. You understand what I'm saying? In the game of promotion we're all alone. The higher you go the lonelier it is."

He laughed. His voice echoed along the cave-like undula-tions of the passage. I followed those echoes in my imagination as if to discover what distance they travelled in this infinity of stone before dying again into silence. All alone? Stephen's words became a question in my mind, and suddenly I did not dare to follow the echoes too far. It occurred to me, also, that Stephen's laughter had sounded as hollow fresh from his lips as it did bouncing off stone.

Suddenly we stopped. Set in the left wall of the passage was an arch. Beneath this, in place of a door, hung a mouldering tapestry.

"In here," said Stephen.

I followed Stephen past the tapestry and was surprised when a light flickered on to reveal a high-ceilinged study, its walls lined with books.

"Electricity?"

"Of course. Too bright for some, but for novices it's very useful and congenial. If you want answers, real answers, this is where you start. Here we have every single volume of importance that has ever been written. This is the true literature of the universe, and it makes for thought-provoking reading."

He drew a sturdy tome from the shelves with an air of reverence compounded with outright fear, as if the object might be lethal not handled correctly.

"*The Autobiography of Money*," he intoned, gazing at its rotten spine. He gave an English title for the tome, though the scrawl on the spine was in some curious worm-like script. He looked up again, scanning the panoply of similar spines. "Yes, they're all here. *The Undying Idols. The Book of Exits. Gleanings of Yxthahl.*"

He seemed lost in reverie. I stepped forward to examine the books for myself. Taking my cue from Stephen, and from the venerable appearance of the volumes themselves, I handled them with extreme caution. Out of the few dozen tomes whose names I perused, there were hardly any that I recognised. The least obscure among them was probably an edition of De Sade's *120 Days of Sodom*, which, to all appearances, was an original. There were works here written in many different languages. My memory has enabled me at least to be familiar with the general shapes of every script in the world, but there were some scripts here I could only conclude were not of the world I knew.

"If I wanted to learn the truth, where would I start?" I asked.

"At the beginning, I suppose, with *The Record of Pnath*. There's a translation into English somewhere by one of those who went deep and never returned."

He hefted the book in question, hoary with dust, from its resting place and passed it to me. It was so large I found it difficult to hold open. Cradling it awkwardly I opened it at random and read the words still vivid as yawning decay on the time-spotted page:

> From the unplumbed aeons that were before Pnath the Uncreated, as a mist about her shattered and inchoate edges, the grey and many half-shapes of Fleeting Things flocked to other spaces. And again, after the clouds of aeons had trailed away, and the Desolation was upon Pnath, and made a waste of her terrible canyons, and there was only the loneliness of a stream whisked from a precipice, and the memory of the Grey and Fleeting Things was only as the memory of deceiving laughter, there came from spaces unknown the dreary spores, and into the blackest recesses of the half-slain Pnath and quickened her with life.
>
> It was a twin life, struggling in the slime of her rock-splintered womb, and which became the final, cataclysmic end of Pnath the Uncreated. And the largeness of creation perished with her. From her split belly spilt the poison of her undoing, the

twins 𝔜xthahl and 𝔐narthrl. 𝔜xthahl was a jelly cloud of darkness and a spitting dragon-tongue of lightning. 𝔐narthrl was a blind and sickly whelp, shivering and pale. And in the instant of their birth 𝔜xthahl knew all and fell upon the puny 𝔐narthrl with her stinging tails of suns and stars, and swiftly settled the battle for all eternity.

I grew dizzy as I read, dizzy with a thin nausea. Perhaps it was the absence of any human figures in the text, or the unpleasant cloudiness of the translation, lending the book a feeling of dusty obscurity that choked me. Or perhaps it was my surroundings, the sense of mildewed antiquity in that one volume multiplied by the spines of all the other books, till I felt myself spiralling into the bottomless well of time. At any rate, I could not read further, but passed the noxious fragment of unknown things back to Stephen, who replaced it with a satisfied air. He then paused and observed me closely for a minute.

"Life is a snuff movie," he said. "If you're not the assailant, and you're not the cameraman, and you're not the audience, you must be the victim. You don't want to be the victim, Brendan. I've shown you a great deal already, but let me show you in simple terms what happens if you let yourself be the victim."

Was he concerned for me? Surely not. Concern would have been against the spirit of his words, and besides, I could find it nowhere in the rapping brittleness of his tone. As he moved over to a roll-top desk I wondered what his motivation could be. From the desk he took out a number of box-folders. He chose one, seemingly at random, and brought it to me.

Inside, in bunches of flip-up cellophane pockets, were numerous photographs with something of the air of police evidence about them. However, though the content was similar, in spirit they were entirely removed from such photographs.

240

The first one showed a human figure curled up on the ground in a protective ball. He was at the centre of a pool of blood. Blood spiked his hair like grease. Something about the way the body was slumped told me, if I couldn't have guessed anyway, that the figure was dead. Beneath the photo, on a label, was the caption, 'Homosexual dance instructor'.

Other photographs with similarly laconic captions of 'explanation' followed. Many of these captions are unrepeatable. As well as photos showing the results of events, there were a great number that showed the events themselves, the protagonists, in most cases, undoubtedly aware of the camera. The scenes revealed to me expanded my imagination horribly and irreversibly with their blank reality. And when I thought my imagination could be expanded no further there would be some fresh horror. My limit of tolerance was very soon exceeded, and, in a husky voice, I asked Stephen to put the photos away.

"Had enough already? Well, perhaps we should call it a day."

Stephen closed the folder again and I saw a label on the front. There were some characters in a strange script, and below these, in English, "Acts of worship."

We left the study. Stephen paused outside, listening, intent, and then proceeded in a direction opposite to that by which we had come. He looked all the time keenly alert. I made careful note of all our turnings.

Before long there appeared a flicker of light up ahead that did not come from one of the wall brackets. Stephen stopped and smiled weirdly.

"I think this might interest you," he said. "It's a kind of . . . workshop. Take a look."

I walked over to the flicker of light. As I did I smelt that cloying, pungent odour again, the odour I had first smelt when the wall opened in the chamber of bullion. Here it was stronger. Both the scent and the flicker of light were coming from a room beyond an archway in the left wall. As I drew closer, I slowed, and my blood felt heavy within me. The tide of silence beat about my ears.

I stood with my hand on the edge of the archway and peered inside. In the dim light it certainly appeared to be some sort of shop. Here, in curiously fashioned braziers, there were spitting black flames like those of the torches, and also the yellow flames of great candles in ornate black tripods. Around the room were shelves and benches, everywhere stacked neatly with red boxes, sheaves of incense, candles. At first this was all I saw, relieved that, after all, nothing here broke the laws of reality as I knew them. Then I saw the head on top of one of the benches. The heavy feeling in my blood suddenly redoubled. There crowded in on me from the flickering shadows of the room all the parcels of horror that for some reason my brain had ignored in the first instant. Now I could not ignore them. Heads, limbs, torsos, all as neat and clean and tightly packed as the other goods stored here. Fingers branched out from narrow shelves, an assortment of claw-shapes, multiplied by shadows, as if reaching out for help, now far too late, or about to crawl away. Legs and torsos sat on separate shelves, the spare parts of mannequins. Here and there on the floor were pieces perhaps not yet sorted, a lone torso like a work in progress. Limbs dangled from the darkness, labelled according to unknown criteria. I wondered whether it would ever be possible to put all these dismantled mannequins back together in their original combinations.

I called these things 'mannequins'. How else could I endure the terrible paradox with which they presented me? It was nothing other than the eternal jackboot paradox of life and death. What was once animated was now mere matter. It was not strange that this paradox should make me imagine things. As I looked I sensed an evil presence that made the objects seem alive. The body itself was evil. It was the sadistic pleasure of the body to betray the individual it once belonged to, betray it with smiling scars and juicy redness, betray it in an affair with the butcher's knife, and thereafter to mock the individual by debasing itself in an orgy of anonymous bits and pieces.

The pieces seemed to crave my participation in that orgy. They had noticed my presence and were turning their attention to me. It seemed I felt the lust to betray me in the various parts of my body, but such great and rending joy was not for me. The room turned convex, bursting out towards me with grabbing, grasping images and bloody shadows. I turned away to escape, but I was weak, as if they already held me in their nightmare clutches and drained away all strength. Stephen was next to me and I heard his voice, once more with that low, projected intimacy it had possessed when I heard it that first time.

"Many people, more than you would believe, pass, living or dead, from the world's memory. Some of them end up here. They burn very well. Those Who Dwell Outside find their light and their scent pleasing."

But I could no longer resist the terrible weight of darkness, as horrible and crushing as the unknown depths of the ocean, that poured into me through the grip of nightmare—the stretching shadow fingers of what I had seen in that room— and I heard no more.

At the tops of tall mountains, in interstellar space, at the centre of a black hole—time passes differently in different environments. This is not mere imagination. Even human science can ratify this fact. I think that, in the realm known only as Outside, time is very curious indeed. It lengthened and wavered as menacingly as the shadows themselves. I cannot hope to write a proper account of my experience there. Time is short and that experience was like the long, long shadow thrown by the tiny speck of my previous life. I can say, though, that I felt my soul dying within me while my body continued to move about intact.

I regained consciousness to find myself supported on Stephen's shoulder, stumbling along like a paralytic. I let myself be carried in this way until we were back in the office, and Stephen gave me a glass of neat whisky. He did not even mention what had happened. He simply told me I could get back to work. I could not concentrate on my duties. I knew that what had taken place was not imagination. My memory is too sure for that. I was left, though, with the disturbing feeling, acrid as a wisp of smoke, that my mind had been momentarily extinguished like a candle flame. Now that the candle had been re-lit, to illuminate its surroundings once more, I could no longer assure myself that the new flame was the same as the old. I went home and collapsed.

I lay shivering on my bed, as if sick. I stared at the ceiling and a great many thoughts went through my head; thoughts that were too vast for my mind to contain. I had started out, it seems, long ago, in the Eden of illusion otherwise called normality, then the world had come to seem uncomfortable, awry. Now this! Now, recalling my mad flight home in all its frantic detail, I wondered how the world had ever seemed ordered and sane at all. Memory is a jigsaw. I had always assumed that because my memory is photographic that it is a complete jigsaw. But my knowledge itself is incomplete. Now I looked at all the different pieces and I could not fathom a single one of them. They were an alien language sinister with meanings I could never hope to understand. I hardly dared venture out the door to be lost again amidst the muddled, disparate pieces of that puzzle.

The ceiling began to spin. I lost track of time. I was vaguely aware of a distant, trifling alternation of light and darkness. It was hunger that eventually forced me from the house. I had not been to work for some days, I suppose, and I could not think of going now, of maintaining that pretence of sanity in a mad world. I wandered the streets wearily. Ate a takeaway on a bench by the river. Wandered some more, shuddering whenever a stranger loomed too near, their very presence a brutal violence in its impenetrable otherness. Contrary to previous instincts, I now found the places where people gathered in greatest numbers the eeriest and loneliest of all. But even in quiet places, everything my eye fell upon seemed so strange and inexplicable that it was a positive intrusion into my defenceless soul, all part of some surreal, inexpressible conspiracy against me.

Since everywhere the same nightmare reigned, I began to care less and less where I went, and drifted like a derelict. It was as I trudged along in this way, lost in the great homelessness that is the world, that I happened to pass by the display windows of an electrical goods shop, and for some reason stopped. I suppose it was the televisions. As is common in such shops, the whole display was made up of TV screens, most of them tuned to the same channel. It is not an original ploy, but obviously it works. Something about a flickering TV screen is like a flytrap for the mind, and when the screens are multiplied, so is the fascination. I wondered dimly what that fascination was. I glanced about me at the grey, beaten pavement, the portentous stillness of the grimy clouds that stretched from horizon to horizon, the slack melancholy of the poky buildings, and the premature dusk that made the very air dismal. In all this the window display was the only splash of colour, the only animation. What it offered was warmth, cosiness, in the midst of the cold and loneliness of the world. I could not hear the sound, but perhaps even more now that the images were mute, I saw in them an exploding rocket, a technicolour extravaganza of pure optimism. For a moment I was uplifted on the creamy, breaking surf of these images, and felt my heart swell as if about to break. Then I saw only the two-dimensional screens, behind which was nothing but the ugly tangle of circuitry. A commercial was playing on most of the screens. The bright world it showed was not the world I stood in. I knew how remote, how empty these flickering images were. It was a moment of vast, quiet revelation, a moment of ghastly loneliness. A terrible reality came into focus. There were these empty, brightly coloured, flickering lies, and then there was the nasty truth of the world. There was nothing in between and nothing else besides. Empty lies and terrible truth.

I stood there mesmerised by these miraculous lies, stood at the very axis of what then appeared to me as the most timeless and the most awesome of dichotomies. Stated simply, that dichotomy was Appearance and Reality. It could go under a number of other names: Advertising and Product. Publicity and Private Life. Innocence and Disillusion. But always the surface is false and superficial, and behind it is something vaster, uglier and more complex. Always we start with appearance, which seems to be all the world, and since it comes first we call it 'normality'. Then we arrive at reality, which is strange because it is not our home. Not my home, perhaps I should say. But we, I, am left with an insurmountable paradox. Reality is the strangest thing of all. It is twisted. It is wrong. It should not be. And that paradox, I realised, was the sinister essence that leered out at me now wherever I looked. Even now I set these things down in wonder, and as a kind of duty or compulsion, useless though it may be, because I know not just their abstract, but also their material truth.

As I stood watching I sensed some vague, grey movement from within the shop and hurried away with a shiver. My sinister vision did not leave me, and was as strong in my home as elsewhere. It was driving me mad, but there was no corner I could squeeze into to escape it. I found myself unable to stay in one place for too long. For some days I lived the life of a delirious vagrant. On one occasion I had stopped to try and find some surcease from my torment in the shadows of some trees in the park, there being the minimum of stimuli there to excite my paranoia. In fact, even the trailing branches and the grass stirred my anxieties, as if they were some subtle creeping death. But I stayed in the relative peace of that place in order to try and collect my thoughts. Then, on the path beyond the trees, I saw something that made me snap. A young mother was pushing a pram up the slight slope. The sunlight fell upon her face as she tossed back her hair. She was smiling in a meaningless, carefree way. How could this be? It seemed to me that I saw the quintessence of madness trundling into the golden sunlight. The mother and her child could only have been a few yards distance from me physically, and yet they inhabited another world. How easy to step over the thin line dividing ignorance from knowledge, but how far, far away the world of the mother and child seemed to me now, and its brightness bleakly infected with shadow. You can never go back. Perhaps it was their vulnerability that outraged me, but I burst from the trees as if catapulted, my heart jagged in its beating, ranting like a prophet with words that leapt from me quicker than my thoughts.

"You! What have you done? You are a monster! A monster of ignorance! You don't even know what an enemy you are to your child, but that only makes you worse. He'll never be able to rip out your poisonous roots from his heart! And you will feed him with your own tender hands into the jaws of darkness!"

I went on, surprised at the hurt, like streaks of lightning, in my own voice, surprised at my own stewed-up, spitting righteousness, my venomous scorn. They were the words of some doom-mongering down-and-out, but I was on the other side of them now. I identified with them utterly. My harangue,

247

however, began to fade. Even as I spoke, looking into her eyes, a silence and a shadow seemed to fall on me so that I could no longer hear my own words. I grew afraid, terribly afraid, and I ran. Maybe the woman thought I was simply a raving madman. I hope so. Perhaps, though, something in my tone and what I said found its way into the recesses of her heart. Perhaps that 'something' will always haunt her. But these are not the only two possibilities. Afterwards I examined the fear that had made me flee. Something had not been quite right about the woman's expression. I thought I had seen reflected in her perplexity a reflection of my madness. But perhaps it had not been perplexity, after all. Perhaps her expression had been a searching one, and she had been looking for something in particular, that she thought she might recognise. It occurred to me that I still only knew the little that Stephen had told and shown me. The world was very different to what I had imagined. There was no doubt about that. But what made me suddenly believe I understood infinity? What made me assume I held greater knowledge than those around me?

So the horror of existence spread outward from its every detail, ad infinitum, in implications and unknowns and possibilities, like some brain-torturing fractal. At the fractal's dizzy centre, I was ready to throw myself away or do myself any injury to escape this garish consciousness. I could not look to myself for the comfort or company that had once been there. I found nothing whose extinction was to be regretted. I stood on a bridge and thought clearly about these things. I knew I could not drown myself in the dark water below, but I looked at my reflection and thought of taking that reflection forever out of the world. Yet the very force that compelled me with greater urgency and more selfless seriousness than I could ever have known before, was also the force that thwarted me and made my self-destruction impossible. If I had faith in a god, it would have been easy. Even if I had an atheist's faith in reason, and the certainty that only oblivion waited, it would have been easy. But I knew that neither faith nor reason would save me, and I dreaded that death might not be the end to this endless fractal of horrifying complications.

These, roughly, were the phases of my wandering. I returned home after that and brooded upon certain memories. I was also forced to confront the present, and, bleakest of all, the future. I could not kill myself, and I could not survive in total retreat. I had no choice but to go back to the bank. As I came to this conclusion I felt certain that Stephen had foreseen this all along.

It was almost as if I hadn't been away. No one exhibited surprise at my appearance or questioned my excuse of illness. I fell back into my routine with a vague feeling of disappointment. It seems my absence had really disturbed no one at all, and now I had to face a backlog of small but necessary tasks that no one else had deigned to take on. If only these tedious chores had provided some distraction I would have welcomed them. But, on the contrary, distracted by other thoughts, I found my work all the more burdensome. Stephen passed by and nodded to me once or twice, but said nothing.

Buried in work I stayed at my desk after everyone else on the floor had gone home. I was in no hurry to go anywhere. My work was going slower and slower, however, and I decided, wearily, to take a break. I went to the toilet, thinking to splash some water on my face. The building was silent. I looked at the carpet tiles as I walked. When I looked up I saw Stephen hovering in the corridor outside the toilets.

"Brendan! How fortuitous!" he said in a voice that seemed to have a hint of the manic about it. "There's something I'd like you to help me with."

I walked closer, uncertainly. He gave a lopsided grin and produced a bunch of keys from his pocket, fitting one into the lock of the door. I saw blood on his shirt cuff and knew that something terrible had happened. And yet I felt as little choice in all I did next as if I had been implicated from the start. Stephen opened up the door and ushered me in. From every direction vision fell upon and seized me. A piece of Outside had been transplanted into the human world. Strange to say, it first met my eyes as a melancholy so deep and sharp I could not keep myself from weeping. Then the crimson became screams, silent screams still echoing in an endless accusation, a last, futile vow of vengeance. It seemed incredible that a single human could yield up so much horror.

"I got carried away," said Stephen in a dead voice.

I looked at Stephen. Indeed he had 'got carried away'. Even as I looked at him it seemed to me that his tenure in his body had become so loose that he might slip out of it at any moment. I could almost see his greasy soul losing its oneness with his frame, becoming a disgusting halo of ectoplasm.

"You're insane," I said. It was not an accusation, or a remonstration. I said it to myself more than to Stephen, in the manner of a private revelation.

"I fear not." He looked at me as he said it. "There are no limits, Brendan, no limits."

This was the closest to sincerity, to one human being talking directly to another, that his tone ever came. Even then it hovered near sincerity only uncertainly. I realised that Stephen was just as lost as I was; more so. He no longer had any use for sincerity, and though there was habitually something mocking in his speech, he no longer had any use for humour either.

"Let's clear this up," he said, after what seemed an age.

"How?"

"It's easier than it looks. We just need to get rid of the body."

"Who was it?"

"Why do you want to know?"

I shrugged.

"It was that bitch Stacy, as a matter of fact." He snorted dismissively.

I looked at her remains. I tried my hardest to see Stacy in the thing on the floor. Instead, what I saw most was an expression of Stephen. It was not just a mangled corpse. It was a detailed record of Stephen's inner sickness. More than the physical fact of blood and viscera, it was the queasy eloquence of these things that horrified. To take what should be the least horrifying of her wounds as an example, there was a purplish-black bruise, like the smoke of an explosion, on her inner thigh. In this bruise I saw the flowering of that lack of respect I had heard in Stephen's voice, and hated, the day he first spoke to me. All of this violence had been contained in that voice all along, and in that body, waiting for the cue to erupt. I seemed to see it now, dripping from his very fingertips, and I hated him afresh.

My eyes travelled to where the face should have been. Stephen's sickness showed itself here worst of all. I was caught in a vortex of unbearable nausea and loathing. I dashed into one of the cubicles and vomited, as if to try and eject what I had seen from my system. I would never be able to.

I felt something fall heavily onto my shoulder. It was Stephen's hand. He spun me around. In his grip I grew afraid.

"Make no mistake," he said, "this is not a game."

He dragged me out of the cubicle.

"You're all the same to me. You know, anyone with Knowledge can spot the weak, ignorant ones, like yourself, Brendan, a mile off. How ridiculous you are, walking about in all your stupidity in broad daylight."

Indeed, as his eyes bored into me, I felt it to be true, and with the unrecognisable corpse of Stacy beside me, I began to tremble violently.

251

All this was business. Of course. And had I not always known it to be so? Had I not long felt that dead dread of the business world occupying the centre of my existence, its abrading shadow eclipsing my heart? This building was a place of business, and Stephen had naturally come into the lavatories to deal with more business.

"Look!"

He shoved me roughly towards the mirrors. There were the reflections of Stephen and myself behind slender bars of blood. Indeed, I looked like a victim. I looked like someone who should never have made it this far alive. As I looked I noticed something in the splashes of crimson. There were signs here that had been made by a hand. They looked like two characters or hieroglyphs. Then I recognised them. I had seen them before in one of those old books Stephen had shown me. They looked like this: [Here Brendan wrote down two squat, baleful characters I am confident no keyboard in the world can reproduce.]

"*Xi Groughl!*" Stephen barked out the words. Without knowing their meaning it seemed to me they were at once a salute, a threat and an imperative.

"'Celebrate!' Literally, 'Reach for Eternity!' That is the one commandment of *Yxthahl*. There is no other. Now, wash your hands and face and make sure the way to my office is clear."

Stephen was quite clearly anxious about getting caught. In this world, he said, things must be kept secret. It seemed to me there was nothing secret about the mess we had to leave behind in the toilets, and nothing secret about the disgusting trail we left, in our hurry, between the toilets and Stephen's office. I was soon to learn, however, exactly how the secret would be kept. In the meantime I noticed, as I had before, Stephen's keen alertness. It occurred to me now that this alertness never left him for a single moment. The brittleness I had taken for easy confidence was in fact bottomless panic.

We heaved the thing that had once been Stacy through the same dark passage as before, that dead corridor leading Outside, and between our grim panting Stephen's words continued, echoing from the emptiness within him like some bizarre version of the last rites.

"You recall how I told you, Brendan, about people passing from the world's memory? Even now Stacy here is moving towards that fate. This is a sad little object we hold in our hands, much to be pitied. She feels heavy now, but very soon Stacy will never have existed."

Once more we knelt before the slab of the hand and the eye. Once more we passed into the chamber beyond. We dragged our burden to a place just before the black idol, and released her. Then, in the hurried, business-like manner of someone defusing a time bomb, Stephen sunk his fingers into the pulpy matter at the top of Stacy's head, and with some low and hastily uttered words in that inhuman Scorpion Tongue, he smeared the handful of blood and gore about the mouth of the idol.

He wiped his hand with a handkerchief. The job was not yet finished. Following Stephen's instructions I took hold of Stacy's ankles once more, while he took hold of her arms, and together we laid her remains in the pool of sticky blackness, which began to suck her slowly down into itself.

"It's a scale model of Eternity," said Stephen. "You see those tendrils forming and unforming—Eternity changes shape! Sometimes, very often, in fact, things that happened are drawn back into nothingness, like the eye of a slug. Stacy is going back where she came from. All of her. She is becoming one with the Waiting."

He showed me his handkerchief. It was perfectly clean.

"Only we shall remember her now."

Stacy had no longer touched any lives but ours. We were the bleakest of mourning parties, the only two souls to witness the lonely end that was all that was left of her. At last the surging blackness closed over her. Last rites.

It was like watching the death of Hope. As the blackness covered her, so I felt something close on and bury me. And, in my heart, I struggled.

"This can't be true!" I said.

Stephen did not respond. My words seemed to mean nothing to him.

"This is too unbalanced. There is too much darkness. Too much. Surely, this is just a nightmare."

"You think there should be equal and opposite forces? You think that's stable? That's *not* a nightmare?" He sniffed. "This is true balance. The majority of existence dominates the helpless and ignorant minority forever. The completeness of the domination creates the sufficient energy, in fear, despair and torment, to fuel the whole thing perpetually. Believe it. Well, since your mind still obviously needs a little broadening, perhaps I should show you what will happen to Stacy."

By now miserably void of any spirit of independence, counting on the dubious protection of my guide, I could do nothing but follow, even knowing I followed deeper and deeper into the inner workings of Hell.

We left that chamber by a different passage than on the previous occasion, though progressing then along very similar passages. At length, since everything that happened in that realm seemed to happen only 'at length', we came to a doorway. It was a simple, but impressive aperture in the wall; straight lines cut into massy stone, widening towards the floor. There was nothing to stop us from going through, but a certain atmosphere would have made me pause at the threshold if it were not for Stephen breaching the dark emptiness with no apparent qualms.

The anti-light flickered in here, too, illuminating, or rendering darkly visible, to some extent, our new surroundings. We were in a broad chamber whose walls joined in a polygon, reaching up to a ceiling hidden from view, and seeming to slant, as if we had entered the perimeter of a black ray. Set in these walls, as far as the eye could see, were lozenge-shaped alcoves, like the interstices of a web. And laid in each alcove was a naked, recumbent human form. The floor of the chamber, too, was half-crowded with bodies, some of them laid on biers, as if for dissection, some of them standing in perfect, unmoving ranks, like terra cotta warriors.

What place was this? The first confused thoughts that came to my mind were that it was something like a tomb, or a mortuary, but there was a quality to these bodies that convinced me they were not exactly corpses. They might have been sleeping, except they did not breathe. The awful effect of the whole scene was as if we had stumbled into the workshop of God, where lay his half-finished pieces, the dumb clay figures into which he was yet to breathe life.

We approached a cohort of these figures, and Stephen inspected them.

"These are protoplasts," he said. "They are perfectly neutral human specimens. Once they had places in history, but all of them have been invisibly extracted from the world. All of them have passed from the world's memory."

He spoke in the Scorpion Tongue to the nearest of these flesh dummies. At once a veil of cognition seemed to fall over the subject, and though it did not move a millimetre, it ceased to be a statue. I just detected a pulse start in its neck. Now Stephen gave commands in English, and the living automaton carried them out. At first I had an impression that the man—for the specimen was male—must be acting. There is something so unreal about such vacancy in a human being that I thought it must be exaggerated. But a few seconds' observation convinced me otherwise. There was no mistaking the authenticity of this object as it lifted its arms, crouched, crawled, curled into a ball, carrying out its master's whims blankly unaware of how ridiculous it appeared. Ridiculous as it was, there was no humour in this spectacle.

Stephen bade the creature stand again, spoke more words of that alien tongue, and then put his hands to its face. His fingers began to work like those of a potter, kneading the flesh about the eyes and mouth. When he had finished, and withdrew his hands, there were no longer eyes and mouth in the face. In their place was blank flesh, imprinted with the marks of fingers.

"Well, that's a small demonstration. The protoplasts are actually infinitely malleable in body and mind. They are the perfect puppets. They can even be returned to a semblance of independent life—and, after all, that's all independent life is—and induced to suffer, through the simultaneous memory of their erased existence and knowledge of their current condition, tortures of the soul perhaps unknown to any other beings in the universe."

"But, what are they for?"

"They're used in certain rituals known to the higher levels, and as reliable slaves. For people like you and I, Brendan, they are playthings."

"Playthings? How can you possibly play with them?"

"Use your imagination. I mean, *really* use it. That would be your wisest course of action from now on. All sorts of transformations are possible here. I can't guide you every step of the way. You're going to have to start taking your own initiative soon. I don't know if you're aware of the favour I have done you. Anyway, you no longer have much choice. I'm sure you realise there's no turning back now."

I had long been reluctant, out of a timidity resembling self-hatred, to voice any of my personal feelings before Stephen. Perhaps it was because he seemed the embodiment of all that was impersonal. Such feelings wouldn't stand a chance in his presence. But now that grudging admiration I had felt for him returned, and with it a desire to sacrifice my already doomed feelings to his impersonal assault.

"Perhaps there is no way back. But there's no way forward either. Evil and darkness—that's all that's waiting."

"Brendan, I'm going to let you in on some very specific information. First of all, I'm really only a neophyte. There are levels to our progression. If you want a goal, the next hurdle is *Qioxtl*, the Seeing Hand with Ultra-Sidereal Eyes, the Will of *Yxthahl*. *Qioxtl* waits as a guardian in the further darkness.

"The real horror of the situation is that there's no end to it. All I want to do is cross to the far shore and immortality. But to do that I have to leave behind the laws of human beings, the conveyor belt that leads to death. I have to move about on my own. I have to wade through blood and horror and madness, like any other god. And this to reach a shore infinitely far. And yet, there really is no choice. You think this is evil, *I* am evil. I tell you, I am good. Why? Because I am surviving. Survival is the only good. I wonder if you understand? I have unique consciousness. The universe would extinguish that consciousness. I shall not let it. That is good. Would it be any better to let the evil universe destroy me? Surely that is relinquishing any claims to moral value and influence whatsoever. Yes, survival is the only good."

Silence fell upon the last of his words. He shrugged and turned away, casually examining the other protoplasts. Perhaps he was looking for his next plaything. I don't know. In the weird hush I felt all left alone and turned to the soulless waste of the chamber, barren as the flinty surface of an alien planet. As if I had taken Stephen's words to heart—and since they came, as it now seemed to me, from the only other human in the universe, murderer though he was, perhaps I did take them to heart—I began to totter outwards, away from the centre of his knowledge and into the bleak, unending soul-death of the ultramundane. With each step came strength and a greater backlash of fear. And the result of this terrible swinging pendulum was that the vast workings of wonder were set in motion. I felt I was beginning to understand Stephen, if only dimly. Newly charged with independent wonder I approached one of the protoplasts where it lay upon its slab. This one was a male, long haired, and, like the others, naked. The eyes were wide open, and even appeared moist. Yet the only thing that was human here was the shape. In fact, I had never seen anything less human in my life. I could only think this must have been due to the anomalous condition of the body. It was not dead, but nor was it alive. It seemed to have been removed forever from those two relatively merciful states. It was an eerie dormancy, suspended on the threshold of a consciousness and animation that was not life.

I passed on, and now I saw a female specimen. Fear was everywhere in that place, but fear of what? Violence? Death? Had I started to believe that fear was merely an omnipresent emptiness like the darkness? But I was soon to learn there are many things to fear Outside. You can never foresee what shape they will take, or recognise the tell-tale signs of their approach until they descend upon you. Of all the things your fevered brain—a pin-cushion pierced through with bristling nightmares—conjured up to fear, there were still so many that you had not imagined.

This protoplast might have been an attractive girl, but to be attractive she would have had to be more than the sum of her parts. Here there were only parts with no spirit to unify them. All the same, there was something about the outlines of the face and body that struck me. They seemed to be saying, There is No Such Person. And yet here was the person, or her twin, or her echo. There was a mysterious nostalgia here, like that which had hovered about the empty chair in the office. And then I knew. It was Kate. Of course, there was no such person, and never had been, but here she was. While the protoplast mocked with its stillness, the real Kate, that is, the non-existent Kate who had once, never ago, sat in that chair a knight's move away from my own, came to life in my memory, perhaps the only place she now existed.

Yes, that's right. Kate. Another human being. She was the first I had met and recognised as such. And clearly she had recognised something in me, too, though I will never know what. And I had had, tentatively, oh so tentatively, a life outside of work and outside of the empty shell of my home. I had shared memories with her. There we were, in her car, parked by the edge of a cliff. Outside, the wind was ripping open the grey bellies of the clouds. Somewhere, out to sea, rain had started. It was visible as a vague, dreary wall that made me shiver. I was almost sure I could see the stipple of the falling rain on the waves beneath. But that must have been my imagination.

I have never been anything special. My greatest instinct in life has always been to keep my head down. That's what I did then, in the car, with Kate regarding me in amused curiosity from the driver's seat. I sat in my accustomed place in the passenger seat and I looked at my hands in my lap, wondering why they looked so awkward. And she extinguished her cigarette in the little ashtray on the dashboard. The seat creaked. She told me to look at her. I did. That's when I realised it's not only me. Perhaps I had learned it from others. People do not look at each other. They do not see each other. But now Kate was looking at me. I was no longer invisible. She knew how to look and how to see. I felt myself using muscles that had become cramped from long disuse as I looked at her. As if I knew, even then, that this wasn't really happening, that it only existed as the memory of a phantom event, everything inside that car became unbearably fragile. Everything inside the car was us. Outside was the blustering wind of the world. Us, as I had once felt Me—that same intimacy. And all so fragile that I grew afraid and shook when Kate's warm hand took mine.

Like Russian dolls, one inside another, that car seemed to contain many other memories of Kate. Some of the memories came chronologically before, and some after, but all were somehow dependent on those moments in the car when we first saw each other face to face. There was no doubt that these memories of something twice-lost were the most, the only, precious things on Earth, in all their helplessness, in all their worthlessness, weak as the most pathetic of lies—precious for being surrounded by a feeling like the end of the world. And all these memories breaking off abruptly like the cliff at whose edge we were parked. They spiralled into nowhere.

There was something else. I have a photographic memory—photographic, but, it seems, not infallible—and I was able to recall the most fleeting daydream from my real history. It was a silly, sentimental daydream of some unspecified girl, a sort of ideal female. It must have flitted across my brain for a few seconds at most. But that daydream was of Kate, and it tallied in every detail with one of the memories inside that car. Most incredible of all, it was a daydream from a time before I could ever have met Kate, even in my phantom history.

Now I stood dumbfounded and appalled over this anti-Kate. I had stumbled across what had 'become of her' in this grave of never-was before I had even known her. The whole revelation fell in upon me as if the far ceiling had collapsed. Not only her present limbo, but how she must have come to this, were thoughts that strewed so much discord in my heart that a loud groan escaped me. This barely human sound must have acted as a sort of summons to Stephen, but I was not aware of his presence till I heard his voice.

"So you've found her," he said quietly.

His tone was slightly changed. It was as if he had been waiting for this. There was something solicitous in his words, and yet now, at his most conciliatory, he was also at his most mock-ing, and I was more afraid of him than ever.

"How did she get here?" My voice almost failed.

"She wasn't happy in the office, Brendan. She needed . . . stretching. I couldn't resist stretching her. Then I felt involved, by extension, with you. I became, so to speak, interested. Now, I wonder if you'll appreciate this very *interesting* situation. I think you want her more than I do. You can have her. She's yours. It's better than love, if you know what I mean. This way you'll win every time."

No insult could have contained a more insinuating sting than this gift. The skin on my face burned. I could not look at Stephen. I looked to the side, my head wobbling on my neck. Very quietly I said, "You are my enemy."

"So you don't want her? Fair enough. I'll keep her instead. And *I'll* have her. Very stupid, Brendan. Very, very stupid. These may be playthings, but this is not a game. It's deadly serious. And you have decided your fate."

He came closer to me; too close. His presence was abhorrent.

"And I thought I was your friend. Imagine, a worm like you turning on me. What are you going to do about it? What are you going to do to your enemy?"

Yes, it seemed to me then that Stephen had always been my enemy, ever since I was small. And now I choked upon the old-est and bitterest hatred that ever was, and as its object jabbed at my chest, its poison rendered me as limp and impotent as I had always been. Once more I was out-smarted, out-muscled and humiliated beyond endurance. And this time, maybe, it would be my end. Stephen started to cuff me. I raised my hands. All about me, like wings, there seemed to beat the final insult, the final sneer that would be my utter destruction. Then he pushed me to the ground.

"I can't even take you seriously enough to kill. I'm going to give you something to think about instead. You can find your own way back. If you try to follow me, I'll crack your skull."

261

I sat there on the ground and listened to Stephen's footsteps disappear into the maze of distance and darkness. Only then did I realise how effective Stephen's presence had been in keeping the terrors of that realm at bay. Now the grappling, thousand-shaped shadows rushed in as if a light had been extinguished. I crawled miserable and whimpering to the bier on which lay the shell of Kate's undoing, as if seeking hope or consolation there. There was not a trace of either. But as I looked upon this form, identical in all but spirit to one strangely dear to me, I remembered the horrible offer so lately made to me, and certain thoughts reared up suddenly before me like monoliths of blasphemous worship. Utterly repulsed, I crawled away.

If Stephen's purpose in acting as he did had been to temper me to the facts of my terrible existence, then he succeeded. At first my instinct was to make myself as small as I could, and I found it impossible to proceed except on all fours. But this method of locomotion was slow and clumsy, and finally made me feel more vulnerable than ever, and I had to stand. Then I moved along touching the walls, like a blind man, though I could see the way ahead well enough. Eventually, I even began to walk unsupported. I might not have done this. In fact, I would almost certainly have remained in the gloom by that morbid bier, screaming like a baby in order to bring my doom down upon me more swiftly, had it not been for one thing. That thing was my photographic memory. I followed it desperately out of that nightmare like Theseus following the twine out of the labyrinth of the Minotaur.

Stephen's office was empty when I arrived there. God only knows what sort of sight I was as I slunk through the building and away.

I went home. I thought a great deal, my mind racing, so that I could hardly keep still for a moment. In particular I thought about all that Stephen had told me, and all he had advised. Perhaps it *was* time I took some initiative. There was no point in waiting. I knew now there was nothing to wait for. I had to act.

I had no appetite, but I forced myself to drink water and tea. I managed to calm myself sufficiently to work out a plan. I went over it again and again, wondering if I had missed anything in my calculations. In fact there were certain factors that simply could not be accounted for, and that was that. I was sweating. I felt so hot I had to undress. All of a sudden it seemed that I could hardly wait at all.

Very simple. Very simple. This was my mantra. Was it really so simple to defy the universe, even temporarily? But there was my secret weapon, that guilty secret that had made me furtive all my life. Perhaps this is what made the difference.

I thought only of the next step. Get to work. There were dangers enough to get through even in this. Then just sit at my desk and make it look as if I were working normally. And wait. This was important. Wait till I knew for sure that Stephen's office was empty. And then would come the next step.

I noticed, in the meantime, that Stacy's desk was not empty. There sat, in her place, a young man with sandy hair called Kevin. He had been working here for some time. Though this was the first time I saw him, I knew this without asking. I remembered it all seamlessly at that moment. Yes, this superficial, mocking surface called the world had come to seem every bit as sinister as Outside.

There was no sign of Stephen, and I was too distracted even to make much of a pretence of working. The strip lights flickered as usual, on and off. How many times a second? Darkness. Light. Darkness. Light. We think it is light, but there is darkness in the light. *More* darkness than light. It squeezes through. The world drifting off course. Lost. I had a terrible, splitting headache, as if it were my head the darkness was squeezing out of. I gulped down some aspirin and water and tried to get a grip on myself.

At last Stephen strode out of his office in his usual manner. He walked briskly past me without registering the least surprise. In fact, he hardly seemed to notice me, as if he had dismissed me completely from his mind. This bothered me, but perhaps it was for the best. Anyway, I had other things to think about. Now the office was definitely empty. My chance had come.

I got up and walked towards the office, trying to keep my pace slow and relaxed. I knocked on the door. There was no answer. But as if I had heard some, I inclined my head and gripped the door knob. Now, impatient and nervous lest someone should think me suspicious, I slipped quickly inside, shut the door behind me, and breathed a sigh of relief. I did not rest long, however. I hurried to the corner section of the wall that twice before had opened to me. Then I put my memory to the test and tried to get my tongue around the sounds that Stephen still repeated in my head. After a few attempts it seems I managed the correct pronunciation.

Then began my long, lone journey, not fleeing, but into darkness. All the way, like some weapon stolen from the gods, for whose theft I expected always a hideous retribution, memory was my skeleton key. The door whereon *Qioxtl*, the Seeing Hand with Ultra-Sidereal Eyes, was depicted upraised, as if forbidding further progress, groaned and gave way before me. Then the first chamber—but something was wrong. It did not take me long to discover the source of my unease. It was an absence rather than a presence that troubled me. An absence of an absence. For the idol of the demon thing had gone from where it once crouched, leaving only an empty plinth.

It was very hard to continue after that, but I had no choice. I followed the twine of my memory inward as doggedly as I had followed it outward. The passages I crept along were empty. Yet when I saw that emptiness, I only thought of the emptiness of the pedestal and quaked. Each corner seemed deadly, poisonous with shadows, yet I made my way at last to that chamber where I had seen the shape of Kate recumbent upon the bier. I stepped within.

I had already seen evidence that the place was not as deserted as it appeared, and I had no way of knowing what the movements of this place might be, or if Kate's facsimile would still be where I left it. If not then I was prepared methodically to search the thousand ghastly alcoves that scaled the darkness, so much of hope weighed for me on her discovery, and so little did I have to lose. I was prepared to go to such grim lengths, but found, to my excitement and great disturbance—for it presented me at once with the reality of my goal—that nothing had changed.

I had got so far and now came the step I had dared consider least. Before proceeding further it was necessary, suddenly, that I think, that I be sure of what I was doing. There was Kate, or her negative, chained in some oblivion neither sleep nor death. Here was I about to break her chains. But why? There had been some ambiguity that tormented me, but now I was determined my motives were not those Stephen had tried to incite in me. Stephen spoke of playthings. Thinking about it, he had acted as if I were a plaything too, an experiment, and perhaps that was even what he told himself. But wasn't his experiment, after all, to see if there were any consolation in the confidence of another being, to see if innocence could withstand his revelations, to find some way out of his loneliness? I cannot know. Only that, in his position those would have been my motives.

And my motives now—just not to be alone. That only! Even though the other thing tempted and made me waver, like the gateway to Immortality and Unknown Ecstasies left ajar.

Ah, but I would make the loser's choice and be damned, even if it were only because I was timid, only stupid, not good. I remembered Stephen's words: "They can even be returned to a semblance of independent life—and, after all, that's all independent life is." So I reasoned to myself, if independent life is only a semblance, anyway, and if I can conjure up that semblance now, what would be the difference?

I could delay the burglary no longer. I summoned up from my memory the shibboleths that Stephen had used to bring the protoplast alive. I spoke them. Just as with the other specimen, a veil of cognition fell over Kate's eyes. Yet she remained perfectly still. Now I hardly dared breathe, but I just about managed my next words.

"Stand up."

She rose from the bier and stood upright, motionless at its side. The impression I had had before, of the protoplast pretending to be under some sort of trance, was here magnified greatly because I knew these features so well. And yet when I looked closely I was certain she was not pretending. She had moved, but still she was not Kate. One look in her eyes and I turned to dust. How could she be so different to my memory of her, when physically she was identical? She was identical to Kate, and yet this was a monster. Her hair, her limbs, her mouth, all of it was monstrous, heavy with a sluggish madness, and I almost reeled away in horror. This was not even a woman. It was more a portal to infinite darkness, a sewer of the soul.

I steadied myself, though a dread greater than I had anticipated had fallen on me. The protoplast was still in some neutral gear. I had to put it back into the gear I knew. Stephen's demonstration had not gone that far, so I had nothing to draw on here. There was one hope. Stephen's instructions to the protoplast after he had woken it had all been in English.

266

"Kate," I spoke her name to her for the first time. "Remember! Remember who you are!"

I could detect no response.

"Something happened to you. I want you to go back, back before you were brought here. Remember me! Brendan!"

Without Stephen, and with Kate in a dubious state of consciousness indeed, my loneliness was dire, and I did not like to raise my voice. I waited awhile in silence. I thought I saw her eyes widen and her pupils dilate. I stared at her fixedly. Her head moved ever so slightly. Her lips seemed about to murmur something. And then the horrible ululation began that shattered those false memories of Kate forever. Whatever might once, in theory, have been true, this was the reality now—a bellowing, animated shell of unknown content. The thing began to stumble and to thrash about. Somehow she, or it, was stuck halfway, but halfway to what I did not know. Even its coordination was wrong. Blundering into the bier it toppled over and crawled upon the ground, all the time making tongueless noises in its throat, like someone drowning in a pitch bog.

I feared this new, unforeseen object, even more than I felt horror at its fate. My purpose now was forgotten. I dashed out blindly, reckless as the dark around me, leaving it to scratch and bray and hearing, as I did, what might have been words intermingled with the loud moans. I say 'might have', because the voice used the words as if they did not contain any fixed meaning. The words were like protoplasts; they could be turned into any shape of plastic monster. There was nothing there of meaning or sense to me. Or perhaps there were hints of a something I dared not recognise as sense.

"... coming, coming, coming ... hand ... no ... don't know ... coming now ... me ... undone ... lies ... coming ... undone ... hand ... undo ... undo me ... coming ... from outside ..."

These were the words that seemed to take temporary shape within the bubbling metamorphosis of the voice.

Out in the passage, I paused. There was no telling what the mad siren of that voice might have awaked. The emptiness of the passage seemed filled with my heartbeat. Then, from the darkness of the way I had not yet been, something, some stirring. At first it was merely a stealthy clicking, like a harsh, arhythmical musical instrument. I stood mesmerised. Gradually the clicking speeded up, in aural imitation of the lashing coils of a whip. Faster. Faster. And with this growing speed came a growing certainty in me, like a paralysing venom stealing through my veins. Faster still. A grating, slithering, like grinding gears, or the belt of an engine slipping off its wheels and screaming in useless revolutions. Like the blade of an impossibly complex moebius chainsaw. Like the scraping and twisting of metal in some terrible accident.

All these sounds were inorganic, mechanical. And yet their overall effect was to give me the impression of a presence, if not exactly alive, then at least knowing, aware of *my* presence. Now I began to see the metallic lashes as the coils of snakes, hissing and rattling; perhaps the deadly locks of Medusa herself.

That petrifying certainty now took the shape of remembered words in my mind. "*Qioxtl* waits as a guardian in the further darkness." *Qioxtl*, the Seeing Hand! From the few words Stephen had let fall and the sounds I now heard, I began spontaneously to visualise a being, an entity, with no knowledge whatsoever if what I imagined bore any resemblance to the thing itself. It started with a literal vision of a hand, but then distorted into a hideous abstract sculpture of mirrors, clocks, pendulums, blades. This insane clockwork seemed to reproduce itself in exponential generation. I saw its jaws open to me, and inside a cosmos-wide museum of pain. Here, glittering, were all the horrors that had been, all that were to come, and all of them eternally now, and all of them inevitable for every soul that ever enters into existence; inevitable if that soul is ever to find exit again.

The vision zoomed in on me, so I was not sure if it were my vision or if I were its. It zoomed in like a hurricane. But just before its glittering jaws could close on me, I broke into flight. As if movement, speed, were my only talisman against this thing, I dashed on madly, bursting. I could not slow my pace for an instant, but bounced myself off walls to keep my impetus, the jaws forever about to close around me. The labyrinth was now a delirium of angles through which I ricocheted.

And then, suddenly, the vision was gone. I was in a cold sweat. My lungs heaving, I leaned with one arm against the wall. Of course, I knew where I was. (It is impossible for me to lose my way anywhere twice.) The passage I stood in led directly to the chamber of the black pool. I was nearly out of that awful place, and I swore I would never return. I stood upright and walked weakly forward. As I did so a sort of wet smacking sound became faintly audible ahead. If that had not been my only way out I would not have advanced another step. Now, the puppet of conflicting fears greater than myself, I yielded to the greatest and inched forward in a crouch.

I came to the mouth of the passageway and peered into the dusky chamber. All was still and lonely, except for that continued smacking, guzzling sound. Then I caught a glimpse of movement. The idol was back on its plinth, but it had changed somehow. Something seemed to be dangling from it. What was it? But soon it was clear enough. The thing that dangled, now a sack of bones and blood, had once been Stephen. The movement I saw in it was not its own, but came in stiff hideous jerks, communicated from the black idol as it chewed and gnawed at the lopsided head. As a preying mantis clutches a cricket in its spiny pincers and feasts without restraint or hesitation, so the idol feasted with relish upon Stephen. Somewhere his lore had failed him. Somewhere he had put a foot wrong.

Tremblingly, I worked my way around the opposite side of the pool, deep in shadow. I was certain the demon thing knew

269

I was there. My fate was already decided. I simply did not know what that fate was. Maybe, as I crept along beside that murmuring pool, I was already the doomed kith of that corpse. But the thing did not even lift its head from its grisly feast. Instead it let me crawl by in a path that seemed to dip into a valley of darkness where it passed opposite, oppressed in my movements by a fear that was equal in weight to death. It seems, at that terrible pass, at least, the lot I had drawn was freedom, even if it were only my own insignificance that saved me.

That is what I thought—that I had escaped. And, of course, I was wrong. Why had the vision of *Qioxtl* disappeared, for instance? Maybe because its jaws had finally closed around me.

The Waiting is here, now. The Waiting is me. The Waiting has already won.

Not much longer now. I must get a hold on my thoughts and write the end. Inside, Outside, it's all the same. Can't move forward. Can't move back. Of course, to get to the next level one must go past the guardian, *Qioxtl*, but I'm afraid I stumbled on the guardian all unready and must face this ordeal an empty-handed nobody. I'm sure many greater men than me have failed.

I came back through the bank, back to the world. *Qioxtl's* jaws still glittered all around me. I stopped at that trap I called a home just long enough to gather a few things, and I came out here, to this broken shelter in the woods where as few people as possible pass.

I know I am not any safer here than I would be anywhere else. There is nowhere *Qioxtl* cannot see, nowhere it cannot reach. Safety is an illusion, and those who seem safest are those whose ends are most assured. But it is quiet here, and I can think of no better place to do my waiting.

The night I first came out here, and slept, I had a dream. The fist of *Qioxtl* closed around me, and I was in its museum of torture. And one exhibit in amongst the many was the Earth, and all the walls were taken away from all the buildings, and Past, Present and Future were laid bare in section, like an ants' nest between sheets of glass. I saw naked reality, and everywhere the influence of the Waiting dominant and brutal. From the playground to the cabinet; from the fleshy indoctrination of the breast to the pale emptiness of the last breath. It was there in hidden bruises and all the secret abuses of the home, in the breaking of glass and footsteps in a tenement building, in hospitals and prisons, in the rod of law, in new diseases and new wars, in loneliness and the living decay of age, in enslaving industry, in accidents, in holy and tyrannical religions, in deformations of body and of spirit, in the quest of science for knowledge, in the urge to reproduce, in sexual mania, in addictions of all kinds, in the ascent of kings to thrones and the establishing of republics, in the exploration of new lands, in the flaming destruction of heathen temples, in riots met with tear gas, in looting, in gang rape, in the protection of the family, in poisons sown in air, sea and earth, in earthquakes and tidal waves, in genocide, in ritual scarring, in business, in entertainment; in all these things *Yxthahl*, the Black Flame, the Waiting, was glorified, and in all these the one dark commandment, Celebrate, was echoed.

As if some great eternal Vesuvius had erupted, showering ash and lava on all history, the human race was shown to me all in one instant, petrified forever in the midst of writhing torments. And I was among them. This museum was a maze at whose every exit stood all the horror enfolded within.

There are only two moments in existence, I think. The waiting, and the end. Each justifies the other so that the end is ever present in the waiting. But what is that end for me? I thought I was ordinary, no one in particular, just another extra

271

in a rational, material world. Now things are gathering about me as if I were the centre of it all. Have I been chosen? Or is this the fate of all?

In my remaining hours I ransack my memory for answers. But now that I know my memory is fallible, even the ground beneath me is no longer solid, and I feel myself sinking hopelessly in quicksand. If I forgot about Kate, how many other things might have been taken from my memory without me knowing? How many added? The past is not a fixed background, after all, but a shifting maze of mirrors. I find certain undistinguished memories coming back to me vividly like a riddle. About them is the same air of mystery that clung to the back of that empty chair. I think about the death of my parents amidst flames and twisted metal. A puzzle with a million million pieces, and yet still with pieces missing, and in their place red herrings. And I have just been so many pieces of a puzzle. And what if those pieces are suddenly scattered so that no trace of pattern and no hope of reassembly remains?

I'm not sure why I write this. I only know I have to. Perhaps my motives are the same I ascribed to Stephen for his interest in me—just to snatch at the remotest chance of communication with another soul. Or perhaps this is my last act of defiance. My soul is lost now, but maybe somewhere in my testimony, like the infinitely fragile memory of Kate in the car on the clifftop, are the last fragmentary glimmerings of a soul; the last twinklings of a dead star, still visible in the sky. And now . . .

Whatever heart beats Outside, it is my own . . . through the trees . . . I am inside, turning a mobile. What is on the branches? A heart that never lived and never dies in the stone. The stone is bellying as if . . . it's getting closer now, whirling in with heart beats, but it is as if . . . I have to get through this to the . . . can see the door again, and *Qioxtl*, the next level. To see it, to reach it, I meant to write the end here, but . . . Seeing Hand with

Ultra-Sidereal Eyes, carved out. I can see my hand writing this as I see everything else. The branches no longer know which order things are somehow. I must try to think, stop something strange is happening to me. I of the trees are spinning outwards, like myself from going into pieces. Now, I happening in. *Yxthahl!* The Black Flame! I can see . . . one . . . Celebrate . . .

This is where the manuscript ends. I think, however, Brendan's life did not end just yet. Of course, it is impossible to reconstruct exactly what happened. There is a sudden change in the handwriting and style of the last paragraph, which makes me think of a refraction of consciousness. Just as dreams seconds long can seem like hours to the dreamer, so I sense this short paragraph seemed several ages to the writer.

The air had grown dusky by the time I finished reading, and there was a vapour rising from the leaf-mould all around. Never before had I felt such a sense of panic at reading words on paper. I told myself, however, that words were all they were, and assured myself that my panic was unfounded. What was it that bothered me so much? Perhaps it was my surroundings, which were obviously those described at the end of the manuscript. I had even seen the shelter mentioned on previous, adventurous walks, but did not feel like looking for it now.

It was not until the next day that I saw the news stories and my panic returned, this time conquering me through intuition and reason both. I hardly have it in me to repeat the gruesome details. A body was found in the woods in such a horrifying condition that no photographs of the thing itself could be printed. In the text of the stories, however, there was enough information to conjure up the scene with disturbing vividness. In the trees the headless, handless, dissected trunk of the body had been impaled on a branch. Entrails hung from other branches in macabre decoration. Elsewhere in the trees was found the head, devoid of eyes. These were eventually discovered along with the hands. Both hands, contracted into claws, had also been fixed onto sharpened branches. Each of them clutched an eyeball.

It hardly needed telling that this was no common murder. In fact, the word 'murder' itself seemed too tame and familiar to describe this abomination. But apart from the unspeakable brutality of what had been done, there was another element to the crime that had equal impact on all who witnessed or heard of it. All were struck, as with fear, by the question, "How was it done?" Police declared it could not have been the work of one man. But even supposing there were many men—a terrible assumption in itself, this co-operation in darkest horror—there yet remained details that defied explanation. One of these was the pattern drawn in blood upon the ground, though elsewhere there was hardly enough blood found to have filled the veins of the body. Although the pattern was drawn with such neatness that it was clearly deliberate and meant to signify something, no one could identify it to say what that thing was. Or rather, no one could say publicly what the pattern was. I wondered how many people knew privately, as I knew, exactly what this message signified. For the photographs of this bloody pattern were as much of the carnage as the papers dared publish. Once a plane had crashed into a snowy mountainside in South America, and its last morse-coded message to the world had been the mysterious word 'Stendec'. Now I knew what it was to understand such a message, for when I compared the photographs with the glyphs written in Brendan's manuscript I found they matched perfectly. Xi Groughl! Celebrate!

Of course, I already know what name they will announce when they identify the body. When I read the stories I could not help wondering if Brendan had still been alive when I found his last testament, or if he had already been dead, and if dead, dead how long? I looked at the photograph and that leafy clearing did not seem as distant, as removed, as it should have. As if the photograph were a window, as I drew closer to it I thought I could see more, and suddenly I saw everything, branches decked with nightmare baubles, spinning, reaching out to grab me with their vivid red horror.

And all this, I think, because I have that manuscript. It was not a good omen that I should find it. It is as if sometimes the world must

274

be reminded of the terror of that which usually reigns in secret; the terror and supremacy of the Waiting. But how long will the world be allowed to remember this? How much of the world will be erased with the memory? I look outside and dusk is falling once more. I shiver. I have never felt so alone. So unsafe. The world is drifting off-course. Lost.

Unimaginable Joys

REBECCA, a name and a posy of yesterday-fresh memories, peering out from the shallow cave of vision onto the world. Walking past the harbour on the way to work. It is high summer and the sing-song of church bells chimes the half hour. The wind is sweet with the barest chill, squeezes blissfully through the leaves of the sycamores on the hill to the left, filters through Rebecca and flows out from the openings of her navy blue office clothes as if it is simply Rebecca herself flowing out into the world any which way.

On the right the cabin cruisers and sailing boats rock in the dips between waves like Rebecca's fingertips lulled in the concave buttons of the keyboard, coated with daylight. A yacht is gliding, white-waked, out to sea. In her chair, at work, sleep in her eyes and sleep like a deep contentment settling heavy as an anchor in her body, her mind drifts off. She sees herself walking to work, thinking of how she will daydream there. The sounds of the office massage her into nostalgic oblivion like the page-turning silence of a public library. The daydream as she walks to work and the daydream at work are one and the same, simply dividing her dreaming selves into different times. Only the minute hand makes its starch-stiff circuit of the clock face as she nods and works and daydreams again. And days circle in the midst of this daydreaming.

Some day she will move on. (A yacht is gliding, white-waked, out to sea.) For now she is at the centre of life. There is no year. Leaves that fall from calendars mean no more than those that fall from sycamores. She does not know it is only the young who feel this sense of infinite possibility as normal life. She does not know what she is going to do. Sometimes she can feel the excitement in her blood. Reading trashy novels and not thinking about anything in particular, just the sea of blood and sunlight in her head. (This trashy novel is the white wake of a yacht gliding out to sea.)

Blinking between sleep and wakefulness, the cat's cradle of sunlight from the office window becomes her hammock for the summer. Of course, like all the young, she is capable of listening to a love song on the radio and feeling as old as the hills. But it is still a pleasant feeling, not the haggard despair that love songs bring when one is truly old and possibilities have all flown, leaving only a sere, withered branch that will never leaf and bloom again. Not yet do such songs strike her with the terror of shock-haired skeletons.

Not yet.

Instead, the minute hand makes its starch-stiff circuit of the clock face and Rebecca makes her circuit of the days, appearing at the same waiting interstices at regular intervals.

The life of places, of unmoving things, that merely witness dumbly: Here is an in-between zone, a little tangle of back alleys that form a shortcut from the harbour to the bus station. It is familiar, but utterly insignificant. "Oh, here I am again!" is as much as Rebecca thinks of such a place. For the rest of her life, when she is not there, it is forgotten. And do the empty diamond eyes of the wire fence along one of these alleys, framing her passing from odd angles, think as much of her?

An in-between zone. But gradually, as Rebecca passes through this short cut in her daily dreaming, that barely noticeable 'here-I-am-again' becomes more and more pronounced, as if this is the part of the dream that makes her remember she is dreaming, and so brings her closer to the surface of wakefulness.

There is a reason for this.

Just off the steep road from the harbour to the high street is a small rectangle of uncertain purpose. Two wooden benches, surrounded by bushes of grass and crumbling away in soft splinters, lean against a wall around the back of the bus station. Over the wall, through a high wire fence, can be seen a mossy, broken-paned warehouse, which is in fact the place where buses are put to sleep at night. In a concrete yard, two buses, fallen into disrepair and disuse, may be seen. Follow the wall away from the harbour and you come to a right turning. Here, along the top of the wall, at about head height, are ragged clusters of valerian and dandelion. And sitting at the next corner, where a terrace of private residences begins, his back against the wire fence, for all the world like another ragged flowering of weeds in human shape, is a boy, or, more precisely, a young man.

Perhaps he does not always sit here, but for Rebecca he has become as much a part of the roof-crowded view as the church steeple, the derelict buses and the gulls squabbling over chimney pots. Unlike such details, however, there is something about the young man that is difficult to ignore. It's not his clothes, though these are motley enough. His untucked shirt is a glossy emerald colour, cascading over the tops of his ripped and faded jeans. He wears an abundance of jewellery and, with a hint of make-up, this gives him a naïvely exotic air, like a child's dream of Egypt. No, it is not this that makes Rebecca self-conscious as she walks past. Nor is it merely the fact that he seems to sit here every morning, as if he has nothing else to do. It's more a sense that of all the people and things surrounding her, he alone does not keep himself to himself, as he should; he alone does not blend in with the camouflage of public existence; he alone is a foreign body in her daydream.

Somehow she cannot even *pretend* to ignore him, as this only makes her more uncomfortable still, and so she has fallen into the habit of deliberately smiling and saying "Hello" every time she passes. He always returns her smile with one of his own—a smile like bees buzzing on a honeycomb, a smile with just a little too much of recognition in it, a smile which both irritates her and makes her half wish she had some excuse to start a conversation.

Today, when she approaches the corner, he is sitting in the lotus position with his head in the air, and he does not seem to see her. At first she is relieved not to have to say "hello". Then, two or three paces past him, she is strangely irritated once more. Surely he should have noticed her? She doesn't want to go any further without the now familiar morning ritual. She stops and half turns. She watches him for a while. He seems completely unaware of her. She thinks for some reason of the phrase, 'head in the clouds'. Perhaps the clouds are blocking his view of her and muffling his ears.

Having stood watching him for this long she cannot just walk away, and yet everything has become awkward and un- natural.

"Hello," she says finally, uncertain.

His body relaxes in a sinking movement, a movement of slow dizziness like the spinning dizziness of the summer sky. His head turns on his neck with smooth, moist slowness. When his eyes fix on her at last, his smile is beatific. What does that smile say? It seems to say, "I know your secret." Or, no, perhaps it is more like, "You know my secret."

"Hello."

A simple word of greeting seems to contain some hidden meaning, some secret humour.

Her smile freezes on her lips. In her mystification she for- gets to move on.

"What's your name?" the boy asks, as if to save her from confusion.

"Becky."

"Ah, yes. Rebecca! I hear the name ecker in a corner of my heart, like dust in a courtyard . . . No, that's not quite right."

He seems to be mumbling to himself now. Is he drunk, perhaps? And yet, he does not seem to be.

"What are you doing?" she asks.

"Nothing really. I've just been looking up at the sky and watching the seagulls. Have you ever tried just looking up at the sky so that you don't see anything else at all?"

"No."

"You should. It's free."

"What's your name? I see you every morning."

"Me? It's a bit strange, but my mother called me Gawaine, like the knight, you know."

"It's a nice name. Very different."

"Rebecca is a nice name."

"No one really calls me Rebecca. Everyone just calls me Becky."

"Then I shall have to, too."

"Well, it doesn't matter, I suppose. It's just strange."

"Where are you going?"

"To work." She looks at her watch. "Actually, I'd better go. I've got to catch a bus. It's been very interesting talking to you."

"Where do you work?"

"Ilford. I'm a typist."

"I'm going to Ilford today. Perhaps we could meet."

"I'm working."

"When do you finish?"

"About five."

"That's okay. I'll be in Ilford anyway. We can meet at the bus station at about half past five."

"Okay. I've got to go. I'll miss my bus."

She does not think about meeting Gawaine in Ilford. She just wants to get away. As she walks briskly down the alley she can hear his voice behind her.

"Bye."

A single word, it would be infinitely sad if it were not softened by resignation. For a moment she feels the sadness as her own. Now she has saddled herself with the nuisance of deciding to keep her word or to break it. What a bother! Oh, forget it! Forget it!

Halfway to the bus stop very different thoughts visit her, as surprising as wild birds pecking crumbs from her hands. Why are people always so afraid of each other? Why is it impossible to talk to strangers? Perhaps people should always talk as Gawaine had talked to her—as if they know and trust each other. Isn't that more natural?

As she steps up from the pavement, where glinting puddles dry, to the bus, she is humming to herself. She feels as though she is waking up.

It's a small, open-plan office where Rebecca works as part of a typing pool. The atmosphere is that of an art-class at school, Rebecca and her workmates trying to look busy between chatting and making any excuse for a break. There are long, tedious periods of serious work, too, when the clacking of keyboards reigns in stiff staccato like the cramp slowly building in the shoulders of the girls.

Rebecca looks up to the clock without thinking. It is already closer to five than to four. She slumps back in her chair luxuriously, her blouse creasing as her body arches. She yawns and stretches, puts her balled-up fist in front of her mouth like an apple she is about to bite. Outside, the sun is still shining. Even though she is still at work, she feels quite free. The tension and tiredness that have hardened in her now thaw in the sunlight, turning into a cool, delicious slush of happiness. Summer is glorious! It seems to go on forever.

The tiredness relaxes into streams of lazy relief that swell until they reach the estuary of five, knocking-off time.

Rebecca slips her arms into the sleeves of her jacket and pushes her chair under her desk. As she walks out into summer breezes she remembers her promise of this morning. She'll probably reach the bus station in time for the five twenty bus. Should she wait for Gawaine? With these thoughts there comes, at first, a return of the nagging, irritated feeling of this morning. She wants to escape. Then, once again, in reaction to this, as if alighting on her from the unbounded openness of the sky, comes the equally unbounded question, 'Why not?' Why not do something new? It's summer and it won't be dark for ages yet. Deadlines are as tiny and trifling as stiles in distant fields.

She waits at the pelican crossing opposite the bus station. Her eyes scan the station nervously for any sign of Gawaine. She sees him, but he has his back to her. He is standing to one side of the public toilets, in front of the benches there, and looking out at the great, sluggish river that flows behind the station. She feels strangely impatient to cross and make him aware of her presence. There is something comic and lovable about his unconsciousness of her. It is also a little sad. She has the odd desire to creep up behind him, put her hands over his eyes and say, "Guess who!" Suddenly it seems to her that that would be the perfect thing to do, that, if she is not going to do the safe, boring thing and get on the bus, then she might as well enter wholly into the spirit of her decision. But she doesn't. Instead she walks up to Gawaine, stops a few feet behind him, waits for a moment, then says, "I'm here!"

He turns around. He smiles. There follows a blank pause in which both of them seem so bewildered by the situation they have put themselves in that they don't know what to do.

At last Gawaine speaks.

"Um. There's something I'd like to show you."

The line is flat, as if over-rehearsed.

"What?"

He holds up a brown paper bag. She takes it from him and peers inside.

"Bread?"

"Yes. You take three slices and I'll take the other two."

"I'm not hungry," she says, puzzled.

"Um, it's not for you. I'll show you. Over here."

He walks to the railings at the top of the wall that rises from the riverbank. She leans on the railings next to him. Below them is the river. It is at ebb tide. As well as the glistening margin of mud banks on each side, there are also little islands of mud in the middle of the river. On the other side of the river are a carpet warehouse and the terraces of private homes. Two hundred yards upstream is a bridge for traffic. Somehow this great, natural gash of mud and water cutting through the chronic, concrete Sunday of the provincial town is exhilarating. It emphasises the miracle of the streaming air. It is a nature reserve for air.

"This is one of my favourite places," says Gawaine, finding his stride after a stumbling start. "I come here quite often. Look!"

"Ducks. You come here to feed the ducks?"

"No. Not exactly. See, there's a couple of seagulls, too. Watch this."

He breaks off a little of the crust of bread in his hand and throws it to where two seagulls are paddling at the river's edge. Immediately the two birds begin to squabble over the titbit.

"Just you wait. In a minute there'll be loads of them. I don't know how they do it. There must be some secret method they have of spreading the news."

Sure enough, after Gawaine has thrown four or five pieces of bread, the gulls come flocking, taking up their positions in the air as if they are part of some complex, invisible mobile. Rebecca, too, begins to tear off little pieces of bread and throw them to the birds.

"Look at that!" says Gawaine.

He hardly needs to indicate. A huge, fawn-speckled gull is hovering some three feet away from them, its beak opening and closing in weird avian meows, its eyes quite as eerie as a cat's. Gawaine lightly tosses a morsel of bread. The gull catches the morsel in its beak and rolls away.

"Here's another one. It's not even moving its wings. It's just hovering there in mid-air. How does it do that?"

The two of them continue to throw bits of bread for the gulls and watch their aerobatics as they swoop to pluck that bread from the air. Now and then they look at each other and smile and laugh.

Finally their bread runs out and they look at each other a little sadly. There is nothing they can do. It had to end. But how strangely unsatisfying it feels now to be empty-handed.

"Shall we sit down?" asks Gawaine. He gestures towards the bench behind them.

Rebecca assents.

They settle onto the wooden slats of the bench and Gawaine produces another brown paper bag.

"I've got something else," he says.

"A present?"

"Yes."

She reaches into the bag and pulls out some kind of heavy confection—a dark filling between thin layers of shortbread.

"What is it?"

"It's a Nelson slice. Have you ever tried one before?"

"No."

"They're really nice. Try it."

She holds it in her fingertips and examines it, drawing her head back.

"It looks too stodgy. You have it."

"My one's in the bag."

"I don't usually eat cakes."

"Try it. Go on. You don't have to eat the whole thing. I'll eat what's left."

Rebecca bites gingerly into the block of bread and cake crumb.

"How is it?"

"Strange. Mmm. It's okay, actually. What did you say it was called?"

"A Nelson slice. Good, isn't it?"

"It's alright."

The two continue to eat in silence, hamster-cheeked.

Gawaine finishes first, obviously practised in the art. Eating in a slow and picky manner, Rebecca still manages to finish the whole thing, quite to her own surprise. She looks across at Gawaine for congratulations on her feat. She finds him staring ahead, a tear rolling down his left cheek. He must know she is looking at him. He seems determined neither to hide his tears not to make a show of them. His head is trembling ever so slightly on his neck.

"What's wrong?"

He stays like that for some time. At length he answers.

"I'm sorry. I'm afraid I've spoilt everything. You'll think I'm an idiot now."

"No, I don't. Tell me what's wrong."

"Do you trust me?"

"Well . . . it's a bit soon for that. I don't even know you."

"Do you want to?"

Rebecca thinks for a while.

"I don't know. Anyway, try it." She echoes his words of some minutes before and he gives a little splutter of a laugh. He wipes away his tears.

"I'm sorry . . . I wanted to show you something, but I think it's all gone wrong."

"What did you want to show me? The seagulls?"

"Well, sort of. You know, for years and years I've never re- ally talked to anyone. I've never said anything I've wanted to say. I've only said what I've had to to survive. But inside me . . . if only I could explain . . . I thought it would be easier to show you my world, but it's just turned into something horrible and concrete. I don't mean you. I like you. I'm glad you're here. I mean me. It's my fault, I think. I dunno."

He pauses for a while as if assessing what he has just said.

"It's like, all the feeding the seagulls and the Nelson slices and the things we've said have all become twisted up bits of metal. You know you get sculptures, abstract sculptures, like climbing frames or something, and it's all just a tangle of metal poles with air between them, and it doesn't mean anything, it's just there, but you stare at it, and for some reason you can't bear it any longer and you burst into tears. Do you know what I mean?"

"A climbing frame?"

"Yeah. Like in a playground or something. Or a sculpture, maybe."

"I think I know what you mean. I'm not sure."

"Well, I get it quite a lot. Anyway, it's like that."

"You're a bit mad, really, aren't you?"

"What?"

"A bit zippy. A bit doolally."

He looks at her, concerned.

"Do you think so?"

"It's alright. I like mad people. One of my friends, Brian, is a bit mad. He'll say things like that after he's been smoking, you know, wacky baccy. But you just say those kinds of things anyway, don't you? You're not on anything at the moment, are you?"

He shakes his head.

"I didn't think so."

"Only this bench."

Another pause.

"I don't know what you think of me . . . Obviously, I don't

286

know you that well, either. But you know, true friends recognise each other very quickly, I think. You can tell by looking
at someone's face. I suppose that sounds superficial, but it's not.
It's just that, well, when I look at your face, I feel you are a
sympathetic person. Do you know what I mean? Perhaps you'll
think this is all a bit weird, but I'm not asking anything of you,
nothing at all, apart from your time and your ear—not literally, of course. Actually, I want to give *you* something, if I can.
It's just the kind of thing I prefer to do with my time—spend
it with someone who really wants . . . wants to know that
they exist, that I exist, instead of just avoiding each other's eyes
and talking about everything else to avoid the most important
thing in the world, which is that we're here, and which is what
is in our hearts now."

He seems to be struggling with his words. They stop as if
blocked and then tumble out all together in disarray.

She watches him as he says all this. She hears his words,
but more than these she seems to hear a message in all the
things that have led to this time and place, and in the round-
shouldered, shallow-chested body next to her. There is something utterly passive about him. Of course, he is asking for
something, but it is quite as if he is asking for nothing. She has
been with other men, as friend or girlfriend, and none of them
have been like this. Most men seem to reach out with their will
as if to take something they know they can have. Perhaps they
don't take it, but they reach out anyway, just to try it on. This
boy does not reach out at all. No, instead he begs with the pas-
siveness of utter resignation for someone to reach out to him,
for someone to come to him. She feels no threat here.

"So, anyway, I won't bore you by talking too much today.
But, if you don't mind, I'll leave you my address and phone
number. There are things I'd like to talk to you about. And
show you."

"Okay."

He looks a little surprised. When he has finished writing his details on a scrap of paper and handed it to her, she tears the scrap in half, writes her own on the empty half, and hands it back to him.

This time he looks perfectly incredulous. He smiles.

✻

Special friends. That is what Gawaine calls the two of them. That is what they become. When she asks what 'special friends' means, he tells her straight.

"When we are together, I am not a boy and you are not a girl. Those things aren't important. You might have a boyfriend some time. I'm sure you will. Girls seem to need that sort of thing. It's okay. That's not my job and I don't want it. When you are having problems with your boyfriend, come to me and talk about it. No matter how many boyfriends come and go, I'll always be here. I care about you. Never forget it."

She can see a flaw in this idea already. It relies on boyfriends not only coming, but going, too. Gawaine, however, really is kind to her. He does everything to make sure she is happy. And when she is not, he only blames himself, apologising and backing down from whatever he has said and done, with such gentle humility she cannot imagine him ever being possessive or becoming an obstacle to her well-being.

He gives her wonderful presents, like rare shells and stones he has collected since childhood, whimsical toys, flower rings, fairy handbooks, old postcards from second-hand shops, favourite sweets, paint sets and indoor fireworks. He writes her strangely folded letters, beautifully written in a childish hand, and full of poems and little pictures and stories. In some of the stories Rebecca is the heroine. In some of them Gawaine is her humble servant. Their adventures together are comically improbable. (Rebecca writes back once or twice before giving up because she can't write "like that!")

All this time Gawaine remains true to his word. He asks nothing of her but her time and her ear. All he ever wants to do is talk or 'show' her things. The things he wants to show her are many and various: poems, paintings, a certain beach where he had such and such a daydream as a child, the house where he first lived, songs that have special significance for him, the moonlight over a particular field, and so on.

There is not the slightest hint in his words or actions of what might be called 'making a move'. And yet, again and again, he shows signs of frustration and disappointment. He says she does not understand what he is saying. Then he blames himself for failing to make his meaning clear. At such times he sighs and frowns and bites his lip. He looks as if he is about to say something more, but sighs again and says nothing. What does he want? Rebecca has a funny little theory about that. She thinks that when he's talking, he's not trying to say something at all. It's as if he's trying to fly, to disappear. That's why he sighs. He thinks he might be able to blow himself out through his own mouth.

One day Rebecca gets a letter from Gawaine that seems impatient, and, in places, almost angry. It's very different to the fey and breezy tone of his usual letters. For some reason it worries her.

In the letter, Gawaine asks if they can meet again at a certain café to discuss something very difficult and serious. She does not know it, but this is the last letter he will ever send her.

Ray received the envelope precisely one week ago. Someone must have noticed his performance. Interesting word that, 'performance', he thinks as he sets to work on his hair with comb and spray in front of the bathroom mirror. It's no co-incidence that it's used to mean acting, like in the theatre, and also to mean how well you do your job. For Ray, the work he does is like acting. When he was at school he joined the drama club, but found the other kids there to be precocious show-offs. Nobody liked them, not the yobs, nor the swots nor the indie-pop rebels. They were luvvies without talent, looking for equally insipid prima donnas to play their boring mind-games with. Most of the time Ray felt like smacking them in the gobs. There were some nice bits of skirt there, though, and since sex gave them plenty of opportunities for drama, they were disgustingly easy to bed.

Since those days Ray has had a deep aversion to any dramatics that have no consequences in real life. A suit and a tie is his costume of choice, business his preferred role. Some people might find it dull, but that's their loss. Anyway, it's a question of attitude. A close shave, aftershave, a perfectly pressed suit—as in business, so in life, if all the right boxes are ticked then all goes well and the role is easy to play. There's no feeling like cleanly clearing one hurdle after another without breaking into a sweat. Once you master the role, you can put your hands behind your perfectly barbered head and put your gleaming, pointy-toed, leather-clad feet up on your neat desk. It is no co-incidence that 'smart' means both 'well-dressed' and 'clever'. There is no such thing as co-incidence.

No co-incidence. That's right. Nothing goes unnoticed. This boy showed impressive mettle in the playground. He won't be too squeamish to make the right decisions. This boy stood in a corner and hung his head. Some day he'll be found, instead, hanging by the neck. Some people find themselves standing in front of the urinal when important words are being uttered; some people find that everyone is quiet when they walk in. Ray knows which group he belongs to. That's why, when the envelope came, pressed between the leaves of other documents, he knew vaguely what it was.

A brown, Manila envelope. In the corner was a rather curious crest, the foreground of which was taken up by a chalice with a human eye on its obverse side. A towering mountain range formed the background. The envelope was addressed simply, "For the attention of Mr. Ray Jenkins." When he first saw that eye stare solemnly out at him from the paper, and his own name there in slightly uneven black type, he felt as though he had just caught a view of another world between vast curtains that had quickly swished closed again after the passage of some unknown person.

Inside was a single piece of A4 paper, folded in three. On the piece of paper were written directions to a certain office, a date and time, and the instructions to memorise those details and destroy both the note and the envelope in which it had been delivered.

The day has come and Ray wants to look his best for the part he has to play. He notices a spot in the crease of his nostril and paints over it carefully with skin-toned foundation. A single blemish like that is a chink in your armour. It is important to appear invulnerable. The illusion of invulnerability is the next best thing to invulnerability itself.

The finishing touches are taken care of. Is there really nothing else? It seems not. In the end all Ray has with which to meet this test are his sartorial preparedness and his wit, both of which are sharp. Such was the sharpness, no doubt, that first got him noticed, like the enigmatic character in the TV commercial whose teeth actually twinkle. He is sharp enough to cut through crowds of normal people.

Now that even the paper with the rendezvous time has been destroyed, everything seems tenuous and uncertain. Has he really had such an invitation? Has he timed his departure correctly? Such uncertainty is what the test is all about. Anyway, time to go. He walks out into the air of the sober street and locks the door behind him. He picks up a broadsheet at the corner shop on his way to the station. As he sits on the swaying tube train, it makes him feel a little more prepared to absorb all the latest information and opinions that are being disseminated about what is happening 'out there'.

At the other end he emerges from the dilapidated underground exit where chronically dodgy characters hang about like flies around the desiccated corpse of an animal. He decides to take a taxi to the building that is his destination.

A hive of smoky steel and glass towers up from the pavement as if some animal has found a way to gather all the soot and fumes of the city and turn them into something shiny and sweet, like a black honeycomb.

Ray pays the driver and steps out onto the kerb of the pavement. He looks up at the building once more, checks his watch, and steps through the main doors. He finds himself in a kind of lobby, neat and anonymous. There is a set of lifts in the wall to the right, and straight ahead is a door, which might lead to a stairway. To the left, an ashen-faced, balding man in a commissionaire's uniform sits behind a curved counter. Ray glances about, unsure what to do next. There are no signs or plaques on the walls. Even the counter is bare. He turns to the commissionaire.

"I have an appointment. My name is . . ."

"It's alright, Mr. Jenkins. Mr. Wilberforce is expecting you. Please go on up to the seventh floor and wait to be called."

On the seventh floor, steel-legged plastic chairs line the corridor. Ray walks up and down looking at the doors of the offices. None of them have names written on them, and most of them are silent. From behind one he hears a dry, dusty voice, which seems to be dictating a letter. Finally, he takes a seat near the strip of window, from floor to ceiling, at the far end of the corridor, and looks out over the gloriously mundane panorama through the smoky glass. He looks for the Post Office Tower, but fails to find it. Of all the buildings, high and low, there are none that he definitely recognises. We need familiar landmarks to tell us where we are, he thinks idly. Where is he? From here the outside world looks like a vast accumulation of litter. There is nothing in Ray's entire field of vision, with the possible exception of the sky, that is neither man-made nor in some way shaped by the hand of humankind. This is what we call daily life. If Ray has faith at all, then it is in the blind architect 'daily life', who shapes the city with groping, sensitive, gargantuan hands.

Off to the right, in a barren spot temporarily given over to destruction, Ray sees the long, skeletal spines of cranes soaring up to the giddy emptiness where no human lives. Who is controlling those cranes? Where do their orders come from? Is there anyone who holds more than a fragmentary knowledge of the whole plan? Is there anyone who knows enough to be sure that the supreme conspiracy is the one he is in on?

Now his gaze turns from what is beyond the window to the window itself. The glass is held in place by a metal frame. A spar of metal divides the window just below the height of Ray's head. There is a screw in the metal, half-obscured by grime. Someone put that screw there. It was a very important job. And yet it could easily have been performed by an idiot. Did that idiot understand the plans for the entire building? Doubtful. But with enough idiots capable of following limited instructions, a miracle beyond the comprehension of any one of them can be realised. All this was a source of wonder, and, if you understood it, and could be a working part of it, pride. All those people down there, crawling about like ants—they don't know what a real miracle is! They don't know for whom they are working, or why!

All these thoughts, not new to him by any means, go through Ray's head as he sits waiting. Despite the quiet, the dullness of the day and the emptiness of the corridor, these thoughts bring to him a sharp tang of excitement that mixes oddly with the stale boredom of waiting. He inspects his shoes again, twisting his left foot so that he can see the leather flank leading from the toe. There appear to be no scratches or blemishes.

"Mr. Jenkins!" A door opens further along the corridor and a man with a thick black beard leans out. "We're ready for you now. Would you like to step this way?"

The man waits for Ray to enter the office and closes the door behind him. The room that Ray now finds himself in is surprisingly small and nondescript. Before him is a desk, behind which sits, in an impressively upright manner, a man in his fifties or sixties with eyes that appear to be mere gleaming shadows in the folds of crows' feet. The bearded man is sitting to the right. Apart from the desk the only furniture in the room is a bookcase and a filing cabinet. Beyond the desk there appears to be a window taking up the entire space from floor to ceiling. This is hard to verify, however, because a type of blind made of white, vertical strips screens the view completely, letting in a half-stifled light in keeping with the shrink-wrap chill of the air-conditioning and creating in total a more intense version of the usual stomach-bug discomfort of being in an office. Ray feels this discomfort for the first time, and wonders momentarily what it signifies. The room is not distinguished or unusual in any way that can be explained, but its very anonymity increases Ray's sense of dislocation. This sealed cell, which is home to no one, is not part of the city he knows. He could be anywhere.

There is a silence while Ray settles into the stiff-backed, armless chair provided for him. Then the man behind the desk speaks. For some reason Ray is surprised by the voice, as if he has suddenly been tapped on the shoulder.

"Mr. Jenkins, do you know who I am?"

"You're Mr. Wilberforce." It seems a safe bet.

"Yes, that will do for now. Why do you think you're here?"

"I received an envelope with the time and place of this interview. I thought you might have some work to offer me. Or maybe . . . information. The message didn't say."

"No. It's not as simple as that. We can't propose, for instance, a position and a salary. Certainly not straight away. We can't even explain what it is that we are offering until you have seen certain things."

His head tilted thoughtfully to one side, the bearded man nods in agreement.

"You mentioned information just now. You're a journalist," continues Mr. Wilberforce; "am I right?"

"I work in the media, yes."

"You collect information and you disseminate information to the public. Perhaps not the same information, exactly, or not all of it. You stand at a sort of intersection of information. An interesting place to be. Actually, the collection and dissemination of information are both things which concern us greatly. In fact, we have a great deal of information about you. More than you perhaps imagine. Luckily, and as you may have guessed, that information is much to your credit.

"There are those who know and those who do not know. Do you follow me? Let us call the former 'us' and the latter 'them'. We have taken great pains to make sure they cannot even imagine the truth."

At this point Mr. Wilberforce slowly extends his right hand in a puzzling, dramatic fashion. It looks as if he is reaching out to grasp something. Or is he trying to indicate something? Or perhaps this is some kind of warning?

"I have in my hand a cup, a chalice."

Ray looks at the hand quizzically. Actually, there is no chalice.

"In the chalice is an unknown liquor. Perhaps it is poison. You do not know. But I can tell you, it is really very good."

The bearded man nods enthusiastically, repeating, "Very good."

"You cannot know what it is like until you taste it. Will you drink it?"

"Yes."

"Why?"

"Well, you just said that it's good."

"Ah, but it may be poison."

"It may be poison," repeats the bearded man.

"Well then, I won't."

"Why not?"

"Because it may be poison."

Ray is beginning to wonder if this is a wind-up, and is trying not to sound irritated. A kind of uneasiness grows upon him that perhaps he has been foolishly taken in by cranks. He experiences a flicker of unpleasant giddiness at this thought. Then he remembers he is a journalist. He has committed himself to nothing. If anyone is to be fooled, it will not be him. And if his tenuous information on this subject proves reliable, and this test is a drama with real consequences, then it would be ridiculous to try and pass this test with an attitude of respect. That would be contrary to the truth he suspects he is soon to learn. At the sight of the mixed senility and buffoonery of the gatekeepers before him, he feels a sudden ghastly loneliness and repulsion. This is not a brotherhood, after all. He must remember that. They spoke of knowledge, but even this was a kind of official stance, a kind of lie. The truth lurks unspoken in the dark shadows of Ray's disdain for this pompous nonsense, and in other such uneasy shadows of the impious and irreverent. If he is to have respect for something, then it must only be for the blind architect of all this. Still, he must not underestimate his interviewers.

"Think about it carefully," continues Mr. Wilberforce. "There might be anything in this chalice. You have only my word that it is good. The decision to drink is yours alone."

"Well, if you drink it first, then I'll drink it, too."

Mr. Wilberforce laughs.

"Very good!"

However, the bearded man seems agitated and, after Mr. Wilberforce is quiet once more, speaks.

"In that case the metaphor doesn't really work. Mr. Wilberforce and I have already drunk of the chalice. We are still alive, as you can see, but perhaps the drink is only poisonous to certain people. What we need is a simple yes or no, and a reason."

"All right, I *will* drink it."

Ray experiences a peculiar rush as he pronounces the word 'will'.

"Why?" Both Mr. Wilberforce and the bearded man pounce in unison.

"Well, I don't think this interview is going to get anywhere if I say no. It's only hypothetical, so I might as well say 'yes' in order to learn what I want to learn anyway."

The two interviewers exchange a glance. His mouth still open, Ray takes a breath and continues.

"In other words, to drink from the chalice is the very meaning of existence. If I pass it up because it might be poison, the result is the same or worse than if it had been poison."

This answer appears to be satisfactory. Mr. Wilberforce proceeds.

"You have made the right decision. I can tell you now what is in the chalice—unimaginable joys. Mark my words—unimaginable joys!"

Ray is suddenly convinced that he understands the pantomime they have gone through with the invisible chalice. It may have been invisible, but there was something very real between those extended fingers, as if they were holding out pure power. Ray is more than a little drunk on the odourless fumes.

"Before you drink, however, there are matters of initiation. I have here a letter. I would like you to read it. Out loud, if you would."

Mr. Wilberforce reaches into his inside breast pocket. This time, when he withdraws his hand again, it contains an envelope. He passes it to Ray. Examining the envelope, Ray sees the address is handwritten, the script large and childish. The addressee is one Rebecca Wilcox. He fishes out the letter it contains and reads the following, hesitating from time to time in what appears to be distaste:

Dear Becky,

This is not an easy letter for me to write, but I'm determined not to apologise. Then again, perhaps that's the wrong way to start. Perhaps I cannot help but apologise. Perhaps I should not apologise for apologising. Really, truly, what I'm trying to do is not so easy. It should be, but it's not. So if I make a mistake, please forgive me. Please don't misunderstand me.

Do you remember the second time we met? We went to the museum and saw the two-headed duckling. There were all those butterflies on pins and birds' eggs in cotton wool. For some reason, when I saw one of those tiny eggs, with the blue, speckled shell, I couldn't help surrendering to daydreams that seemed like they had waited years in dusty places to take me away with them. They took me off to all sorts of cloudy worlds. Books I've never read. Lives I've never lived. How can I explain? In an instant I saw a wild wood, a nest in the branches, a young girl playing there in a dress that was yet another daydream. I saw a mansion nearby where a man of leisure lived. I saw one lifetime of memories cross paths with another. I saw a million landscapes with a million nest-like details in them incidental to a million lives in turn just details in a million other landscapes. And all of these things were full of unbearable longing. It's no use trying to describe them all, but they seemed to be contained in the particular blue of that eggshell from which nothing now would ever hatch. The world is like that. Everything I see is like that egg that will not hatch—full of day-dreams I cannot grasp or explain.

Then, after we'd walked round the museum and come out again into the sunlight of the gardens, I had for a moment a sense of freedom. I'd been thinking about that egg the whole time, but then—do you remember?—I turned to you and said something like, "I find it hard to have normal conversations. Do you mind if I just say whatever I want?" To which you replied with a most beautiful, "No". No, I don't mind. In this case it sounded like "yes", like the best and most blessed yes ever to be blown in a kiss from anybody's lips. I asked if you were sure. Apparently you were. I remind you of this now for a reason. The freedom I felt at that moment comes and goes. I haven't had the courage to take you at your word. I think I must summon up that courage. I don't think my confession will be what you expected.

Well, next we went and bought some ice creams and sat on the beach by the stream. That was when you asked me about my clothes. Strange to think that something like that, which should be so trivial, might prove to be such a key point in my life.

You asked me where I get my clothes from, why I wear make-up, that sort of thing. I think you did say something like my style was very original, but you also seemed to be implying that I was just wearing strange clothes to seek attention. Perhaps you weren't. Anyway, I would deny that most definitely. Such an idea stems from the attitude that it's somehow unnatural to express yourself or wrong to be different.

"And so the story goes
They wore the clothes
They said the things
To make it seem improbable,
Whale of a lie like they hoped it was."

I quoted a certain maligned hero whom I need not name.

Must I imprison myself in the uniform of drabness that is all around, just because other people choose to? Clothes are one very simple way I have of trying to make external what is internal. Why should they contradict my self? They should not. They should be a second skin, a plumage of the spirit. They should not hide, but reveal my true self. How else can we ever hope to heal the human race?

I said all this at the time, and your response, as I remember, was to ask what the 'true self' is. You claimed to be genuinely interested, but I suppose I couldn't help feeling this as a sort of attack. It's not really your fault, but I have learnt to become very defensive on this point. Whenever I mention this 'true self' to other people, I seem to get the same reaction, and it never fails to surprise and disturb me. Am I the only person in the world who can see it? Is everyone else blind? If only I could describe my true self in a few words on request. But however much I try to describe something it seems that it is useless when the other person has been, so to speak, blind from birth. And yet, it seems so obvious. Too obvious for words. Maybe that's why the true self is all but forgotten in this world. I don't know. All I do know is that when I close my eyes and reach inside me, I can feel it there as something definite, as something that wants to live, but has never lived in this world. Don't you feel that?

Since that day when we strolled round the museum and ate ice cream on the beach, finding again and again that words fail me, I have tried instead to show you those things and places in the real world where I find reflections of the true self. I say 'the' instead of 'my', because I always hoped to show you not only my true self, but also yours. That you seem blind to the fact that you possess such a thing saddens me unbearably. Just as I saw dreams in the blue of an eggshell, so I see and feel something more precious than life itself in the colour of your hair, in your clothes, in each never-to-be-repeated expression of your face, in all the shadings of your unmistakable voice, in the stretch of skin between your thumb and your forefinger, in the well-tooled flute of your philtrum. When I think that all this does not know itself, the world suddenly seems a very strange and lonely place to me.

All this is leading somewhere. I mentioned a 'confession' a while back. I can't help calling it that somehow, though perhaps it is more like a secret. I can't tell you what it is in this letter. I have to meet you. My words have to be living things, not dead on the page.

I've kept quiet all my life, but I have to tell someone. I feel as though everything I ever was hangs on this confession. You have no idea how much this scares me and how urgent this is to me. I don't want to force this on you. In fact, if you do not want to hear my secret you must tell me so. Otherwise, please meet me at the Aunt Sally Café at five forty five on Tuesday. I'd very much like it to be you I tell my secret to. Ah, even having written this much frightens me. Perhaps you'll think I'm mad. Enough! Phone me! Let me know—yes or no!

With much love and respect,
Gawaine.

Ray finishes reading and looks up, the corners of his mouth turned down in a wry expression.

"Do people really write letters like that?"

"I'm happy to say, not often," Mr Wilberforce answers.

"What is this, the fourth sex or something? I mean, who writes 'ah' in a letter? You might as well write 'alas' or 'woe' or something. There's even a little flower on the tail of the 'y' in 'Becky'. It's enough to make you puke."

"Fine sentiments, Mr. Jenkins, and well expressed."

"Where did you get it from?"

"We have ways and means, but you'll learn all about that later. This letter is the background to what you might call your first assignment. Actually, it's more like a field trip. This is quite a rare case, and yet representative of much of the knowledge we would like to share with you. In short, it is a splendid opportunity for initiation. We may kill two or more birds with a single projectile.

"We would like you to be present at the rendezvous mentioned in the letter. Your chief task will be to observe, but you may also do whatever you feel necessary at the time. You may, at first, be puzzled by this assignment, but I would not give it to you if I thought it was a waste of time. I won't say any more. Basically, I want you to go and see for yourself, then come back and tell us what you saw."

Trains do not run all the way to Ray's destination. His is a journey of many legs. The last train he takes, running along a branch line, trundles at a snail's pace, stopping now and then between stations for no apparent reason, as if the aged driver has simply decided to take a nap. From the terminus Ray still has to take a taxi, then a bus, then another taxi. As he has left the city behind and let himself be carried further and further into the provinces, a strange gloom he cannot quite account for has overtaken him. While he rides on the grotty bus, looking from the window at passing grassy verges, hedgerows, shelters, war-memorials, flower boats, caravan sites and muddy estuaries, he feels he has arrived in a land of eternal Sunday, a land whose only inhabitants are the retired and the unemployed, a land where the very sun in the sky seems filtered through greying lace-curtains and a murky tranquillity spreads over everything like mould, eating away the last rotting remnants of passion, hope and ambition that may once have served as the fuel for that dynamic process of change known as life. This feeling reaches its nadir just as the bus pulls into the station. Ray feels like he is choking. He wants to brush the mould that infects this place off of his smart clothes. He feels it getting into his lungs, into his blood, making him old and sluggish and apathetic, with that special apathy whose stiff and musty material is despair. How do people spend their whole lives in this silence and stagnation? It is intolerable.

When he alights from the bus, moving his body, he manages to shake off the stale feeling a little. He takes a taxi to the café, consults his watch and finds he still has about forty minutes to wait. He looks around the place, but sees no one who looks like they might be either Becky or Gawaine. He orders a cup of coffee and egg on toast. Then, installing himself at a table, he unfolds his newspaper and waits.

✳

Gawaine swings open the door of the half-empty café and steps inside. He is early and alone, and with his purpose in coming here heavy upon him, this makes him feel strangely vulnerable. He feels he is likely to be apprehended at any moment, though for what crime he is unsure—perhaps for being awake in the midst of a dream, or for dreaming in the midst of reality. Sometimes merely walking about in the open, being conscious, is like being caught in a never-ending, all-involving earthquake. Everything is still, yet everything lurches.

Gawaine is a stranger come to town, and a stranger unarmed, at that. As everything pitches, his swagger threatens to become a stagger. Steadying himself he looks around the shop. No, Becky is not here yet. Instead other faces loom up at him, seemingly uninterested. In the corner a young man in a suit reads a newspaper. He glances at Gawaine coldly for an instant. Gawaine catches a whiff of aftershave. What is it? Together with that glance, the scent seems an expression of pure brutality, like a kick in the stomach. To the left an old couple are eating sausages and potatoes. Next to them is a girl, probably in her late twenties, sitting alone. She is wearing a fake fur coat and thick, vivid make-up. Her gloves lie on the table next to her plate. In the corner diagonally opposite the young man sits a family comprised of mother, father and two young children. Next to them sits a couple wearing leather jackets.

304

That first brutal whiff of aftershave seems to taint the appearance of all present, so that Gawaine is nearly overwhelmed by an air of defensive hostility. Everyone in the room seems to have something to be suspicious and uptight about. For the parents it is their children, for the girl it is whatever her clothes are hiding, for the young couple it is their exclusive relationship, for the old couple it is their loosening fingerhold on a world where their hopes and values mean nothing. Only the young man with the newspaper doesn't seem uptight. No, the hostility that emanates from him is of an entirely different kind. There is a certain purity to it.

But Gawaine has not come here to contemplate the mystery of the English temperament. He orders a single cup of tea at the counter, takes a seat in an empty booth and turns his thoughts to his impending interview with Rebecca. He tries to anticipate in his mind every possible reaction to what he has to say to her, and to prepare his own reaction to each in advance. He has been doing this for days now. And if all goes well, what then? Perhaps this is the biggest doubt of all.

She is seven minutes late. Perhaps she has decided not to come. She has re-read his letter and decided he is a complete idiot. Or, no, she has simply forgotten. Not a single word in the letter or of their subsequent phone conversation has sunk in. She has just forgotten and is washing her hair instead. Just as Gawaine is thinking this, the bell tinkles, the door swings open and Rebecca walks through. In contrast to the other inhabitants of the café, she has grown very familiar. He half forgets the fear he has been harbouring towards her, and in his excitement and gratitude he rises unthinkingly to his feet. Embarrassed, he sits down again.

Rebecca says hello and puts her bag on her seat before making her order, the familiarity surrounding her like the aura of stardom around an actress. Her whole entrance, unspectacular in all its details, is to Gawaine a glittering and magnificent ensemble of gestures, words and other less definable elements. I suppose that is style, he thinks to himself as she returns to her seat and settles in. He sips his tea and smiles, then frowns.

"I expect you're wondering why I've called you all here," he begins.

"What do you mean 'all'? Have I put on weight or something?"

He makes a pained expression.

"No. It's a kind of joke. I've just always wanted to say that. Oh well."

She continues to look at him expectantly. She is dressed quite smartly, in a variation of her office outfit, and this makes her appear all the more attentive. Now Gawaine is lost for words. He just wants to go on sipping his tea, wallowing in the humdrum comfort of the situation and in her simple presence. What he has to do is not at all attractive. It is to get up in the middle of the night and set sail without provisions to an un-known destination. And yet to go on sipping tea, which would be oh-so-easy, is death.

"Okay. I wanted to talk to you."

"Yes, I know. Go on. Thank you."

This last utterance to the woman bringing her tea and scone.

Gawaine looks miserable as he continues. His brow is creased as if he has been struck between the eyes with a cleaver.

"I think I can explain to you what my true self is."

"I'm listening."

"Thank you. I feel like I'm jumping off a cliff, but I've got to do it. First, look around you!"

She does as instructed.

"Yes?"

"What's missing?"

"I don't know. Nothing that I noticed."

"Are you sure?"

"Yes."

"You think this is enough for your needs?"

"This café?"

"Well, not just this café—the world."

"Well, yes, isn't it enough?"

"No. No, it's not enough. It's not even a start. It's nothing."

"That depends how you look at it."

"I've thought about that. To a certain extent maybe you're right. You remember I talked about people being blind? I think the people in this world have a special kind of blindness. When they turn their eyes on something without seeing it, it ceases to exist. You've no idea how much it terrifies me. Becky, I'll tell you my secret . . . I'm not from this world."

She regards him for a moment with more of puzzlement than surprise in her expression.

"I could have told you that ages ago," she says.

"I'm not joking. I'm not using poetic license or metaphor or anything else, either. I mean it literally. I come from another world. I have to hang on to that fact or go blind myself."

"Okay. Fair enough."

"You don't sound at all surprised. Do you realise what I'm saying?"

"I think I've given up on being surprised by what you say. So you come from another world? Okay, go on."

Gawaine frowns and tilts his head in irritation.

"I was kind of relying on your surprise. Everything seems a bit flat now."

"Oh, go on, please. I'm interested."

Gawaine goes on at her insistence, his eyes lowered, stammering, frowning at intervals and making pained expressions. Now it is as if he is telling the story of his life by rote, telling it one last time in the manner of someone who is thoroughly tired of it. All this time, as he begins to stammer, wading wearily through the words he has rehearsed, she feels a strange desire to

307

take his hand or hold him. He has never looked so appealing as at this moment, stumbling apologetically onwards through his words, tired of them all—he has never looked so alone.

It hurts to look at him. She thinks of a time when she was a child and such physical contact as hugging and holding hands had no sexual meaning, was, in fact, a simple requirement, like water. Where does all that go? All these people around her must be starving for affection—not sex, perhaps, but affection. Something about the boy, though, makes her hold back, as if he is a wounded animal. He seems quite beyond her reach.

"The world I come from is the world of the true self. Sometimes I see reflections of that world in this, but they are always fleeting, or hazy."

"What's it called?"

"Actually, there is a name for the place, though really it needs no name. It's called 'Missing'."

A glance up. A nervous, flickering smile.

"Why did you come here, then?"

"I have a mission. Once, a long time ago, this world and Missing were one. But something happened. Some evil power took control and the two worlds have been drifting further and further apart. I'm here to try and bring them back together again."

"Why you?"

"Somebody's got to do it. Actually, you have no idea of the weight of responsibility I feel on my hands. Everything depends on this. Everything!"

"So, what are you going to do about it?"

"I'm already slow in getting started. You're the first person I've spoken to about this in anything other than hints and riddles. I suppose that's because there's something about you that I believe in. To save the world first we must save ourselves. In other words, if I show you the way to Missing, we'll beat a path for others to follow. Somehow I feel it takes two people first of all to make a gateway. So, perhaps now I really am asking something of you. I am asking you to step, of your own free will, over the threshold of my heart. I will say it clearly. I am not asking you to be my lover. There won't be any such barriers between us. You will be playing in my make-believe until it becomes real. I promise I won't hurt you. But the choice is yours."

"Mmm. I don't know. It sounds kind of fun."

"Of course. Of course. We mustn't forget that."

"But I think it could be dangerous. I'm not worried about me. I think I might hurt you, or, anyway, disappoint you."

"We have to take care of each other."

"Maybe you can show me an example. I can try and see."

"Yes, of course. You can do what you want."

"Okay, let's try something."

"Now?"

"Yes." She smiles.

"Okay. Close your eyes and listen to my voice."

Listen to my voice. My voice is more important than my words. What does it mean? Each voice is unique, like the memory of something eternal. That unique something is the true self; it is Missing. It's in your voice as well as mine. After everything else has been measured and explained, that unique something still cannot be accounted for. It comes before everything.

Let's follow it down inside, and maybe it will show us the way to Missing. The voice is a golden thing. It glows. Follow that glow into the heart. In the alcove of the heart, like a living statue, sits a golden, cross-legged child with hands wide open to give or receive. Look at those hands. They are sparkling with gold dust. Look closer. Look at the fingertips. Each unique whorl is a maze. You start to fall into the grooves of the maze, and as you do it becomes a spiralling galaxy. You are lost in golden clouds of space dust. All about you now is this golden colour, like sunlight on closed eyelids.

The smell of summer. The smell of forever in the air. The most ancient time is the freshest of all. Now the clouds part. There is a swinging, swaying motion. The camper van is driving along a winding coast road. Their destination is some halcyon beach where they will hunt in rock pools and collect shells in the sand. All about them the world is full of the simple colours of a Ladybird picture book, paintbox green, yellow and blue for grass, sun, sea and sky. The whole world is written in bold print. Mother passes the lemonade bottle to the back seat. The two girls take swigs, wipe their mouths and pass it back. Then they begin to sing again.

"Becky and Gawaine in a tree,
M-I-S-S-I-N-G.
M-I-S-S-I-N-G.
M-I-S-S-I-N-G."

The words of the song build a stairway of clouds. This is one of the ways to Missing.

At the top of the stairway the song raises great walls and towers. We have come to Me, the capital of Missing, and the greatest city in the universe. It spreads from the clouds to the mountains. Someone has taken a huge wicker laundry basket full of toys and costumes and tipped it upside down and it has turned into a never-ending castle. Time does not follow a straight line here. It changes into different costumes and plays different games. When you wake up in Me, and stretch and yawn, your daydreams are already becoming your itinerary. Everybody knows you, and everybody's famous. No one needs to wear clothes. Naked, they shine like suns. Their souls are visible, external, like the feathers of a bird of paradise, the plumage changing from moment to moment. As you walk through the wondrous halls and corridors of Me, the multi-coloured marble iridesces around you. The castle is made of music, and everywhere your presence is met with beautiful sounds that blush like a mood ring.

As you walk by, the Duke of the Arched Window, who holds dominion of the rays of treacle light that fall into the corridor, invites you to ride with him to inspect his sky-shoals of sea horses and perform and discuss your latest scrapbook of songs, which you composed with a paint box called the Wind. But you decline. You have other promises to keep.

In every room people dressed in the finery of the soul are talking to each other in a language that is made up on the spot, as fluid as birdsong, playing a game of make-believe that is the deepest and freest communion of spirits.

At the heart of the castle is a vast, circular hall whose vaulted ceiling is an upturned view of vales and hills from above the clouds. In this hall is the Fountain of Magic, without which nothing can have spontaneous existence. The waters of the fountain reach up almost to the ceiling. The people of Me come to the fountain to bathe and play. Often they step into the central pillar of water and let it carry them high up in the air. The touch and the taste of the waters of that fountain bring the bather unimaginable joys.

Refreshed by the waters you walk out into the crisp air of the streets, which are cobbled with memories—memories of the past, the future and all times outside and in between. Some streets lead to autumn, to curled leaves and watercolour winds, where romantic detectives are investigating mysteries of nostalgia; some lead to summer, where grasses sway their heads and the days never end and love is as easy as paddling on the beach; some lead to winter, where darkness summons the wolves of the most ancient to begin their chase again beneath the stars, where white breath rises between antlers; and some lead to spring, where everything is fresh from a strange awakening and wonderful with the shivering dew of the first time.

On some streets children are skipping, and their skipping rhymes dictate the movements of worlds and dynasties. On some streets they are playing marbles, and the swirls inside the glass are nebulae and galaxies, and when they collide, a million different fates and a million different realities overlap. And the streets are a fantastic story of a million trillion forks and branches that diverge but eventually lead back to each other.

Some of these streets lead to the great walls surrounding Me, and out between the gates. They turn into paths through forests of bamboo that shine like the moon, and oceans of wild grass, head-high, and mountains of impossibly balanced rocks, and they twine out into the enchanted lands of Missing.

You leave your myriad self behind in the corners and courtyards of Me and pass out through one of these gates. You travel ten thousand miles like a ghost, without tiring, and come at last to a house that glows like a paper lantern in the night. It is perched on the very brow of a cliff, beside a waterfall. Water cascades onto the piled boulders below and mist rises up into the air. Beyond the rocks and the water and the mist, nothing can be seen except the night and the slowly wheeling constellations. This could be the edge of the universe, the stars dropping down forever like the water of the falls. The water plunges swiftly through the air, but the mist and the constant roar, near yet distant, makes everything seem slow and dreamy.

There is no glass in the windows of the house, but even at night the air is not too cold. Inside, in one room, on a floor of straw matting, are one man and one woman. The room is almost empty. There are only some cushions and blankets, a kettle and brazier, a strange, stringed instrument and a chest of drawers. The view from each of the four windows is like a painting. Through one of them, beyond the clouds of forest and mountain, even at ten thousand miles distance, can be seen the walls and towers of Me. Through another, the starry and mist-wreathed abyss. The other two windows show closer views of little streams and gardens dotted with miniature cloud-berry trees and gossamer-drifting lotus flowers. The man sits in one corner, a blanket drawn up over his knees. The woman sits in the opposite corner and gazes into the night. They don't need to say anything. They don't even need to touch.

Behind them, through the window, the layered sweep of ten thousand miles is a scroll that tells of ten thousand years. All the places and the times of Missing are with them as they sit and breathe the warm night air. Ten thousand years pass by as they watch the stars drop down the sky. They hear the sound of water below and their hearts are filled with the same dream. The woman starts to sing. It is an old, old song. As old as the rocks. As old as the stars, slowly rising and dipping like a waterfall-splashed wheel that measures the ages. Her song fades into silence. She looks at the man and they smile.

"Is that it?"

She has waited some seconds with her eyes closed after he finished talking.

"Well, yes."

She opens her eyes and a smile spreads across her face in a beautiful flush. For all Gawaine's talk of overcoming barriers, he is not expecting the reality of such a smile. He does not know quite how to react to it. That smile is Rebecca's contribution to the moment. Its generosity is not a part of his plan. He reminds himself to be generous in turn.

"Wow! That was amazing!" says Rebecca. "It's so relaxing. You've got a perfect voice for that sort of thing. I was completely carried away then. I forgot where I was. When I opened my eyes it was weird to find myself back here again."

Seeing Rebecca's reaction, Gawaine feels as if he too has only just opened his eyes to a world now smartingly vivid. At first, making his confession to Rebecca and taking her on the subsequent journey into the heart of Missing, he kept his voice lowered, not trusting in the dubious privacy of their partitioned space. As he continued he got lost in his own words and he too forgot about the café around them. It was as if the words themselves had made a private booth for the two of them. Now that private booth has burst like a soap bubble, but its presence is still felt in a film that makes the eye blink and kisses the cheek, in a vapour that conjures tiny rainbows in the air. Yes, the vapour of that privacy is mixing with the air around. The vivid blush of their freshly opened eyes has turned to flames and is catching and spreading. These flames are uncomfortable.

Beyond the privacy, Gawaine sees the world loom with fresh imminence. He is appalled at how random and abstract it is. Before him some colossal conglomeration of indescribable impressions is moving, disintegrating, reforming. These are the shapes, sounds, colours and smells that he calls Becky. He has invited this chaos into his heart. He cannot control it. Another sound issues from the confusion opposite him.

"So what's next?"

It is a while before he understands the words.

"What do you mean?"

"That's not the whole thing, is it? What do we do next?"

"I'm not sure."

He looks down and away. He feels suddenly awkward and fidgety and he wants to change the subject, but he can't think how to do so naturally. Why does her enthusiasm upset him so much? Surely he should be grateful? 'We have to take care of each other'—that is what he said. But he is finding it hard to maintain his respect for Rebecca now. Her response seems tasteless, somehow. He feels disdain, and in turn he feels ashamed of himself. He suspects she has misunderstood him, or that she is humouring him. Actually, he simply cannot believe that she believes him, and the knowledge that she is beyond his understanding has thrown everything into disorder. Gawaine feels he is sinking in a quagmire of pettiness.

As if looking for something to hold onto, he casts his eyes about his surroundings once again. Why did he choose this place to divulge his precious secret? It is a place more thickly caked in human blindness than the cooker behind the counter is caked in grease. Few places could be better designed for the extinguishing of the spirit. But then, that is precisely why he chose the place, isn't it? If his message has any value at all, then it must be able to survive any environment. What good is magic if it is defeated the moment it meets a shopping arcade or a car park?

Gawaine's eye falls upon the lightning-white cheek of the leather-clad young man. It wanders over the sparsely haired pate of the father, shiny with sweat, to the little boy eating beans off his knife. He looks at the other inhabitants of this enclosed world, existing in deliberate and mutual ignorance of each other. He looks at the woman behind the counter with her sour, pitted face, and her husband, the cook, his mouth serious under the cover of his iron-grey moustache. Nothing in the universe is more important than here and now. But what here and now is this? Those involved seem to be struggling through the silence as if trying to keep their heads above water. There is nothing else.

Now or never.

Everything depends on this.

Now or never.

Suddenly, pushed to this cruel extremity of the mundane, a new feeling wells up in Gawaine's heart. It seems that in an instant he is granted a God's-eye view of the pores on the bald pate, the muscles twitching in the tense white cheek, the grey sternness of the cook's moustache, in fact, of everything in the whole ridiculous, riddling universe of here and now that has him eternally cornered. Such imminence! Like a cliff! Like madness! The pettiness falls away from him. He cannot help laughing out loud. He seems about to let himself be carried away by laughter, but suddenly he pulls himself up and leaps onto the chair. From there he steps onto the table. Everyone is looking up at him now, and though he struggles to keep a straight face, laughter tugs at the side of his mouth and his expression collapses once again into a smirk. For a while he is unable to speak; all words are overridden by giggles that are close to whimpers. Every time he takes a breath to start again he splutters like a corpsing actor.

"Okay," he says at last, wiping his mouth. Now he holds his head up high as if to receive an invisible crown. "You probably don't know it, but this is what you've been waiting for."

A wondrous calm has descended. Everything is in solemn focus.

"I'm back! I have returned! My spirit went wandering on the shadowy path, but now it has come home again! It's me! Don't you recognise me?"

The proprietoress has dashed out from behind the counter and is waving her tindery arms in instinctive disapproval of this unknown thing.

"Oi! Get down off my table, or I'll get my husband on you!"

"Wait! Stop a moment! You don't have to carry on with this act any more. Don't you understand? I have come now to release you from this act. Maybe you have forgotten, but deep down you know me. There is a first time for everything, and I am it! I come from the world of Missing to set this world free. This is the year zero and a new age starts here radiating from the point where I stand."

Gawaine rips off his shirt and watches in satisfaction as his buttons fly in all directions, like jumping beans. He points to the soft flesh, white as the belly of a trout, on the inside of his right arm.

"Here! This is me! If you look at this spot closely enough you'll see my name, Gawaine, sparkling in letters made of magic dust . . ."

Now Gawaine is being heckled from other parts of the café. At his feet, Rebecca is suggesting in a stage whisper that they leave the establishment. Gawaine must have done something terribly wrong, because now the proprietor has emerged from the kitchen and is trembling with anger.

"Get out of my shop! Go on, clear off before I call the police, and don't come back!"

". . . but this same magic-wand glitter and glue is in your arms and your names, too. It's easy. People think that nothing matters and they think that everything matters. Both of these things are right, but in the opposite way to what you think right now . . ."

Somewhere in the café is the sound of a newspaper being shaken and folded.

"Let me take care of this."

It is the young, smartly dressed man who was sitting in the corner. He has got to his feet and is approaching the source of the disturbance.

"Gawaine!"

Gawaine stops talking and turns to look at his challenger.

"Listen, mate, some of us are trying to read and digest our food. It's not easy with some nutter dribbling his horrible drivel in your ear'ole."

"Hear! Hear!"

Gawaine knows he has told everyone his name, but he doesn't like the confidence with which this interloper has used it. There is something altogether strange and arresting about the poise with which he moves and talks, and about his deliberate use of vernacular.

"I've been listening to you, bending this poor girl's ear. Seems like it's about time someone set you straight on a few things. Well, you want to talk, don't you, so come on, what's your problem? What is it you're after, mate, in words of less than three syllables?"

Somehow his opponent has the advantage on Gawaine. At the back of Gawaine's mind, cogs are turning, trying to work out exactly what's happening here. The barest suspicion that this man is somehow in tune with him seems struggling to take shape within his thoughts. He is doing the same thing as Gawaine in standing up before people and imposing his reality upon theirs, and yet he seems to be concealing this in some way. They are both standing on the same stage, but where did this stranger make his entrance from? Gawaine senses faintly that he is closer to things he has always wanted to know than he has ever been before. But he is stuck for an answer to his opponent's question, and he starts to tremble.

"No? Nothing to say? You're quiet all of a sudden."

"Leave him alone." This from Rebecca. "Come on, Gawaine, let's go."

"Wait a minute, let's just finish our little talk, shall we, Gawaine? What do you want?"

"I just want . . . I want to be myself. I want everyone else to be themselves too. I want to set them free. I'm not anyone's enemy. Is it wrong to want to give my love to the world?"

Ray looks around.

"Do you want his love?"

There comes a dry chorus of 'no's and 'no thank you's.

"Are you being yourselves?"

"Yes."

"So, there you have it, Gawaine. Your services are not required. It seems to me that you're not giving anything. You're just trying to take. You're a parasite. Take a look at yourself, standing there on the table with your make-up and that clown costume that you call clothes. Your mother must weep. What are you doing here, showing your nipples and your potbelly to these good people? These are symptoms of illness, I'd say. Symptoms of deeply ingrained denial. What do you think, Gawaine?"

Now Gawaine is looking off as if into some great distance. His voice when he speaks is very quiet.

"Yes, perhaps there is no use for beauty in this world. I can understand that. Here beauty is seen as an insult to everyone around. But I don't come from this world. I come from Missing. What can I do? Here I am a parasite. My heart belongs in Missing. I need to unite the two worlds. Yes, somehow . . ."

"How are you going to do that, then? Tap together your ruby slippers and say 'There's no place like Missing'? However much you talk about it, you're still here, with us. If you belong in Missing, why aren't you there? You know something, I think you belong here like the rest of us. I think you should get used to it before someone locks you up, mate."

The trembling in Gawaine's body has grown stronger and now seems centred on his head, which he can barely keep still. He appears to have some sort of palsy, and his head jerks to the right once or twice. He looks down and fumbles with his shirt as if to do it up, but only the two bottom buttons are left. His lips are moving, but no sound comes out. Ever so slowly and painfully, as if not to be noticed, though he cannot help being noticed, he edges off the table. His head is still lowered and he appears to be crying. Without a further word he proceeds to the door, his pace stiff and brisk, like that of someone trying not to run. There is the jangle of the shop bell and he disappears, clutching his shirtfront.

Inside the café there is some sparse and sardonic applause at this exit. Ray takes this as his curtain call, and though he does not bow, he turns to his audience with an air of satisfaction.

"Thank you. It was nothing, really."

Suddenly his face is spattered with warm coffee.

"Bastard!"

Rebecca storms out of the café after Gawaine.

✳

"So then, Mr. Jenkins, what did you observe?"

Ray is once more seated in the chair in Mr. Wilberforce's office.

"Well, I can definitely see why you gave me that case. At first it looked like a waste of time, but I really think I've learnt something from it."

"Go on."

"Well, when that gaylord—I'm afraid I have to call him that—when that gaylord was just talking to the fag-hag, his words seemed to have some sort of potency. But when he tried to address everyone his words had no effect. All I had to do was point this fact out to him and he crumbled."

319

"Yes, that's quite right. This kind of rebel, or gaylord, as you term him, basically derives his very limited power from a sense of secrecy. In intimate situations his dreams can appear to take on a certain reality, so for the most part he tries to use very intimate, personal mediums. For him three is most definitely a crowd. Still, he longs to come out of his closet, so to speak. But that is disastrous for his dreams. They die upon contact with the air of the public world. This is the difference between true power and false power. True power, such as that we have access to, is real however many people witness it. Still, we do have a use for secrecy, as I'm sure you appreciate. Remember, it has taken a great deal of work to get things this way. Once upon a time . . ." he chuckles at this phrase, seeming to savour its irony between his dry lips, "Yes, once upon a time things were different. But that's all over now. The scales have swung decisively in our favour."

"Yes, I see. But you know, I have to say I was impressed. I mean, I've really got to hand it to you. You didn't tell me what I should do, but you must have known how things were going to turn out. When I was putting that little faggot in his place, well, I felt everything else fall into place. It was magnificent."

"Yes, yes. It's a bit like meteorology. We watch where the winds are blowing, where the clouds are forming. The big difference is, we can give those winds and clouds a gentle nudge in the right direction. I suppose you could say that, with the data at our disposal, we have the kind of authorial omniscience that allows us to shape fictions."

Ray nods thoughtfully.

"What is it, Mr. Jenkins?"

"Well, you say you can give gentle nudges?"

"Yes."

"There's something I'd like to ask. If there's a price to pay, then name it."

"Your service should pay for most favours."

"That girl, that bitch, Rebecca Wilcox! She made me look bad. Just as I was enjoying my victory she splashed coffee in my face."

"I see. So, what you're asking for is that she gets the treatment?"

"The treatment?"

"Yes. Let's see. She finds herself mysteriously dogged by bad luck. The Inland Revenue ask for two years back payment of tax and just at that time she loses her job. While she's desperately looking for work and trying to borrow money, someone very close to her, say her mother, has a tragic accident. She struggles through her grief just managing to survive in some menial job where her boss takes every opportunity to bully and humiliate her. All the while we offer just enough hope to keep her from killing herself. A gentle, loving man enters her life and they discover something precious together. But this man, too, is haunted by bad luck, and somehow they just can't stay together. They decide it's best to be apart. She tries to find comfort in religion and New Age philosophies, but whenever she looks at her own wretched, empty life she can't escape the knowledge that she is deliberately trying to delude herself with sweet lies. She decides that the meaning of life is to try and help others and so joins some voluntary organisation or other. Being selfless is her sole comfort in life. All this time she has trouble from her landlord, is burgled by people who smear faeces all around her flat, and so on. One year she finds that the cat which has been her sole companion has been tortured to death by some local delinquents. Someone at the voluntary organisation she works for takes a dislike to her and accuses her of abusing one of her charges. For some reason the mud sticks. She is banned from such work. As she walks home one night, crying, she is accosted by a strange man and raped. When she reports this to the police her story is not taken seriously and she is humiliated again. Too late she discovers she has diabetes, perhaps, and she is already starting to go blind. She ends her life, let's say, in a nursing home, where senility overtakes her and she spends her remaining years drifting through the sad scenes of her past in no particular order."

"You can do that, then?"

"Nothing simpler. As long as it doesn't interfere with any of our current projects, and it doesn't."

"What about the boy?"

"I think we can assume an equally dismal fate awaits him even without our condescending to interfere. But now I think it's time for a toast."

"A toast?"

"Yes. Not here, of course. We shall move to different surroundings. Boxwell!"

The bearded man, who has remained silent throughout, stands.

"Please lead the way."

With the bearded man in the van, the three of them exit the office and proceed along a number of empty corridors. Occasionally there comes a muffled voice from behind a closed door, but they meet no one. They arrive at a rather cheerless zone leading to the back stairs. In one wall is what appears to be a goods lift. Mr. Wilberforce presses the call button next to the steel doors and they open onto the raw metal interior, as if the lift has been waiting for them. Mr. Wilberforce gestures for Ray to step inside.

When the doors close on the three of them, Mr. Wilberforce takes a bunch of keys from an inside pocket. He inserts one into a keyhole in a metal plate below the panel of buttons. The plate falls open to reveal a touch pad, like that on a telephone. Mr. Wilberforce keys in a number and the lift starts to descend.

"Have you ever thought that they might have children in Hell, Mr. Jenkins?"

It is Mr. Wilberforce's voice.

"No, sir."

Why is it that Ray feels the sudden need to say 'sir'?

"No, not many people think about such things, do they? Hell is just an imaginary place, or so distant it may as well be imaginary, and its workings are left obscure."

For some moments there is only the sound of the lift sinking down the shaft.

"Do you recall us asking if you were prepared to drink from the cup we offered?"

"Yes. I do."

"As I recall, you accepted that offer. Now, we shall see if the contents are poisonous or not. Some foreknowledge will undoubtedly help you in what you are about to witness. Here's something else not everybody knows: Heaven and Hell are one and the same place. It all depends upon whether you are one of the damned, or one of the overseers."

The lift arrives at the ground floor and continues to descend.

"Mr. Jenkins, you're trembling!"

"Am I?"

"Indeed you are. Remember, it's up to you. Heaven or Hell, Mr. Jenkins."

Not another word is spoken. Apart from the creaking of steel cables, all is silent. In that resounding silence and the creaking that threads through it, Ray imagines he can sense the movements of a giant pair of scales. The last two names uttered by Mr. Wilberforce are being weighed against each other, and the scales are tipping slowly, ominously, first one way then the other. There is no indication which will finally prove heaviest. This swinging back and forth seems to emphasise that, after all, there are no laws, either to restrict or to protect. The lift has been descending into the earth for about one minute. He does not know if it is hot, but Ray is sweating.

There is the shudder of arrival and the doors of the lift rattle open. The thin light from within the metal cage falls upon a passage cut into stone. The sudden cold seems to emanate directly from within Ray's bones, as if to announce his entrance into a different world than that the lift doors closed upon minutes before. Mr. Wilberforce and Boxwell step unhesitatingly into the darkness, and Ray follows as if attached to them by chains. Their moving presence seems to alert a sensor, because a passageway leaps into existence under the coloured illumination of hidden lights. It is no common passageway, but at first seems to yawn toothily in wide, wide, dripping grins on either side. Then Ray thinks to himself in bewilderment that this is like some museum—Madame Tussauds, perhaps—where a carefully contrived display leads crowds of gawpers along a fixed route. But this is not like any museum he has seen or imagined, and he knows that, for all its display, for all its fulfilment of the failed promises of other museums, this is not a place that the public can view for the price of mere money.

The spectacle on either side resolves into a kind of sense. There are carvings here, forming a tableau of some secret history whose figures, and the deeds in performance of which they are frozen, are more striking than the largest figures to loom out of official history, or the mythology that precedes it. It is obvious at once that there is something of great moment here, superseding all archetypes and revealing every story that ever was as a tame little nonsense bowdlerised for children. Nothing now can take the place of these images.

That Ray did not even see them at first is owing to the fact that they appear to be carved out of natural rock formations. Such is the skill with which these carvings are executed, they manage to convey the impression that it is some particularly eerie trick of nature, and not the labour of human hands, that has produced them. As these images claim their place within Ray's vision and his mind, he thinks of that invisible chalice, which was a manifestation of true power.

324

There are human figures here, and semi-human, some with masks and some brazenly unmasked. Bizarre scenes of surgery form eyes in the maelstrom of ritual, revelry and revelation. At the centre of one such whorl, the figure of a surgeon, livid with fanaticism, bends over a struggling female, who is restrained by his assistants. He has taken a scalpel and then a needle to her belly, and it appears that he is sewing something inside her where a child should be. Elsewhere there are surgeons joining living bodies together to create Siamese twins, triplets and so on. Around all this there hangs a meaty odour, which lends the dripping stone skins of the carvings a grotesque lifelike-ness. This parade—august as the carvings of Westminster Abbey— continues on either side for some while, so that the uninvited would have lost nerve before ever seeing the end of the passage. And then the carvings become less intaglio and more bas-relief. And now Ray notices there are holes at certain points in the wall. His attention is caught by one of the semi-human fig- ures, naked, which is depicted as bending forwards and looking back over its shoulder at the viewer with a mocking expres- sion. There is a hole in the rock wall at the place where its legs meet. A similar device has been used with another forcefully restrained victim of surgery. Ray dares to move closer to these apertures and notices a draught of slightly warmer air issuing from them, and bringing with it the same meaty odour.

Eventually, however, this bone-chilling passage, flanked by its stone ceremonial of outrage, comes to its termination in a great pair of double doors, carved with an arabesque pat- tern resembling plumes of coiling smoke. At the centre of each door, wreathed by this mephitic-looking smoke, is a chalice adorned with a single, solemn eye, such as Ray has seen on the envelope containing the letter that first summoned him to this building. A certain cataract-like dullness over the dark- grey metal speaks of the doors' forbidding age. With the eyes and the spirals of smoke, the doors half resemble a scowling face streaked with ashes. At the top of the walls just before the door are two CCTV cameras, but these are rusty and appear to be inoperative, as if long obsolete.

The silence draws in tight around the three disparate souls, as if only they remain in the entire world. Mr. Wilberforce takes something like an identity card from his pocket and holds it against a panel in the door, and these scuffling movements are like a match in infinite darkness, the speechless, sweating focus of all consciousness. Then there is a click and the door swings open to reveal that infinite darkness, almost threatening to blow that tiny flame of consciousness out. But no—the flame holds steady. The air that escapes from within brings with it a heavier load of the stale, meaty odour. Cold silence reigns. Or is there something, a murmur from far off like someone talking in their sleep?

Mr. Wilberforce opens the doors wider and takes a few echoing steps into the gloom. He turns and gestures for Ray to follow. Ray treads forward and breasts the darkness, which seems to swirl inkily about to enfold him. Boxwell brings up the rear.

At some uncertain distance are two points of red light, and their sullen glow gives the barest sense of physical presences— inanimate or otherwise—contained within the darkness. There seems to be an object in which the lights are set whose general shape is that of a cross-legged Buddha, and, because of what he has already witnessed, Ray imagines it must be some form of carving or similar ornament. He is also fairly certain of the existence of a wall behind this object, and can discern a wispy, flowing movement, which he supposes is smoke from a brazier. But then he catches other suggestions of movement around the object. There is something curious in this movement that does not tally with any of the scenarios his mind has projected into the darkness from its available information. And this contradiction gives him a feeling as if he has witnessed a transgression of the laws of physics. But there is also a familiarity here, in some indirect way.

In the next moment a ray of white light bursts forth from some point just beyond the red. So absolute has this world of darkness seemed, that the effect is like that of a bolt of blackness shattering the blue sky of noon. All at once Ray's faculties are stalled by a number of impressions that defy interpretation. Some light from the new source, probably an opened door, has fallen on the previously red-litten object. At first Ray thinks that his guess was right and that this is an idol of sorts, the two red points serving as its eyes. It sits cross-legged with its hands in front of its huge belly. The whole thing seems to be constructed from smaller effigies of shockingly emaciated human beings intertwined. Incense burns in censers before it. It must be the smoke from these that lends the illusion of movement, once more, to some of the statue's details. Heads and limbs protrude from it at disturbing angles. And then one of the drooping heads lifts, and looks at him, and utters a sound.

As if in answer to this sad bellow, there come sounds from the newly opened aperture. They are human voices, and yet they are not human. These screams, hoots and sobs are the sound of walls of experience, perhaps present since birth, falling away to reveal the true limitlessness of reality, in which there is no rescue. They fill Ray's head with fleeting images of a bizarre menagerie. In amongst these voices are others in which there lurks a dry exultation, as calm and terrible as reality itself, like voices at a conference table, lapsing into tones of obscene informality. Both the screams and the other voices reflect the same finality of truth.

Mr. Wilberforce turns to look back at Ray. Some light falls on his face and Ray can see the wet coruscation of the eyes, and in the old man's delicate, sickly smile he discovers a secret understanding that none of his previous words have quite conveyed. There in the wavering tips of the moistened lips is the swinging once again of gigantic scales. A toast. Unimaginable Joys! Heaven or Hell!

Ray feels such inhuman lust coursing through his veins that his hair stands on end. A thought flits across the back of his mind; perhaps the architect is not blind, after all.

He meets Mr. Wilberforce's eyes and returns his smile. He has made his decision. Heaven it is!

She turns the corner of the school building where the path runs alongside the playing field, separated from it by a wire fence. Looking up she falters to see someone on the path ahead. A young man is loitering there, gazing at the empty pitch, one hand clutching at the eyes of the mesh. He does not look like he belongs here, and for a brief moment Rebecca is afraid. Then, even before the name comes back to her, she recognises him. She stops, wondering what to say, but, as if he has not noticed her, he continues to stare at the grass.

"Gawaine?"

Even now she is a little unsure. Perhaps she never really knew this person.

He turns with a certain weariness. He seems unsurprised.

"Hello Rebecca."

She can see his face now, but there is no doubt he has changed. He has had a haircut, for one thing. He has also stripped himself of jewellery and make-up. His clothes are a very plain sweater and trousers. Even these details don't seem quite to account for the change in his appearance.

"What are you doing here?" asks Rebecca.

"I used to come to school here. I just thought I'd have a look round the old place, you know, see if it's changed."

"And has it?"

He nods glumly.

"A bit. Here and there. Anyway, what about you?"

"Oh, I might be getting some work here. I've just had an interview."

"I see."

There is a long silence. Rebecca cannot think of anything else to say, and yet she can't quite bring herself to walk on. Gawaine kicks at a bit of gravel with his toe. At last he looks up again and breaks the silence.

"I'm sorry I didn't write or phone or anything after that time."

"That's all right."

For a week or so after the incident in the café she had been stricken with a strange anxiety for Gawaine's well being. But life had moved on, something else had taken the place of that anxiety at the forefront of her mind, and now it seems as if years have passed and she is meeting a long lost playmate from her school days. Perhaps the setting has something to do with this, too.

"No, it's not. I broke my promise to you. You know, I said I'd always . . ." He seems unable to complete the sentence, "Anyway, sorry. I've let you down."

"No you haven't. Well, look, I've got to go really. Maybe I can give you a ring and we can talk properly later."

He shakes his head.

"I'm sorry, Becky. I can't."

"Why not?"

Gawaine looks up to the sky and takes a deep breath.

"I was . . . I thought I was . . . maybe . . . a poet. A poet is someone who insists on their own innocence as if insisting on wearing nappies into adulthood. When the world laughs and scorns them for this they hate the world for trying to deprive them of their rights. What's wrong with wearing nappies? they ask in defiance, and they become all the more determined. Then, one day, they catch a sight of themselves in the mirror,

329

and they begin to wonder why they are wearing a nappy, after all. It begins to dawn on them that that smell of shit comes from them and not the world, as they had always thought. They realise in horror that they have been quite mad all this time."

"You're not mad, Gawaine!"

"I wasn't quite mad enough. Now I've ended up stranded in sanity."

"I don't understand."

"It's simple. You were right. This world is all there is. What else could there be?"

"What do I know? You don't have to believe what I said. I'm not like you. I say just whatever comes into my head."

"Becky, I can't see it anymore."

"What?"

"It started to fade after that time. You remember I said that whenever I close my eyes and go inside I can see Missing?"

"Yes?"

"Not any more. It's all gone. You saw me before, and now you've seen me after. In fact, you saw me at the very moment the change began. So you see, I can't be friends with you anymore. I don't want to hurt you, but to tell the truth, I can hardly bear to talk to you now."

"I see. So what are you going to do?"

"What everyone else does—get a job, survive, grow old, die."

"It doesn't have to be like that. Maybe the world is a shitty place, but that's all the more reason to be friends, isn't it? I knew I should have . . ."

Until now Gawaine's voice has had a distracted, meandering quality to it. Now, although his words are still slow, he interrupts Rebecca in a tone of irresistible command.

"Rebecca! Look into my eyes!"

She looks. At first she squints a little in puzzlement. Then her expression changes as if she has found something quite unexpected. All the muscles in her face go slack.

"Now do you understand?"

She lowers her eyes and nods, her hand to her mouth.

"Goodbye, Rebecca."

He turns and walks away. Now it is Rebecca's turn to linger by the fence. She watches Gawaine's back until he disappears. He doesn't cast a backward glance. Somehow she feels too dispirited to follow his footsteps. She will leave the school in a different direction. Even this thought depresses her. Rather than dwell on it, she turns her eyes on the playing field, as if searching for what Gawaine saw there. She stands for some time while shadows lengthen. The sun is dipping towards the horizon and the blades of grass are burnished with gold, their ragged shadows black. What is it? There is certainly something missing here. Something . . . Like those eyes . . . The world is suddenly different. She tries to see something in the golden crown of grass. There should be *something* there. Evening is coming. Darkness is growing on the world.

❊

To the corridors of the Castle of Rhyme, many-towered heart of the citadel of Me, a strange darkness has come. Natural darkness cannot resist light and flees at its presence. This darkness extinguishes light as it passes. The many-coloured marble has clouded to patterns of tarry sludge and its song has turned to a whispering, muttering like the bubbling of gases in a swamp.

The Duke of the Arched Window sinks into the floor as it melts away beneath him. He casts about for something to hold and clutches at the treacle rays that have now turned into webs of decay and break away in his hands. His final sounds are a desperate wheezing and gasping without words.

Dust and masonry fall from the ceiling. In the great hall the Fountain of Magic is silent. The castle shudders and lurches like a sinking ship. The basin of the fountain cracks open and the last of the water hisses away into the depths. Amidst the debris lie the erstwhile bathers, the colours of their once bright plumage now faded and drab. Some of them have been crushed by blocks or fallen pillars. Others are mysteriously stricken, as if with plague. Occasional groans rise on the air.

A cruel wind whistles through the heart of Me. The earth trembles at intervals and clouds of razor-sharp grit are whisked up and borne along like swarms of blood-thirty insects. The buildings seem deserted, and apart from the wind there is no sound but here the patter of quick footsteps, there a continuous wailing, elsewhere the banging of a door left open.

The wind sharpens itself on the whetstone of the streets, where there is no light but that of the moon, cold as the cheek of a dead man. It steals through this desolate maze and out of the gates of the city into the far quarters of Missing. It howls through forests of petrified bamboo, whose stalks snap under its onslaught, and over weedy jungles of withered grass, dark mountains of tumbling rocks, and in a few minutes crosses ten thousand miles like a hungry ghost.

There, at the very brow of a cliff, is a house like a torn paper lantern with its flame extinguished. A waterfall beside the house cascades onto boulders below, and the wind whips up its spray and mixes it with the stars beyond, which plunge into the abyss of night.

The house is cold and empty, the few objects within scattered across the floor by the wind. There is a gorge nearby, spanned by a hump-backed bridge, and steps cut in the stone lead down into this ravine where mist from the waterfall fills the air. From somewhere in the mist comes the sound of footsteps. It is the woman from the house. She is running down along the damp wall of the ravine. The man is hesitating just above the level of the mist. She stops and calls back to him, telling him to hurry. There is not much time. He looks back as if he has forgotten something, then follows her, reluctantly, into the mist. He calls for her to wait. Plunging into the mist, he catches glimpses of her on the stairway below. He calls after her again. But the wind is howling and she seems not to hear.

At last she stops running. He sees her quite clearly now. She is standing on a cluster of rocks at the side of the waterfall and peering over the edge into the abyss. Through the spray and the mist are visible patches of star-streaked night.

He slows his pace. She is outlined with painful fragility against the chaos beyond. Somewhere in that roaring confusion, is there an answer?

Suddenly the walls of the gorge begin to shake, and the man is thrown off his feet. His arm dangles over the side of the stairway, and for a while, stunned, he stares into the bottomless haze below. The wind is striking cold against his face. The cold steals through his bones like a lullaby inviting him to rest his head forever on the pillow of endless air. Resisting this strange, seductive cold, he gets to his feet again. When he turns around, the woman and the rocks she was standing on are no longer there. The cold—it tricked him! In a few moments it stole from him the meaning that comes before life itself.

He rushes to the end of the broken stairway. For a long time his calls echo and shatter in the vaporous abyss. There is no reply. He falls silent. His hand against the rock wall, his chest heaving, he bends over, spying into the depths as if about to leap. Then a dullness comes over his features. He sits down, his legs hanging over the edge. As the rock trembles and stars fall from the sky and an unnatural darkness creeps across everything like cracks, he waits.

OTHER SNUGGLY BOOKS YOU WILL ENJOY ...

BLUE ON BLUE
by Quentin S. Crisp

A SUITE IN FOUR WINDOWS
by David Rix

NIGHTMARES OF AN ETHER-DRINKER
by Jean Lorrain

DIVORCE PROCEDURES FOR
THE HAIRDRESSERS OF A METALLIC AND
INCONSTANT GODDESS
by Justin Isis

BUTTERFLY DREAM
by Kristine Ong Muslim

GONE FISHING WITH SAMY ROSENSTOCK
by Toadhouse

METROPHILIAS
by Brendan Connell

THE SOUL-DRINKER
AND OTHER DECADENT FANTASIES
by Jean Lorrain

THE TARANTULAS' PARLOR
AND OTHER UNKIND TALES
by Léon Bloy